The
PURPLE
FLAME

The
PURPLE
FLAME

and Other Detective Stories

FREDERICK
IRVING
ANDERSON

Edited by Benjamin F. Fisher

Crippen & Landru Publishers
Norfolk, Virginia
2016

Copyright © 2016
by Crippen & Landru Publishers, Inc.

Cover design by Gail Cross, based on a photograph by Berenice Abbott
for the Federal Arts Project of the Works Project Administration,
New York City, 1935

Lost Classics logo, adapted from a drawing by Ike Morgan, ca. 1895

ISBN: 978-1-936363-15-5 (cloth edition)
ISBN: 978-1-936363-16-2 (trade softcover edition)

FIRST EDITION

Printed in the United States of America on acid-free, recycled paper

Crippen & Landru Publishers
P.O. Box 9315
Norfolk, VA 23505
USA

e-mail: crippenlandru@earthlink.net
web: www.crippenlandru.com .

CONTENTS

Frederick Irving Anderson
by Benjamin F. Fisher

I

Frederick Irving Anderson (1877-1947) continues to be cited as the author of many first rate crime-detective stories, notably those published in the *Saturday Evening Post* between 1913-1933, some of them collected into hardcover books, yet substantial information about him and his literary career proves to be scant. A longtime staunch admirer, Charles Honce, recalled visiting at the farm Anderson's sister owned, in East Jamaica, Vermont, where she and her brother moved in 1937, after Anderson's wife had died. Honce seemed particularly interested in Anderson's fashioning a sturdy axe handle, without using any power tools. Honce's memory was equally retentive about their spending winter afternoons by the fireplace, drinking whiskey and companionably chatting. He states that even though he and Anderson had been communicating for roughly twenty years before Honce first visited the farm, in 1940, sometimes it seemed to him that, as a flesh and blood human being, Anderson "just didn't exist."[1]

Other recollections are few and vague. Stanley Kunitz remembered Anderson's coming into the office of publisher H. W. Wilson, in the Bronx. In their joint editorial efforts related to the Wilson volumes of brief biographies of renowned writers, Howard Haycraft oversaw the entries for crime-mystery writers, so Kunitz never got beyond the greeting stage with Anderson. Haycraft told me that he didn't remember actually meeting Anderson, nor did he know anyone who knew him. Malcolm Cowley, who was keenly abreast of the New York literary scene during Anderson's years of authorship (roughly 1910-1930s), told me that he had no recollection of Anderson. Still another query, to the firm of William Heinemann, publisher of *The Notorious Sophie Lang* (1925), brought this response: only a few, extremely dry business letters, of no other consequence comprised the sole communication between author and publisher. Frederic Dannay told me that he could add nothing more about Anderson than he had offered in several issues of *Ellery Queen's Mystery Magazine*. Letters from Anderson to Dannay tend to address personal, not professional, topics.[2]

Even Anderson's remaining relatives have few intimate details to share, the only specifics being that Anderson's father, Andrew Anderson, was a tailor, in East Aurora, Illinois, where Frederick Irving Anderson was born, and that Anderson's wife, Emma Helen de Zouche, whom he married 23 March 1908, from New Orleans, was always referred to in the family as "the French woman."[3] If more information concerning Mrs. Anderson surfaced, that would particularly interest Feminists because she pioneered for women's rights. Queries to the town clerk and retired town clerk in East Jamaica, Vermont, likewise brought returns that Anderson and his sister, Mabel Lorena, were remembered, though fleetingly, by a few old-timers.In sum, Frederick Irving Anderson continues to remain a shadowy figure in the chronicles of American authorship, and that despite Hollywood's producing three films, based on the Sophie Lang stories, during the 1930s.

Anderson's career as a writer extended from his early days in newspaper work on through his initial ventures in publishing stories in magazines, between 1910 and 1913. His publications also included articles concerning what during early twentieth-century years were new scientific and technological developments, plus articles and books about improvements in farming. An early story in *Adventure* (June 1912), "Come Ahead Slow," is a parody of westerns, just as Stephen Crane's better known story, "The Blue Hotel," is. In an article, "The French Think Wilbur Wright Is a Bird," we discover a humorous sketch focused on then new technology. In "The Automobilist's Dream," Anderson recommended using electrical engines for better efficiency and less pollution, commenting, however: "In conclusion I may state that I am a writer of fiction by profession, and given to flights of fancy."[4] Anderson also published several series of articles that pertained to the uses of water powered electricity and others focused on soil conservation in agricultural work. He subsequently republished these articles in two books, *The Farmer of Tomorrow* (1913) and *Electricity for the Farm* (1915). Moreover, whether Anderson's knowledge of technology and science in his day was assisted by his resorting to books on these subjects, he in turn employed such information as substance calculated to appeal to audiences who were interested by and caught up in developing technologies, from automobiles, electricity, dairy separators, and telephones.[5]

II

A nderson has been chiefly remembered, however, as author of three books of crime-detective stories, *Adventures of the Infallible Godahl* (1914), *The Notorious Sophie Lang* (1925), and *Book of Murder* (1930), and as a longtime contributor (1913-32) of such fiction to the *Saturday Evening Post*. He likewise published fiction about the theater and music worlds of New York City. Some of these magazines, pulp types, now exist in only a few copies, in library special collections or in the hands of collectors. These early pieces reveal Anderson's experimenting to establish a medium.

"The Purple Flame" (*Adventure* November 1912), fourth and last of several stories in which Mr. White, detective, is central, is reminiscent of Poe's "The Purloined Letter" in that White sees that the revealing clue is what nobody else observes, though it holds the key to identifying the criminal. Thus White manages to frustrate the villain, much as in "The Purloined Letter" Poe's sleuth, Dupin, frustrates the machinations of the evil Minister D——. White's perception of the means of murder also aligns him with Sherlock Holmes (and any other first rate detective) who ultimately comprehends what others overlook. Anderson obviously regarded "The Purple Flame" highly because in a later story, "Beyond All Conjecture," in the *Saturday Evening Post* (29 September 1928), Armiston refers to the earlier story as one he wrote, and Ellery Queen obviously regarded it as worth reprinting, after Anderson's death, in *Ellery Queen's Mystery Magazine* (January 1949). The story had also appeared, as "A Study in Purple," in *The Detective Magazine* (5 December 1924), a British publication, so it was obviously attractive to aficionados of detective fiction.

The first *Saturday Evening Post* story, "The Infallible Godahl" (15 February 1913) initiated a series about the rogue character whose name figures in the title. Godahl descends from E. W. Hournung's A. J. Raffles, another captivating rogue, who inevitably eludes the police. In "The Infallible Godahl" Anderson introduced a second character who, along with Godahl, would reappear in many stories and win fans, Oliver Armiston, who is an "extinct" writer of detective stories. Oliver stopped writing because criminals rapidly came to use his stories as blueprints for achieving perfect crimes. Thus he may remind readers of Anderson himself, as one who created crime stories with many surprises, ditto in the Sophie Lang stories, where the rogue criminal functions in as much limelight as his/her antagonist(s), becoming a fairly sympathetic character.

Anderson's technique in this first Godahl story is subtle. Readers may understandably begin to wonder whether they are reading a story in which Oliver Armiston is simply a character created by Frederick Irving Anderson, or whether "The Infallible Godahl" is fiction created by Oliver himself. In other words we seem to confront a story within a story, in which the nature of story-telling itself is a subtext, thus making "The Infallible Godahl" what now is called metafiction. Elsewhere in the Anderson canon Oliver refers to stories he has written, and in "The Follansbee Imbroglio," a novelette serialized in the *Saturday Evening Post* during July-August 1922, we once again meet briefly Mrs. Billy Wentworth, who was a major character in the first Godahl story, and who in this later piece inquires about Godahl. Anderson collected the six Godahl stories into a hardcover volume, *Adventures of the Infallible Godahl* (1914). Several years later Anderson began to publish stories, the first one, "The Signed Masterpiece," in *McClure's Magazine* (June-July 1921), thereafter the others in the *Post*, in which another rogue criminal, Sophie Lang, is central, always adroitly eluding capture by Deputy Inspector

Parr and his staff. These seven stories Anderson collected into *The Notorious Sophie Lang* (1925), a book published only in England, by Heinemann.

After publishing many stories featuring Armiston, Parr, and their cluster of associates, and republishing ten of them in *Book of Murder* (1930), Anderson in 1937 brought forward, in *American Cavalcade*, yet another interesting character, canny Judge Alan Ebbs. Judge Ebbs is not only learned in the law; like Parr he perceives clues that others routinely miss. Clearly descended from Poe's Dupin and Conan Doyle's Sherlock Holmes, and obviously related to Armchair Detective figures, Judge Ebbs discerns discrepancies in criminals' testimonies, summarily exposing such persons' flawed intentions. Why an extended series of Judge Ebbs stories did not emerge is unknowable, although the death of Mrs. Anderson at this time may have diverted her husband's outlook and energies. Like the earlier Mr. White, no matter how compelling he may be, Judge Ebbs did not captivate his creator's mind and energies as did Godahl, Sophie Lang, or Armiston and Parr.

Readers of Anderson's fiction are allowed to penetrate farther into the minds of Armiston and some others among the gallery of characters who reappear in these stories, e. g., the handsome, debonair Morel or Jason Selfridge and Orlo Sage, respectively the New England farmer who has furthered his formal education, but who combines technical with canny instincts to assist the causes of justice; and the constable of the rural New England area in which many of Anderson's stories are set. No matter that these characters appear in short stories, we confront minds of greater depth than we find in many other, more "cardboard," types (in short stories and in longer works of fiction in the detective vein).

Along with this depth in characterization, Anderson's thoughtful creations in settings impart to his stories an expansiveness that is not mere length and nothing more. Ellery Queen has succinctly emphasized "the dreamlike movement of an Anderson short story," in his headnote to "The Man from the Death House," and that "movement" is enhanced by means of Anderson's establishing excellent background for the ideas and actions of the characters.[6] To a certain degree, many of Anderson's stories offer readers what we might designate as "word pictures," which may indicate that Frederick Irving Anderson was, in part, a literary descendant of the English Pre-Raphaelite painters and poets, and an heir to Poe's techniques. There are, to be sure, in Poe's Dupin stories, as well as others, e. g., "The Fall of the House of Usher," "The Black Cat," or "The Assignation," important pictorial supports for the outlooks and methods of the narrator and, more so, of Dupin himself. Such elements take Anderson's stories far beyond those of mere action driven plots—not that action is lacking in most Anderson stories. Additional texture is evident because Anderson's vocabulary is not severely limited. His diction, which often includes a word or phrase in languages other than English, draws upon what we might call high-brow and colloquial terminology with effortlessness. No stilted expression here. In other ways, too, Anderson's expert command of language surfaces, for example, in his allusions to the writings of many predecessors whose mastery of language was superb, e. g., the Bible, Shakespeare, Sir Thomas Browne, Pope, Dickens, to name but a few. One finds similar techniques in later detective fiction writers such as Agatha Christie, John Dickson Carr, and, even more recent, Denise Swanson or Sheila Connolly.

Anderson's allusions constitute no rarefied expression, intended for a small elite readership, because Anderson leavens his fiction with abundant colloquial language, when it is artistically appropriate, witness, for example, "Wild Honey," which reveals an ancestry, and not just in its dialogue, in the Frontier or Southwest Humor works of Sut Lovingood (George Washington Harris), T. B. Thorpe, or Mark Twain. As in those antecedents, Anderson's stories often pivot on compelling ironies, and Deputy Inspector Parr may owe something to the "half horse, half alligator" characteristics of the protagonists in the older work in frontier humor, though Parr's "frontiers" are usually those of New York City, albeit his visits to Oliver Armiston's vacation home, in New England, expand those frontiers. The comedy in Anderson's stories and those of these predecessors often verges upon or plunges into violence, though Parr also partakes of the Armchair Detective figure, in that he doesn't have to engage hands on with physical violence, but comprehends the nature of a criminal situation or character while he remains physically rather passive. Parr's companion against crime, Oliver Armiston, is even more of an Armchair detective. Anderson's fiction is not part of the hard boiled school of detective fiction that became popular in the early twentieth century.

Overall, despite his debts to previous writers of detective stories, Anderson's fiction manifests an originality that obviously appealed strongly to audiences for the *Saturday Evening Post* and those who read the stories he republished in hardcover volumes. Many types of appeals to early twentieth century American readers whose interests were mirrored in Anderson's fiction, else so many of his stories wouldn't have originally appeared in the *Post*, that magazine with a reading audience of most heterogeneous backgrounds. Farmers, hunters, drivers of the then new automobile and those who serviced it, followers of garment fashion, the arts, financiers, politicians: all might have found compelling elements in Anderson's fiction. Such fiction never grows stale, and Anderson's offers repeated glimpses into American life during the first third of the twentieth century. Those glimpses may remind us that much in life, apart from technological aspects—no cell phones, computers, or electronic banking in Anderson's stories—may not differ drastically in our own era.

NOTES

[1] Kunitz and I spoke about Anderson on October 17, 1985, during the Stanley Kunitz Festival, Worcester, Mass., October 14-17. See also Charles Honce. *Mark Twain's Associated Press Speech and Other News Stories on Murder, Modes, Mysteries, Music and Makers of Books.* New York: Privately Printed, 1940: 53-54. I acknowledge gratitude to Professor William Anderson, University of New Mexico, and to his father, the late Lloyd V. Anderson, for permission to publish and reprint materials by Frederick Irving Anderson, as well as for information about the Anderson Family, and for their encouragement of this project. I also acknowledge my great debt of gratitude to J. Randolph Cox, for assistance in obtaining copies of rare F. I. Anderson materials.

[2] L. H. Bailey. "Anderson, Frederick Irving." *RUS: A Register of the Rural Leadership in the United States and* Canada 2 (1920): 19. Letter from Malcolm Cowley to Benjamin F. Fisher, March 7, 1983; letter from Howard Haycraft to Benjamin F. Fisher, March 6, 1979; letter from Frederic Dannay to Benjamin Fisher, March 6, 1979. The Anderson-Ellery Queen letters are in the Harry Ransom Research Center, University of Texas, Austin. I have examined the will of Frederick Irving Anderson, signed December 1, 1937. Then a childless widower, Anderson named as his sole heir, his sister, Mabel Lorena Anderson. A copy of the will was sent to me, May 14, 1984, by Ms. Wanda L. Fazio, Register of Wills, District of Westminster, Bellows Falls, VT, to whom I acknowledge gratitude.

[3] William L. Anderson, a distant cousin of Frederick Irving Anderson, has furnished me information on the Anderson family history. See also Ron Backer, *Mystery Movie Series of 1930s Hollywood.* Jefferson, NC, and London: McFarland & Co., Inc., 2012: 235-240.

[4] Respectively *Harper's Weekly*, October 24, 1908: 30; *Scientific American*, January 13, 1917: 61.

[5] Information concerning Anderson's uses of books about technology and science has been furnished to me by Professor William L. Anderson, to whom I acknowledge gratitude.

[6] *Ellery Queen's Mystery Magazine* 17 (1951): 82.

The Purple Flame

A T three o'clock in the afternoon Mr. Homer Jaffray cleared his desk for the day and announced to his secretary that he would take the 3:30 train for Waverly. The announcement was not of seeming importance, but he repeated it as though to himself, as he sat gazing absent-mindedly out over the tall roof-tops whose gay plumes of condensing steam told of the clear cold day outside.

There was nothing unusual in his manner, even to the keen eyes of his secretary, who was almost his second self. To look at the dull, pallid face that hung wedge-shaped under the bulging dome of the head, to listen to the crisp, incisive voice, no one, not even his most intimate friend—if this man owned to such—would have suspected that the events of five years had been slowly pyramiding themselves into an apex for this moment. Such was the fact; yet now Jaffray, to whom the next few hours meant life or death, sat idly twirling the ratchet of his watch as he gave a few parting instructions to his assistant.

Before closing his desk he selected a cigar and filled his case from a box in a drawer. From another drawer, which he unlocked, he took a paper of matches that bore the advertisement of his tobacconist. He examined the paper critically as though it were the most important thing in the world at that moment—as indeed it was.

As he bit off the end of his cigar and struck a light, he eyed his secretary sharply as though he were about to address him and were framing his words. But he said nothing. Instead he turned his attention to the match. The match burned out in his fingers, and he tossed it away without lighting his cigar. As he climbed into his greatcoat, he said,

"You will see that the cost-lists of the Class 'B' ultramarines are made up and ready for me the first thing in the morning. Wire Carson in Pittsburgh to pare his estimate another five per cent, if he thinks it necessary. Tell him I leave it to his judgment entirely."

At the door he turned, taking his unlighted cigar out of his mouth, and sniffed the air.

"Is it my imagination, John—or do you too detect an acrid odor in the air?"

The secretary coughed slightly.

"There is something, sir," he said. "It rather irritates my throat. It is probably from the laboratory. Good-day, sir," he added hastily as his employer turned and started running for the elevator, shouting, "Down! Down!"

Ninety minutes later his train set Mr. Jaffray down at Waverly. He was the only passenger to alight; and he smiled to himself as he watched the receding tail-lights of the train. What he desired most of all in the business in hand was to leave a clear trail. And what could be more conspicuous than a solitary passenger alighting from a train at a lonely station?

He walked around the depot, a gaudy little structure of gingerbread pattern to match the mongrel architecture of this new suburb. The depot was deserted. Across the plaza stood a one-story building of field stone with a red-tiled roof, the office of the realty concern engaged in the exploitation of this community. Waverly was one of the so-called "restricted communities" where the party of the second part was provided with culture and gentility and Italian garden effects, along with water, gas and electricity, for a price.

It was rather a cheerless corner of the world at this time of year. A coat of snow covered the whole; the shrubbery and trees, shrouded in wrappings of straw and burlap against the icy wind that swept in from the Sound, described indefinite squares and figures-of-eight across the bleak landscape; and the only evidence of thoroughfares was the double row of gas-lamps that would in and out among the boarded and darkened houses. Only a few lights glimmered here and there to break the gloom; for most of the residents had fled to the warmth of steam-heated flats at the first rising of Winter.

"Can you tell me if Mr. Potter is at home?" he asked of the young man who greeted him as he entered the real-estate office.

"Yes, sir; he came down on the one-o'clock train."

"Can I get a conveyance to take me to his house?"

"It is only a ten-minute walk, sir," said the young man. Through the window he pointed out a structure that stood apart from the others and showed, even in the gloom, a more pretentious exterior than its neighbors. But Jaffray pleaded a fallen arch, saying he feared he would find the combination of snow and ice and the uncertain going too much for him, and the young man called a carriage by telephone.

Jaffray, idling the interim, put a question or two, and the all-seeing eye of the apprentice recognizing this man as a person of affairs, began to talk volubly of the plans and prospects of the Waverly Realty Corporation, and the exceptional advantages it offered a city business man seeking the much desired privacy and at the same time the refined surroundings, etc., etc. Jaffray smiled indulgently, nodding his head occasionally as the talker nailed down his points here and there.

"Let me send you our literature," suggested the young man as the carriage drew up to the door and Jaffray drew on his gloves.

Jaffray shrugged his shoulders indefinitely; but as the other pressed him, he took a card from his case and handed it to him, with a good-natured smile.

"Does this Mr. Porter live alone?" he asked.

"Mr. Potter," corrected the other. "Yes, sir. He is the secretary of the corporation—oh! you are Mr. Homer Jaffray," he broke in as he read the card. "I know you through a cousin of mine employed in your color-works. Would you mind, Mr. Jaffray," he asked ingenuously, "merely mentioning to Mr. Potter that I spoke to you of the Waverly proposition?"

Jaffray bent on him his lean, dry smile.

"You have my permission," he said, "to tell Mr. Potter that you interested me exceedingly."

A few minutes later he drew up at the curb, paid off the driver generously, and presented him with a cigar. He mounted the steps and rang the bell, and a maid-servant admitted him to the library, a long low room whose polished floor and waxed roof-beams reflected the light of the wood-fire burning on the hearth.

He arranged himself with his back to the fire so that his face was entirely in shadow; and when Potter entered, bustling with the made-to-order assurance of his profession—for he was the resident manager—Jaffray did not stir, but watched him intently from under the cornice of his heavily shaded eyebrows.

He had not sent in his card purposely. Potter, he knew, would be accustomed to meet all manner of persons at his home without stopping on formalities, especially during these days of the active exploitation of the Waverly project, and Jaffray had counted on the natural easy inclination of a man without a family turning his home into an office. Thus he came face to face with the man he had set out so ostentatiously to meet—ostentatiously to every man in his path with the single exception of Potter.

Potter took in the outline of his visitor with a sharp glance, a glance keen and penetrating from long training; but the indefinite outline of a figure with only the dull background of the fire, and no other reflections than those of the falling Winter evening, suggested nothing familiar. Jaffray smiled to himself. Still he said nothing.

Potter touched a button to turn on the electric lights, mouthing an easy apology the while for the carelessness of his servant in leaving him in the dark. As he turned and faced Jaffray, he stopped abruptly and stared. He took a step backward, and one hand went involuntarily to his brow.

"Homer Jaffray!" he cried, his breath catching at his throat.

Jaffray nodded, his eyelids closing and opening with the bobbing of his head like those of a mechanical doll tipped over backward.

"Yes," he repeated, "Homer Jaffray."

Jaffray studied the face. His eyes marked the fleeting emotions written there—surprise, hatred, fear. Potter moved slowly across the room, his hand before him, he steadied himself on the arm of his chair before sitting down. He avoided the malignant eyes that followed him.

"I have been expecting this moment—for five—years!" he said haltingly, as he stared at the table.

Then he opened a drawer and took out a revolver and laid it before him. The touch of the steel seemed to infuse new life into him, for he raised his eyes to meet those of the other.

"Sit down," he said, not loud, but with a suggestion of asperity.

Jaffray took the chair opposite.

"We are men," said Potter, studying the other as though trying to divine his thoughts. "We can talk it over calmly."

Jaffray made no response, but stared at the other with eyes so hard and cold that Potter dropped his gaze and let it wander to the fire. And thus, for a full minute while the mantel clock ticked, these two men sat silent and tense.

Potter was the first to stir. He turned and took a cigarette from a tray (a movement the other followed greedily) and began rolling it absentmindedly between his palms. The act in another man might have meant nonchalance, contempt, bravado. Stupidly, as though his thoughts were miles away, he searched his pockets for a match. Jaffray leaned forward with a quick movement, handing him his paper of matches.

"Permit me," he said with his easy though elaborate courtesy.

Potter started and brought his eyes back with an effort. He looked questioningly at the other, but said nothing as he took the proffered matches and struck a light, inhaling deeply as he held it to his cigarette.

Five minutes passed, during which Jaffray, his elbows on the arms of his chair and his head sunk between his shoulders, watched the other through half-closed eyelids. He reached over quietly and picked up the revolver. It was an automatic weapon, potential with quick, sure death. He threw over the cap and saw that the magazine contained a full clip of cartridges. It was still greasy with vaseline, this hair-trigger engine of destruction.

He replaced it in exactly the same spot where it had lain and, walking to the window, he raised the sash probably four inches, letting in a draft of cold air. Closing it again, he studied the thermometer on the wall, as the mercury slowly climbed back to normal. He picked up several pieces of paper that the draught had blown about the room, and when everything was in order again he gave his attention to Potter.

Potter's feet were drawn up under his chair, his knees wide apart; his head had fallen back and his gaze was fixed vacantly on the ceiling. Jaffray exposed one eyeball and pressed it with his finger. He felt for the pulse at the wrist and put his ear to the chest. All the while he was thinly smiling, even when the eyes stared at him. He touched the bell and stepped into the hall, drawing the door shut behind him.

"Your master is ill," he said to the startled maid-servant. "Seriously ill, I am afraid. A good deal depends on your promptness. Go at once for the nearest doctor."

Her eyes and mouth opened simultaneously. Before she could exclaim, however, Jaffray seized her shoulders and turned her right-about-face, saying sharply,

"Hurry, there is not a moment to lose!"

"A very capable woman," he said to himself as she suited the action to the word and dashed out of the house, hatless and coatless.

Five minutes later, when he was still considering the coolness of this female person, he heard steps outside, and he left off strumming his fingers on the table to open the door. A young doctor entered and Jaffray pointed to the huddled figure in the chair without a word. The doctor exclaimed in surprise, and leaned over the figure as he unbuttoned his ulster and drew off his gloves.

With one hand free he picked up Potter's right arm by the wrist, with his finger on the pulse. Between the fingers of the dead hand was the cigarette still burning, mute evidence of how shortly life had fled. With a grimace he took the cigarette from the livid fingers, and looking oddly at Jaffray, he straightened up. Jaffray compressed his lips, but said nothing. He was not interested in abstractions, however weird they might be.

"I happen to be the coroner," said the doctor, laying off his coat. "My name is Jevons," and he looked inquiringly at Jaffray.

"I am Mr. Homer Jaffray, of 1628 William Street," said Jaffray, producing his card.

"Ah, indeed," said the doctor-coroner. "I know you—or at least I know your firm, as I occasionally get supplies through them. This is rather an awkward situation for you, Mr. Jaffray," he added, assuming an official tone. "We officials grow rather callous to this kind of thing," he said, jerking his head over his shoulder at the chair, "but there are certain formalities that have to be gone through with. I will telephone the police, if you will excuse me a moment."

He went to the hall to telephone, and Jaffray heard him say:

"I think you had better come right over here, Carson, and we can clean it up in a jiffy."

The doctor stopped to question the maid-servant, whose frightened face appeared at the turn of the hall; and then he came back into the room, rubbing his hands to restore their circulation.

"Will you tell me just what occurred, Mr. Jaffray?" he said. "If I am not mistaken you have a medical training. Quite good. That will simplify matters considerably."

Jaffray related tersely the circumstances. They had no especial significance, explained nothing. Potter was in the act of lighting a cigarette. He was alive one second, dead the next, that was all. Jaffray had noticed no premonitory symptoms, no spasms, no coughing. In fact he had just come into the room. The face was rather livid. It suggested congestion, did it not? Possibly a blood clot.

"It is indeed most singular," said the doctor. "He had no heart trouble, although he smoked too much by far—had the infernal cigarette habit. I was his physician—had been in fact since he came here two years ago. He was in robust health—lived out a good deal."

He was plainly puzzled, but ventured the opinion that an autopsy would clear the situation.

"You were his friend?" he asked, looking up from his examination of the dead man. "I was rather intimate with him, but I never heard him speak your name. You were his friend?"

"No," said Jaffray.

"An acquaintance, then?"

"Hardly that."

"What brought you here? I am sorry, but you will have to answer some questions."

"I understand," said Jaffray, nodding.

He hesitated as if in doubt how to frame his words.

"Well," said the doctor impatiently.

Jaffray pointed to the revolver.

"Yes, you have already noticed it, I see," he said quietly. "If you wish to know how I felt toward him, you will understand when I say that if the hand of God had not intervened, still one of us would never have left this room alive!"

He turned a look of slow-burning hate at the figure in the chair. The doctor sniffed and looked uneasily about him.

"You are probably surprised at my—at what you choose to interpret as my lack of—respect, for the dead. I can save both you and myself trouble by frankness. It would be idle to show feeling, or to attempt to disguise the situation from the eyes of the police. Listen. I had sufficient and just motive to desire this man's death. And it was sufficient to make me jealous of the Divine Providence that has taken the task from me!"

"Oh, I say—" began the doctor.

Jaffray cut in on him sharply.

"Hear me out," he said. And then, "He took my wife from me—and thrust her aside! She killed herself three months after—"

"I think," interrupted the doctor, rubbing his hands together nervously, "that it is rather ill-advised for you to run on like this."

He paused, embarrassed.

"On the contrary," said Jaffray, "there is no other course open. However, there is only one other thing, and you as a county official, I think, should hear it." He wetted his lips. "I lost track of this man Porter—or Potter as he called himself here—but a strange chance brought us together. He had a great many irons in the fire, as you probably know. One of his investments had to do with an anilin process for which the Ætna Company holds the patent. It happens that I am the Ætna Company. He did not know it; else—" he smiled grimly—"I do not believe he would have involved himself in the litigation to test the Ætna's rights. I, myself, was in ignorance of his true identity until my lawyers brought the information to me."

There came a sound of hurrying feet and the doctor-coroner, welcoming the interruption, hurried to the door and admitted Lieutenant Carson and a civilian companion whom he introduced as a Mr. White—a young-old man, partly bald, with a nose like Louis Fourteenth's, and eyes set very wide apart. The pair gathered the surface facts, and then, as Jaffray, stood apart, the coroner related to them in a low voice the substance of what Jaffray had volunteered with such bloodless candor. Jaffray felt them looking at him from time to time. Carson at length joined him, a queer smile on his face.

"Your attitude is rather unusual, to say the least," he said. "However, that is your own concern. There seems no doubt that this man Potter or Porter, or whoever he may have been, came to his death through purely natural causes, but an autopsy will settle that. You say that you are Mr. Jaffray, the color manufacturer. I will not detain you if you can identify yourself to my satisfaction. The fact that you take occasion to say that you would have done your utmost to commit murder, if Potter had not been so good as to shuffle off on his own accord, is nothing that concerns me. I take it that your mania does not extend beyond this man. It means nothing to me, except—if you will pardon me—to emphasize the fact that it takes all sorts of people to make up the world."

"I am afraid the coroner has put the wrong construction on my words," said Jaffray. "Believe me, I explained the situation to him solely for my own protection. If you find an investigation necessary, these facts—my mania, as you choose to call it—would be the first to come to light."

Jaffray looked at his watch.

"It lacks a quarter of six," he went on in a matter-of-fact voice. "My office force stays late the last three days of the month to get off the foreign mails. If you will take the trouble to call my secretary, you will find that I left the office for Waverly at three this afternoon. I came down on the 3:30 train, and I drove to the house in a carriage which the young man at the office was kind enough to summon for me."

"You seem to have blazed rather a clear trail," said Carson dryly. He made no attempt to conceal his instant dislike for this person. "I will telephone, as you suggest."

Jaffray followed him with his eyes as he left the room. His gaze came back to the doctor who had taken a seat at the table and was filling in his reports. There was an easy contempt in that look. The official scrutiny of these two was irritating, yet at the same time amusing to one who had come by so long a road to so satisfactory a conclusion. He dropped into a chair, his back to the room, and gave himself over to his thoughts.

He was dimly conscious of the huddled form. Something in him, a little higher than the animal, a little lower than the human, vibrated, and thrilled him with a pleasing sensation. It was appeased hunger—that was it. He had often wondered what it would be. He had never been afraid of losing control of himself. He was too sure of himself and his means for that.

But even the beginning, which had destroyed all sense of proportion for him, seemed now dwarfed into insignificance by the finale. It had all evolved step by step, like some intricate formula that had to do with the mysticism of number instead of the fatalism of events. Through it all there had been that dull, gnawing something. And now it was gone. His blood ran cold and placid again, his thoughts flowed crystal clear. The very air he breathed was sweet and pure once again.

Carson's step aroused him from his reverie. Carson was satisfied with the investigation he had made by wire.

"I will not detain you, Mr. Jaffray," he said curtly. "You may consider yourself fortunate, however, because the average man in my situation would have clapped you behind the bars for your impertinence, if for nothing else."

Jaffray turned to hide the flush he felt mounting to his temples. He picked up his hat and coat, saying,

"If anything develops in which I can be of service to you, you can reach me by telephone either at my home or my office."

He nodded curtly to the room and was starting out when he was interrupted by White, the civilian onlooker.

"Just a moment, Mr. Jaffray," said White in a high, thin voice. "Just a question or two. You have half an hour for your next train."

Jaffray turned and eyed White questioningly. He had hardly noted his presence before. Now he noticed with a slight start that White had been interesting himself in the effects of the dead man, and had gathered on the table a collection of odds and ends such as one might find in any man's pockets.

"I didn't catch your name," said Jaffray.

"White."

"Of the police, I presume?"

"No. Newspaper," said White tersely.

Jaffray frowned. He had a contempt for the class.

"If there is anything you wish to ask me, lieutenant," he said, turning his back on White, "I shall be very glad to give you my time. Otherwise, I will be on my way."

"Who is your tobacconist, Mr. Jaffray?" asked White imperturbably, resuming his examination of his trifles. Jaffray was in the act of buttoning his coat. His lips curled in a sneer. He produced his cigar-case, from which he selected one cigar and handed it to White.

"I have to admit," he said, "that my dealings with your class are rather limited. However, I ought to know that cigars of course are usual. I am sorry you had to remind me. Permit me."

White took the cigar, and examined it critically.

"José Mendoza," he said, reading the name on the band. "And a very good tobacconist, I should say," he went on. "There is another formality—in dealing—with my class. Have you a match about you?"

Then suddenly, to the amazement of the other two who stood by, watching White draw sparks from the cold-blooded Jaffray, Jaffray lost control of himself. He glared at White, pale with rage. The muscles of his face began to work convulsively. He launched bitter invectives against the scavenger press and the meddling minions whose callous sensibilities stopped them at no outrage. Carson and the doctor stared in astonishment. White waited until the spasm had passed, and said,

"A match—like this, sir—if you please."

He held up a half-burned match, which he had found in the dead man's fingers.

"I can help you out with a light, White," said the doctor. "And what's more, I won't quarrel with you about it either."

"Thanks," said White. "I think Mr. Jaffray will oblige."

"You impertinent puppy!" cried Jaffray, striding toward the door. Carson blocked his progress at a sign from White. The police lieutenant was in the dark, but he was well enough acquainted with his friend White and his methods to follow his lead blindly and ask questions afterward.

"Stand aside, you!" snarled Jaffray, glaring at Carson; and the lieutenant answered by shutting the door and pocketing the key.

"This begins to look interesting," he said; and he walked to the table and selected a cigarette for himself. "Perhaps you will oblige me with a light, Mr. Jaffray."

"Does this mean that I am under arrest?" cried Jaffray.

The change that had come over him was pitiful to behold. His cool well-poised insolence seemed demolished at one blow. His eyes lost the veil that had given his face so dull an expression; and he turned from one to the other of the three men who were now watching him intently. The effect of this sudden development on Carson was electric. The situation was blank to him. Yet a cord had snapped, somewhere.

For fully a minute the scene was set thus, Jaffray motionless except for the convulsive breathing that heaved his body, and the others watching.

Then Jaffray's eyes wavered, but he brought them back instantly. A shade of color crept into his cheeks. It was a signal for White to step forward with soft tread, holding out his hand.

"If you please," he said, his gray eyes flickering as the only indication that he appreciated the situation his simple request had conjured up.

Jaffray drew a long breath. He had himself in hand again. He produced a paper of matches and handed them to White.

"José Mendoza, eh?" said White, as he examined the advertisement stamped on each stick. "A very good tobacconist."

He tore off a match and struck it and raised it to his cigar, watching its purple flame. He turned his eyes and encountered those of Homer Jaffray, tense and staring.

"You seem—fascinated—Mr. Jaffray," said White.

The match burned out in his fingers and he flung it away and lighted another, still eying Jaffray. The second burned down to his fingers and he flung this one away.

"Do you detect a peculiar odor—in the room—doctor?" he asked suddenly, turning to Jevons and sniffing.

A gasping cry escaped Jaffray. Before any one could move to block him he had reached forward and seized the weapon that lay on the table, and thrusting the muzzle in his mouth, he pulled the trigger!

"I must confess it is beyond me, yet," said Dr. Jevons. "I detected the odor of cyanogen in the air, yes. That was unmistakable. But what had that to do with matches—and these two men who so earnestly desired each other's death?"

"This is the match," said White, "that I found—in Porter's fingers. It had scarcely begun to burn, when his hand fell, extinguishing it. Do you see those tiny crystals—just beyond the burned rim? I don't know what they are. But I never saw them on a match before. Did you? Now, do you see—that blue discoloration on the match-stick? Prussian blue—I should say, eh? And the flame—it was a rich purple."

"Gad!" exclaimed the doctor, the chemist in him coming to the fore. "But how did you know?"

"I searched Porter's pockets—and I couldn't find—another match like that. Jaffray must have given it him; see? When I asked him for a light—he knew—the jig was up. Did you see him—study our faces? He wondered—how much we knew. He wasn't sure—so he took a long chance—and handed me the matches."

"I don't catch the drift," said the unimaginative police official.

"I will make a guess," said White. "Jaffray was a chemist. It was easy enough to strip the paste—off a bunch of matches—and substitute another paste—of his own compounding. Something like cyanid of mercury in it—I should say. Heat applied to cyanid of mercury—evolves cyanogen—the deadliest of gases. One good whiff—the breath, for instance, of a confirmed cigarette-smoker—like Porter here, and—well, you see Porter."

"And he offered you a light!" said the policeman. "I am mighty glad he didn't select me! Now I understand why he watched you like a bird watching a snake."

"You can hold your autopsy," said White, "but I don't believe you will find anything—except possibly a trace of gas—in the lungs. That match was the thing. If it had burned up—as it should have done—Jaffray would have been on his way—back to town—by this time. Poor devil! I wonder—if that was true—about his wife?"

The Phantom Alibi

No! No!" said Armiston, the extinct author, with the air of a sorely tried man doing his best to be civil. He turned to his desk, made a great to-do of being busy and interrupted. He had an impulse to rise and dismiss the persistent visitor with a bow. But he hesitated to be so abrupt. The fellow should take the hint!

"Murder," said the author, "is distinctly not in my line."

Oliver Armiston's visitor smiled, throwing a look of secret understanding at the fat Buddha who reposed among folds of flesh in one corner of the elegant room.

"You turned it to very good account once," he said mildly.

"I recollect your crew did me the compliment to tell me I was guilty," nodded Armiston.

"The guiltiest man unhung!" retorted the visitor, with relish. "You procured that crime! Our moderation on that occasion still astonishes me."

He was a man of fierce aspect, but his eyes had the habit of merriment. Parr, the deputy commissioner, for it was that exalted policeman himself, was recalling an incident in Armiston's career several years gone by, when the famous author of thrillers was gulled by a clever stranger into solving as fiction what proved to be a problem of fact. The fertile author not only contrived (on paper) to rob the unprincipled wife of a diplomat, but when the tale was published, tasted the bitter triumph of finding the clever stranger had executed the crime according to printed direction, not even eliding the murder which to Armiston, engrossed in the plot, had seemed unavoidable. This atrocity, succeeded as it was by a mysterious gift from the grateful perpetrator, had created such a sensation as to drive Armiston into retirement. No! Decidedly murder was not in his line!

Parr rose. Armiston forbore to look up for fear of detaining him. But Parr was not departing. He removed his top coat, remarking it was warm, and sat down again, smiling with sly satisfaction.

"You inspired that crime," said Parr easily.

"Your moderation on *this* occasion astonishes *me!*" broke in Armiston testily. "You arrest a reputable citizen for murder. You admit that the mere statement of the known facts, to any sane jury, would convict him. And then, as an officer sworn to uphold the law, you come privately to me, and say: 'Please, sir, as a personal favor, won't you prove my prisoner innocent.' Is the man innocent, then?"

"Yes."

"Then why arrest him, why accuse him of murder, if you know that he is not guilty? Does the law require a victim? Do you intend to prosecute him?"

"Certainly. I have no option."

"Even if you know he is innocent?"

"Facts, my dear boy. Facts. I can't go behind facts. *I* can't. You can. That's why I come to you."

"How do you know he is innocent?" In spite of himself, Armiston was giving heed. Nevertheless he was determined to smash Parr by logic, if insolence failed.

"How does a bird know North, in spring?" answered the imperturbable policeman, to whom nobody, not even his best friend, would have ascribed the smallest touch of imagination. He dealt with facts, as such; he was incapable of going beyond facts. He believed in shoe-leather and elbow-grease, not divination. Thus he had made his reputation as the very Nemesis of the law. And yet to-day he had come privately to the extinct author, whom he had not seen since that lamented circumstance of long ago, and said, somewhat astonished at his own words: "I am about to convict an innocent man of murder. Indeed I will, I must, unless you can find some way to prevent me." It was a tribute to the cogency of Armiston's fiction mind.

"Just what are the facts?" said Armiston, softening. And Parr, finally convinced that he had struck fire in his quest for subtlety of imagination to oppose his facts, hitched his chair nearer.

"Finger-prints-" he began-

"Bosh! Finger-prints are not facts!" cried Armiston, now fairly in the saddle. "Anybody can counterfeit finger-prints. It's merely a process of photography."

"There you are!" exclaimed the deputy, beaming on Buddha. "I didn't know that. I don't know it yet. Can it be done?"

Armiston daubed his thumb with the ink-bottle cork, and stamped it on a sheet of paper, making his own thumb-print.

"Photograph that life-size," said Oliver. "Print it on a pellicle of gelatine sensitized with bichromate of potash. Soak the gelatine in cold water. What have you? You will find on that pellicle of gelatine, in relief, the exact duplicate of the lines of my thumb. The lines stand up like type. Smear it with ink, grease, blood, anything—leave the imprint any place you want to—on a revolver handle, safe door, window—any place."

"Marvelous!"

"Not at all. Elemental," corrected Armiston dryly. "So much for your finger-prints! It's as old as the art of photography—it's used as a commercial process, to imitate photogravures. The trouble with you, Commissioner is that you don't recognize a fact when you see it. You accept somebody's say-so. A finger-print is gospel to you. It isn't to me. It's the first thing I suspect.

I wonder how many poor devils you've sent up, with your facts." He paused, rather pleased with himself. "Now trot out some more facts." He looked at his watch, as a gentle suggestion that his amiable mood would be of brief duration. Parr settled himself restfully in his chair.

"The murdered man was Sauer—J. H. Sauer," said the deputy.

"A reputable party?"

"No, I believe not. He had a process for making gold out of aluminum. It can be done. I am told."

"Did he do it?"

"Well, he did, and he didn't," said Parr. "He quietly interested a few people—good people—Brown, president of the Elm Park Bank, and Westcott, a technical man employed in the Assay Office, as another. Why is it," asked Parr, "that the clever crook selects the expert for his boob? This one did. Imagine Brown and Westcott, of all men in the world, falling for that sort of thing—the two men who above all others should have been wary. He demonstrated his process for them, and they were convinced he had what he claimed. There would be a pot of money in it, of course. But it meant a costly plant, to start. Well, when he found he had these two hog-tied, when they were willing to back him to the limit, Sauer got cold feet."

"Sauer? That's a new line, for a crook," Armiston, idly whittling a pencil, looked up.

"Wait." Parr was warming up. "After he had convinced the experts, the inventor himself began to have doubts. They were willing to go ahead, but he wasn't. He got the queer idea that he had been fooling himself, that there was a flaw somewhere. There was quite a row. I believe; but he wouldn't go ahead. They repeated that they were satisfied. He told them he didn't think their opinion was worth two whoops. Finally Brown, the banker, who saw riches slipping away from him, asked Sauer if he would be content to call in an umpire and let him decide. Well, Sauer backed and filled, and finally he said if they would call in an expert of unquestioned authority, all right. He would abide by the verdict. He didn't seem to be worrying over the fact that he might be fooling them. That was their lookout. He was afraid he was fooling himself."

The functionary of police chuckled softly to himself.

"Armiston," he said, "you told me once you were interested in electrolytic work. Didn't you study at the Polytechnic?"

Armiston nodded. He indicated a file of electrolytic journals on the bookshelf as indication that this branch of science was one he pursued from day to day, as a hobby.

"You know the big men in that line," said Parr. "Whom would you pick for umpire? Is there one outstanding man?"

"Pettibone—Dean Pettibone," said Armiston, without hesitation.

Parr nodded, as if he had expected this answer.

"They picked Pettibone," he said, turning to smile at Buddha.

"And he took one look, and gave them the laugh," put in Armiston. "I know just how he would do—without batting an eyelash. But what has this to do with murder? And your executing a man who didn't commit it?"

"Patience! I am coming to that," said Parr mildly. "Well, they made several dates. Pettibone agreed to come, not because he took any stock in it, but just to humor Brown. Then our friend Sauer contracted a jumping tooth. And for about three weeks he groaned in a dentist's chair, more concerned about saving that tooth, than he was about his million dollars. Finally the tooth was fixed up, and they had a session. Pettibone handed Sauer some aluminum, and Sauer went ahead with his usual hocus-pocus. When the thing was cooked, or pickled, or whatever there was to be done, he opened up the crucible to show the gold. Not a trace!"

Armiston grinned.

"Count on Petty for that!" he said.

"Well, they tried it again, and again. Nothing doing." Parr regarded Armiston with his dry smile. "It seems Sauer had been furnishing his own aluminum, hitherto. Salted it, I suppose. Those two experts never suspected him. You can get a trace of gold out of any sample of commercial aluminum—not enough to pay, but you can show it. Pettibone suspected what had happened. He handed Sauer a piece of chemically pure aluminum. And he didn't give him a chance to dope the brew. Then he laughed at him. There was quite a blow-up. Brown quit cold, feeling as if he had been made a fool of. So did Westcott. They left in a huff. But Petty stayed behind, Sauer buttonholing him. The last Brown heard. Pettibone was explaining to Sauer, in words of one syllable, just what kind of a crook he was."

"He'd do that—make it a point of honor," agreed Armiston. He yawned. "This is all very thrilling, Commissioner," he said. "But when do you produce the corpse?"

"We don't," said Parr, grimly.

"What? You can't execute a man for murder, in this state, without a *corpus delicti.*"

"We can't produce it," repeated Parr. "And yet, we are going to send Pettibone to the chair."

"Pettibone!" ejaculated the extinct author, now sitting up stark. "You're going to execute Pettibone?" he repeated. "Oh, my dear fellow! Come, this is too much of a good thing—"

"Pettibone was the last man seen with Sauer, alive," went on Parr. "Something happened. Nobody knows just what. The engineer in the basement was roused by a racket. Then water began coming through the ceiling as if there was a flood up-stairs. He called up the office, and with the nightman broke into Sauer's rooms, and found—"

"What?" exploded Armiston, for Parr had paused, smiling queerly.

"Nothing," said Byrnes. "Nobody there. The safe was open, a lot of papers were scattered about the floor. A chair or two was upset and broken; and the city water was pouring out of a broken pipe, from a connection that Sauer had had put in for his experiments. There had been a three-foot length of galvanized pipe over a lead sink. This pipe had been twisted off at the elbow, and there it lay on the floor. Somebody had been bludgeoned with it. On one end there was blood and hair. Otherwise—nothing."

Here the deputy paused again for dramatic effect.

"Have I hooked you on now?" he demanded nasally.

Armiston had sprung to his feet and was pacing the floor. He stopped in front of Byrnes.

"Pettibone arrested for murder! Oh, come, Parr," he said disagreeably. "This is too stupid, even for you." Parr grinned, with no ill-feeling. This was why he had come; he had deliberately played for this explosion.

"But the body—what became of the body?" demanded Armiston.

"What becomes of a lump of sugar in a glass of water?" retorted Parr. "It dissolves." He said in the same odd tone: "Well, that's what happened to our friend Sauer. He dissolved."

"Dissolved?"

"Pettibone's fingerprints were on one end of that pipe," said the policeman.

"Finger-prints, bah!" cried Armiston, angrily. To think that even police bungling would lay a sordid crime of this sort at the door of a man of Dean Pettibone's prestige was maddening.

"I will allow you that," said Parr. "But they led us to Petty. We searched his place. Why, I don't know. Only a fool would expect to find anything there. Still, he was the last man seen with Sauer alive—and something had happened to Sauer. In his laboratory Petty had a big lead tank full of liquid. We asked him what it was. He said it was residues. Residues of what, I don't know. Well, we drained that tank, and we found—this!"

He pushed his clubby fingers into a vest pocket and drew out a tiny ball of tissue paper, which he unwrapped carefully. He laid this small object of irregular shape on the desk. Armiston stared at it. He examined it, under a magnifying glass.

"It's gold, isn't it?" he said, puzzled. Parr nodded.

"It's the residue of our friend Sauer," he said coldly. "It is the *corpus delicti* that's going to convict Pettibone. It is the gold filling out of Sauer's tooth— the sole mortal remains of Sauer, that Pettibone couldn't dissolve in his vat."

Armiston sat down dumbstruck.

"Remember," continued Parr, with painful certitude, "it was only three weeks before, that the dentist made that filling. He used the amalgam process in making the pattern. He has the matrix—and it fits to a crossed T and a dotted I. Furthermore," said the policeman as he watched Armiston with keen eyes, "the dentist happens to have the preliminary rubber impression he took of Sauer's jaw. "You won't tell me you can counterfeit that. Those are the facts, Armiston," he concluded, and he leaned back in his chair to await the verdict.

In his school-days Dean Pettibone had been Armiston's kindly guide and friend, one of those rare teachers who achieve something like saintship in the memory of their students.

"It's—preposterous—" Armiston began, and halted. "Are you going to maintain in court that dear old Petty—why he doesn't weigh a good hundred pounds—carried the dead body of Sauer across town, in the middle of the night, to get rid of him in his vat?"

"Preposterous?" said Parr. "Not at all. It was midnight. Sauer's apartment was on the ground floor—with a private entrance in the side street. Pettibone admits he came and went in his coupé, alone. Nobody saw him leave Sauer's rooms. His laboratory is on a lonely road—I believe there was an element of danger in his research work, and a bad smell—and he had to get off by himself. Now do you say 'preposterous'?"

"Cobwebs!" cried Armiston contemptuously. "Use a little reason, Parr."

"'Reason?'" said the deputy. "There is no reason in a crime of violence. But that!—" He pointed to the tiny fragment of gold, every accidental irregularity of whose surface testified incontrovertibly to its identity. He turned fiercely on Armiston. "What are you going to do about that?"

"You can't establish a murder, with only a gold tooth to show," muttered Armiston.

"Can't I? Take the classic Webster-Parkman case as an example."

The deputy commissioner rose and pulled on his coat slowly. "The jury won't leave its seat," he said absently. "Regrettable, yes, to balance a man like Petty against a cheap trickster." He picked up the particle of gold and restored it to its tissue paper and as he put it back in his pocket, he murmured. "It will send your friend Petty to the chair."

Without a leave-taking he stalked out. In the street the police functionary permitted himself a complacent smile as he looked up at Armiston's windows. Unless he was very much mistaken, he had started a fire.

When armiston emerged, he at once became conscious of something in the air. Not infrequently, even in a city of such involved complexes as this, there comes a moment, an occasion when street-sweeper and applewoman, milady and her maid, stockbroker and greengrocer, think the same thought, as if an idea had become static, and anchored itself over them like a fog. On this day every street corner had its little group, heads together; in the restaurant where Armiston lunched, usually decorous people craned their necks over their neighbors' newspapers; the female cashier instead of saying, "It's a nice day," said, "Wasn't it awful about the vat?"

The latest extra blared in large type—"HELD WITHOUT BAIL!" One couldn't escape it; in the quietest side street the eddies of the news danced and swirled, the vat murder was on the tip of the tongue wherever one turned. The sleuth-hounds of the press, long fretting on leash, were loose, full cry. This single obscure crime summoned into being myriad phenomena of human interest and activity. On every corner stood impatient groups jingling pennies and waiting for fresh extras. It isn't often that the public gets a best-seller. When it does, newspaper circulation must stand ready to expand like a rubber band.

Momentarily there had been doubt, unbelief. But the facts were overwhelming. Then, as if by some common process of thought, the world of newspaper readers became sophists. At Armiston's club his friend Ballard voiced the tone of public debate when he said:

"The real crime was Pettibone's overlooking that gold tooth. He deserves the chair for that. Pettibone, a chemist, tripping up on a solvent for gold! I condemn his bungling after the blow was struck. But for the grace of God— as some one said somewhere," said Ballard, eying the cultivated circle, "you or I might have struck that blow. In each of us is a moment of blind fury, waiting to be summoned. Most of us escape the summons. Pettibone didn't. What then? Should his career of public usefulness be annihilated, simply because instinct overwhelmed reason, for a split second? I say, no!"

"I say, no!" responded several of the circle.

"Pettibone is a man of rare mind," went on the sophist. "He knew what he had to lose. Therefore the more reason to conceal his act. And he, a chemist," cried Ballard in disgust, "trips up on a problem a schoolboy wouldn't have missed—the solvent for gold."

"What is the defense?" asked Armiston, for Ballard was a famous pleader.

"None!" said the lawyer savagely. "Not yet—not for another hundred years. Sauer was a despicable swindler. A decent man, a righteous man, removes him— kills him. And now we, in the name of justice, purpose to annihilate Pettibone, a man with a brain a thousand years ahead of his time!"

Armiston went through a daily ritual before his typewriter. He inserted a recording sheet, lightly brushed his fingers-tips, and gazed abstractedly at the keys. He had great faith in this oracle; time and again, with almost clairvoyant powers, it had solved problems for him. It was probable that the cerebral ganglion in Armiston's finger-tips led him, on those occasions, through the maze of the keyboard. But now the oracle was mute.

"Petty slipped up, for once in his life," mused Armiston for the hundredth time as he stared at the blank wall with opaque eyes, his fingers poised above the keys.

Then suddenly, and without admonitory signal, the oracle spoke! Armiston's fingers, moving mechanically, tapped the keys.

"Did Sauer?" demanded the typewriter.

Armiston felt a queer pricking at the back of his neck. There was something uncanny in the way those two words spontaneously formed themselves before his eyes. He let his thoughts drift. Did Sauer? Did Sauer slip up any place?

That was as far as he could get. The typewriter relapsed into Delphian silence, his fingers refused to move.

"Obviously," said Armiston, "that implies motive, on the part of Sauer."

The oracle refused to be drawn into an argument.

Armiston took a stroll through the Park, conjuring himself to think. But that typewriter had become so necessary to his process of thought in his years of scribbling that without it he found himself stranded.

"Parr," he said to that person of the police an hour later, "who was Sauer? Did he ever really exist?"

"Apparently he was a fact. You might ask Brown, or Westcott," answered Parr.

"Who was he, before he came here?"

"A mining engineer," said Parr. "Brown looked up his references. Sauer wasn't exactly a shade, Armiston. He was flesh and blood enough to be bashed on the head with a bludgeon."

Oliver ignored the sarcasm.

"What did he leave as an estate, besides that gold filling?" he persisted.

"There's a bank balance—about eight hundred dollars."

"That's something. What else?"

This was a demand for material detail, not the flash of divination the deputy had hoped for when first he laid before the extinct author the advance proofs of the now-celebrated vat murder. He drew forth a small bundle of slips, on which J. H. Sauer had, on one insignificant occasion or another, signed his name. It was the handwriting of a habitual draughtsman, as characteristic in its way as that of a telegrapher. Armiston studied the script with the interest of one who, for the first time, comes on the incontrovertible proof of the life and activity of a person who heretofore has existed for him merely as a name.

The sprite here nudged Oliver's elbow.

"Did Sauer?" it whispered, out of the thin air. Armiston departed. Late in the afternoon he presented himself at the home of Dean Pettibone, a little red brick house encircled by a veranda, near the University. Armiston had smoked many a contemplative pipe here, in his school-days, and the sight of the comfortable study with its swept hearth, gave him a pang. Parr had given him a line to the policeman in charge, for the Law had put its seals here.

"I'm trying to help," he explained lamely to the dried-up little secretary, a woman who had not aged by a hair in twenty years, as he remembered her. "We are all trying to help. I want to look round."

"His life is an open book," she said. "You remember his 'log'. They've been through it again and again."

It was a life of an open book, a book of volumes. Dean Pettibone's one marked peculiarity was the desire to set down everything from day to day, as a conscientious navigator would make up his log. Pettibone, with the precise mind of a born scientist, had the habit of saying that, of all the human faculties, one's memory was the least entitled to trust and respect. Endowed with a photographic memory, he never permitted himself to trust it. That Sauer should not have left some premonitory shadow in this human document, which reflected so minutely, seemed absurd—at least from a metaphysical standpoint. But Armiston was not voyaging in the realms of metaphysics, as he turned page after page, under the scrutiny of the sleepy policeman and the anxious little old maid.

A month passed. The rubber band of public interest, measured by the barometer of newspaper circulation, was moving on through other fields of force. The vat murder had subsided. On the side of Pettibone there was nothing to be expected. The Dean had contented himself with a single explicit statement, in the beginning. His respect for words and their uses gave his denial of guilt at once a simplicity and a completeness that were almost classic. Here was a man accused of murder, with no resources save the dignity of his bare word, who made no effort to conceal his contempt for the stupidity of inflexible justice. The little savant passed his days of waiting in a cell amid peace and quiet that he had always craved, but never before achieved. He immured himself and begged his friends to spare him, he buried himself in his books.

The mighty voice of the press even found time to record with much humor how Oliver Armiston, the once popular author of thrillers, absent-mindedly dropped his eye-glasses into a mail-box instead of a letter, rendering himself visually helpless until a postman appeared and permitted the author to paw among the letters for his lenses.

"They never come back!" muttered the deputy commissioner with conviction, as he noted this silly item. More and more, as the days dragged on without incident, the police official regretted having exposed his own fallibility to the extinct author in the vain hope of some super-normal help.

"The state rests."

Fielder, the District Attorney, turned to Ballard, counsel for the accused, and as he sat down he muttered under his breath in a tone that carried only to that man's ears:

"God help you! I have done what I could. Facts are facts!"

Parr sat back in his chair, his arms folded across his chest, looking glum. Judge and jury turned expectantly to Ballard, famous barrister, who had stepped into the case at the last minute. During the presentation of the State's evidence against his client, Ballard had indulged only in formalities; in several incidents it seemed that he went to extraordinary lengths in inducing witnesses to emphasize the damning facts of their testimony.

"Make a plea. We will accept anything in reason," muttered the District Attorney under his breath. Ballard turned on him a look of slow astonishment, and indicated the placid little figure of the prisoner with a slight nod, as who should say: "Can you imagine such a man as that accepting a mitigation of the charge!"

Ballard rose to his feet, stood for a long time surveying the jury, whose appetite had been whetted for one of the great forensic addresses for which this man was famous. The master of sheer oratory, that curious species of hypnotism by which one man moulds the mind of a mob, said only.

"The defense will call only one witness in refutation."

A little thrill ran through the room. Ballard looked at his watch and stepped to the bench where he consulted in low tones with the Court and the prosecutor, and a brief recess was declared. Courtroom and jury box, held in vague suspense, waited; the scene wore that tension of dramatic action momentarily halted. The first interruption was the entrance, somewhat breathlessly, of Oliver Armiston; he dropped into a seat beside Ballard, giving the inquiring deputy a scant nod. Parr noted with surprise that the extinct author sported a badly swollen eye. The green doors opened a second time, and two court officers appeared, followed by a middle-aged man, evidently a person of some position in life. He looked neither to right nor left, as he came down the aisle and stolidly took his place in the witness chair, as the court was called to order again. Then he glanced around stiffly, and when he encountered the face of Dean Pettibone, his eyes lingered there for a moment.

"Your name?" said Ballard.

The witness wet his lips.

"Hilary Jerome Swett."

"Your occupation?"

"I am an inventor," said the man, looking curiously over the jury.

"Do you know the defendant, Mr. Swett?" pursued Ballard.

The witness nodded, and turned his gaze again on Pettibone.

"When did you last see him?"

"In 1912," said the witness, without hesitation. "In the Federal Court."

"What was the occasion?"

"A patent suit," responded Swett acidly. His eyes, as if drawn by fascination, again sought the prisoner's face.

"You were an interested party?"

"I was the plaintiff."

"And Dean Pettibone?"

"He was called to give expert testimony." The man drew a deep breath, and the whole room hitched forward in its seats.

"What was the outcome of the suit, Mr. Swett."

"I lost—my case was thrown out of court." The words were so low as to be hardly audible. Ballard moved slowly back and forth before the witness.

"Was the expert testimony responsible for the verdict?" he asked finally.

"Yes," he said; the witness seemed now to have thoroughly recovered his composure. "Wholly," he added.

Ballard picked up one of the exhibits on the table and examined it absently for a moment. Then he raised his eyes to the witness and asked with great gravity.

"Are your teeth entire, Mr. Swett?"

The effect of this question was like a pistol shot. The Dean, the prosecutor, even the Court, exclaimed audibly. The witness started, violently; he blanched. He grasped the arms of the chair until the veins stood out on his wrists, and turning mechanically, he sought again the now searching eyes of the prisoner.

"Are all your teeth intact, Mr. Swett?" persisted the lawyer, cold and incisive. He held up to view the object in his hand; it was the rubber impression of the upper jaw of the murdered man, one incontrovertible link in the chain of circumstantial evidence that the law had been forging about Dean Pettibone these last three days.

"I ask particularly," continued Ballard, now suddenly stentorian, "about the first bicuspid, of the right upper jaw. Will you please show the jury," he urged, advancing on the witness who seemed to have become stone. Ballard opened his own mouth and indicated with a finger, the tooth.

The answer was unexpected action, almost too swift for the staring eyes to register. With a single bound, Swett was out of his seat; he cleared the steps in a stride and bowled over the obstructing figure of his tormentor. With almost the same gesture he seized a chair, and raising it above his head, charged on Dean Pettibone, crying shrilly:

"You die! You die now! I take you with me!"

It was Armiston, unused to protective reflexes as he was, who fell on the advancing madman as he towered over the little Dean, and the pair went to the floor with a crash. The next instant the court officers had pinioned the struggling Swett.

"Your Honor, and gentlemen of the jury!" rang out the triumphant voice of Ballard over the din of pounding gavel and the shouts of the officers restoring order, "behold the *corpus delicti!* Behold the murdered man, in person!"

"Sauer was a phantom," said Armiston, moulding a cigarette with finished care. He was tasting tribute. This was the first time wittingly the author had ever set the stage of his typewriter with real characters and watched them walk through their parts. "Luckily we were able to provide the *corpus delicti* with an alibi. Else," added the beaming author, turning to the little Dean who sat balanced on the end of a sofa, "our conscientious friend here might have added another notch to his gun, Dean."

Parr took this sally woodenly.

"Ninety-nine per cent of my work is common sense," said he. "I leave the ouija-board one per cent, to the fiction writers."

"Swett set up the fictitious identity of Sauer, with proper make-up, to be murdered," went on the author. "That was his game from the beginning. He took eight years to do it. Once he established the identity, he plotted to be brought to Pettibone, to quarrel with him, to have Pettibone the last man seen with him alive. Then he planted his bludgeon, his fake finger-prints, and the gold filling—and vanished, leaving the rest to Parr. That's all there is to it."

"But how—how?" demanded Parr, who had arrived at the state of openly admiring his own perspicacity in enlisting the aid of the hectic author.

"Habit," said Oliver sententiously. "It's the strongest impulse we have. It's not born; it's acquired. It attacks man's faculties in their weakest spot. If you ask the Dean, he will tell you that man's weakest faculty is his memory."

The Dean admitted as much with a nod.

"But how—how did you trace him—how did you catch him?" insisted the deputy, in his hunger for facts.

"He caught himself," said Armiston. "You went ahead on the belief that it was the Dean who erred. It wasn't the Dean. It was Sauer. You had seventy-three copies of J. H. Sauer's signature, Parr. I dug up thirty-six more. Once he signed it 'H. J.', instead of 'J. H.' There is one thing in the world a man isn't apt to forget—although the Dean won't admit it. That's his own name. J. H. Sauer did. Once! That was enough," Armiston laughed, shaking his head at the deputy. "Parr, it all lay before your eyes, waiting to be picked up."

"Still I don't see," said the deputy. "Swett hasn't a criminal record. How trace one 'H. J. Somebody' among a million?"

"Oh, it wasn't as bad as that," laughed Armiston. "The only 'H. J. Somebody' to interest me would be in Pettibone's log book. I found H. J. Swett's name there. That was enough to go on. Then I found H. J. Swett himself, living obscurely—the discredited plaintiff of a million-dollar patent suit can't exactly lose himself. During the three months J. H. Sauer was dickering with Brown and Westcott to be brought to Pettibone, there was no trace of J. H. Swett. That was another trump card. Then I wanted his handwriting. I schemed all sorts of ways, but failed. Finally I robbed the mails." Oliver shook with merriment. "I saw him mail a letter. After he was gone. I absent-mindedly mailed my own eye-glasses in that same drop-box, and then yelled bloody murder, till the postman came along and opened the box for me. Then with a facility that actually alarmed me, I palmed Swett's letter. There was no doubt which one it was when I saw the handwriting."

The little circle, Ballard, Parr, the District Attorney, and the Dean himself, nodded their admiration at this confession of robbery of the sacred mails.

"That brings us to the final curtain. I wanted to ask J. H. Swett one question—about that tooth. He must have pulled it, to extract that gold filling. Then he probably had another put in, in its place. How to find out, stumped me. I consulted Ballard, who has the direct mind of a child, and some lawyers," said Armiston. "Ballard said, 'Put him on the stand as a material witness and ask him.' Nothing simpler. Swett might reasonably be called as a witness, because he lost a million dollars through the Dean's expert testimony in that patent suit. It jarred Swett when he found where he was. But he had great nerve, and he carried it through, until Ballard asked him about that tooth. Then you saw what happened."

The author tenderly caressed his swollen eye, now rapidly taking on a violet hue.

"Swett had been living pretty retired," he went on. "He was reading all the papers, and gloating—but he stayed behind his shutters. This morning I think he got nervous. He ran out his car and started off uptown. There was only one way to stop him. Ram him! I rammed him! Then I smashed him in the eyes with my fist, accusing him of wrecking me. We were knocking off each other's hat when a cop pried us apart and took us to jail. He didn't dare ask for bail—so we had him on ice, so to speak."

The little group broke up. Dean Pettibone sat for some time with his hand shading his eyes, as he codified his thoughts. Then, "Miss Pruyn," he called, and his little secretary entered. "Will you please take dictation, Miss Pruyn," he said gently, drawing up a chair for her, and taking up his notes. "We have quite a hiatus to fill, haven't we? One must never neglect such things."

Wild Honey

IT was morning, the cool of the morning, the brief ecstatic hour when the sun drinks dew from gleaming chalices and all men are giants. A fugitive moment, this, when the gods in ironic lenity lift the veil from mortals' eyes and let them know their own strength. Hunger, thirst and fatigue are vanished; youth comes again to creaking joints, love warms dried hearts, ambition stirs the blood; and, as the Arabs say of eternal bliss, one holds to his lips the wine of desire, the measure of whose content is one's wish. But unless one bestir himself to grasp it, the sublime and volatile spell escapes him and he is only a man again.

Even old Ezra Beddes felt the stir of the morning. The sour, suspicious heart ticking under his spare ribs was stirred by a thrill in which there was no misanthropy; his beady little black eyes, peering out under a thatch of thick hair pressed tight to his forehead by his battered old hat, gleamed with something that was not hatred of the human race. He sat astride the chopping block by the woodpile, shaving a toothpick with delicate strokes of a razor-edged clasp knife. Now and again as the orbit of his meditations reached its apogee he would pick up a ragged knee in his scrawny fingers and nurse it, while he gazed at the cerulean heavens in which not a single cloud floated. At this moment the little old man, the magic of the dew-drinking hour having lifted from about him the surly cloak in which he clothed himself against human kind, was almost beautiful. He was dreaming of cogs and pawls and ratchets and whirring pinions.

The day before, driving home from the big city, as he called Beldenville—the tiny hamlet in the valley that was the only metropolis he had ever known—behind his old white horse, Kit, with his son Urial, he had paused with carefully veiled interest at the door of the scythe shop. There a group of natives were watching, with sheer bewilderment of unbelief, a newfangled machine that with one dexterous twist turned a stick of hickory into a polished ax helve. It was a new machine, its red paint and gilt letters still shiny; and all day long the curious villagers had watched it, trying to surprise the secret of its eccentric genius. They made way for little black Ez. He could tell them, they knew, if he would. But though his heart thrilled at the sight of this legerdemain he held himself in check. In one swift look through the mat of hair he photographed the thing on his retina, then with apparent indifference drove on. Now, in the wealth of morning, old Ez was taking the thing apart, being careful not to lose a single cotter pin or to misplace a gear, as he sat, alternately whittling a toothpick and nursing his knee, on the chopping block.

Before the greedy sun had slaked his thirst the bright and shiny machine old Ez had taken apart to examine was reassembled, in his mind's eye, to the last rivet of its complicated insides; and he made a pass through the air, as if to shift a loose pulley belt and set its dozens of knives whirring in eccentric orbits.

"There!" he exclaimed in a tone of triumph, so loud and shrill that Gyppie, the velvety black spaniel idling at his feet, sat up and cocked her ears and swiftly made reconnoissance of hill and dale. But there was nothing; merely old Ez finishing a day's work before the dew was off the grass. It was quite enough, to take down and set up a machine he had never seen before.

He knocked out his pipe and filled it with Plowboy's Delight, struck a match on the ax head and applied the light to the bowl with a curious enveloping movement of an animal fending off a storm. From the wood-shed came the song of the separator. Ezra and Urial sold a little cream. A pair of shotes shouldered each other squealing at the trough, waiting for the flow; and a covey of chickens came cluttering up on legs and wings; three scrawny cows with spare udders, drinking their fill at the spring, methodically extricated themselves from the mudhole and, with whisking tails and impatient tosses of the head, wound their way along the deep-cut path through the barway to the cool shade of the woods. A chicken hawk floated lazily overhead; from the alders came the single whistle of a bobwhite; a car in loose-jointed agony passed along the road below the stone wall, rolled across the dry, loose planking of the bridge with a roar that the surrounding hills took up in hollow echoes; away off a mowing machine tinkled; there came the hum of a motor truck a mile away on the main road; the old clock in the kitchen struck eight, and, as if waiting for its summons, a distant sawmill took up its rhythmic complaint.

Old Ez missed nothing of these portents. He codified facts. Orlando Sage's car missed, in the front cylinder—too much oil. Orlando was the town Pooh-Bah. Ed Harrow was sawing maple for a trip-hammer handle; Johnson Benedict was hauling grain to town in his new five-ton truck; Abner Waters was mowing his oats for fodder—and before the dew was off the grass, at that; only Abner, in all this countryside, would do such a thing.

Urial, loose-jointed, long-armed, his long, thin face clothed in the stupidity of a man whose mind moved intermittently, came out of the wood-shed, filling his pipe, and sat down on the chopping block beside his father. His attention as he arranged himself was suddenly attracted by the spectacle of two city fishermen working up the stream; they were amateurs, as was evident from their mincing progress from one slippery rock to another. Also from their clothing, which reminded old Ez, now with Gyppie suddenly alert, of the most recent issue of the mail-order catalogue, of which he treasured a library, which was his only window to the world outside.

Father and son and dog watched the fishermen in silence. There was humor in the situation, too obvious for comment. Ez and Urial didn't begrudge the fishermen their sport—they would catch nothing but the river bottom with their fancy flies and mail-order clothes. This afternoon towards dusk Urial, armed with angle-worms, would cover the same ground with sure feet, dropping his bait into one spring hole after another until he had a basketful of trout, which would be before milking time. He would manage to go by the hotel, and be asked by the city sports how he did it; he would answer with gulping candor and bulging eyes as he examined in detail the lineaments of his questioners.

Suddenly from behind the maples screening the up road came the drum of a sweet-running motor. It was a sleek little green car. It turned in at the gate, changing to low when it struck the sawdust drive. It held a man and a woman whom father and son recognized as the city people, the Armistons, who had recently bought the old Emmons place. They were of some note in the village because of a cow they had immediately purchased from Lemuel Bannon. Lem in clinching his bargain had said that he never yet had been able to get all the milk in one pail, which was true, because the cow always kicked the pail over before the operation was complete.

At this approach of visitors Urial plucked the ax out of the chopping block and started for the woods, with an air of sudden industry. Little Ez meditatively knocked the ashes out of his pipe and headed slowly, with a yawing gait, for the house, Gyppie following stoically at heel. He shut the screen door and locked it, shut the inner door, with its broken glass pane, and busied himself about the kitchen. Urial, watching with vacant stare from the cover of alders, saw the man knock, once, twice, then move to the other door and repeat his summons.

After a long time old Ez appeared; while the man talked Ez watched the river and the mountains and the hawk floating in the sky. The man turned away, evidently discouraged; but the woman sent him back to the attack. He knocked at the front door again. No response. He went to the back door, where at length Ez showed himself with a dishcloth, and after a moment's parley closed the door. When the little car was out of sight Urial returned.

"They are going to shingle their barn," said the father. Urial disposed of the ax.

"Cripes! There's more damn work!" ejaculated old Ez with the air of one completely staggered by the overwhelming demand for his time.

"What you tell 'em?"

"I said maybe—when we get in the oats."

But Urial lost the reply. He was pointing in intense excitement in the direction of the chopping block, his face animated into vivid resemblance to that of an American Indian.

"There's another now!" he cried in a guttural whisper.

Father, son and dog, in rigid attention, stared in the direction of the pointing finger. Old Ez, without relaxing his gaze, reached inside the door stealthily for some hidden object. It was a tiny white box. Clutching it in his fingers, he crept towards the chopping block, Urial and the stiff-legged spaniel at his heel. The object of their breathless stalking was a honeybee, visible only to eyes as keen as theirs. Negotiating the last ten feet on hands and knees, old Ez at arm's length from his goal paused to open his little box, and with a touch as delicate as a lapidary's deposited it close to the ranging insect.

The three crept back to the doorstone. Minutes passed. The hawk still floated overhead; the sun blazed the threat of a blistering day; the tall poplar tree by the gristmill, as if in sudden terror at some unseen danger, rustled violently and then was still. Old Ezra snatched a look at the heavens—it would rain before night, probably one of those crashing thunderstorms that visited the valley these hot days. Father and son smoked a pipe through and visited.

Presently the honeybee discovered the little box, and in its quest for sweets crawled inside. The box had two rooms, one a sugar trap. Eventually old Ezra rose, boldly approached the box and shut the lid, imprisoning the gorging bee. Another half hour passed. Then the great moment came. Old Ezra cautiously opened the trap; and the bee, full to repletion, dutifully bethought itself of home and empty cells. It rose straight in the air for a yard, then began a corkscrew spiral, like an airplane climbing for height, the coils becoming wider and wider. No untrained eye could have followed that tiny speck.

"There he goes!"

The shout was simultaneous as father and son, in the stiff attitudes of pointing scarecrows, strutted forward a step or two, forefingers aimed at an invisible mark against the metallic sky, from which the honeybee was at this instant drawing a straight line—a bee line—to its hidden hive somewhere off in the forest. The next instant, the spell broken, father and son fell into their habitual slouch and shambled back to the doorstone, where they sat down again. Raptly they searched the undulating, leafy surface of the forest rising from the opposite bank of the river. Finally old Ez, casting his eyes on the ground, drew two lines in the dust.

"Right there!" he said. "That's the dead maple on top the ledge of Rocelia Swan's lot."

Urial nodded. "Yep," he agreed.

That dead maple was five miles away as a crow, or a bee, flies. It stood in the midst of a tumble of granite and forest growth, a mile from any made road. Old Ez might have added that it stood at the top of an all but impossible climb. It was a historic tree—it was where the Markhams were shot dead in a bloody battle by a posse thirty years ago, one winter night after they had murdered and robbed 'Gene Johnson, a cattle buyer. Old Ez might have identified the ledge and the tree thus, but it was unnecessary. Urial knew just the tree. Stones, stumps, spars and boles, scattered hither and yon through the lonely woods on every hand, each bore a countenance, a figuration as familiar to these two as the faces of their own cattle, and they could direct each other to an exact spot by a word.

Old Ez curled up under the apple tree and, pulling his tattered hat over his eyes, arranged his mind for sleep. It was a prime day for cutting the oats, only it was a little late to start. Besides, he had done enough for one day. First, that ax-helve machine that he had taken down and set up again while sitting on the chopping block. It wouldn't have been too late to start cradling the oats then, but as luck would have it he had been forced to stop and explain to the city people—who bought the Bannon cow that couldn't be milked in one bucket—that he couldn't help them right now with the shingling. Fortunately, too, that they delayed him, else probably—probably—he'd have missed the chance to line that bee. Old Ez sighed. He had been doing headwork this morning, which, as anyone knows, is the most trying kind of work; it takes the tucker out of a man. That ax-helve machine—probably the man who invented it got, well, maybe he got a thousand dollars.

"I put one together in half an hour—no, fifteen minutes. Maybe not just like his, but it will work just as good as his. And I don't get a cent!"

Ez finished this hurt soliloquy aloud, and Gyppie, nested beside him, looked up, cocking an ear in inquiry.

The bee tree was something else. That old maple was a whopper. Three feet through at the butt. They ought to get fifty—no, a hundred—maybe as much as two hundred pounds! Old Ez began to snore to the tune of the dainty drip-drip of the honey in that bee tree five miles away.

Truth to tell, it had been brain work to locate that bee tree. Armed with a sextant, a compass and a book of logarithms and traverse tables, any midshipmite fresh from Bowditch would have been proud to put his finger on a position by the same method. Two lines would have been necessary for old Nathaniel Bowditch, the original American navigator, and his child the midshipmite. Also for old Ez. Where two lines intersected, on the ocean floor or in the forest, would be the desired position or bee tree, as the case might be. Men were paid for doing just that sort of headwork, and paid well. Bowditch called for a compass and tables; Ez used two bees. Bowditch called it trigonometry and traversing; Ez called it linin' bees. The first line necessary for his calculations he had obtained at the abandoned charcoal kilns one morning a week ago, at daybreak, when returning from bullheading at Spectacle Pond. His cows lowing at the bars and his hogs grunting at the empty trough had had to wait for that bee to climb for height and select its tangent.

The sun rose higher and hotter. Urial in the woodshed gossiped with his pet crow, which was learning to talk. Occasionally he rose to inspect the leaching of a barrel of ashes for soft soap and a crock of potato yeast warming itself by the stove. Flies now and then pestered Ez to wakefulness, as they did Gyppie; as he would fall back into easeful slumber the steady drip-drip of the honey five miles away, nailed down by two bee lines, accompanied him back through the door of dreams.

Once he said very distinctly: "Cripes! I did it in fifteen minutes—and I don't get nothing!"

Afternoon droned on into evening. Ez and Gyppie started for the cows; off on the hills floated the sonorous "Soo, boss! Soo, boss!" of the little old man. When the cows failed to be lured from their cool thickets by his enticing tones Ez became more personal and acid in his remarks to the sly hidden creatures, and shrill profanities echoed from crag to crag with shameless distinctness. Then the milking and evening chores, and supper. Then old Kit was put between shafts, a lantern swung from the rear axle, and father and son, with dog at wheel, journeyed to the big city, there to sit on the post-office porch to watch and listen, and occasionally join in the talk, until the postmaster snuffed out his lamps at nine. Then the solitary lantern wound its slow way homeward through the dark.

The next morning unusual industry pervaded the yard. Axes were ground to razor edges; there was a muster of sap buckets, a riveting of broken bails and soldering of rusty holes. The sugar scoops were polished as bright as new, paddles were whittled out of dry beech, smudge snuffers, an old hive, honey frames added, all the gear stowed in the wagon box and covered from prying eyes with a horse blanket redolent of age.

Old Kit started out at her traditional pace down the road. The neighbors Ezra and Urial met they regarded in surly silence; they had a secret, a bee tree, and they suspected all of coveting it. They worked themselves into a bitter mood over the thought. With furtive glances back and forth, they suddenly turned off through a disused barway into a tangle of briers that had once been a meadow. Instantly they were lost like vanishing animals. For a time the creak of the old wheels, the crack of an ax where they had to clear a path for Kit and the shrill voice of old Ez encouraging or objurgating the patient Kit were the only indications of their progress. This had been an old wood road almost impossible of passage except by cattle even in its heyday; but they crept up and up, till the overwhelming trees suggested the top of the world. Then abruptly the caravan paused and waited in silence.

Suddenly the air was rent with an ungodly chorus of snarls and howls. Through a clearing ahead was a little hilltop meadow lying like a saddle blanket to the sun. Two ancient hounds alternately charged at and retreated from father and son, rushing back from a valiant sally to a decayed old house of some pretension with belching chimney, where near the door a whiskered old man sat sunning himself.

"Who's thar? Down, Jeff! Down, Beau! Who be y'u? Stand out in the open, consarn ye!"

At the sound of the withered old voice father and son instinctively cowered. It was Ezra's father, Ebenezer, a nonagenarian hermit. Years ago Ezra and his father had stopped speaking to each other, for no apparent reason. Gradually the determination had dawned on old Ezra never to set foot on his father's domain while the old man lived. Ebenezer Beddes had been a notorious Copperhead, shunned by his neighbors. His two dogs, Jeff Davis and General Beauregard, were named for his patron saints; they had become his sole companions. It was the talk of the village that the old hermit had a hoard, and that old Ezra, his only son, knew just where to put hands on it when the moment came.

Some sixth sense must have told the feeble old man that his blood was nigh, for he rose on shaking pins with the aid of a knotted stick and shook his fist at the woods.

"You keep off my land! I know ye! You needn't spy round here!"

Ezra grinned sheepishly as he turned old Kit off into the brush and circumnavigated the parent clearing. Once on the other side it was easier going. About ten, cresting a little rise, they reached their theoretical destination. The gaunt dead maple stretched its arms in an attitude to high heaven. The invaders spelled themselves with a smoke.

"Wonder if we can fall it uphill?" mused Urial.

"Got to!" ejaculated the old man fiercely.

He cast an eye on the feathery wreaths of bees floating here and there against the gray old trunk. Their trigonometry, their calculations, their traversing, their distance-and-departure figures, arrived at, not by theodolite, but by two bees going home laden with honey, were correct. They expressed neither surprise nor satisfaction.

At the foot of the ledge they staked out old Kit, cumbered themselves with their gear and climbed up, drawing themselves from one tree root to another. They got out their dinner—cake, pie and sour pickles—consumed the repast in silence. Then they gathered dry leaves and punk and green twigs for smudge, which must be ready at the critical moment. They selected axes, tested edges, spit on the helves and slid the polished hickory back and forth through the eyelet of their clasped fingers to limber their muscles. Then, taking positions opposite, they fell to. It was pretty work, slice to slice.

The great hollow tree boomed and drummed with the alarum of its myriad tenants, disturbed at their peaceful labors. Now and then father and son, working like the two halves of one wheel, would pause spontaneously, and as spontaneously fall to again. The notch yawned deeper and deeper, the majestic spar standing staunch to the wound. Then quietly, like an old man dying, without even a premonitory shudder, the spar nodded, fell— lazily at first, then with gathering momentum and a thundering crash that shook the hills to strange clamor.

Old Ezra, with resting ax, turned to note, with no evidence of pride, if they had felled it true, to a hair line. The next instant with a wild yell of warning he threw himself to the ground and rolled down the ledge with the agility of a mountain cat in spite of his sixty-four years. The great trunk had started to move downhill.

Nothing in the world could stop it now until it had finished in destruction. It passed the cowering pair like an avalanche cutting a swath through the descending forest of the mountainside. A hundred yards below it came to rest, the great trunk broken into three pieces, each opening in halves, from which vomited clouds of dust from age-old punk, and swarms of angry bees.

"Cripes!" ejaculated old Ezra between rage and shame, his face pasty from the breath of death that had passed so close. With Urial he scrambled down through the swath of the catapult, fixing their mosquito netting and pumping their smudge as they ran.

They came to an abrupt stop, staring at a halved section of the shattered trunk—staring, not at the clouds of bees or the broken comb, but at a stranger vision. Gold, swimming in pools of honey!

"Cripes!" gasped the old man. "What's that, Urial?"

"I dunno! What is it?"

"I dunno! Don't you know?"

"How should I know, you old fool? Why don't you look?"

Shaking with ague, striving his best to still his tremors, Ezra dipped in his fingers, grasped a piece of gold. A gold piece! As he picked it up a section of dry combing fell back, uncovering a crumpled tin box, dashed open by the crash; it was disgorging a deluge of gold and bills in wads to the amazed pair.

"How'd it get there?" breathed Urial, eyes bulging. "Who put it there?"

" 'Gene Johnson!" sighed old Ezra, shaking like a leaf now. He brushed off a film of bees. "The Markham boys—no one ever found it!"

II

Treasure! 'Gene Johnson's money! This was it! Ezra was on his knees, brushing aside the befouled honey and rotten wood from the lid.

He pointed, with almost a woman's scream, to the lid.

"There's the eagle—the spread eagle! When I was a boy I seen that. I'd know it if it'd been hidden a hundred years."

Ezra had seen it in life. He had seen it open, stuffed with greasy bundles packed so tight edgewise that they made an even floor.

'Gene had been an enormous, fat, jolly man who drove in a sagging side-bar buggy, cackling like a happy hen as he followed his hundreds of hogs and cattle at a pilgrim's pace along the country roads to market, a host of conscripted boys and men, of whom Ezra had been one, running on either side to shepherd the strays. At every gate 'Gene stopped to bargain and banter, adding to his droves and paying on the nail from this box. The box had come in time to be as famous as the man. Day by day he would follow his slow herds to slaughter and return for more, scouring the country far and wide. The early belief that he would some day be robbed because of this prideful display of his wealth so openly carried had faded as time went on; in its place there gradually arose a superstition that he was in some mystical way invulnerable. Then one night they found him down, in his own doorway, cast like a horse in its stall, weltering in gore. He told them, dying, that the two Markham boys had struck him down and robbed him.

It was a never-to-be-forgotten night. It was here on top of this ledge that the two brothers had been cornered. Squire Wilson, stepping out into the moonlight, calling on them to give themselves up, had been shot dead, his heart all but blown out of his poor body. Dennis Ince in the same volley lost a leg; and twenty years later his family consigned Dennis' patent self-oiling cork limb to the grave with the rest of him.

The younger Markham boy had been found the next morning cold and stiff and bloody from a dozen gunshot wounds behind this same tree; the elder had been crawling higher up the ledge when death came. But no money was found. These two had carried the secret with them to the beyond. The legend grew, from thousands to tens of thousands. And here it lay, uncovered through the fortuitous circumstance, the unheard-of thing of a tree, felled by the hand and eye of old Ezra, not falling true!

"Cripes!" breathed old Ezra, mopping his brow. "How'd I do that?" Then with venomous energy: "What you standin' there with your mouth open for, Urial? Get holt the other end!"

Staggering, they lifted the box out of its nest of dusty sweets, staggering not under the load of it, but from fear and a sudden hatred against their kind that boiled in their veins. They pawed in the sticky stuff for lost pieces and wads of money, filled it to overflowing. They dug a hole under an overhanging rock and hid it with the cunning of animals preyed upon.

"Get the buckets, Urial. We'll lose it all!" cried the father shrilly, and they began gathering what honey could be saved. This done, they set their hive and sugared it; in a few days they would return for the swarm. Then without a word to each other they hitched old Kit, loaded their gear into the buggy box and mechanically started homeward. It was late afternoon. They were in feverish haste, but did not seem to hurry. They left the old road again when they came to the clearing of old Eben, the hermit, and, to the accompanying howls of Jeff Davis and General Beauregard, circled around it, without even a devil's blessing for the old man, father and grandparent to these two, for the trouble he caused them at the moment which meant everything.

Before they turned creaking into the main road again they looked stealthily ahead and behind to see if they were observed. No one was in sight. Farther on they passed neighbors who, smelling honey, and observing Urial's swollen and shining nose fairly bursting with bee stings, stopped to make caustic inquiry. Urial glared stonily at old Kit's ears; and his father was industriously deaf—catch him telling where a bee tree lay!

They were turning in at their gate when Urial said: " 'Gene's daughter is livin' over at Clay Center. I seen her last week taking home Heinz's washing."

He was speaking of the sole heir of the murdered drover, a withered mother of many children, presented as gifts of the Magi to a lame, drunken father named Hines—Huntington Hines.

"Hush up, Urial!" commanded the old man fiercely.

A slashing thunderstorm came up, through which Ezra plodded like a drowned rat after his vagrant cows.

"Goin' up street, paw?" ventured Urial after the evening meal.

"Why, certainly I'm goin' up street. Ain't you goin' to the city?" cried the astonished father.

They must not be missed from the post-office porch. They must not alter their routine by a hair. It had only been habit before; now it became imperative. At nine their lantern could be seen dancing to and fro on its way home through the dark.

When they had turned out old Kit to pick grass for the night father and son took their accustomed places on the doorstone, a skewed square of granite cupped here and there by the touch of feet. Ez planned some day to have this homely shrine mark his last resting place on earth. They listened to the night noises. A creaking wagon passed. They wondered uneasily why Johnny Saunders was out so late, and who had done his milking for him. Orlando Sage, returning from town, stopped by the bridge to say a few words of encouragement to his patient car. Ez shivered at the thought that Orlando might come up to ask for help; and the loose-jointed din that suddenly burst on the night as Orlando cranked up was sweet music in his ears. He even forgot to laugh—nothing made Ez laugh like an old car being urged against its inclinations. Then all was still, except for an owl, an occasional dog and, over behind the pond, a woods fox.

"Ain't there a law—about twenty years, or somethin'?" muttered Urial in a ghostly whisper.

His father gave no sign of hearing him.

A few minutes later Urial, choking with the fullness of elation and bitterness that had this day come to him, burst out in an agony of defiance: "They shan't have it! Findin's keepin'! If there's any right in the world it's ourn!"

His breath whistled through his teeth; his face was horribly contorted. The old man still held his peace, but his little eyes answered the gleam of his pipe.

"It's ourn! Nobody can take it away from us!" reiterated the son.

"They'd ask you where you got it, Urial," said the father softly.

"None of their business where we got it!"

"They'd make it their business, Urial."

The son opened his mouth, paused abruptly, aghast, dumfounded. He hadn't thought so far ahead. How could they spend it—hundreds, thousands? How could they enjoy it, now that they possessed it—they, who had never had a hundred dollars in the world at one time in their lives? Idiotic rage seized him, to be instantly succeeded by a sense of impotence. He turned almost piteously to the old man.

"What you going to do, paw?" he implored.

"I'm goin' to bed," ejaculated little Ezra, springing up and open like a jack-knife. "We cut the oats to-morrow, Urial." He apostrophized the dusty heavens: "Cripes! There's more work, if a man wanted to do it all!"

He looked to the west at the sharp outline against the sky of a high crag on the other bank of the river. His star was about to set, the great star by which, at this season of the year, he kept his watch and clocks true to the second, to the utter dumfounding of his neighbors. Watch in hand, he stood waiting on his star. One instant, its last this day, it twinkled, vast, intense, mysterious; the next it was gone behind the crag, a light blown out. Ezra shuffled off to bed, questioning the faces of his many clocks for any delinquency as he made his way across the house to the far corner, from where, behind the shutters, in daytime he could see up and down the road. His last conscious thought was which barn the city people who had bought the Emmons place planned to shingle.

Up on the Emmons place the Armistons, city people, noted as the temporary owners of the famous Bannon cow, had settled down to a facsimile reconstruction of that historic old nest of hewn timbers. The process would be quite as slow in its geologic deliberation as had been its progress of decay. Aside from the affair of the cow, they developed other peculiarities that made this summer a noteworthy one and caused the tide of talk on the post-office steps nights to linger long after the lamp was blown out. They ripped out the big modern panes of glass, with their frames, and replaced them with punky old sashes retrieved from the barn, sashes set with bleary, rumply, tiny squares of glass. They opened the drafty, crumbling old fireplaces downstairs and up; they repaired the Dutch oven; they scoured the maple floors with lye; they dug in the ruins of the old spring house for hand-wrought nails, which they drove in conspicuous places; they scrubbed the blistered remnant of paint from the crumbling clapboards and replaced it, not with lead and zinc in oil, as was seemly, but with whitewash, tempered with sour milk to draw flies. They had withe rods cut for the apple-drying rack suspended from meat hooks over the dining-room table. In a word, they did a great many things that the village forefathers had learned jolly well not to do for all time to come a hundred years ago.

Oliver Armiston was a finical person with long fingers, a wavy white lock and a general mien of a preoccupied minister. Cynthia, his wife, was a busy little creature who drove from gate to gate looking for antiques, which, bless us, had been swept out of these bins long years ago. Somebody with malicious wit suggested that she call on Uncle Eben, the hermit; but the two terrible dogs charged when she slowed up at the gate, and won a victory that day.

Oliver in his day had been a lurid fiction writer, too lurid. Thieves got the habit of waiting impatiently for his newest creation, to dramatize it to their profit, and the police had requested Oliver politely but firmly to quit. Now he was living on the royalties of past fictional atrocities. His imagination still ran on, however, and just now it concerned itself with the hermit on the opposite hill. For several reasons he resolved to pay Uncle Eben a visit when it could be arranged with the two dogs, Jeff Davis and General Beauregard.

Delving in dusty tomes, Oliver had discovered the tradition that the original Emmons, one day in 1737, having completed his cabin atop the highest hill where he could find a live spring, and being alone in the forest—as he thought—for a hundred miles on either hand, except for his brave wife, was startled by the sound of an ax. Descending his hill to the river, which he forded, and ascending the high hill on the opposite bank, he came on the original Ebenezer Beddes and his woman laying the sills of their cabin about a finished oven and chimney, which sat atop the highest hill with a live spring on their side of the river. Oliver purposed to make the same journey, reconstructing the sound of the ax to his ears, and formulating as nearly as might be the emotions of that original stalwart Emmons threading his way through the primeval forest aisles towards the portentous sound. It was this tale that had driven home the bargain when he bought the Emmons place. Day by day he watched the smoke, across the valley, of Uncle Eben, the hermit.

"Some morning when I feel good," said Mr. Parr, when Armiston broached the girth-reducing journey to his friend, deputy of metropolitan police and famous man hunter, who had been induced to experiment with a week in the wilds.

"The old Copperhead keeps a pair of curs that share in his ideas on reconstruction," explained Oliver. "Are you afraid of dogs?"

"No," said the deputy without mitigation.

It was late September. In the woods as they climbed, their shod toes, punching for a grip in the embankment, uncovered frost powder among the crinkly leaves; in the mowing that topped the first rise the long rowen, stiff with frost, seemed to break like spun glass underfoot. There was the heavy mist of early fall, with a red sun coming up over the far hill, a sun that seemed still chill from the night. It was about seven o'clock. The two wayfarers reproducing the original journey of old Byron Emmons sat down to rest.

"The sound of the ax must have been like Robinson Crusoe's footprint— of no significance in itself, but as a collateral fact of tremendous import," said Oliver. "It reminds me of one of Thomas Bailey Aldrich's projected stories. Every living soul on earth had been destroyed, except our hero, and he sat down to think it over—when the front doorbell rang."

But the great man hunter, frankly winded, was not philosophic or casuistic this morning. They proceeded. It was eight o'clock when they reached the barway on the old back-hill road where Cynthia had paused many a time in her chariot, trying to screw up courage to get down and brave those two dogs.

There were no dogs in sight. Oliver let down the bars with a clatter; he waited for bedlam to break loose. But still no dogs. They could see only a few feet ahead; through the blanket of mist the sun, now come to life, was pumping up out of the grass. Here and there a tufty spiral rose, standing on end like a toe dancer, its upper billows touched rosy.

Oliver laughed.

"If you're not afraid of dogs, Parr, you lead the way," he said.

Parr sniffed the air and gripped his hickory stick; he started forward briskly without asking his less courageous companion for direction. Oliver was conscious of gathering wonder as they proceeded without interruption. They came abruptly on a spiral of mist that was not a spiral of mist at all, but a spiral of smoke, rising from the heap of embers that had been the old Beddes homestead.

In the midst of the area of ashes, as staunch as on the remote day it was built of granite and clay by the original Eben Beddes and his woman, rose the tall chimney and oven—it was all that survived of the habitation of Uncle Eben, the nonagenarian hermit whom Oliver had come to greet this morning as a fellow pioneer from across the valley. Parr was pointing with his hickory stick at an unmistakable object among the charred timbers in the cellar hole.

Oliver was moved to say, "Uncle Eben has journeyed across the valley."

"I'll watch here while you go," said the deputy simply; and Oliver hurried off. It was his fortune to meet first Orlando Sage, the village

Pooh-Bah, who by reason of his multiple office as clerk, poor master, constable, and so on, undertook to carry the news to old Ezra that at last he had become an orphan and inheritor.

Orlando left his car at the gate, not caring to engage the sawdust drive. At sight of the morning caller Urial, splitting wood with the deftness of second nature, shouldered his ax and hurried off to the alders. Orlando smiled. This curious habit had been growing on father and son of late. Their fellow townsmen had taken to calling them Nip and Tuck, so inseparable were they and so sullen in their heed of their neighbors. In another few years, if they continued retreating more and more from contact with their kind, they, too, would be hermits, like the old Copperhead who had been burned to a crisp during the night.

Orlando pounded on the front door without result; he went to the side door and repeated his summons. Then with an oath of irritation he drew the latch and pressed his head in at the door.

"Ezra, you old fool! Come out here! Got something to tell you, quick!"

From within came the flat-footed shuffle of the old man.

"Your father's dead, I tell you!" shouted Orlando.

"My father? Who? Eben, you mean?"

Ezra paused in the act of filling his pipe.

"Yep. Burned to a cinder. Must have ketched fire during the night."

"Fire? Ketched fire?" cried the orphaned son, bending so fierce and malignant a gleam from his beady eyes on the bearer of ill tidings that Orlando involuntarily dropped back a step. "Who says so?"

"The man that bought the Bannon cow," explained Orlando.

"What's he doin' up there?" demanded the old man shrilly. "You tell him he'd better stay away from there!" He thrust out his head. "Urial!" he bellowed. "Yoke up the stags! Your grandpaw's dead—burned up!"

Orlando tendered the use of his car in this hour of sorrow, but Ezra was already arranging the horse blanket on the reach of the wagon. Urial stood at the head of the milk-white oxen with his long whip, and at a signal from his father he cracked the whip and shouted.

Orlando, abandoning his car in one of its spells, mounted beside Ezra, and the cattle took their slow pace forward, turning from the drive into the road with weaving heads, and took up the endless journey to the great city.

Most of the residents of the town were collected at the post office as they came in sight. Old Eben had gone to his reward! There was none so poor to do him reverence. But Ezra was now become a personage. At last he had come into his expectations.

Ezra himself rose to the occasion. As he got down and mounted the steps he was not the shambling, bent old man of yesterday, but erect, resolute, with keen eye, ringing voice. They drank in every word of his sharp instructions to Orlando, who was telephoning the undertaker for him.

"Tell him I want the best he's got! Nothing's too good! Tell him not to worry about who's goin' to pay for it. I guess there's enough for that!"

Urial cracked his whip, and the plodding stags took up their burden again, the son walking at their head. As they rounded the turn to the bridge the neighbors one by one backed their rigs out from the shed, or cranked their cars and followed at straggling intervals.

They gathered in a wide circle about the scene of the night's tragedy, mute, motionless, waiting, as they so often did about an open grave when the fascination of falling handfuls of earth held them spellbound. Orlando indicated two of them to aid him, and they bore away the shapeless form beneath a blanket.

Shortly Orlando returned. Old Ezra, leaning on a crowbar, gazed moodily into the ashes on what had been the hearth of the old homestead. Now and again he raised his bright little eye to the brave spire of the chimney, the forlorn survivor of the catastrophe.

"Comin', Ezra?" said Orlando deferentially.

"Not yet," responded the bereaved son and heir.

Old Ezra lifted his crowbar and let it drop with a metallic clang on the right-hand stone.

"It ought to be right about there, Orlando," he cried, punching the stone again and again. He turned to the overawed Urial. "Did you bring the sledge, Urial?" he demanded.

The sledge was instantly thrust into his hands; the old man spat on the handle, raised the sledge above his head and swung it. At the third blow the stone parted. They were on their knees lifting the fragments away. Now the neighbors crowded about, no longer held off by the awe of death. They saw the wiry old man half bury himself in a hole, grope; they saw him rise, straining, bringing with him an old wooden box containing an ancient doe-skin bag. Orlando lifted up the bag. It was heavy.

A buzz of excitement sprang up like the hum of angry bees. Ezra had found Uncle Eben's hoard.

"I'll have to take charge of it," said Orlando, catching his breath.

Everyone leaned forward as Ezra, grasping the box, shrieked hysterically: "It belongs to me! There ain't no one goin' to have it! I'm my own father's son, ain't I?"

But Orlando held him off, trying to quiet him, for Ezra's eyes were blazing with evil fire.

"Yes; it belongs to you, Ezra," said the mediary. "But it will have to go to court. That's what the law says. You'll get it. Don't you worry, Ezra. How'd you know just where to dig?"

The old man turned, flattered by the question and the hush that followed, and regarded the broad hearth that had seen so many generations of his progenitors reared since that first stalwart Ebenezer, the pioneer.

"I cracked butternuts on it; I roasted chestnuts on it; I dipped candles on it." The little old man's eyes wandered back through the distant years. "When I was a boy I found that hole. I never said nothing to nobody. I always thunk he'd bury it there—if he had anything to bury."

When Orlando started off with the inheritance Ezra and Urial followed at his shoulder, a close step behind. Before getting into a buggy Orlando, it was noted by the enthralled neighbors, wiped his hands on a horse blanket and held them up to the light. His fingers were sticky with honey. The old Copperhead must have moved that precious hoard from place to place as his lonely misanthropic years waned before it came to its final resting place. Sometime or another, Orlando thought, sniffing the bag. Uncle Eben must have kept it with his bees.

III

Deputy parr, Oliver Armiston's guest, was making an effort, in his own argot, to horn in on the post-office steps nights, but with about as much success as a friendly lion in a vaudeville act—though milk-fed and toothless it might be—if it stepped down from the stage to pass the time of day with the audience. The post-office audience was polite but reticent. His eyes were too fierce, his jaw too square, his voice too decisive, his words too short. Try as he might to sheathe his claws, police stuck out all over the famous man hunter. The railbirds did not identify the fact itself, for they did not know the police; but they were acutely, even painfully aware of the physical impression. It was this same physical impression that carried Parr so far in his profession, not only with the unsophisticated but with the knowing as well.

After three or four nights of it Parr confided to his host an admission of failure; he added, "It can't be done—without a make-up." He looked around for an accomplice. His eye passed over Oliver the Elegant—who indeed would have been ineligible because of the Bannon cow, if for no other reason. He picked out Jason Selfridge, Oliver's next-door neighbor. This youth, a graduate of a technical school, had a year ago gone forth to conquer the world; just now he was home, "feeding up again," as his sly neighbors said. Parr closed a professional grip on the bulky young man's shoulder.

"Do you hear dogs howling nights, son?" he asked.

Jason met his gaze level-eyed, and nodded, waiting.

"Did you hear that gunshot last night—off there?" Parr pointed across the leafy hills.

Yes, Jason had heard it.

"The yowling stopped with that shot," speculated the deputy. "Do you reckon that one shot killed the pack?"

"Not necessarily," said Jason. "Not them two."

In spite of his degree of M.E. the young engineer was apt to be colloquial in his farm clothes.

"What two?" cried Parr with the utmost ferocity.

Jason surveyed him in surprise.

"Why, the two you are talking about," he said, meeting that awful eye without a quaver. "They're gun-shy, you know. Or maybe you don't know. Touch off a pop-gun within half a mile of them and they hike for home and crawl under the house."

"Good heavens!" whispered the deputy, as though this simple fact for a moment carried him off his feet. Then quickly through his teeth: "Look at me! Have you ever seen me before?"

Jason smiled indulgently.

"Many a time, sir," he said.

"Good! Do they know—down in the street?"

"No; they've asked me. I said I didn't know. I've been wondering, sir, what brought you up here."

"Don't wonder. There's nothing to wonder about. Son, could they be induced to pry into my identity and find out for themselves?"

Jason considered a moment.

"I think so, sir—if you would mail a package or something."

That evening at eight Oliver and the deputy pulled up at the curb, and the visitor got down and ascended the post-office steps with a cordial good evening, which as usual missed fire. He paused to remark as he looked up at the murky sky that they were going bullheading, and asked an opinion in general whether or not it was a propitious night. Out of the silence one gulping voice said "Maybe." That was as near as Parr came to social interchange. They sat listening to him inside buying stamps and registering his box; and quickly fell into careless attitudes when he reappeared and drove off.

Cordell, the old postmaster, having deposited the box, evidently a shoe box, in a bag for the morning mail stage, turned down his lamp and resumed his seat by the window behind the fly screen.

"What's two-forty Center Street, in New York, Jason?" asked Cordell of the young engineer who had come back home to feed up.

Jason sat up abruptly.

"What do you want to know for?" he demanded in tense tones.

"He's mailing stuff there. That box to-night—and other things."

"What! That fellow?"

Jason swung his feet off the porch; although it was pitch dark, save for his pipe, at his end of the porch, the others could somehow sense the fact that Jason was staring in utter astonishment in the direction of Parr's departure. They all waited, breathless.

"What you say that man's name was—Barr, or Carr, or somethin'?"

"Parr!" Everybody offered the correction.

"Ho!" Jason fairly shouted, unable to contain himself. "Parr! That's Parr, eh? Well, I'm damned! What the devil brought him up here?"

Jason was playing with a relish. They crowded about him, demanding to know what it was all about.

"So that's Parr—the great Parr! Deputy Parr! He's head of the detective bureau in New York! Why, that man's the greatest detective in the world! Two hundred and forty Center Street? That's Police Headquarters!" With sudden rising of blood pressure: "What the devil is he sending away from here in a box to Police Headquarters?"

A profound silence succeeded the outburst. The loungers peering through the dark in the direction of Jason's high-pitched voice seemed paralyzed, as if the concession had crushed their motor nerves. That was their way of taking a great moment.

The tension was relieved by the soft turning up of the lamp inside. Cordell, the postmaster, got down his World Almanac and turned the pages with a wetted thumb. He read sepulchrally: "William J. Parr, Special Deputy Commissioner; in charge of Detective Bureau. Salary, $25,000."

Someone whistled—at the salary; it was incredible. They all strained their ears to listen; the drum of that sweet-running motor was still audible in the night silences; to their minds it had suddenly become sinister.

"Bullheadin', eh?" said someone contemptuously. "I'll bet he's gone bull-headin'!"

A low wail floated over them, high on the night air.

"There's them damned dogs again! Someone ought to shoot 'em. It raises the goose flesh on a man to hear 'em bustin' out this time of night." This from one of the railbirds.

"Someone did take a crack at them last night—about two this morning. Up by the charcoal kilns." This from Jason.

There was a slight rustle at the far end of the porch as two figures moved off, shambling. No need to say it was old Ezra and Urial, Nip and Tuck; their creaking buggy wheels as they backed out of the shed and the luminous white of old Kit told that. One of them struck a match. It was Ezra; they could see his face as he bent to light the wick and snap down the chimney. Then the dancing light took up its slow journey home.

Jason evaporated. When they turned for further enlightenment he was gone. A fine mist was falling now. It was a likely night for bullheads. Jason decided to take a chance. He cut through the woods to a back road, moving through the inky blackness of the brush with a sense of direction that delighted him. He had feared the city smell in his nostrils might have killed it, but it had not. Instinctively he made a detour when he came to lonely Beach Plain; as a boy he had avoided the old grave-yard after sundown lest he be accosted by strangers from another world. Now as he skirted this ancient God's acre he was conscious of a low sigh on the winds. His hair stiffened and he quickened his pace, peering back swiftly for one look.

Shortly he came on the leaden waters of Spectacle Pond through the trees. He knew where Johnny Saunders hid his old boat, or used to. Yes, it was still there, full of water, which he scooped out with a loose thwart, and embarked, pushing the leaky craft out beyond the headland, through the arch of the spectacle into the farther pond. The twinkle of a lantern across the water then directed his paddle. Pulling alongside, Jason related with careful detail the scene on the steps.

Parr's eyes gleamed in his stone visage by lantern light.

"Good!" he said to the last detail. With startling abruptness Parr asked, "Did you pass the cemetery?"

Jason nodded.

"Did you see anything?" pursued the great man.

With an effort Jason controlled himself.

"I heard something. I heard a long sigh!" This in a whisper.

"Just like a human, eh?" mused Parr.

"Gosh! The dogs! They're grievin', eh?" Jason caught his breath.

"Relicts—and remainders!" said Parr grimly, playing with the words in his thoughts. He inspected his bait critically. "Recollect the gold tooth we found in the vat, Oliver?"

Armiston grunted assent.

"Yes, when you tried to hang a man for the murder of a ghost," said the defunct author.

That had been indeed a famous case, the so-called vat murder, in which Parr, frankly beaten, had been set back on the track by the uncanny divination of the imaginative writer. Jason, realizing that through some ineffable favor he was listening in on the moody confidences of the gods, swelled with elation.

"Did I ever tell you about the bank thief"—the deputy was remi-niscing—"who slipped and fell down a cliff in escaping and got wedged between two rocks? They found him months later—some hunter—only the skeleton then, clothes all torn to tatters; foxes, or wolves, or some-thing, had picked him clean."

The huge head of the great man hunter turned at the distant whimper of a hound.

"Tough!" murmured Oliver.

"Sure was!" assented the deputy, bull-heading earnestly. "Funny thing—that skeleton had gimlet holes in the joints and was wired together. That fellow's doing time for another job now. Clever guy, that!" He chuckled.

Jason climbed over from his sinking bark to the comparatively dry haven of the other boat.

"Do you mean to say he dressed up an anatomical specimen in his own clothes—and then forgot to take out the wire?" he demanded.

"Don't ask foolish questions, son," said the great man gruffly. He pulled in a bullhead. "Just take that porcupine off the hook for me, son. You might as well be useful."

"Mister Commissioner," said Jason deferentially, "would you think it very forward of me if I asked what was in that box you mailed to headquarters to-night, sir?"

"Not at all. A very natural question."

"Well, what was it, sir?"

"I'll show you when it comes back. You have the makings of a first-class stool pigeon in you, son," said the deputy commissioner.

The nonplused youth fell silent over this equivocal remark. They fished till morning.

Two nights later the shoe box came back. In one corner was the startling confirmatory legend—Police Headquarters, City of New York. It had been passed from hand to hand. Mr. Parr accepted it casually, tucking it under his arm, and stepped out on the porch. The convention was all there, as usual, except for little Ezra and Urial. This was not worthy of note, because of their recent bereavement. The two, since the splendid funeral, had frequently withdrawn, probably from a sense of delicacy, covering the conventional period of sackcloth and ashes.

"Beautiful fall evening, gentlemen," suggested the genial Mr. Parr, a remark that went by default.

Pipes glowed. Silence reigned. Every man present secretly suspected his neighbor, took an unholy joy at his neighbor—he was quite sure just which one—quaking, at this instant, quaking with terror in the presence of the deputy commissioner, the greatest detective in the world. Also he had civic pride in the thought that his neighbor's crime was big enough to engage the talents of this famous man for a week or so.

"Bullheadin'! Sure, he's bullheadin'!"

They looked at Parr in uneasy derision—and waited.

Mr. Parr sat down, balancing his dynamite box on his knee.

"Let's have some cigars, Mister Postmaster," he called to the shadow behind the fly screen. "The best in the house, for all of us! That skunk cabbage in the right-hand corner smokes pretty good."

A polite titter greeted this sally. Smokes were passed.

"Twelve?" counted the host. "Not all here to-night. Who's missing?"

"Nip and Tuck," said a lost voice.

"How come they to miss a regular meeting?"

Mr. Parr felt he was getting on famously in persiflage.

"They're grievin'," said the same voice.

"Gentlemen," said Mr. Parr, striking a light, "where I come from it is a shooting offense to put a gift cigar in your pocket, no matter what ails it. A man's supposed to smoke it on the spot—if he can."

Several cigars were withdrawn stealthily from vest pockets and pipes knocked out. After all, it was an occasion worthy of a cigar.

Time passed. In one of the long silences a quavering howl floated overhead.

"Someone ought to shoot 'em," said a voice.

On the echo of the words two sharp spats of sound cleaved the stillness. A prolonged "Ki-yi" succeeded; then quiet again.

"Someone did."

"Who done that?"

They listened, as if the night would tell them. It did. A long pause was broken by the disembodied voice.

"Orlo done it."

Parr found himself mystified; such deduction was beyond his talents. Then his ears picked up the sound of a far-off motor. It stuttered. That was it. It was Orlando Sage's car.

"He's coming like hell! Gosh, he'll hit that water bar on Beach Plain Hill!"

They waited for the expected crash. A wild shriek of tortured machinery was heard afar off; but the car, stuttering and barking again, came on like a warrior mortally wounded. With a roar it crossed the loose planking of the bridge over Gray's Brook. The railbirds had risen one by one, getting out their rigs. All was in readiness for a sudden dash, but no one moved. They stood listening, spellbound, to the midnight ride of their Paul Revere. Orlando took the curve at the foot of the hill on two wheels, pulled up sharp, killed his motor with a touch.

"Your damned father didn't burn up at all, Ezra!" he yelled, jumping out. "He was dead and buried without a coffin. His hounds dug him up to-night!" His voice rose in a crescendo of excitement. "I was going by the graveyard—and heard the racket. I shot at 'em—drove 'em off! Then I found the old man!"

Parr clutched his box tighter.

"What's that?"

"Where?"

"How'd it happen?"

"When?"

"Who was burned up, then?"

These questions shot out of the clustering dark like machine-gun spats.

"Ez! Oh, Ezra!" screamed Orlando.

"Ez ain't here! Didn't come up. He's grievin'," said the disembodied voice.

Jason held up his lantern to illumine the ashen face of Orlando; a circle of ghostly visages came out of the dark and formed a closed ring. A car started off. It was a signal. In a moment the assembled conveyances moved at top speed through the dark to the little cemetery back on the plain, where the hounds that had dug up the unburned body of their old master, the hermit, were now crouched on either side; they had crept back to stand guard.

"Shoot 'em!" a voice cried.

"No!" It was the voice of Parr.

"What the devil is he doin' in Dennis Ince's grave?"

A circle of lanterns, suddenly focused on the scene, discovered the fact that this was not the new-made grave in the Beddes' plot in which they had, with some show of reverence, consigned the charred form found in the fire only a few days gone by. The contagion of fear suddenly seized the spectators. Orlando moved over to Parr.

"I guess this is deeper water than I can swim in, sir," he said, trembling. "You take it, sir. I don't know what to do."

"Yes," snapped the deputy. "You men, gather around me!" They crowded close, seeking protection in numbers. "Can you go back and take your places on the steps and shut up?" he demanded fiercely, his eyes blazing in the lantern light. "Anyone that can't can go home and stay there! Not a word. Understand that."

Leaving a squad to care for the uncovered hermit, Parr mounted with Orlando, and the others filed behind, the funereal procession moving at a slow pace. Parr gave his instructions en route. Orlando was to go down and rouse up old Ezra on pretense that some probate papers come by the late mail must be signed to-night to go off in the morning.

The scene on the porch steps was set again as before. Shortly, craning necks discerned the bobbing lantern down the road, then creaking wheels and the luminous shade of old Kit.

"You want me to come too, Orlo?" asked Urial.

"Yep," responded Orlando, and the three stamped up the steps, a sigh escaping the watchers on the porch. Inside, in the sitting room where the postmaster kept his books and his notarial seal, Ezra, who knew the ritual, took his stand, erect, uncovered, ready to raise his right hand and repeat solemnly after the notary, "I swear!"

But the man at the table under the lamplight was not old Cordell. Instead, Mr. Parr, the most famous detective in the world, was facing Ezra unwrapping his shoe box. At the unexpected apparition Ezra looked about quickly.

"What d'ye want me to swear to? Where's Cordell?" he demanded.

He made as if to step back to the door, but Orlando was stationed with his back against it, his two hands behind him on the knob. Still there was nothing alarming in his posture.

Parr, looking up suddenly, with a nod invited Ezra to approach. From the box beside him he had taken two metallic objects, red with the rust of fire, each bearing a ticket with writing on it. These he pushed forward.

"These belong to you, I think, Mr. Beddes," he said gently.

Ezra transferred his eyes with an effort to the two ticketed iron things, his beady little black eyes glittering; he wetted his lips and swallowed hard. Then he shook his head, not at the deputy, but at the two unnamed implements on the table. As the old man brushed aside his matted hair and lifted his chin the deputy had the sudden sense of being about to fail.

"They ain't nothin' of mine," said the old man.

His eyes shot a swift look behind, at the man guarding the door. He drew a long breath. It seemed to restore him.

"Better take a look at them. Maybe they do belong to you," urged Parr, still gently. "Let us see." He spread out the ticket tied to the nearest. "It reads: 'Coffin handle—manufactured by Sprigs & Jessup, Rochester, N. Y.' " He looked at Ezra.

"It's nothing of mine!" said Ezra shrilly, but without a tremor in his biting tones.

He had the nerve of a tiger, Parr thought. Orlando, bending forward, loosed his hold on the knob; his brow was glittering with sweat. Parr picked up the other object; it was a hinged joint of metal.

"This," he said, straining his eyes by the light, "says, 'Self-oiling knee joint. Manufactured by the Patent Noiseless Cork Limb Company, Philadelphia, Pa.' " Weighing it in his fingers, he added softly: "I found these in the ashes, Mr. Beddes, of your father's homestead."

He let the thing fall with a clang as Orlando gasped out uncontrollably: "Dennis Ince's cork leg—the one they buried with him."

Urial with a shriek rushed at the door, but Orlando thrust him back into a chair.

Old Ezra straightened up, murder in his face.

"They ain't nothin' of mine, I tell you!" he shrieked. "Let me out of here! Where's them papers to sign, Orlo? Who is this man? What's he got to do with me?"

With the foulest of oaths he advanced on Orlando with so frightful a mien that the constable's courage oozed and he deserted his post.

But Jason Selfridge, hiding in the closet for just such an emergency, interposed his big frame between the old man and liberty. Ezra fought like a demon, reviling them and all the world.

Parr felt utterly sick. There was something horrible about the hopeless courage of the little old man, whose shrill vituperations seemed without end. But suddenly they ceased. It was the long, quavering wail of a hound floating on the night, with eerie modulations, that worked the magic. The lashing form on the floor seemed to sink within itself as if struck lifeless. Jason and Orlando released their hold. Parr played his last card.

"They're bringing in your father, Ezra," he said. "The hounds dug him up."

Ezra drew himself painfully to his feet. All eyes were on him as he stepped over to the table and picked up the leg iron which had betrayed him.

"Cripes! How'd I do that?" he asked himself aloud.

Then with a single spring, like coiled steel suddenly released, before anyone could intervene, he dived through the window, carrying sash and all with him. There were wild cries outside of "There he goes! Get him! Get him!"

But they didn't get him, not until next morning, when he floated up among the river trash on the swale below the bridge.

Urial's ravings rang through the clamor:

"We didn't kill the old man! Grandpaw just up and died on us when we was hidin' him in the coal kilns! We ain't done murder! The money's ourn! Findin's keepin'! 'Tain't no crime to burn up a dead body!"

For months after the neighbors, spurred on by the knowledge that the hoard old Ezra had so cunningly uncovered under the hearthstone was the treasure not of Uncle Eben but of the murdered drover, 'Gene Johnson, dug and dug throughout the old foundation. But the doeskin bag, with its wealth taken from the bee tree and concealed by the little old man where he might opportunely find it again as a rightful inheritance, was all the Beddes homestead ever yielded.

Armiston was driving Parr across the hills to his train when they turned out for Huntington Hines, the drunkard cripple, 'Gene Johnson's son-in-law, driving a new horse to a lather.

"There goes the logical conclusion of your tainted hoard," ruminated the deputy, looking back after the braggart husband of the sole heir of 'Gene Johnson, the drover. "First, the old drover, who cheated his poorer neighbors with his sharp trading; then the Markham brothers, who murdered him for it and were slaughtered; then old Ezra, whose chance discovery of it in a bee tree turned him into a ghoul. And now your town drunkard, as an epilogue, scatters it in the ditches of the highway."

The Footstep

T
HE orders are absolute," said Stetson, the impresario of this gorgeous vault of jewels—a magnificent person who spent two hours over his toilet every morning. His handsome face had the impassivity of an idol's; but behind it his curiosity was examining the woman in detail. He was thinking that he should know who she was, and it irritated him to find that he did not. "Orders are absolute," he repeated, essaying a smile. He indicated a slightly raised dais in one corner, where a company of slender chairs stood waiting by a rare table. "Unless he is seated at his desk, no one may approach him." He lowered his voice discreetly; he was sure he was addressing a personage—a personage at the point of fading into the dusk of age, but still retaining that ineffable elegance of those who are born to be great.

Stetson noted these things while he suavely assured her, "His moments of abstraction grow on him. He is old, old. His memories occupy him."

Ludwig Telfen—for it was the old lapidary they were talking of as they stood in the midst of his spendthrift atelier which had come to be known, curiously, as the Whispering Gallery for its trick echoes—was plainly visible to the naked eye, but utterly, so it seemed, unattainable. He was in his celebrated cage under the skylight, mooning over something. It was said that he kept a gem or two back there that he prayed to.

The woman looked wistfully at the old lapidary. And she was frankly bewildered that she should be denied. A queer little smile touched her lips.

"But if the place should be robbed—or a fire—would he still be unapproachable?" she said.

Stetson shrugged, smiling; such remote contingencies had been insured against before the sumptuous monolith that was Ludwig Telfen was off the drafting board.

"Might I not stand so he could catch a glimpse of me through the bars?" she pleaded. There was color in her cheeks; there was a little sense of pleasurable excitement about her.

Stetson was adamant.

"If he could hear my voice he would lift his head!" she exclaimed, and she raised her voice slightly; it was so full and rich that it filled the vaulted chamber and roused resonant echoes in ghostly responses. Stetson thought that he surely must know who she was. But the identity persistently evaded him. He made a point of knowing personages. It was his whole career. But she came to his rescue providentially in her distress.

"If he knew that Velma Ilseng had come to see him!" she implored.

"Velma Ilseng!" ejaculated Stetson. He started back. "But—"

He could have bitten off his tongue for that "but." He would have sworn she was dead. Velma Ilseng was only a legend now, like Patti and Jenny Lind! Stetson, with a supreme effort, regained his mask of impassivity. But his curiosity still peered out through his slits of eyes.

"Come!" he cried impulsively. "We will break the rules—for Velma Ilseng!" He bowed low. "Or at least," he amended, "chip off a piece of one corner." He laughed silently. He led her to the dais, indicated an inlaid chair; she disposed herself exquisitely. She was aglow with the acknowledgment. "You can be seated, waiting for him," he whispered. "He usually comes here about eleven." He glanced at the clock; it lacked a few minutes of the hour.

There were a number of curious things on this table, for Telfen always retained his youthful enthusiasm for surprising his clientele with storied trifles. Her fingers idly explored them while her eyes watched the bent figure of the old man behind the bars, vaguely wondering what held him there within sight of the world, yet a thousand miles distant in space. The clock softly intoned the hour; and the old man, shaking himself free from some thought, arose, unlocked the gate of his cage and, turning the key in it again with smiling precaution, wended his slippered way to his desk. Velma Ilseng, savoring the meeting, arranged herself with some deft little touches of vanity that women carry with them to the very grave. Stetson, satisfied of her preoccupation, lost himself among the tall vases and marbles in the diagonal corner where, unseen, he mounted a little winding flight of bronze stairs hidden behind a screen; it took him into a tiny cubicle of lattice and grille on the mezzanine. There was a red-haired woman sitting there doing nothing, and when she started in surprise at the apparition of his head in the stair well, he cautioned her with a slight gesture.

"Velma Ilseng," he whispered. He was forming the syllables with his lips. She stared at him. She peered down through the ornamental metal work at the posterlike picture of the woman in silks on the slender chair by the table. She turned, bewildered. He nodded and sat down beside her. The pair of them watched, heads together, too close for a good-looking girl and an impassive idol. She took up her stenographer's notebook and pencil, held the pencil poised—but her eyes still drank in the woman who should have been dead a generation gone by. With a businesslike air, she looked at the clock—11:02. She set down the time at the head of the page; the date, September fifteenth; the name, Velma Ilseng.

"I recollect now," she said below her breath. "She married again recently. Some boy. Half her age."

"Reginald Baker," immediately supplied the card-index Stetson. He needed only this word to supply the missing page out of the Blue Book. As a rule, pages of the latest edition of these *archives de la haute noblesse* were indelibly photographed on the retina of his memory. That was his calling. Stetson had frequently picked up titbits of vast value to, at least, his enormous curiosity in this cubby-hole. It was an asset in his business, just as his two hours of toilet was. This was the home of the trick echo. There was a little accidental parabola in the dome just above that table which picked up the slightest breath, a pin drop, and conveyed it undiminished to the little mezzanine alcove. It was the task of the red-headed girl to make pothooks of every syllable waited up from that table. Telfen himself had so ordered, because he was getting old and a typewritten transcript sometimes came in handy, especially as his clientele spoke in terms of five, six or even seven figures.

The scene opened rather tamely to the eavesdroppers. But great scenes between great actors rarely read well. Old Telfen took Velma Ilseng's hand and retained it, covering it with a cage of trembling fingers lest it escape. He gazed up at her as he was wont to gaze at the few gems to which he was addicted, though not so humbly, for this was a happy moment. Here was Velma Ilseng in the flesh again. He thought of her as Manon, because it was as Manon she had appeared to him last, years ago at the Paris Opera. He had sung a small part. Few people knew that the savant had been an aspirant for operatic honors.

"You and I," she said in a soft, luscious voice, "wander like ghosts among our tomorrows."

The red-headed girl, taking this down in prosaic pothooks, arched an eyebrow.

"God," said the old lapidary, "has given us this easy condition," which the red-headed girl thought she had heard before, but she didn't know just where. The two lovers—they seemed almost that, from their rapturous regard of each other—prolonged their moment in a silence stirred no doubt by the most cherished of recollections.

"You have married again," said Telfen.

"Yes," she shrugged.

"A fine fellow," said he, wagging his head. "But I have now and then found time to pity him; he has seemed always so irrevocably doomed to success," said the old man whimsically.

"Whatever he touches turns to money," she said. Her lips parted in a sigh, as if deploring the material side of her last hour of romance. "I came to him rich. He has doubled my fortune in the two years. I don't know where it will end." This with a captivating lowering of the eyelids. "He is just now engaged in breaking up my fortune for my children, Roger and Eva. Most young husbands engage themselves in breaking up fortunes for themselves," she put in with a bright smile. "He thinks I should have the happiness of seeing them in good estate while they still have me. We will reserve a morsel for ourselves," she added with a gay little laugh. "That is what brings me here." She paused on the thought, sighing. "Do you remember, twenty-five years ago you sealed up the collection of jewels which are my artistic rosary?"

He nodded dreamily, naming them not as gems but as rôles—Marguerite, Manon, Lucia.

"Not pearls, rubies, diamonds, but triumphs—the tears of achievement," he murmured.

"Together we buried them," she said. "I have never reopened the casket." She dabbed at her eyes. "The time has come when I have determined to part with them." As the old man started forward with protesting hands she exclaimed, "As souvenirs? Never! They are the dead ashes of the past. They, with their secrets, will pass into the possession of strangers. I will sell them all."

"Ah!" exclaimed Telfen, his eye glistening with a counter thought. There were several pieces—he dropped his lids upon the fire of eagerness. "The uncut ruby? Ah, it has been my prayer I might again touch it with my eyes!"

"Yes," said Velma Ilseng stoically.

"The black pearl?"

"Yes. All! They are nothing."

His tones tremulous in spite of himself, "The Talisman?" he cried. "The unrivaled Velma would part with her Talisman?"

"Yes," said Velma Ilseng. "The Talisman was the touch of the scepter!" she cried, the flame of romance burning bright, visioning the imperial donor, the great Alexander of Russia. "The prince of patrons! An emperor—and yet a man!" she sighed. "So," she laughed, shaking off the mood, "I arouse even you to cupidity. Well, my friend, you shall feast your eyes once more. It is you, and you only, who shall break the seals you placed upon my trophies."

The pothooks on the stenographer's pad in the mezzanine moved scrawlingly to the final apostrophe; the pencil paused, poised. The red-headed woman and the impassive idol exchanged covert smiles.

"You will sell them?" asked the lapidary.

"If I have the courage," she said.

"Not courage"—he shook his head—"but perspicacity in choosing the buyers. Only those worthy shall assume their care. I maintain my own Index Expurgatorius," he added slyly.

The amazing Velma Ilseng had literally declined to be a memory. When she had stepped from the stage she had condemned these gems, souvenirs of high moments, to be exiles in outer darkness. She had been cruel. She had locked them in a cold vault, denied them the light that was their life. It was like banishing friends from one's heart who had erred only in dearness.

"They played their part exactly as I played mine. Together we disappeared," she said to the old lapidary. "Why live in sentimentalities?"

"If one can forget, yes," said Telfen, wagging his head. He was thinking how great a pity for a mortal to move from one existence to another without drinking of the waters of Lethe. But here was no ordinary mortal. Her glorious past must always overwhelm her.

"The market is at the top," Velma Ilseng was reminding herself. "I am supposed to be a shrewd business woman; and it is good business to capitalize my fame while I am still alive. I am having the collection moved to Manhasset, where we usually spend our summers, you know. But," she said, with a hopeless reversion to her mood, "I could only pray that they be turned to dust when I break the seals. So come, Telfen, and lend me courage to confront them."

She outlined the preparations. Reginald Baker, her husband, methodical and exact to the *n*th degree, had specified she was to speak of it to no one. In these lawless postwar days one does not cry aloud when a quarter of a million is moved in a hand bag, and there must be some proper receptacle for them. So Baker, departing on a prolonged tour of the West—on his eternal business—had sent down a great elephant of a modern safe, a thing swathed in cotton batting like an incubator baby. It was too big for any doors or windows fashioned on earth; and it had been necessary to broach a hole in the south wall to bring it into the boudoir. Masons had been pothering for a week, opening the gap and closing it again. There had been a pretty penny to pay for caution, and in the end it appeared it might have been cheaper to set the thing down in a field and build a new house around it, as one does with an old fireplace chimney he cherishes. The diva laughed merrily. In a few days the packets were to be removed from town. She was going away for a week to screw up her courage for the confronting. Would he come to her this afternoon, two weeks? She bowed her head, and he saw to his surprise that she was crying.

"Have I been foolishly sentimental, Ludwig?" she asked, drying her eyes.

"You shall see for yourself," he replied, and like a magician Telfen said to some third person, who apparently occupied the empty air about them, "Let me have a transcript at once, Miss Pastor."

Velma Ilseng looked her bewilderment. No one was about. The old man smiled. He loved his little tricks, and never went to the trouble of explaining them. In a few minutes the red-headed amanuensis came down with some fluttering sheets of typewriting; and Telfen, solemnly folding them, handed the sheaf to the diva.

"Here is your confession," he said.

That day two weeks the old man went down to Manhasset, somewhat excited at the prospect of this audience with regal gems which were to be brought up from long exile. Only addicts in the lore of historic stones knew of the few famous gems that had been lying all these years in Velma Ilseng's dungeon. She drove in from Lakeville, with a maid as her sole companion, an hour late. Roger, her son, and his two fine children were there to meet her, had been there awaiting her for several days; and Eva Sarien, her daughter, the oratorio singer, had come down. Only her husband was absent, and he would be home in the morning.

Her spoken wish that the contents of those precious packets might be turned to dust in exile when she broke the seals was not to be realized. It was much simpler than that.

Velma Ilseng, pausing in her sitting room amid the gusts of welcome from her children, had said with a little start, "Marie, where did you put my emeralds this morning?" And Marie, the maid, laughingly had turned back the laces of her lady's throat to disclose the gorgeous string nesting there. There was a merry laugh, the diva joining in at her own expense as she gave the string to the maid to put away. Then, suddenly, the household was electrified by the maid's wild shriek; the members of the family, rushing into the dressing room, found the girl cowering, emeralds clutched against her breast with one hand, and a shaking finger pointing at the niche in the wall where the safe had been installed with the aid of so many skilled artisans. The niche was empty. The safe was gone. It might never have been there, so completely were all traces of its going erased.

It was beyond the talents of the local police. The mere mention of the sum, a quarter of a million dollars, precluded them. Wells Martin, of the Martin and Martin Agency, went down and looked over the ground with a coldly professional eye. He shook his head, with a curious smile.

"It is not the type of case we care to handle," he answered. Something in his tone roused the ire of Roger Ilseng.

"What exactly do you mean by that?" he demanded with heat.

"I repeat," said the expert with patient emphasis, "it is not the type of case we handle."

Reginald Baker had not arrived home the next morning as had been expected. He had been shunted off to the north among the hard woods, and a telegram failed to reach him until two days later. Then he came by airplane. There was something staunch about Baker in a storm. He went to the Corlears people, who did handle this type of case. But they had a polite excuse.

II

Captain broadbill, he of the delicate, confidential and strictly private detective agency, had been kept waiting for half an hour in young Baker's anteroom along with a dozen others, when young Baker came in late and in a hurry and not bothering to use his private door, but plowing through the morning levee without a look. The waiting chairs stirred expectantly, but Baker had already disappeared, and the pneumatic bumpers of two doors thumping gently behind him notified the listeners that he had taken refuge in his private-audience chamber. There was a long silence. Broadbill, the delicate, confidential and strictly private, turned his capacious visage on his elbow neighbor and surveyed him gingerly. He was a dapper little fellow from the architect's office, with a roll of sketches. The detective knocked the neighboring elbow; he covered the loose corner of his mouth with a discreet hand and remarked, in a voice audible to all the room, "He thinks he is the Angel Gabriel." Getting no reaction, he added to the empty air, "I've got a waiting line of my own."

He arose, took his hat and moved threateningly to the exit. The clerk at the desk continued writing, the chair warmers relaxed, as if relieved at the prospect of being one less. Captain Broadbill got as far as the water bottle. He paused to quench his thirst from a dainty paper cup. Then he returned to his place and sat down. More silence. The buzzer sounded, causing a general start. The clerk emerged from his pencilings and gave Captain Broadbill a curt nod. Broadbill dusted himself off for the audience, and as he passed on in he gave the envious group a broad wink.

Baker was a man of, say, thirty-five. He presented the general effect of the man whom commercial artists strive so successfully to depict in collar advertisements. His wife was thirty-five years his senior. People invariably added this qualifying clause in speaking of Baker, as if it were only fair to the third person of a transaction to put this card on the table, no matter what others they held in the hole. His wife, the great Velma Ilseng, had retired to private life with a fortune to match her fame. But nothing now remained of the diva's voice except her records, which were capitalized in six figures. This suite of offices in the Bourse Building represented Velma Ilseng, Inc., with Baker as chief of staff. The waiting list in the entry room any morning was evidence of the ramifications of the incorporated legal person of the extinct singer. Baker was, always had been, a high-priced man; yet his stewardship had been so successful, not only for his wife but for her married children as well, that it was generally admitted that she had, as usual in all her dealings, struck an exceptional bargain.

Captain Broadbill, the delicate, confidential and strictly private, closed the last door behind him, tiptoed across the room to the witness chair, his hat dangling loosely in one hand. Baker was too well bred for Broadbill and made the detective ill at ease; but Broadbill had enough insolence to bridge the gap. He waited.

"Have you anything to report to me, Broadbill?" asked Baker.

Broadbill, after a moment's thought, shook his head and smiled.

"No," he said, and stared straight into the gaze of the man at the desk.

"You have been on the case six weeks," said Baker.

"Yes; six weeks Thursday."

"What steps have you taken?" asked Baker.

Broadbill contrived an admirable expression of surprise.

"None," he said. He drew the lazy breath of a fat man in a chair that fitted him. "You didn't expect me to do anything, did you?"

There may have been an instant of breathless thought on the part of the well-dressed man at the desk, but the keen eyes of Broadbill failed to detect it.

"No," said Baker. He touched the buzzer for the next visitor. The door opened and the little architect came in on the heels of the clerk.

"Good morning, Sutro," said Baker, nodding. He got up slowly. "Put in your final statement, Broadbill," he said. "Our vouchers go out Thursdays. If you get it in before then you will have your check this week."

"Final?" said Broadbill, as if in mild surprise. "Oh, no," he expostulated good-naturedly, "I expect to be on your pay roll for some time to come."

The amiable Baker shook his head the while he was unrolling the sketches from the architect's; they were the preliminary draft of plans for a sun parlor for the house at Manhasset.

"Unfortunately, no," he said, smiling. He turned to his clerk. "See that Broadbill's account is closed this week without fail," he said. Broadbill was on his feet, kicking out his baggy trousers. He dropped an expressive eyelid over his left eye for the benefit of the little draftsman, who flinched. "Oh, I don't lie awake nights worrying how to collect what you owe me, Mr. Baker," he cried expansively; and with this amiable tribute to the financial rating of the husband of Velma Ilseng, he took his departure, a deep-sea roll to his gait.

Baker was saying, as the door shut, "This means we shall have to go into the south wall, doesn't it?"

"It will have to be tied, yes, sir," said the draftsman.

"Curious. I hadn't thought of that."

The architect said nothing. His thoughts were cynical. He had supposed that that was just what Baker was scheming to do—to mutilate that wall. It had been the gossip of the drafting room.

Baker shook his head.

"No, we can't disturb it now," he was saying; and, as if everybody in the world didn't know about that wall by this time, he went on, still studying the sketches: "We broached that wall last September to move in a safe for my wife's jewelry. Last month somebody moved the safe out again without so much as nicking the wall paper. Until we find out how he did it, we shall have to leave that wall undisturbed."

His tone was the easy conversational one that made him so many friends among the lesser folk who came to him shivering in awe at the thought of his importance in big affairs. The little architect knew all about the baffling robbery, of course: it was—had been for weeks—one of those notorious unprinted stories that newspaper readers glean between the lines. To hear it thus casually referred to by the young husband whom everybody was whispering about was too much for the little architect. He was leaning forward, rapt, his eye gleaming with eagerness. Baker turned to him, and Sutro, abashed in having his thoughts surprised in his face, dropped his eyes in confusion. There was a pause. Baker was frowning and handing back the sketches.

"That is all," he said. "We will hold everything in abeyance for the time being. Thank you very much for letting me see the drawings."

When the man had gone Baker sat for some time frowning at his paper weight, a fragment of Balaklava cannon that Victoria Crosses are made of; it was one of his wife's gifts—in her career of thirty years on the Continent she had accumulated many odd things. He picked up the bit of metal and examined its fractures minutely, as if they alone claimed his thoughts. His mind traveled to the waiting list in the entry room. Most of these people he didn't know. But he knew why they had come. Recently people got in to see him on the flimsiest pretexts, apparently just to look at him, hear him talk, as if his recent notoriety had marked him as something more—or less—than a man.

He told his clerk to turn the callers over to the office manager, and putting on his hat he left by his private door. As he drove uptown he smiled with a hard-drawn grimness at the thought of those people who waited so patiently. He caught sight of himself in the mirror of the car, and he examined his own features curiously to see if he, too, could detect something there to excite the morbidly curious. There was nothing to distinguish him from the common herd. Yet he was aware that should a newspaper announce that Reginald Baker would call at the district attorney's office at ten in the morning, hundreds of people would be jostling about the door just to get a glimpse of him; if they did see him their day would be made thrilling by the mere fact. Does guilt, crime, notoriety, blame, suspicion stamp the person of its victim with some intangible symbol visible to all eyes but his own—like the black smear on his nose which identifies the villain in a Chinese play? He laughed harshly.

His car drew up in a side street in the old residential Fifties. Oliver Armiston, the householder, was surprised to receive this visit from Reginald Baker, with whom the exigencies of city life had restricted him to a nodding friendship for several years past. Years ago they had been intimate enough. Armiston had known Baker at school. Even then he had stood out among his fellows as one predestined to success. First he had been secretary to a money baron. Then he had been invited into an important directorate, and as its youngest member straightway became its most distinguished. The success myth grew up about him before he was thirty. Then he had married Velma Ilseng. And now, this notorious robbery!

Oliver led the way into his study and pushed over a paper box of cigars. Old Buddha, as big as a mountain, sat there toasting his august shins. Buddha listened with a tight mouth to many strange confidences in this room. Armiston, as a fiction writer, in his day had created rogues so plausible that rogues in real life had followed their lead and the police had politely asked him to desist. It was then that Deputy Parr, the versatile man hunter, had stepped in to make use of Oliver's hectic imagination to solve some of his most baffling mysteries. Results had been so startling in several instances that the chief of the detective bureau regarded him as clairvoyant.

"I haven't seen much of you lately," said Armiston.

"Doubtless you have followed me in the papers," said Baker.

Baker had always been in the newspapers. Never seeking publicity, yet he possessed the knack, or the curse, of first-page prominence in the day's news. It was the success myth translated for breakfast-table consumption.

"I have come for your help," said Baker. Oliver nodded and waited. "Oliver," went on the husband of Velma Ilseng, "you are the first man who has looked me in the eye for weeks. It is a curious thing that when a man harvests contempt and opprobrium, his fellows avoid his gaze. Not an hour ago a man walked into my office and informed me that he expected to blackmail me for some time to come. Not in so many words, but his meaning was unmistakable. A few nights ago in a theater the comedian got a big laugh in a trance-medium act by asking the spook if it could move a ton safe through a stone wall without his wife finding out. Oliver, I have become a gag. People point me out in the street as the man who robbed his wife of her jewels." He paused, smiling grimly, but his eyes were agony.

"And your wife?" Armiston said. It was some time before Baker replied.

"That is the most painful part of it," he said. "She is sailing for Europe on twenty-four hours' notice."

"She usually winters at Baden, doesn't she?"

Baker shook his head.

"Not on twenty-four hours' notice," he said.

"And Roger, your stepson?" asked Oliver.

"Roger was to have spent the winter with me, with his children, at Manhasset. This morning he telephoned—or his man telephoned—that he had taken a house in town. He is sending down for his things, not coming for them himself. At breakfast his sister, Mrs. Sarien, spent an hour trying to explain to me palatably why the rats were leaving the sinking ship. Oliver, is it that you don't know," he cried abruptly, "or is it that you do not believe it?"

"What?"

"That I robbed my wife! Isn't it obvious to you that no one could have gone through the hocus-pocus of dematerializing that safe without my connivance? It seems perfectly clear to everyone else. Every newspaper I pick up blares it at me between the lines. They have a smart way of putting forth their innuendoes, their unprintable stories! I wonder how many poor devils the newspapers have driven to death by the stories they print between the lines. There is no fighting back. You can't pin them down to a word that is actionable. Yet it is there for every fool to read and gloat over. They love to see the bubbles burst. A man is a poor judge of his own acts," he mused absently. "We are apt to warp our consciences into place as we go through life. I suppose there is no scoundrel, no matter how black, who does not somehow justify his own acts. I try to stand aside and look at it dispassionately, to judge myself as I would judge others. I ask myself not am I a thief, but have I done anything to justify the world in his belief that I am a thief."

Oliver was fingering his single white lock.

"What was in the safe?" he asked suddenly.

Baker started irritably. He laughed mirthlessly.

"The inventory has been printed a thousand times," he said. "Every street-corner loafer knows the list by now."

"The jewelry?"

"Yes! Yes, man!"

"Did you see it there?" persisted Oliver.

"No. I never saw the safe."

"Did your wife see the jewels in the safe?"

"Yes," almost barked the distraught man. "She signed for it. They were delivered from the safety-deposit vault by armored car."

"How was it delivered? In packages?"

"Yes."

"Did she open the packages?" queried the author.

"No."

"Why not?"

"I see what you are driving at," said Baker. "It's no use, Oliver. There isn't a chink anywhere that you can pry a doubt into. The stuff was sealed by old Telfen himself, years ago, when it was insured. The seals were intact."

"Why did she not open the packages?" insisted Oliver.

"It was an ordeal that she dreaded," said Baker. "These were the mementos of her career. It is a terrible thing to live beyond your fame. These things were symbols of her great triumphs. They were mostly gifts—from kings and queens." He shrugged. "She had all Europe at her feet. She dreaded to stir the ashes. It was with the greatest reluctance that she brought herself to the decision to dispose of them. She asked old Telfen to come down, to be with her when she confronted them—confronted," he repeated oddly. "She continually used that word 'confront,' as though she were a guilty person about to face her accusers. A foolish qualm, you may say. But it existed in her mind. These artists are all poets."

"How long were they there?" asked Armiston.

"About ten days, I think."

"Did anyone know of it?"

"I had especially cautioned her not to speak of it to anyone. No one but old Telfen." He shrugged away this absurdity. "She had gone to him about two weeks before, made an appointment with him for the day she came back from Lakewood. You don't suspect old Telfen, do you, Oliver?" Baker's set features, for the first time, relaxed. Oliver shook his head.

"Let us assume," said Armiston, "that there was nothing in the packages when they arrived, that the seals had been broken and counterfeited."

Baker laughed harshly.

"If you please to do so," he said idly. He looked up. "Then why would the counterfeiters give themselves the trouble of dematerializing an empty safe?" he demanded.

"To accomplish just exactly what they succeeded in accomplishing," said Armiston—"to make it appear that you robbed your wife. They have done that, haven't they? There isn't a chink, as you say, into which you can pry a doubt. You are almost ready to doubt yourself."

Baker was silent. This man doomed to success was hard and fast aground, like a great ship fast on a shoal. He would live on forever, a monument of error.

"Has the insurance company paid?" Oliver asked.

"No." Baker looked significantly at Armiston. "They are making their own investigation."

"And this blackmailer? Who is he?"

"A miserable rat named Broadbill."

"I know him," said Oliver. "Nothing to worry about. His whole business in life is capitalizing suspicion. He makes a very good living at it. Reggie, will you give me a week?" he asked.

Baker took his hat and arose. He laughed sardonically. They clasped hands. He departed.

III

"Orders," said the elegant Stetson, who took two hours to his morning toilet, "are absolute. He is not to be approached unless he is seated at his desk."

He indicated with a nod the cluster of waiting little chairs about the rare table on the slight dais in the corner of the vast gallery. Behind his idol's mask he was secretly examining Oliver Armiston, annoyed that he could not quite recall him. This person had an air about him, what with that distinguished white lock and a slender æstheticism, and his clothes were undoubtedly well cut.

Armiston considered the situation: and, as usual when he considered, he fixed his eye on the person who happened to be at hand, Stetson in this instance; he looked on and through him as though the things he saw existed, if they existed at all, only for his eyes. Stetson squirmed inwardly under the impact of the stare. Finally he took refuge in speech.

"You have personal business with Mr. Telfen?" he asked.

Oliver nodded, still staring vaguely through the elegant impresario of this feast of jewels.

"I am entirely in his confidence," suggested Stetson delicately. "He is old, old. We try to spare him routine as much as possible. If you would tell me the nature of your business—" said Stetson, and he paused, leaving the sentence to finish itself.

Oliver turned on his cane and surveyed old Ludwig at his oblations; there he sat as plain as day and as inaccessible as a fish in a glass tank. Oliver swung around again and eyed the elegant Stetson speculatively. He leaned closer, pinioning the man with his stare.

"I am of the police," he said in a low tone, his lips scarcely moving.

It was the first time in his career as the occasional assistant of the great Parr, the man hunter, that Armiston had ever gone so far as to brevet himself with authority. In the titivating confidence of this moment no great harm could come of his presumption. He was feeling his way. He had dropped in to look things over, to test an unknown quantity, x, with various reagents; to see, for a start, if he could narrow it down to a known genus.

Stetson stood like a man galvanized. He seemed for the instant incapable of utterance. Oliver reached out and touched his arm in caution, to forestall an outburst.

"Easy!" breathed Armiston. "Don't let anyone suspect us. Listen to me. I must have a word with him. There must be no possibility of my being overheard. Do you understand?"

"Police?"

Stetson seemed finally to have found his tongue. Still the idea seemed incomprehensible, a sacrilege.

"Police? Here?" he muttered, looking about with wild eyes. Oliver nodded confidentially.

"It involves the house," he said. "I must see him at once."

Stetson's eyes moved to the old man behind the bars, oblivious of the impending catastrophe—for police, here, spelled catastrophe, desecration. He appeared to defer. His eyes wandered to the clock; finally they came to the little dais, and then to Armiston. He motioned him to follow.

"Come," he said; "this will be the place. You can be waiting here for him. He usually comes about eleven."

"We will not be disturbed?" said Oliver.

"I will see to it personally," promised Stetson.

He moved off, assuming a careless air. Fortunately, it was not the brisk hour. The place was empty, save for the few distinguished salesmen, attired like Stetson in correct morning wear, who busied themselves over their separate concerns. Very cleverly the efficient Stetson moved from one to another, and with a suggestion here, an order there, gradually herded them into the far corners. A redheaded girl appeared against the opposite wall from behind a bronze screen, and Stetson, approaching her with the magnificent tread of an undertaker at a funeral, said something that caused her to vanish. Oliver waited. The clock intoned the hour; and the addict of gems, recalled from his oblations by the sentinel of time, arose from his chair, where he crouched over a steel drawer; jingling a bunch of keys, he opened the gate and let himself out like a jailer; he turned the key in the lock, smiling to himself over some pleasant image that he had not quite banished. He approached the dais on slippered feet, and perceiving Armiston he gave him a sharp look and a formal nod of greeting as he sat down. Only privileged people were permitted at this table, and he trusted the efficient Stetson for that. Ludwig Telfen opened the drawer and busied himself replacing some curious objects that lay on the desk.

"I am of the police," said Armiston, leaning forward and speaking in a tone scarcely audible to the old man. The hand that was lifting a jade paused for a moment in air, then continued its task.

"The Velma Ilseng robbery," said Oliver, very low and distinct. He watched the room in a mirror that hung on the bars of the golden cage; Stetson had moved off-stage; there was a sepulchral calm in the picture. The old man picked up with a pair of tweezers a paste stone, a replica of a famous diamond and placed it in a case which he transferred to the drawer. Oliver leaned farther over the table.

"The gems were stolen in transit," he whispered. The old man was looking at a cameo, a thing of no great value, but with an interesting history. Oliver said, scarcely moving his lips, "Your seals were tampered with. Counterfeit packages were delivered."

There was a long silence. But for a slight, almost imperceptible lift of the eyelids, Oliver might have believed that he had been talking to a man stone deaf. Telfen after a time shut the drawer and leisurely arose; he hooked a hand through Oliver's arm to take him with him, and they started off together like father and son. Telfen brought him to a pause in front of a marble fragment of Rodin, and smiling over it, felt the thing with fingers that did not quite touch it.

"You are from Deputy Parr?" said the cunning old man. "I recollect you now. You were here with him the night of the robbery of the Dolgoda pearls." The lapidary sighed. That famous instance had very nearly cost him his philosophy of life, so cleverly had a confidence woman duped him on that occasion.

He urged Oliver on to a sacred case filled with Cellini mementos, and he leaned over it, tracing with his finger on the glass, as if explaining the contents.

"What does he wish me to do?" he asked as he bent forward.

"Nothing," said Oliver. "He wanted you to have word of it. He will keep you informed."

"He is a very able man," said the old lapidary, "but sometimes I think"—he tapped his forehead, smiling—"he has flights."

They paused at a fresh group. It was slow progress across the room, for they must pause, and pause again, to explain to a barbarian that one must be a dreamer to dwell in these marble halls. Finally they came to the street door, which obediently rotated on its axis, and as Oliver admitted himself to the stile to be conveyed into outer air the old man waved a courteous farewell to him.

"Parr," said Oliver Armiston, addressing the fiercely scowling visage of the great policeman, "I have been amusing myself with a little qualitative analysis this morning. I have been applying reagents to an unknown solution, x. It might be anything. The mathematical possibilities are infinite. With the aid of my reagents, red, blue and green drops, however, I am enabled by simple tests to isolate it as to genus, then as to family group. Once having determined the family group, I seek to identify the individual. And I think I've got him," he added dryly.

Parr said nothing.

"I have just come from the Whispering Gallery. You recollect the Whispering Gallery?" asked Armiston.

Parr's great head turned on his massive shoulders like a gun turret.

"Telfen's?" he said curiously.

"Telfen's," acquiesced Oliver. "Do you recall the old man in his dotage may be addressed only when he is seated at a certain table, on a raised dais? Do you remember why?"

Parr stirred uneasily in his chair.

"There's a trick echo, isn't there?" he said. "He has a stenographer hidden in the mezzanine to take every word down in black and white. That's what you are driving at, isn't it?"

"Correct," said Armiston. "So there can never be any dispute as to any transaction enacted at that desk. Now listen, Parr." Oliver was plainly in his best vein. "I walked into Telfen's today with my mind clean, sensitized for impressions. I was accosted by a man named Stetson."

Parr nodded. He recollected this elegant gentleman very well as a functionary he had had to reckon with in an episode in the career of the notorious Sophie Lang, a confidence woman.

"It might have been anybody else," continued Oliver. "As I say, I was dealing with an unknown quantity. I was very mysterious. I could see him trying to place me. He didn't remember me. So I took out one of my little vials—I am speaking in allegory now, Parr—say, some of the red drops. I put a drop in his ear—a word. I whispered it. 'Police!' He reacted instantly!"

"To what?" queried Parr mildly.

"Fear!"

Oliver sat back, preening himself. Parr grunted.

"Certain families, in the table of human elements," said Oliver, continuing his metaphor, "react to that reagent, fear. The mere sound of the word, uttered at an unexpected moment, causes a change of color. This man went pea green!"

Parr, rubbing his bristly chin, was examining in great detail the ceiling above his head. He was groping, but he had no clew.

"And then what?" he rumbled impatiently.

"Well, having isolated my specimen and identified him as a member of the fear family, I feed him another drop—that is, I whisper in his ear again. I tell him I must have a word with Telfen, with no possibility of its being overheard."

"And how did the specimen react, professor?" drawled Parr.

"Beautifully!" cried Armiston. "It all goes to show the exactitude of qualitative analysis. He set me down in the one spot in that room where he himself could overhear every word I said. Do you recollect the lay of that room? There is a bronze screen and partition in one corner, diagonally across from the Whispering Table. Behind that screen there is a little stairway leading up to the cubicle on the mezzanine where the stenographer sits. Well, that's where he went, quite casually."

Parr brought his chair down slowly to all fours.

"What did you tell Telfen?" he demanded.

"I told him that Velma Ilseng's jewels were never delivered," said Armiston; "that Telfen's seals were tampered with, and dummy packages substituted. Parr, that safe was removed to cover up the fact that the robbery occurred in the armored car that made the delivery."

Parr sat silent a long time. He shook his head.

"No," he said. "They wouldn't take a chance on the packages being opened and inspected on delivery."

"But they didn't take a chance," interjected Oliver. He beamed. "They knew that they wouldn't be opened. Velma Ilseng went to old Telfen two weeks before the robbery—and at that same table asked him to be there when she opened them. They would lie in that safe for ten days unopened. That would place the robbery indisputably in the house."

"How do you know that?" demanded Parr fiercely.

"I have seen the transcript of the testimony," smiled Oliver. He told how old Telfen, in a moment of childish enthusiasm, had presented the diva with the typewritten transcript when she asked him if she had been saying anything foolish. Parr pondered.

"Stetson?" he muttered. He was dubious. The man had too assured a position to attempt such a coup.

"This jewelry had been shut away for twenty-five years," said Oliver, as if guessing the thought passing in Parr's mind. "It would be difficult to identify it—that is, the stones, if they were removed from their settings."

"The girl would be involved, of course," snarled the pessimistic Parr.

"A red-headed woman—a Russian, I think," agreed Oliver. Parr smiled.

"They say a Russian woman is equal to three ordinary females," he remarked dryly. He touched a button. A shabby little fellow named Pelts, who seemed to have been cooling his heels outside for such a summons, appeared and stood uncomfortably under the portentous scowl of the great man.

"Look up the members of the armored-car crew in the Ilseng robbery," he said. "See if one of them was blind at that time."

"Blind?" queried Oliver, puzzled.

"That safe was cut up by a torch," said Parr. "Those fellows usually wear goggles when they use a torch. The old hands get careless. They take a spell of blindness for their carelessness now and then. Get along, Pelts."

Again Parr touched the button. This time a man named Morel came in—a handsome man, whose specialty was women.

"Morel," said the deputy, "there is a red-headed stenographer at Telfen's. See if you can get her bumped in a street accident on her way to work some morning and kept in a hospital unidentified for a day or two."

Morel was gone. Parr was on his feet, pacing the room, on the *qui vive* now. During Oliver's discourse he had been skeptic enough; now he was a bigoted convert.

"Sometimes, Oliver," he said, "when you leave me I feel for my watch to see if I still have it. I lay back on the oars in this Ilseng case. It had all the earmarks of a family job. You have caught the thief!" he cried, aiming a pistol finger at Armiston.

Oliver was not so sanguine. Parr brushed his objections aside. It was a mere matter of gathering up the loose ends now. His eyes twinkled.

"Now I will take down my little red bottles," he said. "Having isolated the specimen, we will feed him some more drops. We will let him worry a couple of days over this woman disappearing. Then we will put a clumsy man on his heels as a shadow, so that he will know it. Then I will call on him."

"But you can't accuse him until you get something more definite to go on!" protested Armiston.

"Ha-ha! I won't accuse him," laughed Parr. "I will let him react to my little drops—let him accuse himself. I will call on him some night. I will announce myself as Deputy Parr-r-r! Police! He knows who Parr is! They all do." The deputy's jaw shut with a snap. "When he comes in, I will stare at him right between the eyes. I'll keep on staring. I won't say a word. He'll talk! Oh, they all talk! Just give them the gaff. Oh, simple, very simple!" Parr waved an airy hand.

Four nights later Parr mounted the steps and rang the bell of Stetson's house, one of those old frame structures that still cling precariously to the sidehill above the river in the Heights section. He gave his name to the servant with a ringing snap—and he spelled it, for fear she would fail to get it. He went in and sat down and waited—and waited. Finally he heard a step on the stairs—Stetson coming down. The step faltered, halted. There was something eerie about its hesitancy. Parr could almost see the man trying to hearten himself for the interview, moistening his lips, swallowing painfully, trying to steel his nerves that were turned to water. Finally the step came on again. Whatever doubts might still have assailed the man hunter, that lagging footfall had dispelled. Whatever flicker of courage the doomed man may have summoned in that faltering moment, fell from him like a cloak before the stern accusation in the visage he confronted. It proved pathetically simple. He made a clean breast of it—the jewels had been sent to Amsterdam for recutting before being offered for sale. Stetson thought the woman had played him false.

The House of Many Mansions

NEXT to the squealer," said Parr, the man hunter, making thoughtful repairs on a stogy, "the little tin god of coincidence gets all my joss. The average crook spends about two-thirds of his life in jail simply because, though he might beat the cops, the long arm of coincidence is longer than the long arm of the law. If it wasn't for chance," said the police deputy, his eye roving over the street crowds—and doubtless some mechanism in the back of his head clicking now and then as he identified some familiar face—"if it wasn't for chance, Oliver, I'd be a tailor—or maybe a shoemaker—like that fellow in the window."

He took off his hat and mopped his brow. It was one of those days of late winter when, though the city pavements are swept bare of every flake of snow that falls, there hangs in the air the smell of thaw from distant stream and wood. They paused for cross-tide traffic and there came alongside of them a shabby little fellow in two or three pairs of pants and a coat or two too many, who hugged himself, in addition, to keep warm. Parr regarded him as a strange bug.

"Yes," he went on, "one of those shoemakers in that window." He laughed. "Recent remedial legislation designed to put crooks in jail and keep them there," he said, "has thinned out the good shooting in my district, I admit. Still, with squealers and coincidence, I manage to bag a good trophy or two now and then." His eyes followed the little fellow, who, as rich in choice as any tramp with all time for his own, drifted over to the window where sat three shoemakers half-soling shoes for the edification of passers-by. Quite a little crowd stood watching, because city people are simple and easily amused.

Oliver Armiston chuckled to himself. Pelts! That shabby little fellow was Parr's man Friday, Pelts. The man hunter had undoubtedly recognized a "mug" out of his mental rogues' gallery in that shoemaker's window and had sent Pelts back to look it over. The deputy commissioner never walked abroad without this fellow Pelts trailing behind to keep watch of the wake, and his side partner, Morel, the handsome man, moving ahead as a scout. Pelts was undoubtedly a tramp at heart, whereas Morel looked like a society man—a profession requiring, as a starter, good looks, fine clothes, and a big income. No one would take either for a police detective.

"Coincidence is *verboten* in your business, isn't it?" said Parr, turning to his companion, the extinct author, as they moved forward again and swept into the Avenue. "Why?" he asked. "Is it because it is so true to life? Or because it isn't? Which?"

"It is the lazy man's way," explained Armiston.

"It keeps my jails full," said Parr complacently.

"It's not dramatic," said Oliver.

"Oh, isn't it? Listen! There was a famous porch climber who eluded us for three years—and all the time he was busy climbing porches. How did we get him finally? We didn't. He got himself. He accidentally stepped on the grass in the Park! That's a misdemeanor, punishable by a fine or ten days in jail if it is flagrant. A sparrow cop picked him up and brought him in." Parr chuckled, "Clever, eh?"

"Clever of your desk lieutenant to recognize him when he was brought in," agreed Armiston.

"No; clever of the coincidence!" cried Parr. He produced his cane, which had been standing on its head in a very deep pocket of his ulster, and marched with it alongside. "Here is another! A crank writes a threatening letter to the President when he was in town last. Threatens to kill him. We trace the letter to the district it was mailed from. He probably votes. Such a man is apt to regard the franchise as a solemn duty. We examine the polling lists in that district. We find he has given his pedigree and signed his name in the same handwriting as the letter. Careless of him to mail that letter in the same district where he voted."

Parr's eyes moved this way and that, never still. He saw strange things in crowds, unseen by other eyes. Crooks knew him to the last hair. They studied him as rats study a cat they would like to hang a bell on. It was a legend that a ripple of fear accompanied Parr wherever he went.

"Here's another!" Parr was harping on the same string for the edification of his author friend. "Did you read of the holdup last night?"

Oliver nodded. It was one of those atrocious crimes that leave the city aghast. Pay-roll bandits had backed a messenger into a hallway and shot him dead without a word. They escaped in a stolen car held in waiting. Around the corner they changed to a second car, also stolen. Half a mile farther on they changed to still a third car, which they picked up in passing. Thus the police had no description of the third car for another hour, when the owner reported his loss.

"A cunning get-away!" said Oliver.

"Except for one thing," agreed Parr. "The second car was cold. It didn't start very well and they were in a hurry. One of them got out and pushed. He left his fingerprints for us. We happen to have copies of them downtown." Parr turned his cold eye on Armiston. "It is stylish among your type of philosophers," he expounded, "to say that nothing really ever happens, that things always occur. Isn't that a fact?"

"It is a fact that there is no effect without cause," agreed the bookish Armiston. "If that is what you mean."

"That is exactly what I mean," said Parr grimly. "Tell me, Mr. Philosopher, what induced this particular crook to get out and leave his mark on that car for me. It might just as well have been one of the others."

"Have you got him?"

"I will have him shortly," said the man hunter easily. His eyes beamed. "I expect to be decorated by the French Government when I turn him in."

"Oh! Who is he?"

"Aristide Leblanc." Parr's tone was just above his breath.

Inwardly Armiston recoiled as if at a shot. But outwardly he preserved his poker face. In fact, he managed a humorous twinkle to the smile and bow he gave some friends passing in a car. To walk and talk with Parr one must be imperturbable; there was no telling how many eyes stared at them from ambush.

Aristide Leblanc was an apache who had cunningly obtained employment in a wealthy household as a butler—the family of Worthington Horn, a banker. He locked the family in the wine vault and abandoned them to die miserably beyond the reach of help, while he looted the house and walked off. Horn had dug his way to freedom literally by his finger nails, and just in time, too, for his wife had been at the point of succumbing. So terrible had been the ordeal that the banker pledged his life and his fortune to the running down of the apache and bringing him to justice. At present Horn was in Paris conferring with the French police.

"He was in hiding here, then?" exclaimed Armiston, shading the incredulity in his voice. Where could such a marked man conceal himself! Never had there been such a price on a man's head, such a hue and cry.

"He's never been away," replied Parr.

"I'd have gambled he was following Horn," said Oliver. "Just one step behind, in the shadow of the pursuit. That would have been the safest place for him." Then he added with conviction, "That fellow has finesse as well as cunning. You'll never get him!"

"He's left his card," said Parr, smiling.

"He makes no effort to cover his tracks! He seems rather proud of them, in fact," put in Oliver.

"I'll have him shortly," reiterated Parr confidently. "The percentage in favor of the bank is beginning to work against him. He can't beat coincidence. It's Fate! There comes a time when these things work out very simply, in spite of you fiction writers. Hello! What a magnificent fellow we have here!"

The exclamation was evoked by the sight of a door opener, in the regalia of a Dahomey potentate, handing into her landau a woman in gorgeous furs—a woman of the type known among dressmakers as a "larger" woman, as distinguished from a stylish stout. There is something particularly menial about opening doors, it seems; and people who can afford the indulgence have it done with as much pomp and circumstance as possible. This truly magnificent fellow was as tall as a Swiss Guard, and he wore a clanking cloak plastered with medals. He bowed and bowed to the lady, and when he shut her in with a final polish of the door handle he continued to bow and back away as if etiquette prescribed it.

"What a crib to crack!" muttered Oliver Armiston, looking up at the embellished façade and identifying it as that most opulent of recent apartment hotels, derisively known as the Golden Shekel. "Did you ever have a squeal from there, Parr?" he asked.

Parr shook his head. No. He stopped at the next corner, looking down the Avenue and tapping the curb with the point of his stick. A taxi that might have been stalking him immediately drew up and proffered itself. Parr was in the act of stepping in, when a blond young man of the type the English call a nob came to a halt in front of the mail box and began frantically searching himself. It was evident that the dumb letter box had just reminded him that he was to mail a letter, but he had forgotten the letter. Parr looked him over with a smile of pride.

"That door-knob polisher," he was saying to Armiston, and he stepped into the taxi—"that door-knob polisher—" and the taxi rolled forward. The young man was still canvassing his pockets for that letter. It was Morel, Parr's society specialist, called in for orders.

Oliver, for his part, would have liked to continue on foot because of all the rabbits Parr could kick up along the road. But the deputy evidently had something else on his mind. They ran into a traffic semaphore set against them, but they swung into the center of the Avenue with an angry honk and their car was put through, to an accompaniment of peremptory police whistles, as if it were the King of the Belgians in town on another visit of thanks. They had gone five blocks before the stalled traffic resumed. If Parr had been followed—as he usually was—this regal procedure snuffed out the lurking shadows. Half an hour later they arrived on foot at Oliver Armiston's home in a quiet side street in the lower Fifties.

Since the deputy had taken to calling on his friend Armiston, the extinct fiction writer, for an occasional *tour de force* of the imagination to help out in refractory cases, Parr had been coming here more and more, usually by some such devious route as he had just pursued. During the run of what was known as the insurance-widow case—in which one crook had obligingly snuffed out another for him—Parr had installed a private wire here in Armiston's study, and he had conveniently neglected to remove it. It connected directly with Central Office. Many of his most famous cases had been brought to a successful conclusion in the seclusion of this quiet side street.

The deputy had hardly arranged himself in his favorite elbow chair before the fire when his telephone muttered discreetly. It was Morel reporting.

"What's that? You say you never saw him before!" cried Parr with the utmost ferocity.

Morel expatiated; as an added precaution he had turned the well-thumbed leaves of the rogues' gallery, pages that swung on hinges, like museum specimens. But the deputy was not to be mollified.

"Go back!" he ordered. "Wait! Better get yourself invited to dinner. Can you?"

"I think I can arrange it, sir," said Morel meekly.

"Good! Find out what a crook is doing there as lookout. And don't tell me he isn't a crook!" He hung up.

"The carriage starter?" asked Oliver. "Did you recognize him as a crook?"

"No! He recognized me. Didn't you see how careful he was to keep his back turned to me?" cried Parr.

There must have been an unholy glamour about the person of the deputy for crooks, big and little. In their dread they were always fearful he would recognize them. And in their childish vanity they were almost afraid he wouldn't. So they were forever revealing themselves, torn between vainglory and terror. This fellow gave himself away. The hours passed.

Shortly after eight o'clock that evening the figure of a lithesome young dancing man such as any hostess might have been proud of emerged from the Golden Shekel and decided to walk a little, for the air. It was Morel. He must have passed some secret office, for hardly was he out of the block when a magic invisible curtain of espionage fell, without a rustle, about the house of many mansions. In another ten minutes so closely was the Golden Shekel invested by the police that not a shadow would have emerged unobserved. Comings and goings continued apparently as usual, but with each departure a shadow detached itself, unseen.

The telephone muttered again discreetly. Parr listened; his eyes glowed like dull coals.

"Good!" he cried, and hung up. He turned on Oliver. It is more of an art to hold a poker face on good news than bad. This was triumph.

"It's a den of thieves," he said. "The place is crawling with crooks from cellar to garret."

"I thought they were all post-deflation millionaires of the most noisome type!" cried Oliver, aghast, getting the feel of the excitement.

Parr guffawed.

"Oh, not the tenants!" he roared. "The help! Waiters, hallboys, maids, chefs, clerks—they are all crooks! And apparently on their good behavior. A kind of sanctuary!" Parr's face wore the smile of a benign cannibal. Then he added in his *coix blanche*, "Your friend Aristide Leblanc is the maître d'hôtel."

Towing this hand grenade into Oliver's lap, he sat back smiling and bowing.

Even the clocks for the moment seemed to forget their occasions and cease to tick; then they all began again, thudding on Oliver's eardrums. Parr, with the light touch of a watchmaker, deftly broke off the ash of his stogy. It wasn't often things fell out so nicely. He eyed Oliver.

"Rot!" snorted Armiston. He glared at Parr.

"Wait," counseled the deputy. He breathed triumph. Morel should be here any moment.

"He is hiding there—Leblanc?" cried Oliver, unwilling to believe.

"Could you think of a better place to hide?" beamed the deputy.

Oliver pulled up sharp. "By George, you're right!" he exclaimed excitedly. "Nobody ever goes there! They are social parishs! Parr, that apache has more than low running! He has brains! If it hadn't been for that lookout—"

"Haven't I been telling you?" interposed Parr. "A crook can't beat coincidence! Its arm is too long."

It was almost laughable that the vanity, the craving of that petty crook on the door should reveal the *abri* of the crafty Leblanc.

"Is he disguised?" demanded Armiston, breathless now.

"I suppose you would say so, yes," said Parr complacently. "But not for Morel. Morel spent two years in Bertillon work. You couldn't fool an anthropologist with a faked Piltdown skull, could you? No. Well, no more could you fool Morel with a faked Leblanc. Here he is!"

The housekeeper, all smiles, was ushering in a faultless young man, done over for evening. Oliver, who knew Morel well, was amazed when he got out of his coat. He looked so much like someone else, anyone but himself. Even if the matutinal Morel had been known among crooks—and Parr was very careful that he should not be—it would have taken an anthropologist now to pierce the disguise which he seemed to have put on by the mere act of dressing for dinner. Some women do the same thing merely by going to their hairdresser's.

"You managed your get-away all right?" asked Parr, eying Morel narrowly.

"I think so, sir, yes," answered the young dandy. There was a slight tremor in his voice, as if for the first time he let down. The bare question may momentarily have shaken him. If Armiston had doubted before, he was without doubt now. He knew these two and he detected the swift interchange between them. Inured by the many dangers they had faced together, they used unconsciously a pantomime that was beyond words in moments like this. This was touch and go!

"Is everything tight?" muttered Parr.

Morel nodded.

"I left Burke in charge, sir."

"And Pelts?"

Morel shook his head. He didn't know.

Armiston had a momentary vision of the last he had seen of Pelts—the forlorn little fellow pressing his nose against the show window while he watched, with glazed look, that shoemaker. If Pelts had one fault it was that he was hard to call off, once he had the scent.

Morel explained the disposition of the men. Various effects, geographical and other, contributed to perfection in this investiture. In the first place, the Golden Shekel, rearing fifteen stories into the air, stood on a corner opposite the Park, behind whose wall a whole regiment could be planted. At a signal from Parr as their Roderick Dhu, those drear winter thickets would suddenly become alive with bonnet and spear and bended bows. Only a stone's throw away stood the old arsenal, a windy old police barracks, where reserves were held in readiness for any emergency."

"Now, let's see. Who are our neighbors?"

"On the street side," said the complete Morel, who seemed to have chinked every crevice before coming in, "is a private dwelling occupied, it so happens, by your colleague, Deputy Konhelm of the Automobile Bureau. I put two men in his cellar. I thought they might crave a back burrow under the walls."

Parr roared with delight.

"The little tin god of coincidence!" he cried. "As you say, it is the lazy man's method, Oliver! See, I sit here and let it work for me. ... Go on, Morel."

"On the other side," said Morel, "is new construction—the new Towers the McClintick people are erecting. It's up to the twentieth floor."

"Yes. Nothing but a steel skeleton yet. We might put in our own gang as watchmen."

"I made the arrangement, sir," responded Morel.

"Remember, there are eyes looking out as well as in," cautioned Armiston. It fired his imagination, the way this curtain was drawn.

"Now tell us what you had for dinner," said Parr between his teeth. Now they came to the crux of it.

II

Every little while certain rich people decide that nothing available through the regular channels costs quite enough. The weight of ready money is appalling. Their constant craving is for something more expensive, to distinguish their taste from that of the lower strata. When they reach the peak of extravagance still unappeased, in very desperation they paint the lily for themselves. Sometimes it is a motor car, especially designed from sump pump to door tassels, of which a limited edition of signed copies is privately issued—much as a forbidden book is circulated. These hand-tooled vehicles seldom run, but at least the curse of cheapness has been circumvented.

The Golden Shekel was an expression of this yearning for the reek of wealth in housing. Impossible as it may seem, every apartment had a private entrance and a private automatic lift. It was really a house of many mansions piled one on the other.

The subscribers shared the same servants, breathed the same air and used the same street; also they had a common *salle à manger*, where, dressed for one another, they dined in the evening. It was said the food was gold plated. Otherwise each lived in his own automatic niche.

Morel bathed and changed, and dug up an acquaintance to take him in. One had to be taken in, it was that exclusive. In lugubrious state, amid the overstuffed splendors of the banquet hall of the Golden Shekel, Parr's handsome man readily passed inspection. He had a way of looking the perfect sap instead of the sophisticate, quite a trick of countenance when you may be under an observation as shrewd as your own. It was a mask ordinarily as impenetrable as the one of black silk Morel wore mornings downtown when he reviewed, with his Bertillon eye, the crooks brought in for the line-up.

So far, so good! Morel turned in response to a murmured question in his ear involving a technic of gastronomy and found himself staring, nose to nose with Aristide Leblanc—whom Morel, too, believed to be just one step behind the suddenly implacable Worthington Horn in Paris. It was an emergency there is no school for. One must be endowed with an iron nerve and a coordination of all the faculties that bespeaks the perfect subconscious state.

"A pheasant's egg—a little high, gentleman, crushed in the sauce," the maître was suggesting, with that flattering assumption of equality some of these distinguished gentlemen can sometimes confer.

In that moment Morel, the perfect collector, found himself examining, with the utmost fascination, the point of Aristide's jaw, which in this specimen, as rarely occurs, suggested a pair of mandibles united by a central suture for a chin, instead of the single inframaxillary. Also he noted methodically the alveolar and auricular points, and the asterion and the angle of the condyles—trick signposts in the voodoo of craniometry. To the eye of the expert the face had been insidiously lifted: A plucked eyebrow replaced the distinctive lowering effect of the erstwhile child of Nature; a slight tightening of the lower eyelids gave the face a wholly new regard. There is a beauty doctor who does this thing for the trade. Morel canvassed these improvements with artistic valuation.

"Crushed through a fork and whipped into the oil!" urged Aristide seductively; he lowered his voice: "It is for the *gourmet* only, gentleman!" he said. His baleful gaze, in turn, from force of habit took Morel's cranial points to pieces, but with less-informed analysis.

Morel shook his head. If it must be egg in the sauce, then a near-by hennery white. He could order a dinner to allay suspicion in any quarter; nevertheless, he drew the line on high flavors.

Morel sat tight from soup to nuts, his amazement growing. Just as Lloyd's, of London, list missing ships year after year, so the police post among themselves the names of big crooks who sink without a trace in the ooze of crime. This attrition is continuous, because crime breeds its own virus and takes a bigger toll of its votaries than do the forces of retributive justice. Else, Parr would need more than squealers and coincidence to keep up with the parade. There is no port of missing ships. But here, under the ornate roof of this blatant house of many mansions, was such a cache of jailbirds as might win the chevrons of a whole police force. In fact, Morel at the first blush of this embarrassment of riches could hardly restrain his impulse to dash out and call the wagon.

The apache himself was a day's work for anyone. The man on the door, whose vanity had inadvertently touched off this bonanza, was a mere jackal following on the heels of the lions who lolled inside. The first familiar face Morel had encountered was that of Manny Sheftels, deep-sea card sharp, who had conveniently disappeared over the side in a recent winter passage. Some of his victims would not be too happy to find him safe on earth and brought to book, for Manny had a sly talent for making his accusers appear contemptible. Redrawn, it is true, but still unmistakably Manny to a Bertillon eye. He seemed to occupy the position of social prompter here among these innocents. Elegance under this roof being of a variety such as only a movie director could beget in the sins of his cinema palaces, the dapper Manny fitted admirably as *arbiter elegantiarum*.

With more of a trade flavor, there was Little Joe Mangin, soup expert— safe cracker—recently out of Leavenworth—under the walls, not through the big front gate. He was the checker on the kitchen door, his valued fingers tamping rubber stamps instead of nitroglycerin during the interregnum.

The cigarette girl was Pin-Point Annie, manipulator of a dozen night-club cloak-room holdups. She was noted for her nervous trigger finger. She was out on bail; overdue, in fact. Among the elegant waiters were such mellifluous art- ists as Tony the Plasterer—with an arm like cordwood—Soft-Shoe Ferry, the Human Fly; Killer Depuis; hovering over a lady from the oil fields, apparently oblivious of her lavish display of ice—platinum-mounted ice—that decorated the horizontal bosom, was Spanish John, the garroter. So the roster ran.

But most astonishing of all was the unveiling of a recent acquisition to Parr's collection of rare prints downtown—in the person of the resident manager. At first sight his face did not quite isolate itself for filing in the well-ordered card index in the back of Morel's head. Then it came to him. It was Vincent Delby, absconding bank cashier from Seattle—one of those rare birds who build up a lifetime of rectitude for one single splurge of crime. Delby had walked out on his board of directors one fine day after shipping the portable assets of his administration ahead of him.

Morel came to a pause at this point in his recital. The great man hunter, who had never drawn such a net as this before, shook his head, smiling with that look of foolish incredulity which denies an overwhelming event.

"Vincent Delby!" he repeated. His lip curled. "The amateur! Do you imagine for a moment he knows where he is? He does not!"

Usually these amateurs, for whom the police had such scorn, did not get very far. Too late they learn that thieving is a trade that requires an apprenticeship. Crooks shelter one another; the amateur has no place to go. Yet someone somewhere had reached out and touched this bank wrecker on the shoulder and guided him—and his loot, you may be sure!—to this haven of refuge. Now he was using his undoubted talents to promote the splendors of life for the subscribers at the Golden Shekel, in return for the protective coloring they, unsuspecting, gave him. A retouched Vincent Delby, but undoubtedly, if Parr knew the breed, a quaking fugitive suspicious of every footfall.

There was a long pause, each peopling it with his own thoughts. Morel was consciously smiling, as if laboring under the flattery of great personal achievement. Parr scowled villainously at the fire. Oliver tugged at his single white lock.

"Who's running it?" asked Oliver. "There must be a head."

"I couldn't make out," said Morel. "Delby is the front, of course, but he is only the stuffed shirt. There is someone else."

"Leblanc," said Parr grimly. "He knows the business. It takes a man of superb endowments to get away with it there. And it takes a cold-blooded killer to hold that gang in leash. Think of the tons of stuff under their very noses!"

There was another silence. Through it there came the long-drawn-out wall of agony of a fire siren, like the cry of a panther; it rose on the air, flooded every crevice with clamor. All heads turned as if stirred by some atavistic dread. The eerie cry sank to a whimper, then died away. The staccato exhaust of some great cannonading fire truck smote the resonant air of night with blows like the hammer of Vulcan. Then the horrible siren cry rode the wind again. A great many indignant people have written letters to *The Times* asking "Why do you make so much noise going to a fire, when the streets are empty?" The answer is for children: "To remind you not to play with matches!" From near and far came the clang of bells, screams big and little, echoing and reëchoing among the empty streets.

"That's near by," said Oliver.

Parr's telephone rang. Burke speaking.

"The Towers is burning. I thought maybe you'd want to know, sir."

"The Towers? There's nothing to burn—nothing but steel girders."

"It's in some falsework—planks and timbers—that the workmen use. It's two hundred feet up in the air."

"Sew up the block with the reserves!" commanded Parr. "Let no one come in, not even a reporter!"

"But if they have to get out—out of the Golden Shekel! What then? Embers are falling all around it!"

"I expect likely," laughed the deputy. "Well, they can't. I'll be right over."

He hung up. He arose and put on his things, as did the others.

"My little tin god is working overtime for me tonight," he said, laughing. "I didn't want to pull that joint until daylight, so we could see just what we were doing. Now we've got a nice fire next door. We might dig up a little panic in the Golden Shekel and drive out our precious lambs, one by one, into our waiting arms." He usually chose the simple way, avoiding, as much as possible, the sensational exploitation of his acts in the press. "Well, we'll see what it looks like first," he said grimly.

They hurried on, Morel running ahead. When they turned the corner into the Avenue the spectacle in its rare magnificence broke on them as if framed for a picture. High up above the roof tops, like something floating unsupported in the night, the bud of flame gently swayed in a graceful fire dance. It was one of those nights with no moon, and there were no low-lying clouds to reflect the luminescence of the city streets; the fire blazed placidly against the clean background of the night. Now and then a balk of timber—probably a 12 by 12 that the big derricks up there handled like toothpicks—dislodged itself and fell, a blazing plummet, to the street below. Or some lighter stuff, with little plumes of flame blowing this way and that, wafted in spirals like a falling leaf. But the spectacle was all up above.

It was the theater hour, when just before midnight, for a brief moment, traffic in the Avenue surges to full tide, to die away as suddenly. This traffic, all northbound, people going home, was jammed against the rigid police lines ahead. The passengers in their gay wraps crowded the sidewalks with cries of amazement and delight.

"Look at that!" cried Parr, halting and pointing in sheer admiration. "Did you ever see a shot like that in the movies? No, you didn't!"

His jubilant cry was occasioned by a new aspect to the picture. Against the dull outline of that skyscraper skeleton, on top of which the pyre burned, there now appeared crawling fireflies. First a single one, then another, several, six and more. They moved slowly, with a stop and go, climbing floor by floor, up and up toward the blazing timber. They were firemen with lanterns and fire extinguishers, mounting by scaling ladders. Climbing with a scaling ladder is the test for a fireman. When he stops doing that he stops being a fireman, goes out to pasture.

The deputy broke into a run; the boy in him got the better of him. Oliver hung to his heels. They pushed aside the crowd, the bulldog visage of Parr winning for them a breach in the police lines that otherwise stood like a rock. Burke was evidently taking no chances until his chief arrived to take charge. Inside the sacred vacuum of the police lines there stood only the highly privileged Golden Shekel, with a newly swarmed clump of police plugging its every exit. There was about it all the sprawl of fire apparatus. Directly below, the spectacle was dwarfed into insignificance. This was only a seven-minute wonder, after all. Parr, with a sigh, saw that he could not turn it to account, that he would have to wait till daylight to back up his wagon. He passed the word to Morel: Not a soul was to be permitted to emerge from the Golden Shekel—those were fire orders! The patrols and hose wagons, and odds and ends that trail along with such noisy jubilance whenever a fire calls, were winding in their hose lengths, folding tarpaulins, gathering personnel and backing off and going back home for another wink and nod. There was no chance to get water up there in the clouds. It was up to the scaling-ladder crew.

Parr wandered over to the hook-and-ladder truck that mothered those intrepid climbers.

"Well, Jerry, my old pal!" he burst out happily. He seized the grizzled old captain, who had a megaphone strapped across his face, and wrung his hand. "Why, Jerry, I thought you were retired and out to grass years ago!" cried the enthusiastic Parr.

Capt. Jeremiah Gilhooley, who had followed the trucks through snow and ice for forty years, started back, stung to the quick by such an insult. The deputy, quick to see his mistake, turned the subject.

"Those are fine lads you've got there!" he cried heartily. The lanterns were still crawling up and up in that interminable climb, painfully slow and small now.

"And why should I retire when I can climb a pole?" cried the outraged Captain Gilhooley, not to be diverted. And to prove it he snatched a scaling ladder off the truck, hooked it onto the cornice above him with a single thrust and started up like a monkey. Gaining the first horizontal girder, he clung there precariously while he drew up his ladder and swung it above his head for another hold. And up he went another notch. He roared through his megaphone to the fireflies above him, "Step lively, ye terriers! I'll be treading on yer tail!"

The first firefly lantern was on the level of the fire now; then the second and the third winked out as it crawled out of sight over the ledge. Those crawling fireflies below continued to ascend, winking themselves out one by one, over the top, the brave captain with the rest. Then, of a sudden, as if from some great ghostly hand clamped over it, that blazing pyre aloft—that must have shone like a beacon for ships at sea—died down and whipped out. The fire was out! That was all there was to it!

After an interval a lantern looked over that high ledge and the descent began. It was even more breath-taking, their climbing down, than going up.

"I'd better fade out of the picture," laughed Parr. "That fellow Jerry will want to fight when he gets back. Never, Oliver, suggest to a cop or a fireman that he is old enough to retire!"

Parr moved into the background. Morel came up.

"All snug?"

Parr, as he asked the question, let his keen eyes explore the outlines of the precious Golden Shekel. The face of Vincent Delby, the bank wrecker out of Seattle, could be seen pressing itself against the barred windows giving on the street. That amateur fugitive was doubtless the prey to the most terrible fears, even now when the excitement had died down and the chances of his being driven into the open seemed remote.

"All snug, sir," reported Morel. "They are like a herd of cattle in a burning barn. We'd have to go in and drag them out if we wanted them!"

It was all over. Hook and Ladder Truck Number Thirty Blank, Capt. Jeremiah Gilhooley, was departing, its bell tolling gently its farewell hymn and its siren murmuring *sotto roce* as it gathered speed. It cut a path through the jammed crowd behind the police lines with a sudden threatening snarl of a panther aroused, but in another moment all that came back on the night air was the rhythmic purr of its sweet-running motor. There is nothing so tame as a fire truck going back home.

Now there were police whistles sounding, and sharp commands; then the police lines broke and let the flood through.

"Keep them moving, Burke!" commanded Parr. "No jamming in front of the place, remember! I'll see you at daylight."

Parr and Oliver walked home. It was only a few blocks and there was a zest in the night air for tired brains. Inside, Parr folded his hands over his ample girth and settled back in his favorite elbow chair for a wink and a nod. This was one of those nights when he would take a hot towel in lieu of a bed. Oliver, for his part, had suddenly become wide awake. The tips of his fingers were itching. A sure sign! He did most of his thinking with the tips of his fingers—an old trick from his days of story writing. He softly opened his desk and brushed the keys of his faithful typewriter, letting those gifted cerebral ganglia in the fingertips waft him hither and yon, on the wings of fancy. As he wrote, there gently nudged his thoughts the low wall of a fire siren. Suddenly he came to a halt and shook Parr violently.

"Parr! Wake up, Parr!"

"Yes—yes—"

"Are you awake, Parr?"

"Yes!" said Parr, in that abused tone of the guilty.

"You'd better telephone your friend Gilhooley—"

"Eh? What's the—"

"See if he's got home yet, Parr!"

Oliver frantically shook the deputy.

"Wake up, Parr! Wake up!"

He seized the telephone and jammed it into Parr's hand.

Parr suddenly was wide-awake; with one sweep he seized the phone. He called for a connection through Central Office. Before he asked his question he knew what the answer would be. The answer would be no. In that swift moment, like a man drowning, the whole panorama floated before his eyes.

Aristide Leblanc, the apache! The apache climbed over from his own roof and set the fire in that pile of plank and timber! Then he and his murderous crew lay in wait for the scaling ladders to come crawling over that parapet one by one. One by one! Oh, it was poetically simple! Aristide Leblanc took care of that crew of firemen, one by one, as they came over the top.

Then Aristide calmly put out the fire with a squirt of the extinguishers, borrowed the firemen's helmets and coats and scaling ladders. And down there in the street Aristide borrowed that hook-and-ladder truck, and with the bell tolling gently the farewell hymn and the siren muttering *sotto roce*, under the admiring eyes of Mr. Parr and his cohorts Aristide drove away, till even the soft purr of the engine was lost to sound. Where were they now? Where? What difference did it make? Who would think of stopping a rampant fire truck, no matter how much noise it was making, no matter where it was going?

"They don't answer, chief."

"They are not expected to," responded the deputy wearily. "Flash Morel for me!" He rubbed his head, felt of it tenderly to see if it was there. "Morel!" He snarled, he swore horribly. What the shocked Morel, who had been playing pinochle at the arsenal, waiting for dawn, got out of it was that he should go at once to the roof of the Golden Shekel and find there the dead bodies of the crew of Hook and Ladder Truck Number Thirty Blank.

Parr arrived on the scene in person before Morel found them. The hovering Delby, the amateur, who, it seemed, had been left behind, along with some others too old for the climb, followed them, tremulous, hoping against hope. There were so many doors and shafts to guard the magnificent isolation of the subscribers that it was some time before they found the right chute to take them to the roof. The crew of the fire truck had been stored in the penthouse, just big enough for the purpose. They were tied tight, Captain Gilhooley and all his bra' men. Each sported a welt the size of an egg over one eye, the fruit of a soft-nosed bludgeon wielded by the unerring apache. Otherwise they were unmarked and all alive. They had no story to tell. They had simply been extinguished one by one as they came crawling over that parapet. Parr's men were sweeping up the agonised Vincent Delby and the others, and were leaving. When all was said and done Parr turned on Morel with curling lip.

"So you didn't make your get-away all right, after all?" he snarled.

Morel would have taken oath that he had withdrawn without disturbing that picture. Certainly that villainous apache, in his guise of maître, had not visibly turned a hair under Morel's scrutiny.

Parr, snatching at straws, asked savagely "Where's Pelts?"

No one had seen him. Pelts, the scent in his nostrils, was probably fatuously chasing that shoemaker that Parr had set him on earlier in this fateful day.

At midnight an abandoned fire truck was reported loitering in Pelham Parkway, Westchester. At two there came a cipher message by wire from New Haven. Parr raced to Curtiss Field by auto.

An intrepid flyer, in his pajamas, said, "We don't take off at night. We can't make a landing. That's elemental!"

"We'll hover till dawn!" commanded Parr, with so much pent-up venom in the words that they took off at once; they arrived over Boston just when the first pink of day showed beyond the Light.

It was shortly after eight in the morning that a long low rakish-looking parlor-car motorbus, of trunk-line vintage and as squat as a long-wheel-base hippopotamus, rumbled softly down the runway and entered the terminal. It had been delayed in leaving New York this night by tire trouble, and most of its passengers had gone over to a rival. But fortunately, passing through City Island, off Pelham Bay, it had picked up a dozen emergency passengers. So the trip had not been a dry haul after all.

Parr and two hundred men, the finest the police force of Boston affords, enveloped the motorbus as it came to a soft stop and carefully extracted therefrom Aristide Leblanc, the apache, and ten companions, together with their luggage, which was very heavy. This luggage contained all the portable loot to be had on short notice from the Golden Shekel.

"I'll take care of this little fellow," said Parr, taking out of the line-up a shabby forlorn creature in two or three pairs of pants and a coat or two too many. Since dropping overboard with that message to Parr at New Haven, Pelts had been curled up in a chair behind the apache, to all intents, asleep.

"Chief," cried the exultant Pelts, "you are a wonder! That shoemaker— remember that shoemaker you sent me back for? He was the outside man for this gang of crooks. Every so often he went up there and looked their place over, to see if it was all right. He was the one that tipped them off and started the fire on the roof. I was pinned to his tail!" said Pelts with the feeble smile of a shy man who nevertheless has his pride.

Hangman's Truce

A T thirty-seventh Street, where the Avenue begins gently to fall away from the knobs and peaks of Murray Hill to the mosques and minarets of the garment zone—a climb more arduous, for an ambitious man, than the eye suspects—Deputy Parr of the police, taking his daily quantum of afternoon sunshine on foot, with a scout ahead and a scout behind, paused in his methodical pavement pounding stride and let fall a brawny arm like a tollgate pole across the path of a tall, well-turned-out gentleman of middle years who was coming up the hill. The advancing pedestrian was beguiling himself with some daydream of so pleasant a nature that his rapt smile bespoke the finishing touch to a castle in Spain; he was so oblivious of his surroundings that he only became aware of the obstruction when he ran against it and found it rigid. Then, instead of looking up, with an expression of amused expectation he looked down and examined the arm thoughtfully, as if, for the moment at least, it was the tollgate itself, rather than the person who operated it, that interested him.

At this unusual reaction Parr's companion, Oliver Armiston—who had been entertaining himself recently exploring conundrums of behaviorism, with the aid of a slide rule and textbook—gently detached himself from the scene, turning to a palatial show window in which a nut-brown maid with pasted-on eyelashes demurely poured batter cakes on a hot griddle to provoke a sales effect of hunger through the eyes of the beholder.

Oliver, however, was not hungry. He gave his entire attention to his friend Parr and the intercepted foot passenger, as they stood reflected in the mirror-like surface of the window. The intercepted gentleman was of the sleek, fit type we denominate as successful business man. The term implies something more than a mere stroke of good fortune; that could happen to anyone with brains enough not to stand in the way of luck. The term implies that success had worn a path to one's door, that it has come again and returned; and includes that easy air of prosperity that derives from long use. You seldom see this person on foot these days, especially at this hour—mid-afternoon. Men of this breed are too busy downtown, have too many appointments waiting in line, to turn thumbs up or thumbs down, like Roman emperors. Later in the day, when the ticker has caught up with the market, some of the more elderly will come gravely walking up the Avenue, by their doctors' orders. But the prime ones, if they come here at all, will usually be in limousines, talking or listening very intently, or dictating to a stenographer—such is the poverty of time among the princes of success.

This one, on foot, and for the instant wholly engrossed with the obstruction in his path, let his gaze stray up Parr's arm until it was met and held by that of the special deputy commissioner in charge of the detective bureau. Parr's face was illuminated by his versatile smile—versatile in the sense that it could mean anything, depending entirely on the point of view of the individual who, through good or ill luck, was its object.

"Hello, Eddie," said Parr suavely.

There was a minute though distinct hiatus.

"A crook!" Oliver sensed, with a thrill. "It goes to show there is no such thing as a criminal type." He mentally amended this by the qualification: "Or if there is, it pervades all classes."

"Hello, sarge!" said the intercepted gentleman.

That "sarge" redrew the picture slightly, redated it. Parr hadn't been a sergeant for at least twenty years. And this title had come to have an entirely different significance. They were shaking hands. That in itself might mean everything—or nothing. Oliver smiled to himself over it. In Parr's business there seemed to exist a sort of hangman's truce, at which Armiston, in spite of his long association with the deputy and familiarity with his methods, had never ceased to wonder.

"Well, well! It's twelve years, isn't it, Eddie?" exclaimed Parr, with an extra shake for good measure. "I've heard of you now and then," he added blandly, as his cold eye felt the tug of some passing face in the crowd. "They tell me you are rated A 1 in the big books, Eddie!"

Eddie laughed pleasantly and gazed down over the heads of the crowds that swarmed off to infinity to the southward. "Double A 1!" he corrected, his eyes coming back to Parr in a firm, searching look. "And you are the big fellow himself now, eh?"

"Yes, this is my town now, Eddie," admitted the deputy.

"You'll always be the sarge to me," said Eddie.

"It's good to hear you say so," replied Parr. "Oliver!" he cried, and drew his friend and collaborator into the charmed circle. "This is Mr. Armiston, Eddie."

"Oh, indeed!" exclaimed Eddie, conferring an implied distinction in the best drawing-room manner. He thrust out a hand and Oliver found himself ceremoniously gripping it in his best drawing-room manner. "This is Eddie the Clam, Oliver," said the deputy, adding, as his never-ceasing eye trailed through the crowd: "In his day there wasn't a better man with the soup, soap and blanket. Walk along with us a bit, Eddie, if you have a few minutes."

The safe cracker—for such Oliver took him to be, from the elaborate kudos bestowed on him by Mr. Parr—looked first at the sun, then at his wrist watch—a platinum affair of the recent self-winding type. He fell into step with them and they were off downhill. They were two handsome men of the Central Office type, and Oliver, too, was not without his air of distinction; so people turned and looked after them enviously.

Eddie raised a quizzical eyebrow. He turned to Parr.

"You are not taking me downtown, are you, sarge?" he asked.

Parr chuckled.

"I'd like to, at that!" he confessed. "Just to show them a little class in the line-up!"

It may have been a too fervid imagination on Oliver's part, but it seemed to him that Parr's implied tribute caused Eddie to inflate himself a little.

"I don't suppose they would know me from Adam," he said, a lingering satisfaction in his tone. "I had business downtown in the Street this morning," he added. "I crossed the old dead line!" He paused; he and Parr exchanged a swift look. "Believe it or not," he went on, "I got quite a kick out of it. Nobody knew me! It was like Rip van Winkle coming home." A shade of what might have been wistfulness crossed his handsome face. "Are any of the old crowd left, sarge?" he asked.

Parr shook his head.

"Not outside," said he. "The turnover is pretty fast in this business—on both sides of the fence," he added significantly. "Barney, my old doorman, is still with me. You recollect Barney, I guess."

"Barney! That little fellow you used to send out to bring me in? Very well!" He laughed heartily. "I have cause," he confessed. "It's odd, to look back," he went on soberly, "and note how great decisions were influenced by trifles. Stupendous effort usually flops. Like the French mob storming the Bastille to rescue their friends and finding it practically empty. It's the little things that count. Barney cured me. When you took to sending Barney, your janitor, to bring me in, instead of a platoon in a wagon, I began to think that maybe I wasn't such a wonder as I'd been telling myself. I decided it was time to quit."

Oliver was drinking this in—the idea behind the sending of a janitor to bring in a vainglorious crook wasn't such a trifle, he was thinking.

"Is there any of my old bunch left?" asked Eddie.

The deputy ran through part of his mental gallery.

"It's a young man's game," he said. "Only Chick Galey is left, I think. He's bouncer in a swell night club in Fifty-fourth Street. He is fat and bald, and wears a green sweater and patent-leather shoes!"

"Does he still catch flies out of the air between his thumb and forefinger?" asked Eddie.

"Yes, he still works that gag."

"You mean a fly—an insect flying through the air?" cried Oliver, entranced at the idea of such virtuosity.

"Yes!" cried Eddie. "When he was good he could stand on a handkerchief and you couldn't put a glove on him on a bet. I'll look him up while I'm in town, and hand him a piece of change."

"No," said Parr decidedly. "Let him be. Prosperity might upset him."

They came to a stop at Thirty-fourth Street. Human beings banked up against the curb like a log jam; on the other shore crowds faced them, straining at the lines. They waited. Parr saw everything without seeming to see anything. He passed those myriad faces under scrutiny, as if they composed an endless cinema film which he must inspect for flaws; something corresponding to a Geneva escapement in the back of his head undoubtedly clicked now and then. He tapped the point of his stick absently against the curb. Parr had begun life in a telegraph office as a boy and he never got far from the dots and dashes of that enchanted period. A woebegone little fellow, down at heel and out at elbow, squirmed through to the front rank and looked up hopefully for a cup of coffee or some such manna in this wilderness, but stony looks were all he got on this shore. He turned away with a sailor's tug at his waistband. Armiston applauded inwardly. Pelts, he thought. On the *qui vive*. It was indeed Pelts, the deputy's flank scout, called in, doubtless, for instructions, duly delivered under their very noses. But as usual, when Parr passed the "office" to one of his scouts en route, the hand was quicker than the eye. Oliver searched the other shore for some sign of the handsome Morel, the scout who always ran ahead; he didn't find him.

Red lights blinked to green, traffic whistles bleated, and like a circus of trained fleas, the myriads that moved east and west broke and paused, and north and south united and began to flow again.

"Prosperity doesn't seem to worry you," observed Parr, picking up the thread of talk again. Eddie didn't reply at once. He walked on for several paces. When Eddie responded, it was in a masked tone.

"I had a horrible dream the other night," he admitted. "I dreamed I had come back!"

"That would be your hard luck, Eddie," said Parr.

"This is my first trip to town." Eddie was still philosophizing on his mental state. He added: "And my last! I keep dragging the crowd for bulls."

"Do you see any?"

"No. But I think I do. That's part of the disease. You jarred me back there, sarge, when you put out your arm. I got the old chill of the catch! I felt the ice water trickling down my spine." Nothing in his tone or manner suggested the weight of his words. He returned the salutation of a prosperous business man flashing by in a limousine.

"I sell that fellow carbon black," Eddie explained. "I bought some low-grade oil wells to sell stock. But it is better business to burn the stuff and to sell the soot." He and Parr had a little smile over this. He ran over his other activities. He reclaimed rubber for ten-cent-store novelties; he worked up veneers for storage-battery separators; he manufactured maple platens for paper cutters—in this unsuspected side line one could use up a sizable forest of hard maple every day. He made door hangers; he had a grubstake in a rare formula for bookbinder's glue; he made rake stales and tool handles out of sawmill edgings; in short, he hovered around the outskirts of the great industries, investing time and money in accessories, all indispensable and unheard-of. He was pleased to recount the sources of his prosperity to an old friend, as if inviting him to share the secret of it. It was difficult, while he talked, to believe that this was a retired crook who had given up the racket in a pique because Parr had sent his janitor to bring him in, instead of going himself with a platoon and a wagon.

Eddie consulted his platinum self-winding wrist watch.

"I'm breaking away," he said, pausing.

"So am I," nodded Parr, and held out his hand. A taxi pulled up, tendering itself, and Parr pushed Oliver ahead of him and got in. It was like a magician turning up his sleeves—he was concealing nothing, so he seemed to imply delicately. Eddie watched them off with a good-by, which he repeated again and again. Not until their taxi was lost in the mêlée did he turn away. He methodically dragged the crowd from force of reborn habit, shivering slightly to find himself the slave of those long-forgotten reflexes, and in thoughtful mood he traced his steps up the hill.

"I thought you said there was no such animal," said Oliver, turning to Parr.

"As what?" demanded the grim deputy.

"A reformed crook. There's one now!"

"Where?" cried Parr, turning swiftly, as if missing something. He went on without a trace of cynicism: "Oliver, there is such a thing as a mad dog, I suppose. I've never happened to see one. Have you?"

"You mean you've never seen a reformed crook?"

"Yes"—Parr made an ugly grimace—"there are such animals, but I never happened to see one. I've handled crooks in carload lots. I've never seen a real crook that would go straight if he had a good chance to go crooked."

"You are not averse to giving them the chance, are you?"

"Why should I be?" asked Parr complacently.

"That comes dangerously close to *agent provocateur*, doesn't it?"

"I'm not afraid of the word," retorted Parr. "If it is a real crook—"

"Ah, you begin to qualify!" There was something of the schoolmaster in Armiston, for all his ideality. "Who is to decide—you?"

"There is no difficulty in deciding," said the man hunter. "When a man has been up the river three times, like your friend Eddie, he is pretty nearly incurable. We give them three breaks. Then, on the theory that he has pulled ten jobs for every one we caught him at, we say, 'The next time we get you,

Eddie, we will put you away in our home for incurables.' That's what Eddie is up against—the promise of going up for life the next time he side-steps. Do you think it will deter him? Not a bit of it. Ten to one, Eddie thinks we haven't even got a sporting chance!"

"There is no doubt," remarked Oliver distastefully, "that something of the *bouquet de bagne* sticks to you fellows too. Do you ever give a poor devil an even break when he is making an honest effort to go straight? Or do you scheme to meet him accidentally in the street and tip him off to where he can find an old pal, if he happens to have anything on the fire?" Armiston added with some venom: "Chick Galey, for instance."

"In ten blocks, this afternoon," replied the deputy, "I counted ten men, first offenders, whom we are nursing along, helping to go straight. Anyone can make a misstep once, maybe twice. But after the third time we're through. I'll make you a bet." Parr looked at his watch. "About now Eddie has begun to test himself for a shadow. Eddie isn't under any delusions of magnanimity from me. He knows I'll check him up. That doesn't worry him. It rather flatters him. Being seen walking down Fifth Avenue with me would have been quite a feather in his cap a few years ago."

"That's part of your game," Oliver was thinking. "What is the bet?" he asked.

"In about ten minutes Eddie will discover Pelts," said the deputy.

"Naturally! You called Pelts in so Eddie could get a flash," laughed Oliver.

"Yes," admitted the shameless man hunter. "Pelts is hard to shake. I'm not sure I could do it. Eddie can—and will! It'll take him about half an hour. How are you betting? Will Eddie lose Pelts?"

"Why should he?" demanded Armiston bluntly.

"I don't know," said Parr. "But he will!"

Doubtless there was a good reason; several, in fact, why, as well as why not. It was one of those double-bitted problems the casuists love to work both ways from the middle to opposite conclusions, equally sound. If man-hunting is the most thrilling game in the world, isn't it fair to assume that the hunted gets some kick out of it too? He plays for bigger stakes. Eddie had everything to lose. Yet Parr, without indulging himself cynically, seemed to entertain not the vestige of a doubt of the ultimate end of Eddie. A few blocks down the Avenue Parr changed to another taxi of the same color and generally flea-bitten condition, but, nevertheless, a different animal altogether. They continued on their way.

"He has been behaving himself since the last time, hasn't he?" said Oliver.

"I'll let you answer your own question when we get downtown," said Parr. They proceeded in silence. Oliver thought of Chick Galey. Somehow, though he had been given only a line for Chick's portrait, it was astonishingly vivid, like one of those frugal Frueh caricatures.

Chick had undoubtedly been a punching bag in somebody's stable of prize fighters in his time. Probably he was walking on his heels now, as happens to the cauliflower gentry, the best of them, from blocking too many punches with the point of the chin. But he could still pick flies out of the air between his thumb and forefinger for loose change. Oliver would like to see him do that.

They drew up under the portico of Central Office and went in. This was a one-way street for the world of the shadows—so many went in who never came out. Shadows haunted the corridors—wretches waiting their ordeal and scheming desperately what to answer to the eternal "Why" of retribution. It goes on every hour, every day, with never a dearth of human material. Barney, armed with a dustpan—his ægis of office—held open the door for them to enter Parr's private sanctum.

"I saw an old friend of yours uptown, Barney—Eddie Reel," said the deputy as he passed in.

"Did you, chief? I'd like to see him!"

"You will," said Parr. "Hello, what are you doing here, Pelts?"

Pelts tried to explain. Parr silenced and dismissed him with a gesture.

"Let me have the dope on Eddie the Clam," he said to his clerk. It was a thick pile of several hundred sheets, yellowing toward the bottom. The top sheet, dated only the day before, told of Eddie being picked up by unseen hands, off the Broadway Limited, and escorted to the Waldorf, where he registered and ensconced himself in a bespoken suite on the third floor, Astoria side. Eddie would have to drag his crowds with a finer mesh. As they dug down through the pile they came on things about Eddie that even his mother couldn't have known. There was what the French police call a *portrait parle*, which overlooks nothing—not even the matching of a porcelain filling. When a man has been up the river three times, everything about him is news. He had been sent up twice for safe cracking, once for forgery—Eddie could sign your name for you with his eyes shut. But for the last twelve years there had been no entry in red ink in his ledger. There were lapses of weeks, months during that time, but sooner or later somebody would come along and look him over through a peephole. He must have been conscious of it; no one could fail to sense that malign scrutiny.

Oliver found himself fighting against the cynical certainty it all implied. He could even hear Eddie again, with no emphasis to reveal the weight of his words, saying: "I had a horrible dream the other night. I dreamed I had come back!" and Parr's casual rejoinder: "That would be your hard luck, Eddie."

"There is nothing to show he hasn't been on the level," protested Oliver, "since his last time out."

Parr handed Armiston a sheet of foolscap—his record. It contained thirty-three typewritten lines, every line a separate crime for which our prosperous business man had been intercepted by the police in his heyday and brought to the bar of justice. In the column marked Disposition appeared the legends Discharged, Disagreement, Not Guilty, No Complainant, *Nolle Pros.*, and so on. For Eddie, Justice seemed always exercising a reasonable doubt.

"Would you say that that leopard changed his spots?" asked Parr. Oliver said nothing. "Or would you call it a typical case of police persecution—hounding the poor devil because he had a prison record?"

Parr was exercising his sarcasm. Somehow Armiston couldn't picture Eddie as the poor devil the professional reformers talk about when they are collecting funds for the underdog.

"Eddie is too slick for us," said Parr—"that is, nine times out of ten. You ask me, hasn't he been behaving himself since the last time out? I say I don't know. I simply wait—and watch!" His jaws shut with a click. "He wins nine times out of ten, but the tenth time he slips up."

"If Morel needs any help," said Parr to his clerk at dinnertime, "tell him to use Sangree." He put in confidentially: "You might tell Pelts, on the Q. T., to keep away from me for a few days."

Oliver smiled over this. If Eddie hadn't lost Pelts, Parr would have been disappointed. But Pelts having lost a track, he must be disciplined.

"I remember the first time you brought him in, chief," said Barney, opening the door for the big fellow. "Big Bill says to you, 'Did you bring this fellow in alone, sergeant?' and you says, 'Yes, chief, but you got me wrong—I ain't a sergeant,' and Big Bill winks at me and says, 'Don't correct your superiors, sergeant!' "

"I suppose I should be charitably hopeful," said Parr, getting in his taxi. "Eddie brought me my first promotion."

II

This was one of those rare occasions when Parr bunked downtown at headquarters and went to bed by the simple process of taking off his shoes. There were times when the big fellow, for no reason apparent to less-gifted mortals, seemed to sense some sort of psychic density in the atmosphere, and when this happened he ate and slept on the job, patiently waiting for something to break. It was the general belief that something would break, and it usually did. But in the present instance there was none of the voodoo of prescience to mark the incident. The explanation was simple enough—Eddie Reel was in town.

Eddie slept late. But others were up all night for him. At six in the morning—that shivery hour when conscience is at its lowest ebb—in a bleak side room in West Fifty-fourth Street, where waiters were counting their catch of silver and attendants were hanging up their uniforms and calling it a day, a gigantic, blond, peaches-and-cream young man with guileless baby-blue eyes, in perfect evening dress, was occupying comfortably two chairs alongside a wooden table, and engaged in some sort of betting game with an elderly person who was fat and bald and wore firemen's suspenders over a green sweater and patent-leather shoes. This latter was Chick Galey, one time the Phantom Kid, and he was picking flies out of the air at one dollar a fly. The gigantic blond young man, with a skin that would put a rouge pot to shame, was known around here after two in the morning as Roy, and all women instinctively mothered him. He was of the type which, neurologists tell us, enjoy an indefinitely protracted period of childhood due to an overactive thymus gland; and so difficult do these overtimed children find the problem of adjustment to their mature environment, that they are prone to turn to crime as the easiest way to put themselves on an even footing with their fellows.

No one else paid heed to the game. Two pasty-faced waiters, having made their reckoning with their floor captain, had turned to with what was left and rolled a pair of dice in a life-and-death struggle at another table. Roy stripped a dollar bill from a bookmaker's sheaf of money and passed it silently to Chick as one fly after another bit the dust. Finally Chick missed and had to pass a dollar back. Although Roy had shot almost his entire roll by this time, the blond giant now roused himself from his patient attention to the legerdemain and burst into a shrill cackle of triumph, pointing a finger of derision at the discomfited Chick; Roy pushed his elephantine bulk perilously against his fragile pair of chairs and called on all to witness that he had won. He dared Chick to try it again. But Chick, it seemed, had run out of flies, of which he brought a fresh supply in a little box for each night. The young man accused Chick of being a quitter, and made such an outcry that several waiters, still counting silver, bade him angrily be still.

A petite girl came in from an inner room, drawing on a chiffon dress over a dance set, but as she was one of the regular floor girls who nightly disported themselves as water nymphs inside, no one noticed her. She caught Chick, to his chagrin, in the act of ironing out his pile.

"Give it back to him!" the girl commanded. "You know you promised me!"

"He quits when my luck turns," complained Roy with abused dignity.

"Give it back to him!" repeated the girl, and she calmly helped herself to Chick's pile and hid it somewhere about her person.

"Hey! Hey! Hey!" cried Chick. "What's eating you? I was only fooling the kid."

"You darling baby dumpling!" cried the enraptured girl, patting the smile-wreathed Roy. "They would draw your milk teeth if you didn't have me to mother you. Now I'm going to get my things. You sit perfectly quiet till I come back."

When she had gone, a door-knob polisher who was hanging his clanking cloak behind the door, leaned over the dull Chick—who was nothing without his flies—and smiling expansively, said in his ear:

"Hey, fellah, I was told to tell you something. The Clam is in town. Does that mean anything to you?"

Chick didn't seem to get it. Several seconds passed. Then he lifted his eyes and stared fiercely at the messenger; then furtively around the room. Dropping his eyes to the table again, he nodded several times—yes, it meant something to him.

"Who passed that to you?" Chick asked.

"I dunno," said the carriage starter. "Some guy in a top hat."

"Say, can you do that thing you was telling me about?" Chick suddenly asked, leaning over the table toward Roy, his eyes fixed on him intently.

"Certainly I can do it!" exclaimed Roy contemptuously.

"Stick around for a day or two," urged Chick. "And don't tell your mother everything you know!" he threatened out of one corner of his mouth; a trick he learned at table up the river.

The nymph returned, dressed for the street. Roy got into his coat and put on his top hat. If all women envied him his complexion, all men begrudged him his tailor and his knack of wearing good clothes. They went out, and one by one the other night birds drifted away, to hole up for the day. Presently a grimy stoker came slinking in to put up the shutters to exclude the heretic sun. He and Chick held casual converse, ending by a protracted silent scrutiny, each of the other. Chick was sending out word, to be passed along to the old-timers, that the Clam was in town, after all these years. If Eddie had any notion of guarding his carefully hoarded reformation, he would have more than one obstacle to overcome.

The first thing Eddie did on arising was to arrange for a chartered car for his brief stay in town—an imported Belgian with the heavy withers of a prize bull and a commodious expansiveness that preëmpted one hundred square feet of precious traffic space in downtown streets. Eddie, coming down to inspect it, on the Thirty-third Street side, gave particular attention to the chauffeur. Only a jealous matinée idol could have objected to this young man, who was as handsome as Eddie himself, and younger. He was as trig and well set up as any of those pampered young men Parr hand-picked for his famous detective school. In fact, he was one of them, Sangree by name.

Oliver Armiston telephoned Parr, via private wire, at ten.

"Are his income-tax returns available? So I could see them?" he asked.

"My dear fellow," cried the deputy, "there are some privacies even we must respect!"

"How about 1924 and '25?" asked Oliver. "Returns were not so sacred then, I seem to recollect."

"We've got them. Come down and have a look," said Parr.

Meantime Eddie was driving out. He made several calls in the upper terminal zone, where capital is beginning to aggregate in pay lodes. Then he drove downtown, pleasantly conscious of his own splendor, of the trig man on the box and the city crowds that surged about wherever he turned like so many colonies of busy rotifera under a microscope; he identified a familiar figure in Morel, who had replaced little Pelts yesterday. Also there were other faces that seemed to fit into the pattern. Eddie was lunching at India House, with a gathering. He picked up a Solomon Deer, jobber in soles, uppers and findings, in a gloomy crypt under Brooklyn Bridge, where leather, for some unknown reason, aggregates. He next called for a Mr. Monkton, a reinsurance specialist in William Street, where risks and actuaries hive.

They turned over into Nassau Street where, nights, sand hogs dig a Subway that bores like a mole among the steam-jacketed and poison-gas-screened vaults of the Federal Reserve and Subtreasury. Eddie smiled wistfully as numerous cross references sprang unbidden in his brainpan. Crossing Fulton Street, he was conscious of the premonitory rising of the hackles, or what evolution had left of them, on the back of his neck. There was a pause just above Maiden Lane for traffic.

"That's the old dead line," said Eddie, meditatively rubbing the back of his neck. "Would it surprise you," he went on, "if I should confess that not so many years back I was not permitted to go south of Fulton Street?"

Solomon Deer laid a cold marble eye on Eddie.

"Why not? Who'd stop you?" he growled.

"Bulls!" was Eddie's simple rejoinder.

"Police?"

"Police."

"You were a crook, you mean?"

"Yes. And a good one!"

A chill silence supervened. Sangree felt the cold on the front seat. Finally Solomon Deer demanded gruffly: "What's the idea of telling us?"

"Part of the consideration between us will be good faith," said Eddie. "I expect you to look me up. I certainly will look you up before I finally sign!"

The jobber in soles, uppers and findings, and the specialist in reinsurance exchanged a swift look. The car rolled on up the little grade to Pine Street. Here they stopped to pick up a Mr. Silas Kildrif, specialist in cats and dogs in bale lots—this is a derisive epithet applied by the Street to worthless securities, for which, it seems, there is a constant and legitimate demand. At India House they were met by several other specialists, making a final party of eight.

"What did they talk about at luncheon?" asked Mr. Parr of Morel later in the day.

"The bull market, of course!" laughed Morel. "Does anybody down there talk of anything else? They went to Kildrif's office after, for their palaver. We drew blank on that. Eddie left them, still in session, at three and—"

"Just a minute," said the deputy. Parr studied the list of names. Morel turned to the swinging leaves of a rogues' gallery section that stood against the wall, giving particular attention to this rueful book of sin. It was habit with him, with all of them—they never came in without dipping in it, although they knew it by heart, like a priest his breviary.

"Get me reports on these," ordered Parr, passing the luncheon list to a clerk. "Better get photographs."

Thus it happened that seven prosperous business men came under the ultramicroscope of the police—more, were subject to being clandestinely photographed as if for some little élite rogues' gallery of their own. There is a saying that a good fellow never goes to the devil without taking several good fellows with him. Certain it is that no thief ever comes under the scrutinizing cognizance of Centre Street without tainting everyone, no matter how remote, with whom he comes in contact, with the soil of espionage.

"This fellow," said Morel, tapping a panel—"if he didn't have that saber slash under one eye, he might be jobbing soles, uppers and findings in Gold Street."

Parr's eye kindled—there was some big game in his woods!

"That's Heidelberg Max," he said. "I'm afraid we'll have to let him have his saber cut—that's his diploma. But, my dear boy, if you ever bring him to me, you can have anything that papa owns!" He studied the surly, slashed visage of Heidelberg Max. "How are his teeth?" he asked curiously. Oliver, sitting back and taking no part, felt an odd stir.

"Solomon Deer's, you mean? Very good—especially good!"

"Have them dig up Deer's dentist—get me a chart of his mouth," said Parr to his clerk, and he added by way of explanation: "Max had a perfect mouth. He was as vain of his teeth as any woman. Now, what about Chick, Morel?"

"Chick Galey's got something on his mind," reported Morel, the clearing house. "He has passed word along the line to find the Clam for him. Chick is nursing that fat boy. By the way, the stoker up there, hiding out in the cellar, is Kid Link. I'll have him brought in later."

Those hopeless wights, thought Oliver, sitting back and watching the pattern weave itself; they come swimming to the gill net wherever it is laid.

Meantime Eddie was continuing his day uptown, seemingly oblivious of the fact that he was living the life of a goldfish. He knocked off at 4:30 to sit through the andante of the Fifth Symphony at Carnegie Hall; this was in accordance with the latest theory that a little emotional stirring up of the endocrine system refines the motors of thought. He wanted his to run with a silky purr just now.

He dined alone, and shortly after eight Mr. Kildrif, specialist in cats and dogs, called for him. They were moving out through the dulcet fragrance of Peacock Alley when the ever-receptive Eddie became conscious that he was about to be tapped on the shoulder—with the concomitant trickle of ice water—the chill of the catch—on his spine! He paused and turned, and found himself levelly surveying, for the first time in his life, the gigantic youth known as Roy in Fifty-fourth Street after two in the morning. Roy was beautifully turned out for the evening and presented himself with all the poise and assurance of a pampered child.

"Mr. Reel," he said, "I have a message for you which I am to deliver at once. Could I see you for a moment?"

He bowed to Mr. Kildrif, bowing that gentleman out of the picture. He presented his card to Eddie, and with a continuation of the same gesture, he cunningly picked an imaginary fly out of air, inspected the insect and released it, and watched it off. They stepped into an elevator, bowing an apology to Mr. Kildrif. The lift arose with a deep hydraulic gurgle.

"Delightful!" said Roy. "How this place preserves the flavor of old wine!"

Eddie took him in from tip to toe—his suavity, his pinkness, his baby dignity. Eddie was on the hair trigger. Chick Galey! Quick work.

He knew too well the grapevine telegraph to ask how it could have been done. Unlocking his sitting-room door, he bowed Roy in ahead of him.

"Better lock it," suggested Roy, and Eddie complied. Roy produced a package wrapped in Christmas tinsel and seals, for it was the holiday season. It contained a book of elongated octavo proportions—say an inch thick. Mutely he indicated that Eddie was to examine it. Eddie lifted the cover gingerly with a finger nail, let the book fall open. It was the signature book of some bank. It contained hundreds, possibly thousands of signatures, alphabetically arranged, each in facsimile, in enlargement, and in typewriting. An odd whistling sound at his elbow Eddie identified as coming from the windpipe of the young giant—the child was not so calm as he wished to appear; he was seething. Eddie turned the pages, still using a finger nail. He shook his head.

"This means nothing to me," he said.

"I suppose not," replied Roy, sneering contemptuously. With a fat hand he pushed over the leaves to a selected page. "I suppose this one means nothing to you!" he drawled, indicating an atrocious scrawl of ink under which stood a typed name of such magnitude that even Eddie, artist in the reconstruction of the chirography of the rich and great as he had been in his day, checked his breath and held himself hard. "Or this one? Or this?" said Roy, pushing the pages over. "Here! See that dot? That has been tried, over and over again, but they all forget the dot—think it doesn't belong. Well, it does! Here! Look at this one with the smudge—the smudge is part of it!"

"Are you leaving it?" asked Eddie politely.

"Not while I've got my health," said the giant. "You'd take a photograph of it and tell me to jump in the drink."

"What if I should take it away from you?"

Eddie's lifted eyebrow actually awaited a sober reply.

"I'd scream," said Roy. "They'd find it on you."

Eddie had to smile. Parr never planted this one. It was too good! He seemed to consider everything in detail, through a long pause.

"Can you put it back as deftly as you extracted it?" he asked mysteriously, eying a window. He was wondering what perversion of luck had ever enabled this great ninny to walk off with the very keys of the treasury. He pushed open the cover page with a finger nail and read the name of the bank, an odd smile on his face.

"Absolutely," replied Roy. "And produce it again on demand! That's what you want, isn't it?"

He tied up the precious tome in its goodwill-on-earth-and-joy-bells wrapper. He had hooked his fish; his air of importance considerably increased. They descended together to the foyer in silence, and there bade each other a ceremonious adieu.

"That boy is—is familiar. That boy, I think, is in my bank," said Mr. Kildrif as they got into the tonneau of the imported Belgian, the faithful Sangree at the wheel. "A clerk, I think."

"I told you this afternoon, as a matter of precaution to myself, that at one time in my youth I was not permitted to go below Fulton Street," said Eddie. He turned and stared at his companion as if to prepare him for what was coming. Kildrif seemed momentarily hypnotized. He recovered himself.

"That's over and done with, sir," smiled the dealer in cats and dogs. "Don't refer to it again, I beg."

"But the melody lingers on," said Eddie, catching an apt line from a current song hit. "I shall prove it to you. I haven't been in town in twelve years. I am spotted in my first twelve hours."

Kildrif's face became suddenly gaunt.

"By the police, you mean?" he cried.

"Naturally," laughed Eddie. "But that doesn't worry me. This is something far worse. I am spotted by my kind—by some old wolf of the pack! Word is passed along the line that I am back. Somebody finds something for me to do—something that is peculiarly my *métier*. Do you follow?"

"That boy, you mean?" gasped the astonished auditor.

"Yes. He was sent to me. He brought the signature book of your bank under his coat. God knows how he ever extracted it! I sometimes wonder how banks get by, the stuff they leave lying around. I suppose it is like working with dynamite—they get a contempt for the stuff."

"Wait! The signature book—" Kildrif was stuttering in his excitement.

"Yes. A bound book containing the signatures of depositors in photostat or electrotype. It's for the tellers to consult to verify signatures."

"I never knew there was such a book!"

"Neither did I," confessed Eddie, adding naïvely: "I'd like to have had a copy of it while I was in practice!"

"This is terrible, terrible! Something must be done!"

"If I were you," said Eddie, "I wouldn't waste any time. I'd get in touch with my bank tonight—quietly tip them off."

"Stop at the Century Club. I'll run in there and see if I can't find someone. It's inconceivable!" he was exclaiming. "What are the surety people doing? They are supposed to be on watch!"

Kildrif was stepping out at the curb in front of his club.

"Go easy on the kid," cautioned Eddie. "This kid is really psychopathic, you know. He's overchemicalizing, if you follow me," he said with a grim smile. "Remember, you can't cure them when they come that way. Just put him some place where he will be safe. That's all you can do. Don't pin a crook label on him; just guard him from being one."

Kildrif hurried in. For a moment or two Eddie sat still. Then he stepped down and walked up and down in front of the door. Passing his car on one tour, he stopped and stood, hands in his pockets, balanced on his heels, regarding his trig chauffeur.

"Did you hear that?" he asked abruptly.

Sangree, in spite of his best efforts, batted an eyelash.

"Yes, sir," he had to admit lamely—"about the boy, you mean? I did overhear some of it, yes, sir."

"I am being framed," said Eddie the Clam. "I don't intend to let them get away with it!" His teeth snapped with a savage click.

Kildrif came running out.

"He's here—one of the vice presidents," he said excitedly. "Would you—will you—we'll have to leave our evening in abeyance," he stammered. "We have to move fast! You'll excuse me, I know. You're pretty white, I'll say—you're pretty white, sir!"

"I'm protecting myself," replied Eddie coldly. He watched the door shut on Kildrif; then he turned and stared at his chauffeur long and fixedly.

"You are going to be my alibi, young fellow," he said finally. "You and I travel all night. I'm sticking to you closer than a flea, brother! I'm too old a bird to be framed by any of this particular bunch." He looked at his watch. "I think we will start at once, for, say, New Haven. How does that suit you?"

"May I telephone, then, sir?" asked Sangree obediently.

"If you can arrange it without letting me out of your sight!" snapped Eddie. "But you are to account for my every minute from now till the bank opens tomorrow morning."

It was not until they reached New Haven, after midnight, that Sangree was able to get on the telephone. He was in a booth, with Eddie sitting outside in full view, but out of hearing. Parr had moved from Central Office to field headquarters, uptown in Oliver Armiston's study in the Fifties, and the connection was put through there by private trunk.

"You are a little slow on the draw," said the deputy, after listening to Sangree. "The fat boy was picked up in a Tenth Avenue areaway an hour ago, with his head busted in."

He hung up, smiling; he regarded his friend and occasional collaborator.

"There you are!" he said softly. "I told you Eddie was too slick for us. He never drew a straight breath in his life! He picks things off right under our noses."

III

It was late in January. Barney, the wizened old door man, in holiday attire, got off the train one bleak dawn at Tupper Lake Junction and waited an hour for an accommodation that would take him still deeper into the woods.

"Honest, chief," Barney said later to Parr, "it was so cold my breath froze and I could hear it drop on the snow!"

The accommodation took Barney in an ambiguous manner in a generally northerly direction to a desolate little factory siding which, the conductor asserted, was his destination. The village lay there, buried like a huddle of Eskimo dogs that had been snowed up while they slept. There was a big turning shop going full tilt, a smoking stack at each end. This was the shop where Eddie the Clam, a versatile fellow, turned sawmill edgings into rake stales and tool handles. Barney followed a hard-beaten path to a door marked Office, and, without knocking, turned the knob and entered. Eddie sat there with several clerks; there was an air of industry, and from within came the hum and grunt of machinery. They all looked up. Barney slowly unwound his muffler.

"Why, hello, Barney!" cried Eddie, springing up, beaming.

"Hello, Eddie," laughed Barney. He took a hand out of a mitten and seized Eddie's hand; they held the grasp through a long smiling moment, checking up the toll age had taken in each other.

"The big fellow wants to see you," said Barney. "He asked me to stop by and tell you."

"I was going down this afternoon, anyway," said Eddie. "Take off your things! We've got three hours. I'll show you around, if you want."

Inside were machines and men—young men of a type Barney didn't know—clear-eyed, clear-skinned, stalwart young fellows who nodded pleasantly and treated him like a father when he asked questions.

"This would be a good place for my boy," said Barney. "He's a little wild."

"Send him along! We can take care of him," said Eddie.

Going down on the train, Barney fell asleep after lunch, like a healthy baby taking too big a gulp of fresh air on its first long trip abroad. After reading for some time, Eddie put down his book and browsed in thought. This gave out and he got up and went back to the club car and made a fourth at bridge. Even in the narrow confines of a vestibuled train, he had certain subtle means of testing himself for shadows. Ruefully he made one dry haul after another. There was not a single trace. Barney had come alone.

He smiled at his own reflection in the buffet mirror. He stared down into a deep ravine they crossed at slackened speed. At the bottom a black stream cut a winding path through snow-incrusted banks. Possibly, on the jet surface of that placid pool, he had a momentary true vision of himself in all perspectives. Possibly, for it is said that even the most happily insane are haunted by tiny instants of time through which they are permitted to peer, horror-stricken, at their real selves.

Possibly he saw something in that dark pool which reflected only the shadows of earth. But probably not. The chances are, he was thinking again, for the hundredth time since the episode of the signature book, that Parr had not given him so much as a single line of press on it; hadn't even telephoned him; and that now Parr had sent little old Barney to bring him in—Barney alone.

When they reached Grand Central the next morning, it was the delicate Barney who suggested they part company. Eddie could take himself downtown. Nobody knew him when he came to Central Office. It was unfamiliar to him. In his day he had always done business in the old Headquarters at 300 Mulberry. So, actually, he found himself asking his way to Parr's office, and being shown there by a policeman with such deference as even a policeman will show to a gentleman who was so obviously a prosperous business man.

Parr's room was empty, except for a huddled shadow in a chair who, on turning, proved to be none other than Chick Galey.

"Chee, Eddie, you look good to me!" cried Chick, his leathery face wrinkling with happiness. They shook hands, Chick treasuring Eddie's slender hand between his two big mitts. "Kosh! Like old time, boy!"

"You're not back on your heels, Chick," said Eddie by way of compliment. He held Chick away from him and looked him over with a professional eye.

"Not so bad," said Chick; he walked a few steps to show.

"Are they giving you the rap, Chick?"

"Say! Certainly! What do you think?"

"What can I do, Chick? I'll do anything."

Chick's face cracked in another smile, so blear-eyed as to be almost a sob. It was his pride—the staunchness of Eddie his friend. He shook his head. "No, Eddie. They get us good now, when they do get us." He searched Eddie's face. "What the hell! All the gang is up there. It won't be so bad going back this time." He jerked his head toward an inner door. "You can go right in, I guess, Eddie," he said. "They're all in there."

Eddie pushed open the door and walked in. The seven prosperous business men—dealers in findings, reinsurance, cats and dogs, and various other specialties—were grouped in more or less of a line in the middle of the room, which seemed to be a police gym; and wandering around them like a group of tourists in charge of a guide in an art gallery, were twenty or thirty men, all of a size and cut and age, and all masked except the cicerone himself, who was delivering a lecture, pointing out the high lights with a rosewood baton. This was Mr. Parr.

"This one," Mr. Parr was saying, as he came to a pause before a short, heavily built person with a marble eye, "is Heidelberg Max. He has been rebuilt. His own mother wouldn't know him. He's had a slab of skin grafted from his hip onto his cheek, to cover up a saber cut you could lay your finger in. His line is leather—soles, uppers and findings—mostly findings. We found a sheaf of Liberty 4's from the Kaltenstall holdup in a consignment of shoe boxes he was shipping to a carbon-black plant in Texas. Open your mouth, Max, and let them see your teeth."

"This one," droned the cicerone, moving on down the line with his little stick, "is a first offender named Kildrif, dealer in cats and dogs and skunks. He sells them by the bale. Open a bale and you'll find it salted and peppered with some gilt-edged stuff the police are looking for. He not only specializes in worthless stuff the bucket shops can't sell but in gilt-edged stuff a crook can't sell after he has swiped it! He's like all the rest of this bunch—a receiver of stolen goods—and he ran a good business as a blind, so he could receive stolen goods and dispose of it behind his bank account and Bradstreet rating without being questioned. He left a telephone number at the Century Club the other night that we could trace him by. Otherwise he'd have got away with a signature book that fat boy swiped. He's been operating for years, would have gone on indefinitely, except that Eddie the Clam had to come to town and show us how slick he was and do business under our very noses. Now, look at Kildrif's crooked nose—look at the angle of his jaw—look at the droop in his left eyelid. Walk, you! See, he's covering up a limp in the left leg.

"And this one," intoned Parr, motioning Eddie into the picture, "this, men, is Eddie himself—Eddie the Clam. Read his record! It's good reading! He's never drawn a straight breath in his life. He's so slick he practices on himself when there's no one else around to bilk. He is the"—Parr paused, his lip curling—"he is the great mind of this undertaking! He's been great-minding for the past twelve years. It occurred to Eddie, just like that, that the average crook was not getting a fair deal out of the stuff he swiped, because he wasn't rated in Bradstreet. So he organized a syndicate—this bunch! all of them rated—any of them can deposit ten thousand dollars without being asked where he got it. He was the clearing house for the syndicate. He kept his business broken up in small units, scattered all over the map. They handled cash and negotiable securities for yeggs on a fat commission basis. If it hadn't happened that we had a bright young man on our consulting staff, who suggested we check up his audits against his income-tax returns, he might be doing business yet. Eddie, you slipped up there!

"Look well, you wolves!" intoned Parr. "He's been up the river three times and he's on his way now to the home for incurables! But don't take anything for granted with Eddie. Know him when you see him again! Moreau, go over this fellow's points for the boys, will you?"

Parr turned to the other members of the syndicate.

"Take 'em away," he growled. They were herded out. Eddie lifted his head and submitted himself to Moreau, the Bertillon expert, who stood by him with a little book opened at a particular page; he read from this book while he drew imaginary lines on Eddie's cranium with a little stick. The masked gathering gave breathless heed like a clinic of medical students.

Finally the demonstration ended. They went inside and Eddie sat down by Parr's desk.

"Just where was the break, sarge?" he asked.

"Heidelberg Max," said Parr. "That was a dumb trick for you, Eddie."

"He was pretty well rebuilt; he fooled me!"

"His face, yes," agreed the deputy. "But his teeth, man! That broke your back. When I found him in your nest, I took a chance and broke open the stuff all of them were shipping to you. That batch of thousand dollar Federal Reserve notes out of the express-company robbery—that was pretty raw, Eddie! To put them through the way you did! We've got you on any one of a dozen counts."

"There is always reasonable doubt," ventured Eddie, the experienced.

Parr shook his head: "It ain't like it was, as Chick would say."

"What about Kildrif? Did he double-cross me with that bank signature book?" asked Eddie.

"He didn't have a chance," said Parr. "We picked up his gang before they had a chance to put that book in circulation. Kildrif is some actor!"

He chuckled; Eddie smiled. The door opened. It was Barney, back in regimentals, armed with his dustpan—his ægis of office. Seeing the room occupied, he was retiring.

"Oh, Barney!" cried Eddie, and Barney came in. Eddie took out a card and wrote something on it and handed it to Barney. "Send your boy up there, Barney. You won't know him in a year. That's a good bunch! They'd do anything in the world for me."

Barney, through dim old eyes, read the card. He thrust out a hand.

"That's sure white of you, Eddie!" he cried. He moved slowly off, studying the magic card.

"They are all for you, Eddie," said Parr harshly. "I don't get you, at all. All these little towns where you've got your factories—you had a good living in any one of them for the asking. But you wouldn't take it! You'd rather be a crook. How do you figure it out, Eddie?"

Eddie smiled again, an absent look in his cold gray eyes. What worried him, at the moment, was not how to go straight, but how to beat this break. He was thinking about lawyers, wondering whom he'd call in. This break was a little worse than the others. There was no bail this time! And there was life in stir staring him in the face if he coppered the wrong card. He repressed a shiver, felt the drip of ice water. But what the hell? Lawyers were still in business, weren't they, with their lawyer-made law? They'd been writing it for themselves for the last hundred years, plugging the loopholes, widening the get-aways, nursing their inalienable, sacred Presumption of Innocence, Burden of Proof, Reasonable Doubt, the holy right of Trial by a dumb Jury. In Eddie's experience, all a crook had to do was to keep his mouth shut and let the law protect him. Any good lawyer—Eddie smiled, amused. Eddie wasn't downhearted—nine to one was a good bet.

A clerk came in and laid a yellow slip on Parr's desk, the big fellow wrinkling his brow over it. He touched a bell that clanged dismally outside somewhere, touched another that brought a man in uniform who stood at attention. Parr got up and took down his hat and coat, shoved the yellow slip in a pocket. A big murder had just broken uptown. Parr put on his over-shoes. For a moment, as he buttoned his greatcoat about him, the deputy studied the bemused Eddie.

"Lock this fellow up," he said to the uniformed man, and he went out, picking up Morel and Pelts in the corridor.

Vivace-Ma non Troppo

W HAT's become of the red-headed girl?" asked George, the clerk in the delicatéssen store at the first corner. "I haven't seen her for a long time—two weeks. Do you know what she ate for lunch? An apple, a pickle and a doughnut."

He was ladling out loose milk for Wicks, the overseer of the apartment house on the river brim—one of those most recent shoe-box skyscrapers that specialize in one-room suites, to be had as low as a thousand dollars a year. Wicks was as vain of his kingdom as the mayor of any *arrondissement*, and when he came in here for loose milk he used the back door.

"She wore a plaited skirt that swung like this," said George, gently moving his dipper from side to side. "Where is she? Is she gone away for good?"

"'Good'?" repeated Wicks suspiciously. He didn't like the word, and he didn't like to talk about his people.

"Has she gone away?" said George. "That's what I mean. Can't I ask?"

"Sure, you can ask," said Wicks, and he took his can of loose milk and departed by the rear door.

Other people had asked about that girl. Her name was Lucena Wirden. The gas man had said, "Doesn't she use any gas at all? I'll have to take her meter out, unless she begins again." The milkman had said, "I want the empty cream bottles from 26 R. They won't answer the bell." Wicks, before setting down his milk, looked at her electric-light meter. The hands hadn't moved since the last reading. He knew, because this house bought electricity wholesale at four cents and retailed it to tenants at seven and eight.

He called her by telephone. He could hear the buzz as the girl at the board prodded with her plug. No answer. He stood by the wire, waiting. Her picture came more and more distinctly to him. Her eyes were not blue, as one expected, but a deep brown, almost black, with a glint of red behind them which made her red hair very striking. She had a lilt to her walk, and a quick toss of her head like a bird when she talked. Her skin was so white one thought at first it was glazed with powder, like a Spanish woman's. When she moved in—in a taxicab, as most of his tenants did—she had paid her rent in advance for a whole quarter. The check was drawn on a bank that required a minimum cash balance of three thousand dollars. The pickle she ate for luncheon was not parsimony but regimen. She was working hard with her voice, and the pickle had something to do with it. He wondered about the apple. Some of these advanced students, when they reached a certain stage, went into the chorus for what they called hardening, and they had to give up apples and gum—it made them fat. She wasn't fat. The whole block as far as the bus station for cross town knew her and her swinging little skirt whose bewitching oscillations George had depicted with slow movement of the milk dipper. Her mail had the unmistakable air of a person who is asked out in society. The envelopes were never two of the same size—to the despair of the post-office canceling machines—and the inscriptions were scrawls of painful, loose grace. Once, standing in the elevator alone, Wicks saw one had come unsealed, and he slyly looked inside. It contained a tissue-thin card with some grand name on it, and in one corner was written a single word: "Tea?" He remembered particularly the question mark after the word "tea." It struck him at the time as very effective.

Consuming his milk, with loose bread, Wicks went upstairs and outside, and stood by the river wall, watching his people come and go, as was his prideful habit. He wouldn't have anything happen to this house for the world. It had a good carriage trade. Taxis were on the come and go. There was a taxi stand at the river wall. Most of the tenants were beginners in the artistic professions who, by hook or crook, had scraped enough money together for that final finishing splurge in the glitter of theater, concert hall, gallery, and editorial room, which they so confidently plotted to crash. One wonders where all the money comes from to outfit this army that moves so valiantly on New York every fall. They must all have establishments of their own; for part of the game is to appear prosperous and in no hurry. They always moved in, in a taxi, with a floor lamp or two, an elderdown quilt, and that inevitable war bag, the hatbox. Sometimes a wardrobe trunk too. In a day or two, along would come several pieces of heavy furniture of the overstuffed variety—on the installment plan—and a grand piano of expensive make, always rented by the month. Window hangings and floor coverings came gradually. They came so bravely, departed so forlornly. One of them, a little doll of a girl with a voice as hard as china, had said to Wicks, when she departed yesterday, leaving all her furniture behind for the installment collector to repossess:

"Some day you will see my picture all over the opera programs and the Sunday papers. Now I have to move into a thirty-dollar flat."

They flowed by like eddies in the river just beyond the jagged rocks. He looked up at the lights, gay curtains, the receding terraces of his shoebox skyscraper domain. High up, almost out of sight, he caught sight of what he knew, from previous inspection, to be a brace of mallard ducks hanging outside of a window. Instantly he tossed away his cigar, walked in and entered the elevator.

"Have you taken up that girl in 26 R?" he asked.

The elevator boy shook his head. He was a Bermuda boy, had been there only three days. Was there any mail for her? The boy took down a few letters, great and diminutive as usual. He said there was a big batch of it when he came; he had climbed up and tipped it over the transom into her hall.

"Nobody answered?"

"No," said the boy; he looked at Wicks. He anchored at her floor, watching while Wicks pushed the bell and listened with one ear at the door panel. The boy edged over beside him, and they eyed each other, breathing a little faster. They started when the elevator buzzer sounded. The boy closed the gate, looking back till he was out of sight.

A door opened down the hall and a young man came briskly out. It was a tenant by the name of Van Halen. He was a writer. He had come to town, so he would tell you if you were interested, to be on hand when things finally broke. He carried a fat brief case, the contents of which he would distribute in person at the various offices in Park Avenue, just north of the depot, where volunteer manuscripts are sorted for the market.

"Nobody's home there," he said.

"How do you know?"

"Who should, better?" replied the young man. "Have you never heard her scream? You'd think someone was strangling her. She doesn't make tone any more. She's advanced beyond that! She is limbering up her throat. Ar-rgh! Ar-rgh! Ar-rgh! Like that." He gave a clever imitation in a half voice. He added: "Except that she lifts herself up on the piano in thirds, you'd swear dirty work was going on."

"How long since you've heard her? When did you hear her last?"

Van Halen considered before he answered. He looked around.

"Remember that night the lights went out all over the house? About two weeks ago," he said. "She was screeching then—I swear I was on the point of calling the police. Then the lights went out. She stopped like that!" He snapped his fingers sharply. "What made the lights go out?"

"We submeter in this building," explained Wicks. "A fuse blew on the street side. It happens. Give me a leg up, will you?"

With the young man's help he drew himself up and stood with a foot on the door knob to peer through the open transom. He hopped down.

"I can't see anything. I'm going in," he said.

He took out a bunch of keys, from which he selected one, a strange key. It was a master key. There were times when one had need of a master key in a house like this.

"You've got no right to go in there!" said Van Halen.

"You come with me," said Wicks, turning the key in the lock.

The young man recoiled.

"I will not!" he cried. He suddenly rasped, "What are you doing here anyway? Springing another strangling scandal? Well, you can't rope me in!"

He retreated to the elevator, punched the bell. "You want a witness? Well, call a cop. Or a coroner!"

Wicks wouldn't go in alone. He telephoned police headquarters.

"Give me East Fifty-first Street," he said.

"For what?" inquired a bland voice.

He explained clumsily. One of the tenants—a good-looking girl—hadn't been seen for two weeks—didn't answer her bell.

"I'll give you the homicide bureau," said the flat voice. "Don't touch anything till we get there."

"No, not the wagon! There may be nothing! Send one man," Wicks pleaded. A thing like that would kill this house. He thought of one famous case. They had found the girl strangled with her own gauzy silk stockings, lying across a couch. Nothing was missing, nothing ever came of it, they never even found out who she was. It had killed that house; it would be years before people forgot.

Shortly a man came from the homicide bureau.

"I go first," he said, entering without taking off his hat. "Touch nothing. Step in my tracks. There are more clews destroyed in the first five minutes than can ever be raked together afterward. You fellows smear everything."

The entry hall was strewn with letters—the ones the elevator boy had pushed over the transom. Wexler, the homicide expert, stood on the threshold examining the floor with a light torch. He picked out a spot to step on, then another, and hopped across to the door of the studio. This was hung with a curtain. Using a pencil, he pushed aside the curtain and looked in.

"Nothing here," he said, chewing thoughtfully. "When you've been through as many of these things as I have—"

Wicks touched his shoulder and pointed to a hall tree on which hung her street things.

"That's her hat and neck piece," he said. "I never saw her wear anything else since she came."

"That clock is twenty-three minutes slow," said the man of murders. The clock stood on a mantel above a fireplace in which lay some ashes. It was an electric clock plugged in on a light socket. It ran in synchronism with the sixty-cycle turbogenerators in the central station; it might drift a few electrical degrees ahead or behind momentarily, but ordinarily it was on the dot. However, a fuse had blown one night recently. The clock had stopped then, of course, and would not start up until the current came on again. That would account for the twenty-three minutes. While Wicks explained this the homicide expert watched him with steady gaze. When Wicks ceased speaking, Wexler continued to gaze at him, as if waiting for more. This disconcerted the manager.

"Everything in the entire house went out?"

"Yes. The fuse quit. That cut off both sides."

"And stayed dark twenty-three minutes?"

"About that, yes."

Wicks mentioned Van Halen—indicating the apartment to the right—and the screams that night. The screams meant nothing. She screamed at all hours of the day and night. There was nothing like the pertinacity of the creatures working at music. No ordinary laborer could have stood the hours and toil.

"The lights went out in the midst of her screaming?"

"She stopped, yes."

"For twenty-three minutes?"

"According to that clock, yes."

"Isn't that pretty good evidence?" demanded the expert.

"Unless the clock had been tampered with."

"Apparently she hasn't come back to tamper with it," remarked Wexler, his doubting gaze going over Wicks' face. He said: "Did you ever hear of a law requiring an emergency storage battery to carry the load after thirty seconds of darkness? A lot of panic can happen in a crowded house in thirty seconds. Where was your battery?"

"I never heard of such a law!"

"You will," promised the detective. He turned and studied the great room. The space suggested opulence—until you learned there was nothing beyond; it was all there was. There was the usual trick setting of period furniture, the grand piano. Wexler stepped from one tiny rug to another, Wicks carefully following. Everywhere was pleasant disorder. One tiny table held cigarette trays, with a day's run of ashes and stubs; throat pastils; a book of powder papers such as girls use to freshen their faces. Another table held a Satsuma bowl full of pennies—hundreds, thousands, it seemed; probably for poker parties.

"Did she run a game here?" Wicks thought not. How did she pay her rent? Did she sign the check, or did the cashier? Was it a cashier's check? Wexler's doubting gaze hovered about Wicks' eyebrow. He, Wicks, had never thought of a cashier's check before, and its possible significance. It might have been; he didn't remember, hadn't noticed if it was. All this stuff was good, Wexler said; it didn't look like the usual installment layout that was constantly being repossessed and dealt out again. She had money from somewhere. The bathroom was in the same pleasant disorder, suggesting the occupant had only now gone—except that one tap had dripped and accumulated a stain of iron rust on the white porcelain, which spoke of the time gone by—since the electric clock had stopped and begun again.

"Touch nothing," Wexler kept saying. "All this stuff will have to be fingerprinted."

"But there is nothing!" protested Wicks, who had long since come to regret his precipitancy.

"Don't worry, there will be," retorted Wexler placidly. "Maybe she went out the window."

He looked down the seventeen stories, a dizzy drop. The turbulent river just below the Island, where prisoners could be seen crawling about like ants, seemed directly below. As a matter of fact, anyone falling from here would have been dashed to pieces on the rocks many feet from the water's edge. Wexler lifted the brace of mallards that hung below the sill, inside. He carefully arranged them on an open newspaper. These two birds were full of implications for the experts who would follow his reconnaissance. The birds were frozen stiff.

Concealed beyond a jog in the hall was a so-called kitchenette; and still farther on, where the hall bellied out, was a so-called dinette, with a dining table folding against the wall.

"Who's next door?"

"The young man—Van Halen—this way."

"And the other way?"

"Nobody, ordinarily," said Wicks.

"What do you mean, ordinarily?" Again those doubting eyes explored Wicks face.

"It's rented, but it isn't occupied," said Wicks. That sounded queer. He had never thought it queer before. "They live out of town. They use it to dress for dinner or for the theater. I don't think they ever stay overnight." The fixed gaze compelled Wicks to go on. "I'll give you the name when we go down to the office," said he. "It's Wylie, or Slylie, or something like that."

"And you'll give me the date and the hour when you blew the fuse," said Wexler, a slight smile appearing momentarily.

Lastly they inspected two closets, large and well filled. The clothing was mostly dresses hanging on forms; it exuded the pleasant odor of a well-cared-for person. It bore good names: Juleph, Davide, Arnov, Salm Sœurs, Merphy, and so on. Wexler went through it with his pencil. There was a mahogany chest of drawers, which he looked at closely without touching. Finally he said he had enough for a report. He pushed Wicks out ahead of him, stepping from island to island, to avoid disturbing anything. His last act was to reach back from the outer hall and fish out the letters, one by one, being careful not to let his fingers touch them. He gathered them in a newspaper with his busy pencil.

"But she'll come back and find them gone!" protested Wicks.

"She won't come back," said Wexler. He fixed seals on the door; and then, to Wicks' horror, he brought up a policeman in uniform and set him on guard. Wicks, nervous and regretful, hovered about. He had been too precipitate. It was not the fate of the girl that bothered him. It was the fate of the house. The house would never survive the stigma.

II

"The odd thing about it is," said Parr, the police deputy, dropping a bundle of imposingly big and little envelopes on Oliver Armiston's desk, "that none of these people can tell us anything about her. She was merely one of hundreds, possibly thousands, they use to fill in at their parties and dances and dinners. Society is a good deal like the movie business—they keep extras on hand to dress the stage."

The man hunter drummed on the desk, smiling to himself. It was the unexpected, weird flashes of life that appeared as though illuminated by a lightning stroke which gave him pause. Parr had long since ceased to be cynical, although his men invariably were.

"She had mahogany-red hair and black eyes shot with red, and an ivory skin. She had a walk—" Parr paused, shifted his gaze to old Buddha in bronze listening from his nook by the fire, Oliver unbound the bundle of fancy envelopes and examined them one by one. "Have you seen this new Spanish dancer—"

"Perez? No. I have a card. She has a million-dollar back, I hear."

"Not Perez. Hilaria, I mean," interposed Parr. "When she walks across the stage the audience breaks out in *braras*; they think it is part of the program. I don't know your Perez. Is she the one they have brought over for drawing-room presentations?"

Oliver nodded, taking out the cards of invitation one by one. They were all grand names begging the presence of a girl none of them knew.

"Hilaria is not new," he said. "I saw her eight years ago. I know what you mean," he added with a sly smile.

"Everybody does," said Parr. "Lucena wore a little plaited skirt that swung as she walked." Parr undulated his hand gently like a conductor indicating *vivace ma non troppo*. "Everybody noticed it—the delicatessen boy, the fruit man at the corner, the bus man, the janitor."

"Ah!" said Oliver. "That impalpable sway which the French call the tempest in the glass of water! Belasco worked six months getting that walk into one of his stars."

"One touch of nature makes the whole world kin," said Parr. "That brings me to what I am driving at. A few weeks—a month or so—before she disappeared, she dressed up in the best she had and went downtown to call on Lacolmbe, the banker, to thank him for paying her rent."

"Lacolmbe was paying her rent?"

"Don't use that tone of voice," cautioned Parr. "He didn't know it himself. He maintains a fund for real people who can be helped. He is the most kindly and generous of men—under cover! The most onerous thing about giving is the acknowledgment of your gratuity, the insistence on thanks, which, of course, simply inflates your credit with other beggars. His wife and daughter do the picking and tell him what's required. He arranges for the funds in cashier's checks, so they can't be traced. Well," said the deputy, in parenthesis, "we traced this one! He was the most surprised man in the world when she walked in on him. He didn't know her. It hit her in a heap, evidently. Imagine yourself—thinking you are a coming genius whom he has had the discernment to recognize, consumed with the desire to tell your benefactor how grateful you are—and then finding that he doesn't know you from Adam!"

"That's good theater," nodded Armiston. "Somebody ought to use that scene. What did she do?"

"He said she couldn't believe it," went on Parr. "She started to speak, but the words refused to come. It was like a dash of ice water! Instead of being the favored protégée of a rich patron, who would recoup in pride and satisfaction some day when she crashed the gate of fame; she probably saw herself in his eyes—as merely another grafter, one of the measly string that trails every millionaire, always asking for more. Do you get the picture?"

"Very well. What then?"

"She turned and walked out without a word." Parr gently swayed a hand from the wrist, conducting *vivace ma non troppo.* "Lacolmbe was wild, of course!" he said. "He thought she was playing him, that she had come downtown to parade herself. She was too pretty to be left around loose, you understand. He gave his wife and daughter the devil! But they were rather vague about it. You know how such people are. Lacolmbe was so worried about it he set a private detective agency on her track. But she turned out to be just another dummy of this fellow Cristème."

"Dummy?"

"Yes, dummy. Don't you know about this fellow Cristème?"

"The coach? The music teacher, you mean?"

"Yes. That's the way he feathers his nest. Do you know the one I mean? Have you ever seen him?"

Oliver nodded. The vogue of Cristème among women was because he was so distinguished, so—so Continental!

This Cristème made a business of collecting budding Carusos and Melbas from among the thousands of aspirants who move on New York every fall. His primary object in his skillful selections was not the creation of a new star as the glorified product of a limited group of discerning philanthropists. That would be too much of a gamble. His business was organized on the more secure basis of bleeding his rich dupes through the long years of labor that must intervene before talent comes into its own.

No one could deny his musical judgment. With each fresh discovery he would whisper to some favored woman in his large feminine following, and confer on her the privilege of paying the bills—twenty dollars an hour—and found. Just a little encouragement and help at the right time! It was thus the Lacolmbes, mother and daughter, embraced the cause of Lucena. Such things are kept concealed. Lucena didn't know.

"Did she have a voice?" asked Oliver.

"Apparently just enough to keep her hypnotized. Cristème carries them on his rolls as long as he can. Then he launches them—gives them a debut!"

Yes, Oliver had seen those debuts—the papered house, the drilled applause, the property flowers run down the aisle after the first encores, the rich patronesses splitting their gloves. It was all calculated to complete the dream. Then came the gradual letting down, the drift back to earth. Talent is so rare, genius is an epoch. Most of them were never heard of again. The aftermath was always the same—small roles, teaching, the radio.

"I like that joke about the radio," said Parr. "The fellow who went to the service station and said, 'What's the matter with my radio? All I can get on it is sopranos.'"

Oliver took down the Social Register. She was listed there, alone, with no hint of who she might be. This was not unusual. In these lists of who arrives socially, husbands may appear without wives and wives without husbands, or even a child without parents. With Lucena, the omission of her parents from among the socially possible suggested volumes.

The year before, the address was care of a leading bank in Paris, which meant that she was traveling abroad under exceptional auspices. The year before that she was set down in the list of dilatory domiciles as at Neuilly, and there was a note in italics, "*see Cambrel.*" Under Cambrel there was listed a large family, with adult sons and daughters and two juniors; and finally, in brackets, Miss Lucena Wirden.

"I get the picture now," said Oliver, putting back the books. "She lives among the rich, in parenthesis."

He sketched what he conceived to be the portrait of Lucena. From good family, with gentle rearing, yet she was poor—poor. Somehow, probably through exceptional intelligence or a lucky scholarship, she enters college—Bryn Mawr, Vassar. There her misfortunes begin. She is taken up by rich girls. One of them picks her as a chum—with the usual result. The rich family take her up, carry her around with them as daughter's chum. They dress her, feed her—not a penny does she spend but what comes from them. They indulge her like a daughter. When they are through with her they drop her like a hot brick.

"This isn't romance, Parr; it is everyday fact," said Oliver. "I have seen rich people with stupid daughters deliberately pick such a girl and carry her along for years. She is the ready coach who supplies the lacks of grace in the other. If she has tact she gives the dumb daughter an imitation polish that no school could provide. She isn't a companion or a tutor—that would humiliate daughter. She is daughter's chum. Actually she occupies the place of a highly specialized companion, without pay. She is thrown among rich young men. But they don't marry her. Their doting mammas have other plans for them. Eventually she grows a little faded and drifts to the level of social secretary."

"That's a good print," said Parr, nodding. "The private detective agency Lacolmbe had set on her trail turned up just such a story. Esther Cambrel, her college chum, finally married a count and no longer felt the need of her around the house. Lucena, after testing the splendors of the upper ether, came back to earth with a jolt. She had to make her own living. She had a voice of a sort, and she could dance. All this social experience and travel, the languages acquired during winters in the Sud—in brief, all the acquirements that gilded the lily, told heavily with Cristème, when he discovered her and started her on the highroad to fame and fortune again."

"And now she wakes up the second time—finds she is only a dummy again," mused Oliver. "Poor little devil! I don't blame her for walking out on it. That's what has happened, isn't it, Parr?"

"Possibly," admitted Parr. He eyed Oliver grimly. "But you can't sink like a stone without somebody asking questions," he said. "She hasn't any folks. Nor friends either—except this bunch!" He jerked a thumb at the big and little invitations. "It is up to us! We don't want to have to drag the river for her." Parr paused, drummed the desk. "That wasn't a fuse that blew. It was a circuit breaker that opened. Those things don't open on a whim," he said.

III

Here in town we make a good deal of a pose of not knowing anything about our neighbors. We see them and hear them, of course, but we sedulously avoid the pretense of doing so. We profess ignorance of the names of people who live on the other side of the wall; and when we meet them outside we try to remember where we have seen them before. These things must be, in city life, else the intimacies of living would become unbearable. So we affect not to know them. Nevertheless, there is a subconscious espionage going on all the while, accumulating impressions, like the minute but continuous sedimentary deposit of a swiftly flowing river. So, when something extraordinary occurs, all those trifles we have been subconsciously laying up are brought forward and come to have astonishing significance.

As to Lucena, her background was an open book. Without knowing it, she had taken care of that herself. That day when she started downtown to interview old Lacolmbe she began unconsciously weaving, fettering herself to her somewhat ironic past, so that when she woke up she would find herself tied, like Gulliver himself, with filaments of delicate spinning as fine and strong as cobwebs, than which there is nothing stronger. That prying *dossier* of the private detective agency was a perfect revelation to the eyes of the sophisticated. So was her every act up to the moment she stepped off into the void. There the record stopped. Parr, as he had said, didn't like the business of dragging river bottoms, so his scientificos applied test tubes and microscopes, till they came to the end of their resources. It was then that the deputy went to his confidant, Oliver Armiston. He wanted to know something, without seeming to inquire, about Lucena's neighbors—the two young men who occupied cubicles on either side of her.

"Of course, we can break in and paw over things," said Parr. "In fact, that's what we have done," he added gruffly, with a little shrug of self-forgiveness. "Wylie said he never knew her. But we found her fingerprint on a tumbler in his bathroom. The maid who took care of the suites on that corridor may have replaced a broken glass in his bathroom by an extra one from hers. So much for that. Van Halen, on the other side, didn't know her either. So he says. There seems to have been a feud between them because of her eternal caterwauling. But the janitor thinks he remembers seeing the pair going out together."

Doubtless these two had both made observations, conscious and unconscious. Wylie would probably be the harder nut to crack. On inquiry, he turned out to be the Wylie of Broadway; a person of some distinction who exercised certain extraterritorial privileges over there. He brought over European artists for private showings. For instance, those of us who are seeing Perez, the dancer, this winter for the first time are always surprised to be told that she had been seen on this side of the water before; that she was brought over last year, smuggled in, as it were, in bond—like a great jewel that is for sale—for private inspection by the very rich. That sort of traffic is going on all the while—these very lucrative private seasons of great artists. The idea that is capitalized by Wylie and his kind is that the very rich be given a chance to see them before the bloom is worn off by popularity.

Oliver, considering Wylie, passed him up for the time being as probably too nimble a liar for their purpose. No matter what he might know, he would lie. The prospect of anyone, either in public or private life, waking up some morning to be greeted by a line in the newspaper that he "had been questioned by the police in connection with the mysterious disappearance of Lucena Wirden, a young music student," was not pleasant. The mere statement of the fact would suggest conclusions to the minds of readers that would be irrevocable. Therefore Armiston, in the role of observer, assigned him by the deputy, turned his guns on the less adroit of the pair of neighbors. Until the moment arrived when publicity and newspaper notoriety would have to be called in as allies the unofficial Armiston was in a better position to uncover what either of these two might know than the police themselves.

Several days later Alexander Van Halen, who had come to town from a little upstate Dutch village to crash the gates with his mighty pen, found himself the recipient of a card from Mrs. Billy Wentworth. Everybody knew who Mrs. Billy Wentworth was. Mr. Wentworth, although a former ambassador, was always referred to as Mrs. Billy Wentworth's husband. In one corner stood the engraved word "Friday"; under it stood a single word, in scrawling handwriting, "Tea," followed by a question mark—a very fetching, fat little interrogation point bursting with naïve innuendo. Alex did not ask himself why he was the recipient of a card from Mrs. Billy Wentworth. He believed he knew.

He understood that certain hostesses of the *haut monde* were in the habit of making discreet inquiries as to the more possible of the newcomers on the beach of Bohemia each season, and trotting them out for inspection. If one withstood the ordeal, there was no telling how far he might travel. It was a thrilling afternoon for Alex Van Halen. He met a man he had always wanted to know—Oliver Armiston, the author. Oliver had long since ceased to write thrillers, but his stories had gone into textbooks and been analyzed by professors of the craft, and all students knew of him.

"Come around and see me," said Oliver cordially, not for an instant suggesting that it was he who got the card for Alex.

"Are you trying to steal my lion cub?" cried Mrs. Billy, in passing.

"Might I fetch along a story?" begged the budding author.

Oliver shook his head. He explained that it was against union rules to ask writers to read each other's stuff.

"Bring your pipe," said Armiston.

Young Van Halen waited not on the order, but rang Oliver's bell the next evening.

"How," said he, getting right down to the meat of the interview, "would you go about breaking into big time with our type of story?" He included Oliver in the same category as himself.

"The same way I'd go about breaking into the front page of a newspaper," replied the extinct author of thrillers, seeing the prospect of an opening.

"Murder, you mean?"

"Yes. In a front-page manner. Or, if you are squeamish about committing murder—even in fiction," said Oliver—"try dropping like a stone into the void, without leaving a trace. A good-looking girl! That always takes. The technic is much more difficult than murder, however."

"Would it hurt if it were true?"

"The effigy of truth," said Mr. Armiston ponderously, "should hang before your eyes."

"I've got a story I'd like to write," said Alex, thoughtfully polishing the bowl of his pipe. "The only trouble is that it is true, and you've probably observed that true stories never end—they always keep on going. I've got the beginning and the title. I call it Repossession. That's good, don't you think?"

"It's positively Russian!" Oliver smiled vaguely, twiddling his single white lock of hair on his forehead. "What does it mean?" he asked innocently.

"You see ads," responded Van Halen, in no wise disconcerted, "of repossessed autos, repossessed furs, furniture, clothes—anything that is sold on installments and taken back because of nonpayment. They sell the same stuff over and over again. Of course, it gets a little shopworn as it goes downhill." He looked at Oliver keenly; Oliver sat back, waiting. "In my story it isn't overstuffed furniture or hand-me-down autos that is repossessed. It's a girl!" went on the rapt Alex. "She is poor, but beautiful!" He shrugged deprecatingly. "Those elements are necessary to fiction, one must admit. Hers is the fatal gift of being taken up."

"Taken up?"

"Yes. Patronized by rich people. She moves in the best circles. Why? She looks the part! She has all the elements to reflect glory on a commonplace background. She thinks she is putting herself over big. As a matter of fact, she isn't selling herself at all. They are merely using her—renting her on the installment plan. After she has served her turn she is dismissed without a qualm. Then she has to look for another bidder. Meantime Lucena is getting a little shopworn."

"Lucena?"

"Yes, Lucena. That's her name. As a matter of fact," said Alex, looking round and lowering his voice, "that's her real name. This is her real story. Isn't that a bang-up setting?"

"Yes, but what happens?"

"We're coming to that. She lived next door to me."

"Lived?" repeated Oliver, stressing the tense.

"Lived," responded Alex. "I never knew her from Adam. You know how neighborly we are in this town. You know, sometimes," he said, shaking his head with a wistful smile, "at our age, a whole lifetime of events will occur in one day. A whole epoch! Well, I blundered into Lucena's orbit in the middle of that day. She had been hit so many times that day that her knees were sagging, and she was hanging on, but she wasn't out yet, as they say in the ring. She had been working two years with her voice. That morning, to begin with," said Alex, pausing to relight his pipe, to let it go out immediately thereafter, "some kind friend, in whose judgment she believed implicitly, told her that the voice which was to make her fortune had just three notes, three golden notes, as a foundation—and nothing more! There never would be any more!

"And then," said Alex, "to blacken both of her eyes at once, this kind friend added: 'But of course you don't need to worry, because you've got one of those self-filling bank accounts.'

"This fired every drop of blood in her veins. Some rich patron had been putting up for her. It had been cleverly impressed upon her from the first, by Cristème, her teacher, that she must not inquire too closely. Her part in it now was to work—work hard. When she became famous, yes, she was to know who was the patron. Return it? Yes, by supporting other beginners. It had always been plausible enough.

"Well, she made her exit smiling," said Alex. "She went straight to her bank and demanded to know where her money came from. Who was depositing money to her account? As long as she thought she was going to be famous and pay it back some day, it didn't matter. But now she knew that her voice was a fake, she wanted to know. The cashier didn't know. Anybody can bank money in an established account, with no questions asked. It's when you come to draw it out that they ask you who you are. She went to the president. He said in his fatherly way:

" 'I know who it is. Isn't that enough for you? You should be happy and flattered to know there is a generous and disinterested person who is confident of your future, and ready to help you over the rough places in the cause of art. The actual money means nothing to him. But the satisfaction means much! Now can't you humor him to that extent?'

"She said, 'But I have no future. That's what I want to tell him. It must cease. I can no longer accept his bounty.' The old man said kindly. 'Let him be the judge.'

" 'You refuse to tell me?' she demanded. 'I have no recourse. How would you like to see your daughter living on one of these self-filling bank accounts? Her friends would probably smile a little when she said she didn't know her benefactor. Mine are beginning to.'

" 'Now, now,' protested the embarrassed banker. He gave more advice. As Tchekhoff says, everybody is anxious to give us advice when we are in trouble, but only about half of them have ever been in trouble themselves. Well, greatly perturbed at the directness of the girl, the banker finally blurted out a hint of some famous philanthropist as her backer, a man with a charity list longer than most orphan asylums. She put two and two together. A great light came. She knew who it was. She jumped in a taxi and went downtown to break the news to him that she was only a deadhead on his pay roll, had been for the past two years. She got in to him, but never had a chance to say a word. The old man took her to be an adventuress, a blackmailer. It staggered her. She turned on her heel and walked out, absolutely dumb."

"How do you happen to know all of this?" asked Oliver Armiston, eying the narrator curiously. Alex was bursting with his yarn, drifting unconsciously from fact to fictionizing as he moved through it. Now he looked up, surprised.

"She told me herself," he said bluntly. "Wait! I'm coming to that. Her first impulse was to go back to her conservatory and blow it up. She was only one of a hundred dupes in this game. That was Cristème's game! Something told her to wait, the night would bring good counsel. She came home, next door to me, and to work off her nerves she sat down at her piano and began her dumb-bell exercises with her nose and throat. Have you ever heard those really advanced students putting on muscle? It's like a parrot cage."

"There is a woman who works on Caro Nome every day across the street," said Oliver, with an understanding smile.

"Well," continued Alex, "I had a job that day, writing a folder at a cent a word. When she began to shriek I went to her door and called her out. It was a matter of a month's rent to me. I said, 'Is there any particular reason—' and she cut in with, 'I am beginning to think not.' She knew who I was, of course. We'd gone up and down in the elevator together. She looked so lonely and woebegone, I told her if she'd rest her nose and throat till I got through I'd let her go to dinner with me around the corner, to the brewery. She said all right, if I'd let her pay for her own food.

"Half an hour later I called for her and we went around there. They sell near beer at that brewery. Do you know it? It has ether in it to make you feel stupid, and the crowd think they are getting the real thing. They line up six deep at the bar. Yes sir, a bar! Barnum was right. The food is good, though. We had pig's knuckles and sauerkraut and beer. The place was jammed and blue with tobacco smoke. Carriage trade, actors from Broadway—all of them come over to break the law and wonder why the joint isn't padlocked. You can get away with anything as long as you make it look illegal, in this town. … Does this interest you?" Alex asked solicitously.

"Proceed," said Oliver, smiling his vaguest smile.

"Well, along in the middle of the meal a fellow got up from another table and moved over to the end of our table. He nodded to me as if I were an old friend. I'd seen him somewhere, but didn't know where. Then he turned to my lady friend and said:

" 'Madam, could I speak with you a moment? I think you will be very much interested in what I have to say. Your escort will tell you who I am and assure you that I am all right!'

"I shook my head—couldn't place him. He said, 'Why, you sat in Morris Gest's office this afternoon when I came in, and he introduced us. Your name is Van—Van—Norden—Bulen. My name is Wylie.' "

"Wylie," said Oliver, sitting up at his desk and making cryptic lines with a pencil on a sheet of paper.

"Yes, Wylie. Do you know him? He is somebody, I believe," said Van Halen.

"No," said Oliver. "When was this? The date?"

"The last week in September, a Monday night. Well, this fellow Wylie pulled up a chair and sat down facing Lucena. His lips were close to her ear. He began to talk to her in an undertone. I don't know what he said. Her face never changed. It was lifeless. She'd been telling me about her day, and her eyes had that dead look. You know, that latest school of acting—utterly expressionless? Well, her stare was mostly fixed on the floor at the far end of the room. While he talked he examined her side face; his face was utterly blank. When he finally ceased speaking, there was a slight pause; then her eyes came slowly back to me, sitting there watching them on the other side of the table. Without lifting her voice out of a half whisper, she said to me crisply:

"'Don't wait for me. Leave my check.'"

Alex smiled, the corners of his sensitive mouth a trifle raised; he shrugged with that ineffable gesture of youth for a moment passed that could never be fully recalled or renewed.

"What would you have done?" the young man asked Oliver, an eager note in his voice.

"I would have left her check," said Oliver.

"I did," said Alex. "It wasn't exactly like abandoning her in a dive. There were a couple of hundred people sitting around, most of them wearing diamonds—people you know and I know by sight. I was a little hot," he admitted. He paused, thinking.

"What then?"

"Nothing."

"But you saw her again?" Oliver leaned forward.

"Oh, yes. But she never saw me. Just looked a hole through me. And shriek! How she did shriek!"

There was another pause. Then Oliver asked: "Where did you get your idea of repossession?"

"Oh, that was hers. Not in those words, but the idea. You see, it happened I picked her up when she was ready to boil over. She had to talk! She had to tell somebody. So she told me."

"What did Wylie want?" asked Oliver softly.

"The impression I got," cried the young man, "was just as if one of these lordly movie moguls had walked up to a woman in the street and said, 'Pardon me, but you are exactly the type I've been combing the world for. Will you accept ten thousand a week under my direction?'" Alex laughed awkwardly. "She was in that state of mind when a million a week wouldn't have stunned her. She didn't even look surprised. She only looked up and told me not to wait."

"And that is the end of your story?" asked Oliver, gently prodding.

"Oh, no! She stayed on for weeks. One night the lights went out suddenly. And she went out with them! Talk about a stone dropping into the void! There's never been a trace of her since." He stopped, regarding Oliver strangely. "Have you ever noticed," he asked, "how many people disappear after a catastrophe? It is as if they lay in wait for the chance to disappear. She left everything behind. A fuse blew or something, they said. At that moment she vanished. The police have been there. Not a trace! I think somebody blew that fuse so that she could walk off in the dark. That's the way I'm writing my story anyhow. Lucena repossesses herself!" he recited grandiloquently. "She steps into her new life! Funny thing," he said suddenly, "there is a suite on the other side of her which, they tell me, is rented by some rich commuter, who uses it to dress for dinner! Queer slants we get on life in this town! Several times, in going by that door, I thought I heard her voice. In Spanish! Someone was coaching her in Spanish. She was repeating proverbs. Spaniards have a way of making a proverb mean anything. You know how they can dress it up with a shrug. '*Gran sabor es comer y no escotar*,' quoted Alex, rolling his vowels and striking an attitude. "I was born on the Canal Zone. I know Spanish. My father was an engineer on the Canal. I don't know who that tenant was, but I am positive I heard her voice over the transom."

"Did you tell this to the police?" asked Oliver.

"Why should I?" replied Alex shortly.

Why should he, indeed? A wild impulse to believe the most incredible was beating against Armiston's brain. He slowly revolved in his swivel chair and absently took down a telephone—Parr's telephone; a private wire running to Parr's desk. Parr had it installed in this private study during the run of the insurance-widow case—a murder—and had carefully neglected to remove it since.

Oliver, looking straight at the puzzled Alex, talked in undecipherable riddles. He proposed—to some unnamed person who seemed to have been waiting for him on the other end of this wire—he proposed cables—cables, not castles—to Spain. And other incomprehensible things.

Of course, the ending—that Alex didn't see yet, so he couldn't write it—follows on. You can hear it coming. Mrs. Billy Wentworth is giving one of her exotic entertainments. The lights are dimming. For some time past you have been turning your head occasionally, conscious of a beat on the air. Six-eight time. Or is it five-eight, a broken lilt? It comes nearer, floats to the surface, emerges from the surrounding counterpoint, dominates the themes, is the theme itself—like the tramp of *Chu Chin Chow*, of the footstep on the stair in *Don Giovanni*. Then everything is hushed. The curtains part, and there stands Perez, her million-dollar back flat against a pilaster, and Mrs. Billy's moment of triumph is at hand. Perez doesn't move when she finds herself thus discovered; only turns her head slightly and stares at the audience, the eyes glowing somberly, with a red glint behind them, the corners of the painted mouth a little uptilted. There is a deathly silence, painful in its tensity.

Alex put his hand clumsily to his throat, pulled at his collar. Oliver shook his head slightly, not daring to take his eyes off Perez.

"Quiet! Quiet!" he warned in a whisper.

She took one step, put down a foot as supple as a swan's neck; she took another step, another, and another. Then the guitars began, pluck and strum. It was Perez!

This evening, at the Wentworth presentation, Perez danced four little numbers, the same dance but a different tempo each time, like La Svengali singing Mironton, Mirontaine. *Andantino; allegro appassionato; presto con fuoco;* and *vivace ma non troppo.*

"Could I slip back to her alone?" begged Oliver, the favored one. Mrs. Billy reconnoitered cautiously, smuggled him in. He came on Perez adjusting a fluff. She looked up at him, looked down again. She gave him her hand to kiss.

"Lucena! Lucena!" whispered Oliver over the ivory hand.

She said to her don, a handsome, bold fellow, with a little shrug and a spoiled smile:

"Quien lejos ra á casar, ó ra enganado ó ra á anganar."

"Si," agreed the don thoughtfully. *"Ó demo á os suyos quiere,"* he added darkly. The shade of a smile touched her lips, and she looked down demurely, smoothing her bodice with her two hands. She bowed to Oliver to acknowledge his compliments, gave him her hand again. Oliver bowed over it a second time. He whispered:

"We just wanted you to know that someone cared enough to make inquiries. Everything is all right."

The corners of her mouth tiptilted a little more than usual, her penciled eyes lengthened sleepily. The don watched narrowly as she murmured to Oliver:

"Si la locura fuese dolores, en cada casa darian roces."

Oliver laughed outright. He knew that proverb: If folly were a pain, there would be groaning in every house. She bowed to him and walked away, *vivace-ma non troppo!*

That was the end of it. Except that one afternoon Morel, Parr's silk-stocking satellite, picked up Wylie, the *entrepreneur* who imported foreign artists for private showings, and brought him downtown to his chief. Parr asked him how he was making out with Perez. The adroit Wylie waxed voluble. She was magnificent; had never been younger; the season was an immense success. Parr handed Wylie a cablegram; it was from Spain, and read:

"Perez still here. Has never been away. She has sold out her name and retired to her mountain home to grow herbs and brew tea for her rheumatism. She will dance no more."

Wylie said, as if in continuation of the cablegram:

"She welshed on me at the last minute! After all my contracts were made! I had to buy her out at her own price and put in a ringer. Fortunately," said the adroit Wylie, lifting one hand and gently swaying it from the wrist, *vivace ma non troppo*, "I was able to produce an artist die-cast for the part."

That gesture saved him. Parr had been about to question him severely as to the mysterious disappearance of Lucena Wirden, a young music student. Instead, he said gruffly:

"It will be all right this time. Don't do it again."

Thumbs Down

Parr, the police deputy, settled himself in his favorite elbow chair by Oliver Armiston's desk and selected a stogy from the cardboard box at his elbow. For some time he was lost in contemplation.

Finally he said, "You won't have seen the evening papers yet, Oliver?"

Oliver shook his head. It was not yet noon. He knew, of course, that morning papers are put to bed at ten the night before, and Sunday editions for the hinterland closed on a Thursday. Yet he never could reconcile himself to an evening that impinged on his breakfast. Parr lighted his stogy and drew several puffs; the best puffs, which, unlike the kisses of paradise, are not eternally renewed. He examined the book trough, finally lifted out a volume—a tall, fat dictionary that could stand alone on its own feet. He set it upright in front of Oliver.

"That is a telephone switchboard," he said. "You are the operator."

"Male or female?"

"Female."

Oliver regarded the *pro tem* switchboard.

"That's a very exacting role you are asking me to take on a moment's notice," said he. "Do you realize, Parr, the lady acquires a highly sophisticated mental habit? She is listening all day and all night! She accumulates scraps, fragments of picture puzzles. Did you ever think of that, Parr?"

"I'm thinking of it now," replied the deputy casually.

"Is this a hotel?" Oliver asked, a little anxiously.

"An apartment house—fifteen stories and penthouse."

"You overwork the penthouse motif. Thieves and murderers and suicides are like theatrical producers—that is, they are like sheep. If one makes a hit, they all make duplicates. Can't we vary the location?"

"This is a maisonette," said Parr.

"Ah! At last! I've been waiting for a maisonette—or a doctor's apartment with private entrance on the side street."

"This is on a corner," said Parr. "Three stories and basement, with high stoop."

"Basement?"

"And high stoop," said Parr. "Keep that in mind. It may take a trick. Any evening after the dishes are done, you can—could—go by there and see the butler, with his coat and shoes off, sitting in the basement window behind the bars, reading the sporting extra by the light of the street lamp."

"Why the street lamp?"

"To save electricity, of course," said the deputy, opening his eyes with great obviousness. "We come to that—there is an odd thread of thrift woven into the whole pattern. For instance, the apartment house itself takes city steam. Not so the maisonette. It is heated by an old-fashioned furnace, and the ice man comes over every morning to stoke the furnace and carry out the ashes."

"Incredible," said Oliver. "Where is this atrocity located?"

"Over by Kips Bay."

"I once knew a truck driver over there," mused Oliver. "He was an active member of one of the gas-house gangs. He told me it always had been a good neighborhood until the swells moved in and roughed it up."

"It's got worse since," said Parr, chuckling. "This house occupies the site of a building I know well. Many's the time we backed the wagon up there in the old days and moved out a whole houseful, from cellar to attic, and ferried the whole bunch over to the Island to cool off. It gave me quite a kick to go back there this morning. It's a swell joint now—the shine kind, with flunkies downstairs and foyer dinettes upstairs."

"But three stories and basement," protested Oliver.

"No shine about that," admitted Parr. "Back in the 80's there was a fellow named Red Gallagher—it's a good name over there yet. Well, this Gallagher went West. He promised his old mother when he came back he'd buy her the finest brownstone house in town. That was his idea of grandeur.

"Well, when he came back, six or seven years ago, there wasn't any mother—but there wasn't any brownstone either. So he bought an old house—many is the head he broke there in the good old days—and he built his own brownstone. Being a frugal soul, knowing well the cravings of capital for fixed charges, he had them build a fifteen-story apartment, with penthouse, around his brownstone to pay the ground rent. He sits out on the front stoop on sunshiny days, regretting, like your truck driver, the decadence of the neighborhood. The swells think he is a caretaker. They don't suspect that he is the dour old party who takes them to court when they don't pay their rent."

"You're not going to kill off old Gallagher just when he walks on the first time, are you, Parr?" pleaded Oliver Armiston.

"No, indeed. Gallagher and his old woman are making a cruise! Being thriftily inclined, as I say, he sublets to a young architect—not so young—an architect named Alexander Phiesan Whitter. Did you ever hear of that combination? No, I guess not. He made it up. He was born Jeremiah Cline—good old Irish Cline—he went to court to change his name. He designed this house and put it up—including the three-story-and-basement maisonette—for old Gallagher, and he knew a lot of things about it that old Gallagher didn't."

"Did he take over the old butler, in his stocking feet, and the other servants?" asked Oliver, fingering his white lock of hair. He was getting the picture very vividly, because he knew his town and its side streets and the people who lived in them.

Parr shook his head.

"No. Red Gallagher staked his servants to a trip to the Old Sod. Whitter moved in an outfit of his own, that slept out. That's part of the picture. Now," said Parr, clearing the desk at his elbow for more room as he glared ferociously at Oliver, "it is 1:10 A.M. Your switchboard is in the lobby behind a grille, to the right of the street door, and you can see everybody who comes and goes." He added as an aside: "It's the shank of the evening for this bunch. There is a certain type of woman who picks the hours from one to three for any rough stuff she has on hand." Parr snapped his fingers for action, camera. Again: "It's 1:10 A.M., Oliver," he said sharply. "You get a flash on the board from Maisonette A. Now let me see you do your stuff."

Parr leaned back in his chair, eying Oliver. He was wholly in earnest.

Oliver put aside a hypothetical book he was reading, glanced at the hypothetical switchboard, and noting the location of the hypothetical lamp that burst into a hypothetical glow, he exclaimed in the voice of a blasé telephone girl:

"Well, look who's getting as common as dirt!"

Some hypothetical person standing by seemed to express curiosity.

Oliver said airily: "Mr. T. Square, who sublets the gold-filling suite on the corner of the house. Hasn't he got a wire of his own, that he's got to wake me up?"

"Eh?" muttered Parr. He sat up as if shot. "Eh? What's that?"

"I ask you why," said the hypothetical telephone girl. "He certainly has a nerve. He's got a telephone trunk of his own, hasn't he? Why put a call through the house mains? Not to save time, surely. To make the call more difficult to trace? Possibly. But I think not. The girl keeps a record of every call—or is supposed to. Why, then? Not to avoid notice, surely. To attract it, I should say, on a guess. Whoever is calling wants to establish the fact that he—or she—is there, in the maisonette, at this hour. See, the girl puts it down automatically on her call chart as she takes the call— Pardon me, he's getting impatient." Oliver explained to Parr, aside: "The light is flashing on and off."

"Is it?" cried Parr.

"Isn't it?" demanded Oliver.

"Maybe, but how do you know?"

"Simply by using the intelligence the good Lord gave us telephone girls," cried Oliver. "It's of a superior order, I don't mind telling you."

"Wait a minute," said Parr. He took down his own phone—a private wire to his desk which he maintained here at Armiston's study at all times. He lifted off the receiver and began talking into a waiting car:

"Was he in the habit of using the house phone, Morel? Go through the chart and see how many calls he put through by the switchboard since he has been there. Then look up his calls over his own wire. And here's something else—ask the girl if the lamp merely came on and stayed on, or did he prod it to hurry her. And, Morel, will you please tell me why we didn't ask these elementary questions ourselves, without waiting to have them spelled out for us?" He hung up. "Proceed," he said tartly.

"Number, please?" inquired Oliver gracefully. He waited, eying the board malevolently. "Number?" He prodded viciously with a hypothetical telephone plug. No answer. He leaned back in his chair, resumed his paper novel.

"They haven't hung up yet," said Parr sharply.

Oliver nodded.

"It's alive, isn't it?"

Oliver fixed his mind on the other man; both listened intently.

"Do you hear anything?" whispered Parr.

"Not a sound."

"Do you hear anyone breathing? Or footsteps?" Parr bent over. "You didn't hear anything that sounded like a shot, did you?" he asked.

"Nothing at all."

"Maybe the receiver fell off the hook," suggested the man hunter.

"And then picked itself up and prodded? No. Someone lifted it off. For a purpose." Lowering his voice, Armiston went on: "This happens frequently—I mean, the light comes on and stays on, and no answer. Usually the householder finds the receiver off the hook and puts it back on. Sometimes they have to send around a man. They can't put in a call from the outside until it's fixed. ... What happens now, Parr?"

"Well, an hour passes," said the deputy. "The light is still on. The assistant manager—an ex-hotel clerk—quite a gadabout, comes home. They tell him about it." Parr took the dictionary and restored it to its place, to conclude the séance. "His name is Troy." Parr told what happened:

" 'Somebody's there. They are having a party. I think,' said Troy. 'The whole house was lighted up from cellar to garret—it was just now, when I came by.'

" 'It's been lighted up all evening,' said the door opener.

" 'Has there been any company?' asked Troy.

" 'I've been busy on this side,' said the door opener.

" 'You'd better run around and tell them,' said Troy. 'We might want to put a call through, ourselves.'

"The door opener came back almost at once."

Parr and Oliver looked at each other.

" 'Funny thing,' the door opener whispered; 'the street door is on the latch.' They stared at him. He added, goaded on by their silence: 'The house is empty!'

" 'Did you go in?' asked Troy.

" 'I did not. I looked in. I listened. I—I wouldn't go in there alone for—for a million dollars.'

" 'What's that on your thumb?'—it was Troy's sharp query.

"The telephone girl shrieked—one of those ghastly, helpless shrieks of a woman suddenly gripped by horror. The door opener was staring at his thumb.

" 'The door knob—it was wet!' he was gasping.

" 'Call the cop on post,' ordered Troy. 'No, wait.' He took up the telephone. 'I want the police,' he said. To the first voice he heard, he was saying: 'We've got a telephone off the hook up here that looks bad'—and they switched him to the Homicide Bureau. He was saying to a tired voice that made a living out of this sort of thing: 'We've got an unlocked street door with blood on the knob,' when at that instant the switchboard lamp, at which they were all staring as if it held some strange hypnotical power, went out. Someone in Maisonette A had restored the receiver to the hook."

Parr smiled rather grimly. "We were there in three minutes," he said. "Morel happened to be at Fifty-first Street."

"And your dead man?" invited Armiston.

"Dead woman," said Parr dully. "Shot through the head. Powder marks on the skull."

He was eying Oliver sharply. It was his method, in consulting his highly sensitive oracle, to pay out his rope of facts inch by inch, never giving any slack. The idea was to avoid blurring any images that might be forming, and to avoid a double exposure, so to speak.

"Oh, not Aleck?" cried Oliver.

"Not quite," said Parr. "We found Aleck with his head bashed in, unconscious, in a closet in the same room. The door was locked on the outside, and the key was in the lock." There was an almost imperceptible pause. "We've got him in Bellevue Hospital. I think he will pull through."

"It would be a tough break for Aleck if he didn't, with an alibi like that," remarked Oliver. "Who was the woman?"

"We don't know," admitted Parr, frowning. "We found a name—Flora Kinsel—with an address in East Fiftieth Street, printed in indelible ink on the inside of her pocketbook. We found a Flora Kinsel at that address. It was not her pocketbook. She never owned one with her name in it. And she never heard of these people. Odd about some dead people," mused the deputy. "They borrow apartments for murder or suicide—and frequently are very exacting about it. I don't see any reason why they shouldn't occasionally borrow somebody's name."

There was a long silence. Parr had a great deal more to tell, but he hoped, if he went slow, Oliver would probably tell it to him from an entirely new viewpoint. Oliver sat up in his chair and made an imaginary design with the tip of a finger on a pad; he pushed the pad aside.

"Parr, if I were writing this story," said the extinct author, "I'd find her finger prints on the key turning the lock of that closet door; on the knob of the street door; on the blackjack that bashed Aleck; on the gun that was pressed so close to her skull when the trigger was pulled; and on the telephone receiver that was lifted off the hook to summon help."

"We've done that," admitted Parr casually. "Oliver, just when did she lift that receiver off the hook to summon help?"

"Not before she was shot," said Armiston. "Your telephone girl would have heard the shot. Even with a so-called silencer, it would have been heard. And she didn't lift it off after she was shot. She was dead then; she didn't need help. It was the man in the closet who needed help. He didn't want to be left to bleed to death after going to all that trouble."

The police deputy relit his stogy, drew a few more puffs preliminary to abandoning it for good.

"That is substantially our case," he admitted—"that is, gliding gracefully over a few insurmountable obstacles. I have been given to understand that there are such things as forged finger prints. I have never seen one to pass inspection."

"These won't be forged," said Oliver. "They are hers."

Parr gave Armiston a shy, hurt look.

"Sometimes it occurs to me, Parr," mused Oliver, opening a desk drawer and taking out a lacquer snuffbox, "that you share, with many other truly great men, a positive genius in selecting lieutenants. You couldn't have done a cleverer thing this morning than coming here and selecting me as your telephone girl."

Parr gave him a short look and winked secretly at the old bronze Buddha toasting his shins at the fire.

"Let me have your watch," directed Oliver. "First, be sure the crystal contains no incriminating finger prints."

The deputy, smiling, polished the crystal of his watch with his handkerchief; not until he satisfied himself it was perfectly clean did he pass the watch to Oliver.

"Whose finger prints would you like to find here?" asked Oliver, with a vast air of legerdemain.

"Mine," said Parr blandly.

"Elementary, Watson," said Oliver, chuckling. "Lest you gather the wrong idea, I confess I have your print here, Parr." He took several pellicles of what appeared to be sheet gelatin, about the size of postage stamps, from the snuff box, and with the aid of a magnifying glass selected one. "This is it," he said. "Watch me." He breathed lightly on the pellicle and pressed it gently on the watch crystal for a moment, and passed the watch to Parr. Parr studied it with the glass. He nodded.

"Is there any reason why I couldn't leave that print on a gun, or a black-jack, or a telephone receiver?" demanded Armiston.

"It's a perfect forgery," admitted the deputy.

"It is not a forgery," protested Oliver. "It is your finger print. That is, it is a photographic reproduction of your finger print, printed on bichromatized gelatin, so that the image stands out in relief and accepts ink like a litho-graph. In fact, it is the basis of an old method of printing that antedates the photogravure. First get the finger print. Then photograph it. You left yours on a drinking glass the other day. I must confess I have been stalking you for weeks. I never realised, before I started stalking, how few finger prints are readable—most of them are merely smears. I suppose all of hers were perfectly readable?"

Parr took down his phone.

"Is Ferrault there, Morel?" he asked. "Ask him how good those prints are. Are they suspiciously good, Morel?"

"Very good," reported Morel a moment later. In an aside, Morel said, "It seems to annoy him, to find how good they are. He is taking another look."

"Ask him what fingers he got," directed Oliver.

"The right thumb in every instance," came the answer.

"Not a very versatile fellow—this Aleck," mused Oliver.

Ferrault had taken over the phone at the other end. He was talking fast. Evidently, being a true scientist, he was further qualifying some previous statements. He made such free use of subjunctives and semicolons that the deputy, winking at Oliver, said soothingly, "All right—all right. I'll come right over," and hung up.

Parr smiled pleasantly to himself. He had a trained troupe of scientificos of whom he was inordinately proud; with their test tubes and microscopes and X rays, there was no wall too dense for them to see through. But they were as temperamental as a cageful of prima donnas.

"This fellow is annoyed with himself," said Parr. "On second look, it appears that all these prints are upside down. The lady must have been hanging from a chandelier to make them."

"Beautiful!" ejaculated Armiston. He sprang to his feet, seized his hat and coat, pushed Parr ahead of him. At the last minute he ran back for his snuff box.

They found a taxi around the first corner, shining its brasses and enjoying a quiet smoke. And it seemed perfectly in accord with what one knew of the deputy to discover that it belonged to him. When they got in, it made off at a great rate, knowing just where to go. They passed through that down-at-heels section, of many children playing in the street, known derisively as the Near East, which interposes itself between the more elegant portions of midtown and that slowly spreading film of culture, refinement and high rents that is taking possession of the old gas house neighborhood along the river.

"Architects use bichromate for blue prints," said Oliver. "Remember our syllabus on vocational tools of murder, Parr? We had a dark-room operator using cyanide in a unique way. We had a polo player bashing a head accidentally with a mallet. We had a great swimmer luring his victim out beyond his depth. Every man makes use of the tool with which he is most familiar. Here we have an architect—"

"Using a blue print," said Parr dryly.

"You anticipate me."

"Do I indeed?"

"Parr, we have a great many estimates—mostly by public-spirited reformers who do not like you—of how many murders go undetected. Have you ever seen a reliable estimate on how many murders go uncommitted?"

"Now, there is something for the parlor penologists," exclaimed the deputy, with mock enthusiasm.

"Uncommitted for lack of opportunity," pursued Oliver. "Some prospective murderers are capable of calm deliberation, high police opinion to the contrary notwithstanding."

"Yes, but somewhere along the line he looks back and begins to hurry," said Parr. "There is something about the mere decision to murder that stampedes him, drives him on helplessly to the act itself. The more he deliberates, the more mistakes he makes. That is why premeditated killings are usually easy to solve. Whereas crimes of sudden passion may baffle us. This fellow is clever, Oliver. He plants it as a crime of passion—a woman, coming secretly by night and striking him down, then killing herself. Even the lifting of the phone off the hook is clever—and unlocking the street door—women have a horror of lying undiscovered."

"Did she put the phone back on the hook an hour later?"

"I admit that annoys me," said Parr, scowling.

"You say this architect used a blue print for a lethal weapon, Parr. That is a very profound thought, and opens a new vista. … Parr," cried Oliver, "Aleck built that house! Aleck superintended the construction! Aleck was there morning, noon and night! Have you ever watched those fellows? They snoop around noons, when the mechanics are at dinner. Parr, if Aleck wanted to use that house for murder, to provide himself a get-away, is there anything in the way of a loose brick or a hollow wall that he could not have planted?"

"We have gone over every inch of that closet—if that's what you are driving at—floor, walls, ceiling."

"Aleck was a protégé of the old man," pursued Oliver. "Was it Aleck who maneuvered this world tour for old Gallagher, so he could move himself in and get his job of murder done?"

They drew up at the maisonette. Though there was a high stoop and a basement area-way for old time's sake, the façade itself was integral with the skyscraper. A curious crowd stood staring fixedly at the place, as if the mere fact of tragedy had in some subtle way changed the brick and mortar into something strange and horrible. Morel came down the steps and opened the door.

"Get in," said Parr shortly. The dapper Morel drew out the jumper seat and, fastidiously disposing of his coat tails, sat down facing them. "Is there a connection, on any landing, to the apartment itself, so that anyone could enter without passing through the street?"

"No, sir, but the plans show break-out spots in the walls on every floor, so doors could be put in easily," said Morel.

"Morel," said Parr, "consider this: He brought her here to kill her. He had everything ready for his own get-away. Remember, he built this house himself. That implies preparation over a long period of time—years. What does that suggest to you?"

"A wife," said Morel, without hesitation. "A woman long since abandoned, who must be rubbed out before he can put into effect some long-cherished plan."

"That fits your hypothesis, Oliver," commented Parr. "And what is this long-cherished plan, Morel?"

"An ambitious marriage," said Morel, concealing a surge of elation. This was a moment of triumph, but he took no credit to himself; it was Parr's trick of putting a question, at a certain stage in the game that implied its own answer. Morel stared out of the window, signaled absently to a man in the street to push back the crowd that was edging nearer. He looked at his two companions. "Odd," he said, "how everything begins to dovetail when the break finally comes!"

"Well?" said Parr impatiently.

"There was a girl—a very self-possessed young lady—here about an hour ago," said Morel. "She thinks she should have him removed from Bellevue to a private hospital. She thinks he will get better care with his own doctors. Her name is Shannon. She is Red Gallagher's niece. There's your ambitious marriage."

"Well," said Parr, "I'm afraid Aleck will have to content himself where he is until he decides to come out of his coma. I want a talkie movie of Aleck when he comes to. I have an idea he is rehearsing his lines right now. After that, we will let her have him. I want him very confident, sure of himself, before I surprise him. Morel, your job is to trace that early marriage. Probably under the name Cline. Drop everything else."

They got down and went in.

II

One afternoon late in March, some weeks after the opening of the maisonette murder—which enjoyed a run of a week on the front page and then, like a new play that failed to click, was folded up and carried to the storehouse—Parr's taxi, after its usual maneuver to shake off spies, turned into Oliver's quiet side street, and pausing at the curb to deposit Mr. Parr, started off again for new customers but pulled up around the first corner for a quiet smoke. Parr glanced up and down the street. It was his fond hope and belief that this hideout of his was unsuspected by the criminal classes who studied him and exchanged information concerning his interesting habits among themselves, much as if he were a rare bug and they entomologists. In the street now there was only a street sweeper hopefully waiting for a wind to blow some litter his way, and a nurse girl in a white cap with blue streamers and cape, *tout entièrement français*, riding herd on a rich underprivileged child that played lugubriously with some toys on the sidewalk. The coast being clear, Parr punched the bell, successfully got by the scowls of Oliver's housekeeper—who had her own ideas about policemen wishing themselves and their nefarious goings-on on honest folk—and entered Armiston's study. He nodded curtly to Oliver, took his usual chair and selected a stogy. Then he said:

"I saw a friend of yours driving in the Park just now. Aleck! Yes, first time out. I think Aleck put more English on that celebrated forehand stroke of his than he realized. I was afraid, for a time, that he was going to pass out."

He lifted his head, listening. The doorbell was ringing. The housekeeper was opening the street door; there was a mumble of voices, then silence. The housekeeper entered with a card.

"Maureen Shannon," Oliver read.

Parr considered this, drumming the desk; finally he nodded.

"All right. Let's see what she's got," he said.

It was the nurse girl with the blue streamers. As the study door opened, she was offering the child to the housekeeper. It seemed quite the usual thing for this child to be left with servants, for it suffered itself to be led away without surprise or protest. The nurse girl closed the door and stood facing the two men who had risen.

"I borrowed the dear little thing and this costume to come here today," she said. And then, fixing her Irish-gray eyes on Parr, she asked with an odd directness:

"Are your men shadowing me?"

"No," said Parr.

This gave her pause, but she was not convinced.

"Are you sure?" she cried.

"Perfectly," said Parr. To Oliver's surprise, Parr took down his phone and spoke into it. "Back-track her when she leaves here," he said. "They are getting a report on her."

She sank into a chair Oliver put out for her, and they sat down.

"Oh, you don't know how good it is to be here! I've hardly dared think my own thoughts for weeks," she murmured. "It is about my uncle. I have been trying for days to reach him." She paused, and they waited—a trick of Parr's that Oliver had picked up—and she began to speak again: "I think my mail is being opened. I must get word to my uncle. He will be home almost any time now. He must not enter that house without being warned."

"We have already warned him," said Parr, smiling. "Being a Gallagher from the gas-house district, his idea was to come running. But I think we have persuaded him to let us handle it." He lowered his voice. "What have you found?" he asked.

She said, in a tone scarcely above a whisper: "I have been getting the house ready for him. The lights have been changed in my uncle's bathroom. I had an electrician look at them. He was very much surprised. He said they were connected to the 'high' side—the 'high' side of something in the street—whatever that meant. ... Oh, I had to see you! There is no one I could talk to. What did he mean by 'high'? The word terrified me! What with that closet door—"

"Oh, you did know about the door, did you?" muttered Parr, eying Oliver.

"I saw that it opened inwards," she said. "I don't think I had ever seen a closet door open inwards like that one. I saw he could lift the door out of the frame from the inside by taking out the hinge pins."

Parr said, in his hypnotic undertone: "Was that your first suspicion?"

She pondered her answer, gazing moodily at the fire.

"I don't know," she said finally. "Now that I look back, in the light of what has happened, it seems there was always a suspicion in my mind. Nothing tangible—just a woman's feeling about it. It's—it's rather difficult to put in words. You know he expected to marry me. Do you know that?" she asked with her swift directness. Parr nodded. "He hadn't spoken yet. I don't know what I would have said to him. I suppose it would have been yes. My uncle, I think, counted on it; he was very fond of Aleck, and wanted to see me settled."

She paused again, watching the fire absently.

She said, with a wan smile: "There was something charming about Aleck. Uncle depended on his judgment in many things. It was always good. And apparently disinterested. Aleck had almost a child's sense of right and wrong—which is pretty likely to be a true one. It seems incredible he could plot evil."

"And yet you always suspected him," said Parr.

"Yes," she said. "I had a feeling he was holding himself back all the time. Maybe it was caution—he was afraid to lose everything by being too precipitate." She looked full at Parr. "Do you really believe he plotted to murder my uncle?" she asked.

"If your uncle had stepped into the shower room in his bare feet and reached up to turn on the light, he would have been electrocuted—like that!" Parr snapped his fingers. "Twenty-two hundred volts. That's a fatal dose. Very cleverly done, too—it would have looked like another leaky transformer shorting to ground."

She rested her chin in the palm of her hand and regarded him thoughtfully.

"That was his wife he murdered, wasn't it?" she asked, with that startling directness again. Oliver had never seen Parr subject himself to question before, and he was keenly enjoying the spectacle.

"What makes you think so?" asked the deputy.

She smiled vaguely. "Nothing else fits," she said. She shot another question at his head: "Have you found out who she is yet?"

"No," admitted Parr. He was watching her closely.

"Would you think it presumptuous if I made a suggestion?" she asked.

"Help yourself," said Parr.

"We have been terribly poor," she said earnestly. "When my mother was alive, just before uncle came back, we were wretched. I know the shifts the poor are put to, to save their miserable pennies barely to keep alive. They are forever moving from place to place, running away from their little debts. Obscure?" she cried; she laughed bitterly. "There is nothing obscure about poverty. Try to flee from it! The trail clings like the trail of a cuttlefish. There is no one easier to trace than a poor family. Aleck was poor before uncle picked him up," she added. "Do you follow me?"

Parr shook his head. "Proceed," he said.

"Take a gas bill—two or three dollars," she said, tapping the desk. "We've got to have gas, or starve. We're always slipping away, leaving gas bills over and above the deposit. We apply for gas in the next place, changing our name slightly, thinking they can't trace us. But one day someone knocks on the door, or comes in without knocking, more like. And there's the collector, come for the old bill! Oh, they have reduced it to a science! Now you follow! That was our life. That was Aleck's life, too, I guess." She leaned forward, her eyes holding Parr. "Mr. Commissioner, could you get me a job in the gas-company office as clerk?" She was suddenly breathless. "Some of those records must be in existence yet! ... Leave it to me! I know my East Side! Get me the job! We'll find out where he lived, and how."

Parr took down his trusty phone. It was like the magic lamp; he could summon whomever he wished through it. This time, after a few preliminary passes, he got the ear of a personage whom he called George—there was no doubt about its being a personage.

Parr said: "George, I want to put a girl in your accounting department, where she can have access to the records of unpaid bills and forfeited deposits. Her name will be—her name will be Katie McGovern. She will be a mahogany brunette. And she will call on you at nine o'clock in the morning. Thank you. I'll say a good word for you in court some day."

He put up the phone and faced the young woman sternly.

"Were there ever any cops in your family?" he demanded.

"My father was a cop; he was in Eldridge Street for twenty-two years."

"Not the mick on post in front of the Tub?" ejaculated Parr.

"The same," she said.

"I was thinking you talked our language!" exclaimed the deputy. "First, tell me this—did anyone follow you here today?" He scowled at her with the utmost ferocity.

"I lost them," she said, smiling. "I lost them in the Roosevelt. Then I picked up my child and uniform, and came here to wait for you."

"Is there any reason why you should go back home?" asked Parr. "I want you to put on a disappearance act, child. Get the idea? Return your child and vanish. ... Here! Get an eyeful of that street cleaner out there!" Parr pointed out through the window. "His name is Pelts. He'll always be in reach. Do everything he tells you. If you want to tell him anything, write it on an old envelope and toss it in his garbage can." Parr eyed her speculatively. "Have you got the nerve?"

Her eyes blazed. "I've had the nerve to face your Aleck every day," she told him. "Nothing you can think up now will worry me."

"You'd better get a cheap suit, and a hall room somewhere in the East Twenties. Want any money? With your uncle away, who will miss you?" he asked. "Who is apt to ask the police to send out an alarm?"

"Nobody but Aleck," she said rather pathetically.

She took out her vanity case and retouched such purely hypothetical damage as had marred her beauty during the interview. A tear or two may have escaped at some point in the ordeal, thought Oliver, studying her as she searched her own countenance in the tiny mirror. She arose, adjusting her nurse's garb, and calling for her child, took her departure.

Oliver's first reaction to Alexander Phiesan Whitter was that his topcoat was too loose at the shoulders and too tight at the hips. Certainly he could not have sat down in it without unbuttoning it. Odd, he thought, what insignificant trifles one selects to hang a prejudice on. Aleck had an unquestionable distinction in manner and appearance. His neck may have been a shade too round, his hair too well-behaved, but the devil had undoubtedly made this disciple glamorous to both men and women.

"I know who you are now!" said Aleck, taking off his gloves to shake hands. "I see you at concerts, recitals and first nights. I have heard it said there is a dependable phalanx of ten thousand souls who may be counted on, month in and month out, to support music—with students to fill in the dry spots. I believe I could cut the number down below that. I think I know everybody by sight downstairs. You always sit on the left side of the house, wherever you go. That might fit into one of the mystery stories you used to write."

He finally got his glove off the right hand and offered it—the hand—to Oliver. Oliver thought, when he took it, of the words he had heard the Shannon girl speak, when Parr asked her if she had the nerve: "I've faced your Aleck every day!" she had retorted. Oliver took the hand without qualms, smiling to himself.

"I wonder why the commissioner asked me to meet him here, instead of downtown," said Aleck, getting out of his coat and placing it carefully across a chair.

"I thought it was you who called him," said Oliver.

"It was. I called him for an appointment. Why didn't he let me go downtown?"

"He is a great man," said Oliver, shaking his head. "Never ask him why. He always has a reason, but it is for his own use. You were sending out a confidential alarm, weren't you?"

There may have been the barest pause.

"Yes," Aleck replied.

"Is there any reason why he shouldn't want you to be seen entering headquarters—seen by the reporters, I mean?" went on Oliver smoothly. "You know no one gets in or out down there without being spotted."

The telephone rang—not Parr's, but Oliver's.

"Hello!" said Oliver.

"I've got an idea," said Parr. "How would you like to extort a confession from the murderer?"

"Oh, I say!" cried Oliver, in a panic.

"He thinks he is your sort," said Parr glibly. "He has been trying to kid himself that he is a first-nighter. Did you shake hands with him?"

"Yes," admitted Oliver.

"Good! Could you—could you accidentally—if I am delayed and you have to stall for me—could you accidentally show him your fingerprint collection? Explain some of the pitfalls for prospective murderers. I'll call up a little later. Oh, by the way, he is not armed. We frisked him, without his being aware, on the street car coming over. Have you got that gun of yours in your table drawer?"

Oliver, who had regained some of his sang-froid, laughed, and said: "Yes. But I've never used it, except in a gallery."

"Is it loaded?"

"No. I keep it for moral effect."

"Let him see it quite casually," instructed Parr. "Let him gradually edge over within reach of it. We won't be far. ... Ta-ta!"

"Wait! Wait!" cried Armiston, prodding at the phone.

But the deputy had withdrawn beyond reach.

Oliver had frequently been in attendance with Parr or Morel when a murderer was brought to the point of confession. But he had never been pushed on the stage alone before. He sat down, frowning. He was quite conscious of the cold scrutiny of his visitor.

Aleck leaned forward.

"Was that by any chance the commissioner himself?"

Oliver nodded. He said absently, "He is delayed; he will be along directly," and he lifted his gaze to Aleck with the air of mild surprise, as though seeing the man for the first time in some strange new light. He continued to look at him for so long a time that Aleck, finding himself growing uncomfortable, resorted to the first refuge of the motion-picture actor in a situation that requires acting. He took out his gold cigarette case, selected a cigarette with finical care, closed the case and put it away; it was quite a ceremony. He tailored the cigarette to his liking, he busheled it and tamped it elegantly on the edge of Oliver's desk. By the time he came to lighting it, he had outgrown his uncomfortable feeling. He looked inquiringly at Armiston. Drawing a puff and exhaling it, he said:

"After Stokowski's little foreword the other day, I found one or two spots in Stravinsky that I could listen to without ear muffs."

Oliver said absently, "Is this—is this confidential alarm for the Shannon girl?"

Aleck's scalp lifted all but imperceptibly, as if he had suddenly shut his jaws together.

"Oh, you know about that!" he said.

Oliver smiled vaguely. "We knew about it before it was confidential," he said quietly. Now he avoided looking directly at Aleck Whitter, as one avoids looking directly at an animal in the first stages of training. He ran on quickly: "Set your mind at rest. Maureen is not missing. She is missing only for the benefit of the murderer. Parr has her up his sleeve. He will produce her at the psychological moment."

Oliver reached over and drew open the middle drawer of his desk, revealing inside two objects, one a glittering revolver, and the other the Chinese-lacquer snuffbox. He took out the snuffbox, leaving the drawer open.

"When you know Parr as well as I do—as I hope you will some day—you will understand why no murderer who deliberates can escape him. Murder of passion, yes. That might—in fact, frequently does—elude him for the time being." He paused. "Because there is no residue," he added. "But in a deliberate murder, the more the murderer deliberates, the more tracks he leaves—if you get me?"

Oliver lifted his gaze for the fraction of a second.

"Don't let the idea of time bother you," he said. "Time is always on the side of the police—against the fugitive. It lulls him; he relaxes his vigilance in spite of himself—the fugitive, I mean. Even terror can be made commonplace by time. Parr uses time scientifically. If you will take the pains to understand that, you won't grow impatient over this maisonette murder.". Oliver paused on the word and softly pried up the lid of the snuffbox. He emptied the contents on the table—a dozen yellow pellicles of sheet gelatin made limp by some process. He examined them under a magnifying glass, and selecting one, he passed it to Aleck, holding it high.

"What do you make of that?" he asked. "Take it. Look at it under the glass."

He counted ten by the clock before Aleck's dull voice muttered, "Is it a thumb print?"

"Yes, a thumb print. My right thumb. Some of us know a great deal about fingerprints. Some of us only think we do. That is my right thumb. An exact duplicate, made by a photographic process."

He inked the pellicle of gelatin on an ink pad and made an impression of it on a sheet of hard paper.

"If you don't believe that is a print of my right thumb," said Oliver, apparently enchanted with the plaything, "look at this." He tamped his right thumb on the pad and made a print of it alongside the other, for comparison.

Aleck studied the two prints for a long time—for so long a time that Oliver looked at him and saw that for the moment, though he seemed to be staring at the prints, his eyes were tight shut.

"You see what I am driving at," urged Armiston quietly.

"Yes—oh, yes. Very clever, I say!"

"You don't see at all," said Oliver reprovingly. "You know this one is the print of my right thumb, because you saw me make it. You know the other is a print of my right thumb, because I tell you it is. You take my word for it. Look again, more sharply. Don't you see, they are identical—but reversed!"

As though on impulse, Oliver suddenly seized Aleck's arm, and Aleck shrank back, his eyes staring wildly.

Oliver did not appear to notice it. He went on rapidly:

"Note the lines in the knee of the curve below the main vortex. One points to the right, the other to the left. Those lines always point inward on every hand. On the right hand they point to the left; on the left hand, to the right."

Aleck rested his elbow on the desk and shaded his eyes with his hand. He said, drawing a deep breath:

"I think—I think maybe I'm stupid. I don't follow."

"In the maisonette murder," said Oliver, tapping out the words meticulously, "they found good prints of the woman's thumb at every single critical point in the layout. Pause a moment to see how dumb that was. In the first place, it was always her right thumb. Odd, that out of ten possible finger tips, that was the only one which registered. Point No. 2: The prints were found only at the critical points—on the telephone, the key, the door knob, the gun, the blackjack. Wouldn't you think any moron would have been versatile enough to let her touch something else, just to keep within the bounds of chance? These two slips alone are enough to hang him," ran on Oliver.

Aleck was staring dully at the fire.

"Aleck," cried Armiston abruptly, and he felt the man start violently at the word, "there is no possible way a human being could have left those fingerprints! Every print was reversed, upside down—like this one!" He jabbed the impression of the gelatin pellicle with his finger. "Even if she had hung from a chandelier, if she had stood on her head, she could not have left those finger prints on the scene of the murder. They were not made by her finger tips! They were made by a photographic reproduction of her finger print—like this one! They are not the same. One is always the negative of the other. It's the difference between print and type. This consummate idiot never saw that he reversed the prints in the process of photography. She couldn't have left them. ... Here; try it yourself!"

As if actuated by sudden thought, Oliver seized the bright and shining revolver, and buffed it swiftly with a silk handkerchief to remove any possible marks.

"Here! Try it on this!" he cried, and he thrust the weapon toward the staring Aleck. Oliver sprang to his feet. He paced down the room, listening with all his ears. At the far end of the room he stopped before his radio and turned it on and pretended to listen for a moment. Then he turned it off again and sauntered back to his chair and sat down. Aleck sat staring at the carpet. He had broken open the revolver. Conscious of Oliver's gaze, he held the empty chambers up to the light and laid the weapon gently on the blotter.

"I supposed it would be stretching your hospitality too much for me to hope for one shell," he remarked sardonically.

One of those unfathomable pauses intervened. Finally Aleck looked up.

"I get it now," he said slowly. "To get a clearer print, I photographed her finger print instead of her finger tip itself. That's when I reversed the image." The vanity of the artist asserted itself. "Who noticed it? Parr's man?"

"With my assistance," replied Oliver.

Aleck turned on Oliver stolidly, saying, "I didn't know you were in the business."

"I dabble," said Oliver. He turned his head. "We have company." He went to the door and held it open. Maureen Shannon and little Pelts came in. Pelts was strangely clean, for him, and tidy, as if, in the springtime, his fancies stirred.

"Why, Aleck; I didn't know you were here," said Maureen. Still playing her part, she went to him, offered her hand. Aleck got up. A tall, graceful fellow, Oliver thought, with a strange tinge of envy, as he watched the scene. Whitter took the proffered hand and held it for a moment without a word.

"No use keeping it up," he said as he relinquished it. "I seem to have left residues all over the place." His eyes strayed but came back to her. "Where have you been, kid?" he asked.

"Down in Grove Street, Aleck; looking for this," said the girl. She opened her pocketbook and took out a slip of paper and gave to him. "That's a copy of your marriage certificate. I found it in the rectory of the old church down there. I traced you, through an old gas bill and a deposit slip you indorsed."

He looked casually at the paper and gave it back to her.

"I've been running out on gas bills all my life," he said. "There was all that money to be had for the taking. I'll give you a tip, kid. Look in your room— that is, the blue room on the third floor, with the porcelain bath. Eventually you were going to occupy that room as the mistress of the house. Have the electric wiring looked after. ... Ah! Here comes the commissioner! I expect I will get better acquainted with him now—that's a fact, Armiston."

He sat down and was studying the reversed fingerprint when Parr entered. Parr looked sharply at him, and then at Oliver. Oliver nodded.

"Take him away," Parr ordered. At the clink of the shackles, Aleck looked up. Two men stood beside him.

"Coming," he said, and held up his hands.

The Two Martimos

I T was raining—gently, pervasively, economically—as if, having long since achieved utter saturation, it now contented itself merely to hold the dew point and make no gain. The road, a one-horse road, picked its way down a hill, really a mountainside; here and there it side-stepped with shuddering abruptness a fall into eternity; now and again an aged water bar would rise up and wipe the wishbone with an awful crunch that localized itself in the pit of the stomach. The ancient flivver, one of the original fifteen million, an indispensable part of the tackle for this trip, cost Oliver thirty-five dollars as is at the railhead, and was acquitting itself beautifully, having been brought up on this sort of thing. If one must have hothouse trout that rose wantonly for Coachman or Professor, it was necessary to suffer. It was required to penetrate beyond the uttermost limits of the week-end carriage trade. This was it. This thoroughfare, so-called had been especially engineered for planetary transmissions. Anything more advanced in design left its engine pan and tie rods five miles back, and retreated on foot.

Eventually, with smoking reverse, the flivver reached the foot of the hill. It entered a sea of bean-soup mud, panting. Then the myopic headlamps, that waxed and waned like a firefly on a hot summer night, suddenly burst into an almost incinerating state of bedazzlement as the little high-vaulted cohippus unexpectedly climbed out of the mire onto a flat rock and halted trembling at the very brink of a non-fordable flood. It was a native creek, out of bounds. The top rail of the fence was just going under.

Inured as they were to week-end hardships, Armiston and his companion, Parr, the police deputy, settled themselves deeper in the soppy folds of their oozing horse blankets, prepared to watch out the night; they were sustained and soothed by a sort of hair-shirt ecstasy to be achieved only by chronic fishermen in the barbless-hook stage of the disease. The frugal Oliver turned off the ignition to save gas, and later he turned off the lights to save the battery. Still later, sometime after three in the morning, Parr aroused Oliver with a gentle nudge and muttered lugubriously that they were about to have company.

Without doubt, someone approached. Having heard that sound once, one could never mistake it. It was a patient tin lizzie methodically plowing through muck and mire with the perseverance of fate itself. The loose-jointed clangor came nearer, against the background of dripping leaves. Fortunately it came head-on, was not sliding down the greasy mountain road on its haunches to ram them in the small ribs. Listening, they pictured the struggles of the earnest creature. Now it raced breathlessly, with an unexpected easing of the load; then it would hang agonizingly on a dead center, and they held their breath to help it over. Then abruptly, as if some cosmic hand had snatched the coal sack of night from in front of their eyes, two unblinking headlights stared at them owllike from across the swollen creek. The last of the rail fence had disappeared by this time.

Oliver kicked on his own headlights by way of welcome to a fellow creature abroad in such weather. He prodded the rubber bulb under one elbow and evoked a certain damp halloo on his horn. In the radiance of their crossed headlamp beams, they watched the driver extricate his lank form from behind the wheel and step out with spineless case.

"If I had children," said Oliver, "they'd join a circus and learn the back bend."

The fellow was coming across the creek, walking the submerged top rail of the fence.

"I'd rather do that than be President!" muttered Parr, but he knew the White House would be easier of attainment for him.

The equilibrist came up the bank. He politely illuminated his visage with a momentary spray of light from a torch. It was the usual hawklike visage of the indigenes.

"How'll you swap?" he demanded.

Oliver fairly shrieked his tickled ecstasy. "Even!"

"Get out of my car, then," said the man gruffly. "I'm the sheriff. You're obstructing the law."

It was amazing how these few simple words restored their drowned-out interest in life and living things. The sheriff helped them unload. He seemed to know by instinct where fishermen hide things. As a final, and what proved an unnecessary precaution, he prodded the excelsior cushions with a sharpened skewer, explaining that he wanted to be sure he wasn't getting anything that he didn't pay for. He shouldered their dunnage and walked it gracefully across the fence rail to the other shore.

"What worries me," said Parr, who knew this country and its illegible roads, "is how we're going to hit that blind turn on a night like this. You ought to have a traffic cop on that corner," he said to the sheriff.

"We've got one," responded the sheriff. "Listen."

They listened, but heard only the dismal drip of the rain. The sheriff unlimbered a villainous-looking revolver. He fired it above his head, and the explosion seemed almost to bring down the heavens on their heads. When the last reverberation had quenched itself they heard a dog barking a long way off.

"Turn sharp right when you get to that dog," said the sheriff. With a dexterous twist of the wrist he brought Oliver's thirty-five-dollar car to life, listening for a moment to its heartbeats; then with boneless ease he deposited himself behind the wheel and started up the hill without the usual formality of turning around. Probably, thought Oliver, that hill could not be taken except in reverse. Fascinated, they waited till his headlamps winked out behind the last turn.

"That's what I call efficiency," said Parr. "Glad he ain't after me."

"What do you suppose he is sheriff of around here?" speculated Oliver. The attenuation of population up here approached that of flies in a cathedral.

"Whatever it is, he knows his shrievalty," said Parr. "Did you notice how many useless questions he didn't ask?"

They looked wistfully at the submerged fence rail but kept to the road; the water came up to their armpits. The tin lizzie meekly awaited them, idling pensively. With the deputy directing traffic with a flash light, Oliver turned the creature around and they set out with light hearts toward the barking dog. It was four o'clock when they finally got to the faithful dog, and turned sharp right onto a harder road, into a deeper and darker woods. The dog continued to bark. They felt sorry for this, but there was no way to turn it off, and the dog undoubtedly derived solace from its own noise. The storm was suffering a change of heart, but so dark was the path through the woods that the wayfarers had no knowledge of it until, coming suddenly on a straightaway, they were amazed to see the newly risen sun staring at them, in cool candor, down the long tunnel of trees. They were almost dry again at six o'clock, when they turned into a wood yard carpeted with chips, behind a cottage of rived shingles at the edge of a soapy-blue pond, from which shreds of mist arose languidly.

Nate Alden was in the act of decapitating a resigned hen at the wood block. His wife softly opened the kitchen door and let out, together with a dignified cat, a benumbing aroma of crisping bacon and coffee boiling over. This hair-trigger effect of inciting a ravenous man's hunger belt to riot could be timed perfectly when the wind was just right. Then, as you approached the end of the journey through the woods, every passing zephyr tore off a bulletin of your progress and sped it on ahead to listening ears.

Nate and his wife were, as always, scrubbed and pressed and darned with faded completeness. Nate shaved himself well up in under the heavy thatch of his hair so that one thought at first glance he wore a wig. The old guide and his wife must have known how distinguished was the clientele that wore a path to their humble door, but they never mentioned it, at least to the clientele itself. There were great men in the world outside who would have given their eye-teeth for the privilege of hanging an old suit on a peg in the attic. But the visiting list of this camp was closed. The rich and great of this earth are a clannish lot. When they find some simple pleasure exactly to their liking, they go to no end of pains to bottle it up, fence it in, to keep out the hoi polloi. This club, of which Parr and Armiston were members, owned everything up here, from the barking-dog corner on the south to the Gravel Meadow on the north; and, east and west, from the state line to Tunxis Stream. They preserved it. Even the jagged rocks that arose in the wheel track, to eviscerate any low-hung car of modern vintage that poked its nose in here, were part of the picture.

Nate's wife held open the kitchen door for them to enter, shaking her apron at imaginary flies. She told them they were going to get out of their wet clothes before they sat down to eat. She told them she had laid out their old clothes on the bed. Even with that vicious breakfast at large to taunt them, they meekly obeyed the mild, masterful woman. There was little talk over the meal, and that purely of a secondary nature. The rigid law of the logging camp, where deep-woods guides get their start in life, prescribes that a man address himself solely to his food and let his neighbor do likewise. It is a good law, and works out like the old axiom never to interrupt a dog with a bone, no matter how well you think you know the dog. The better part of an hour passed when Nate—with the same delicacy as a hostess in some marble palace might signal her guests—pushed back his chair and lifted the horns of his luxuriant mustaches. He neatly dusted off the nether side with his napkin.

"The pond's working," he remarked. He filled his pipe and lighted it with a spill. Oliver got up and staggered to the porch and fell into a hammock, sound asleep before his head touched the pillow. Parr's eyes fell shut. He reopened them with an effort.

"How long have you had traffic control down at the corner, Nate?" he asked languidly.

"Three weeks, Thursday," said Nate.

"It's a good dog," muttered Parr, nodding. "If there was some way to start and stop it, I might use it in town."

"He starts easy enough," said Nate.

"Who owns that dog, Nate?" asked the deputy.

The woodsman shook his head, troubled. It was incredible to him that any living thing, man or beast, could exist for twenty-four hours in these parts without his knowing its life history. There were fishes in the pond he had put there as spawn; there was a family of skunks in the woodpile that ate off the kitchen doorstep every morning; there was an old bear on Honey Ridge he gathered beechnuts for every fall. But in three weeks' time he had been unable to scrape acquaintance with that dog.

Nate's wife paused in lifting the stove lid, and they, husband and wife, regarded each other in surprise. Some vagrant zephyr of the morning was bringing a news bulletin to them from windward. Parr, the famous man hunter, who was deaf, dumb and blind up here away from his city streets and tenements and card index of wrongdoers, slumped in his hickory armchair, his chin on his breast. He was sound asleep. But when, immeasurable ages later—the table had been cleared and draped in fly netting in the interim—the kitchen screen door thumped softly and a strange step fell on the floor, the man hunter instantly opened his eyes, wide-awake for any emergency, like a wild animal that is never wholly off guard.

The tall sheriff entered. His ragged hat, rent either by time or the bullets of hostiles, brushed the apple hooks in the ceiling. He leaned against the slab mantel and whittled tobacco from a bone-dry disk of cut plug.

Parr, in consonance with the pantomimic implications of the scene, mutely proffered a cigar. But the sheriff declined it with a shake of the head, and ground his whittlings between two horny palms; he studied Parr with the air of a man who would eventually have something to say and was speculating on the best mode of approach. He winnowed the stuff with a stout puff, filled his pipe and lighted it; he hooked a kitchen chair with a prehensile boot toe, and sat down, riding the chair backward. Parr lit the rejected cigar for himself.

"Are you reneging on the swap?" he asked casually.

"No," said the sheriff. "Oh, no. That's a good car."

Nate said unexpectedly; "Always was, Adam. She bites a little easy, that's all."

The sheriff dismissed this constitutional failing with an airy wave of the hand. His boy, Seth—who, he suggested by modest inference, was something of a gyp with flivvers—could make it eat out of his hand. It appeared that the thirty-five-dollar creature Parr and Oliver had swapped to cross a stream, in defiance of the adage, was not unfavorably known in these parts, had indeed passed current through many reincarnations.

A pleasant stillness settled down. Nate arose and, with no sense of shame, permitted his wife to tie him in a checkered apron. He dried and polished the dishes while she did the washing. The sheriff asked, addressing no one in especial:

"What's the first thing you look for when you enter a house without a warrant?"

"Dog," said Parr sleepily.

"Dog goes with him!"

"Where?"

"Nobody knows, except the dog."

"Follow the dog," advised Parr.

"Can't—this dog," said the sheriff; he shook his head and almost smiled. Parr was asking himself just what type of moron would try to hide out up here in the woods—and when he went visiting, where would he go? There was no place to go, nothing but timber everywhere.

"Doesn't he plant anything for you to find?" he asked. "No? That's not artistic."

"My boy says I don't know what to look for," said the sheriff. "What do you look for, mister?"

"Laundry mark," said Parr.

The look of bewilderment that met this suggestion told him the geographical significance of clews. They didn't know what a laundry mark was. In his bailiwick a man could change his name, lose it—but a laundry mark had a way of sticking to him to the end. Most men, though they didn't suspect it, were allotted only one to a lifetime. There were men in the big house up the river because they forgot this trifle.

"If he is a crook, or an actor," said the man hunter with a vague smile, "look for his press notices. That's one thing he never destroys. Get hold of his coat. Look for newspaper clippings of his past triumphs. They'll be there." Parr smoked for a time, his two companions waiting silently on his thoughts. "I doubt if he is a crook," he said. "When a crook hides out, it is always in a town—the bigger the town the better. Most of them steam for New York. Is there any man, beast or flivver within twenty miles in any direction that you don't know personally, sheriff?"

"I don't calculate there should be," said the sheriff.

Parr chuckled. "This is a grand country for a stranger to stake himself out in, with a dog to keep off marauders!" he exclaimed. "It sounds interesting!" Parr checked himself abruptly. "Of course you understand I am not practicing. I'm out of my jurisdiction. I'm up here fishing—"

"The pond's working," put in Nate. "There ain't no fishing." He turned a face full of secret understanding on the sheriff. The sheriff then said what he had come to say.

"If you'll look him over I'll drive him out in the yard at four o'clock this afternoon."

He got up and knocked out his pipe and departed without another word. They heard him wind up the flivver. It started with uncontrollable vehemence, but it knuckled down meekly enough when the sheriff got in and let in the clutch. Parr wandered languidly into the kitchen and watched with sleepy fascination the long curlieues of potato peelings that wound out of Nate's wife's fingers into a dish pan. He was irresistibly drawn to the horsehair sofa—which no well-dressed kitchen should be without—and when he awoke, hours later, the late resigned hen was coming out of the oven and the dinner bell was ringing.

At four in the afternoon the man hunter stretched himself at full length behind the break of a knoll that rose at so advantageous a spot at the depth of the woods that the log shack at the barking dog corner lay, a mile away, in a notch in the tree tops. That notch ranged the target perfectly like a gun sight, and Parr, as he focused his telescope, decided that man had somewhat aided Nature.

The sheriff lay alongside, holding a watch; and when the second hand touched the top of its circle, at the hour of four, he looked up expectantly. As if in response, three quick gunshots sounded from a remote point in the forest, a point that Parr roughly estimated to be about one hundred and fifty degrees from where they lay, using the barking-dog cabin as the center of a hypothetical circle. The shots echoed through the leafy stillness. Parr cocked an ear. The faithful dog was barking. The first few bars were ferocious. But shortly it settled down to a monotonous "Ow, ow," that might keep up for hours.

Parr, at the telescope, saw the cabin door, that swung on a harness hold-back, slowly open. The mysterious gentleman in residence stepped out into the yard without haste or alarm. He had been interrupted in the act of shaving himself. He had shaved the left side of his face, and as he paused for a moment, he applied a lather brush. He locked the door with a key. He moved without haste across a little back yard that contained the inevitable woodpile, and sat down behind a clump of junipers at the edge of the woods. At an alarm he could step into the brush and be lost. He listened, looking up at the sky; and so significant was that gesture that Parr, too, took his eye from the telescope and looked up. The sheriff did likewise.

The wary occupant of the shack being satisfied, for the moment, with the six points of the compass—including the Aztec up and down—and his dog now having settled down to a mere unemotional repetition, he resumed shaving. He was a young man, of military erectness, and very obviously not a man of the woods.

After a while a third person joined the watching pair at the break of the hill. It was the sheriff's son, Seth, who had fired the shots. He was as tall as his father, and almost an exact duplicate, except that he hadn't begun to shave yet.

"Can you get Oliver?" asked Parr.

"He's down in the swamp for a mess of bullfrogs," said the boy. "I guess I can toll him out."

A quarter of an hour passed. Then Oliver came cautiously crawling up the bank. Parr passed him the telescope. The dog's "Ow, ow" was still metronomic in its iteration. But the wind was changing, and the sound dimmed. The man had finished shaving. But he did not relinquish his hiding place. He spelled himself with a song in pantomine. He swayed from side to side. It was unmistakably tango time. Oliver could count the syncopated beat with its characteristic pause. Odd, he thought, that the Spaniards never get far away from that idiom in their everyday music. Oliver put down the telescope, with that peculiar look of bewilderment of one whose mind leaps fantastically ahead of his perceptions. When he rolled over on his back, and studied the sky, from horizon to horizon, the sheriff nodded, almost imperceptibly, and winked at his son. Oliver took up the telescope again.

"Who is he?" said Parr, in the peculiar hypnotic tone he used on occasion.

"If he's got two fingers off his left hand. I'll tell you."

"He had," said Parr.

Oliver put aside the glass. "What's the latitude and longitude of this place?" he asked. Without waiting for an answer he said, "I'd like to see a map."

Seth said: "I've got one in the car. I'll fetch it."

Oliver smiled. "No, son," he said. "Not a road map. I want a Mercator projection."

The boy arose. "That's what I've got," he said. "I'll get it."

The sheriff pulled grass, his hatchet face utterly blank. Oliver said slowly: "Wait a minute, son. Are we anywhere near the great-circle track between Le Bourget and Roosevelt Field?"

"It lies about five degrees south of us, sir," responded the sheriff's son. His eyes fell before the stare of Deputy Parr.

Parr said to the sheriff, with an odd smile. "I don't see as you need any outside help, sheriff."

The sheriff maintained his poker face; he said, pulling grass thoughtfully: "The boy is all right. But this thing goes outside my jurisdiction. I didn't believe him, until he showed me this Cuban's pictures in the magazine. I didn't take any stock in it."

"It's Martimo, the Cuban aviator, all right," said Parr. "I ought to know. I rode up Broadway with him, after his South American flight. I wonder if he faked that too."

"Martimo was in Paris yesterday, according to this morning's paper, trying out a new engine," said Oliver. He looked through the glass again, a long while. "Oh, it's Martimo, all right. Nobody could doubt that," he said. He plucked at his white lock of hair smiling. "The hare and the tortoise, eh? I've always wondered why some crook didn't try it out. There is a million dollars for the first man to make a solo flight of the Atlantic from east to west."

"Who makes it, or fakes it!" amended Parr.

"If that's the game this fellow isn't alone," said Oliver. "He's been planted here and told to keep out of sight until the signal comes to hop off. Where is the rest of the bunch?"

"Don't know!" exclaimed the sheriff, with a frown.

"Where's the nearest take-off for a single-seater?" demanded Oliver. "It wouldn't require a long runway. He could take off with a hundred gallons, or less, to carry him to New York."

"There's Gravel Meadow," said the sheriff. "That's twenty miles north, on the river."

"Anybody there?"

"Well, nothing but what we know about," said the sheriff. "They say they are working the gravel for tourmaline. They are putting up shacks for half a dozen men."

Martimo, the Cuban ace, was returning to his abode. He must have given some signal, for the barking of the faithful dog abruptly ceased. The swinging door had scarcely closed when the dog—an oversized bull terrier with an unorthodox black nose—came bounding into the yard and opened the door by leaping enthusiastically against it, and disappeared inside.

"If that is Martimo," mused Parr, "who is the gent standing on tiptoe at Le Bourget in Paris, to hop off?"

No one had an answer for this.

"I wonder what my friend Martimo would say," remarked the deputy, "if I staggered in on him, right now, weak from thirst, and demanding succor in the name of humanity?"

"That dog would probably ask for your card at the front gate," said Oliver, "and report back that the boss was out to lunch."

"But I am desperate with thirst," persisted Parr, a steely glow in his eyes. "A desperate man wouldn't let a mere dog stand in his way."

The sheriff shook his head. "You'd never get to him," he said. "We've tried it. He'd see you coming. His job is to keep out of sight till he gets the signal."

"You could drive him out into the yard again, for me," said the hopeful Parr. "I'd be parked in the junipers, to welcome him."

"Not with that dog," said the sheriff. The dog, in spite of its not sporting a pink nose, impressed him well.

Parr turned to the sheriff's son. "How would you run this, Seth?" he demanded.

The boy flushed slightly. "You mean if I were you, sir?" he asked.

"Well, let us say I place myself at your disposal," agreed the deputy with a smile.

"I'd send him a fake signal to hop off," said Seth stoutly.

"And let him land in New York?" said Parr fiercely.

"I'd meet him with a brass band!" cried the boy. Taken back by his own presumption, and the emotionless faces that waited on his words, he glanced shyly at his father; but that stern parent was pulling grass. Seth was strictly on his own. He embroidered his theme: "To do it right," he said, "you should fetch him up Broadway in a ticker-tape cyclone—with Grover Whalen to greet him, and Hector Fuller to read a scroll, and Jimmie Walker to present him with a rubber key to the city."

It was obvious that in part at least his erudition derived from a close perusal of headlines in the metropolitan press.

"Meantime," suggested Parr encouragingly, "at Le Bourget—"

"—the dummy crew would be still testing out the dummy plane—and waiting on the weather to hop off. They would get their first inkling that they had made the nonhop flight of the Atlantic from the news dispatches."

Parr settled himself comfortably on one elbow, and regarded Oliver and the sheriff with a look of indolent vacuity.

"Proceed," he urged softly. "How'd you get their code?"

"That's up to the French police," replied Seth.

"Oh, you're using the French police, are you?"

A hurt look showed on the boy's face. "You were kind enough to place your facilities at my disposal, sir," said Seth. "I assume you have a working agreement with the police of every country in the civilized world. So you could call on them at a moment's notice." He paused, but no one offered to take up his burden. "The French are crafty at decoding cipher," he said. "At least so I have always heard. That's the logical place to do it, over there, under the guns. The messages will originate there. There's plenty of time," he added hopefully. "This flight won't take off till July. They can't buck the winds till then."

He ran on breathlessly. Favorable weather was a necessity, even on a fake start that would end as soon as they got safely out of sight of land. A flight would not be undertaken in the face of adverse winds. He had canvassed the possibilities of intercepting the cipher at this end; the air was jammed with code and phone and machine sending; not to mention the ham stuff, with its mush and hash and raw a. e., and—especially in the amateur bands—the CQ parties. He smiled shamefacedly, but forbore insulting the intelligence of his audience by interpreting the cryptic abbreviations. They weren't transmitting at this end—at least not yet. It seemed he was sitting up nights, sweeping the circumambient ether with a direction finder; his compass loop gave him a zero point of not to exceed ten degrees of arc, and with this for a pick-up, he worked into a double-detection unit, peaked at fifteen hundred kilocycles, with four stages of impedance-coupled screen-grid i. f. and a space-charge detector on the front end that could detect a mosquito sneeze; he had been using this contraption as a mine sweeper, for bootleg phone stuff, but hadn't got a nibble: for c. w., he had a local heterodyne to "beat" the signal frequency—

At this point in the monologue the boy's father came to life. He held up an admonishing finger and said, "Keep your feet on the ground, son."

"Don't interrupt!" said Parr, looking daggers at the interruption. "Has Martimo got a receiver down there?"

Seth nodded. He was off again. Martimo—or someone who was a good enough ringer for the Cuban ace to fool Parr, under the magnifying gaze of that spyglass of the sheriff's—had one of the late-model broadcast receivers, with four stages of tuned r. f.

"Not short-wave, then?" said Parr, who could talk this lingo to some extent.

"That spiggoty is a born ham!" cried Seth, his eyes blazing at the thought that here was someone who understood the English language. "He uses this B.C. outfit as the intermediate bank of a super that he feeds from a short-wave converter. He works it upside down—that is, he tunes it through a thousand k. c. band, by shifting the i. f., and leaving the oscillator be." Seth was gliding without effort into a beautiful mathematical exposition of the principles involved, but a mere drooping of an eyelid on the part of his parent brought him back to earth. Seth, however, had one last fragment of treasured information he must get off his chest.

"There is some transatlantic stuff coming through in daylight, around fifteen and seventeen megacycles," said he, for such of the audience as had intelligence enough to comprehend. He shook his head. "It's not reliable. I doubt if they'd take a chance on direct communication. They probably cable to New York, and then relay it here by short wave."

Parr took up the glass again. "We'll get a finger print out of there," he said.

"We got one," said the sheriff. When Parr turned to stare at him he swallowed. "The boy thought you might want it," he said apologetically.

"Have you any other children?" asked the deputy politely.

"Yes. Oh, yes!" exclaimed the startled parent. Like old Adam of the antiquities, this Adam indeed had many children, but Seth in particular.

"I rather like your idea of a nonhop flight," admitted Parr, turning to Seth. "Where is a telegraph office?"

"The boy can take care of you," said the sheriff, with a truly remarkable effect of casualness.

"To Paris?" cried Parr. He glared at the pair with the utmost ferocity.

"Yes, sir," said Seth meekly.

That, is, maybe not direct, but in effect, yes. Due to the idiosyncrasies of radio communication—especially amateur radio-relay communication—it might be necessary to loop the message around through, say, New Zealand, or Egypt, or Cape Town. Due also to the rather chilly encouragement accorded transmitting amateurs—*réseau émetteurs*—by the French Government, it might be necessary to approach the frontiers in Holland, or Germany, and smuggle it across the line by bicycle or telephone. Seth, it was to develop, held conversations with persons of his own age and ilk over the entire surface of the earth, at seven, fourteen and even twenty-eight megacycles, nightly. In fact, the rotund earth was a pitiably small pellet for one of his capabilities, and if it had not been for the purely hypothetical Heaviside layer of ionized atmosphere—which, it was privately believed by this tribe, inclosed the earth like a fly net, and kept the signals in—Seth would have put through, without batting an eyelash, a person-to-person call to Mars.

It was four in the morning, in the radio shack—an erstwhile smokehouse—when they finally routed the message. It was in cipher, and explained in detail, to one Alphonse Gubinard, the details of the proposed nonhop flight, and the nature of the coöperation desired. This Gubinard was a savant in crime, whose time and interest had been the property, through his lifetime, of the French police. On several occasions Deputy Parr had visited the great man personally. As Seth took up the cipher message, and turned to his telegraph key, Parr said, in a low tone, as if the walls could hear:

"Won't Martimo get this, on his machine?"

"No, sir," replied Seth, fanning his key. "Dad is chasing him out in the yard while we are sending."

This impressed Parr. Next to that hair-trigger dog, he would have given worlds for a pair, in his bailiwick, who would even roughly approximate, in versatility, the tall sheriff and his son.

Parr, at home, always slept with at least one eye open, sometimes several. It might be his penumbral shadow, Morel, a handsome lively young fellow, who could have made a good living as a tailor's model, or a society man, if he hadn't preferred the police. Or it might be Pelts, the other half of the inner shadow, a shabby little fellow who in all his time on the police force had never yet put on a police uniform; indeed, it would have taken at least two of him to fill a blouse.

Pelts had been boarding in the west-side subway for several nights, on an assignment. There is a race of human moles who save room rent by riding back and forth in empty trains in the small hours. For meals they watch the vending machines, picking up here and there an unappeased penny. On a morning in the last week of June, Pelts was being thrown out by the porter at Long-acre; a bundle of morning papers that were to be given a ride uptown for the usual nickel at that moment came tumbling down the cement stairs and burst at his feet. His eye caught the headlines, and he managed, in passing, to steal a copy. It was the *Morning Times*; it had replated its first page at 4:06 A.M., an hour when even the most metropolitan of its circulation was on its way to the ultimate consumer. Six minutes later Parr picked up the telephone beside his cot in Little Central Office uptown, where he had been riding out the current murder for the past three nights. Pelts read him the headlines. Martimo, the Cuban ace, took off unexpectedly for the transatlantic flight at eight A.M., Paris time this morning.

Concurrently the wall telephone rang. It was Morel with the information that the lobster trick in the *Evening World* had a flash from Paris that the great hop, which was not to have started for another three weeks, had to the consternation of its backers and handlers, as well as to absentee reporters and photographers, taken off at eight A.M., on a spur-of-the-moment decision to take advantage of the especially favorable weather conditions prevailing over the Atlantic.

There came, simultaneously, a cable-gram from M. Gubinard. Decoded and expanded beyond its terse brevities. Gubinard informed his esteemed colleague that from the beginning of this affair he had assumed that the American police were the victims of misinformation; and that this morning, at the moment of departure, he had assured himself of the correctness of his opinion, by shaking hands—left hands—with Martimo, the courageous Cuban ace, who was essaying an east-to-west flight in which so many brave men before him had failed—and it was his pleasure to report that at the moment of saying farewell to terra firma, M. Martimo had two fingers missing from his left hand. Further, Gubinard himself had placed the official seals on the barograph that accompanied the flight, as proof of genuineness.

"There's a boy to see you, chief," reported Barney, the doorman, as the deputy studied the accusing message from a police savant who, he had reason to believe, never made a mistake.

"Boy?" said Parr absently.

A wide-awake boy of high-school age entered and gave a snappy salute. "A radiogram. Mr. Commissioner," he announced, "by courtesy of our amateur organization, sir. We have sixteen thousand active members in this country, and affiliated organizations in every civilized land on the face of the earth. Our Paris-Shanghai chain is functioning especially well this afternoon, and if you have any friendly messages—"

"A moment," begged the deputy. He tore open the envelope. The message was orthodox in every way. It was on a printed form, in upper-case typing: to preserve the flavor of cosmic encompasure, the time was given as Greenwich, 0858. That was eight minutes before *The Times'* last-minute replate. The message was signed Adam, and read:

"In view of premature take-off, will abolish traffic control, and hold for instructions."

"Any reply, sir?" asked the active member of the Tribe of Seth, laying a blank before Parr.

"Not to this fellow, unless I've got something to say," replied the deputy. "How does he come in? Pretty good?"

"Very QSA—through strong QRN, at that!" ejaculated the accomplished amateur. "I have him an R9 on his fourteen-meg sigs."

"Indeed!" said Parr, lifting a surprised eyebrow. On second thought, he had something to say. He wrote:

"Two fingers unexpectedly missing, at Paris this A.M., at moment of departure."

There came a shuffling of feet outside. The latest murderer was being brought in. For the next six hours Parr's immediate concern was not of the skies and the wayfarers thereof, but of the earth, and the regions thereinunder. Shortly after ten, Oliver Armiston came in, with a roll of early extras under one arm.

"You had better dust off the rubber key to the city," he remarked. Parr glanced over the extras, scowling. While he had been in camera this morning with an egotistical murderer, newspaper headlines had suddenly expanded from normal to the elephantine, afflicted by that weird epizootie of gigantism which attacks the press without warning, and causes ordinary one syllable words to hurst the column rules and crowd a page. It usually subsides very quickly. This one was still in the expanding stage. Even since Oliver had come in and sat down, a fresh extra had exploded in the street. Martimo had circled low over a British tramp ship in the Channel off Lizard Head. Parr could read the headlines across the street, where a frantic newsboy waved the paper at the staring passers-by.

"It's a good trick, if he can do it," mused Oliver. Parr nodded, an odd smile on his face. The weather was perfect. All those meteorological bunkers and traps, and such other hazards, as had combined to thwart all previous attempts in the east-to-west flight seemed to have been brushed aside by a sort of miraculous dispensation. From every ship in the steamer lane came messages of soft scant airs, such a calm as that which lay o'er Eden in the cool of evening. The old earth seemed to have taken her toe off the gas. At any rate, whatever accounted for it, there was a decided tapering off of the anticyclopic breezes the earth customarily stirred up in her wake as she spun on her course through space.

"It is the irony of fate!" mused Armiston. "On the one occasion when heaven and earth conspire for success, the flight is a fake! Isn't that a beautiful thought. Parr! Why is it that a born crook will deliberately refuse a prize to be had honestly, if he can possibly figure out some way to get it dishonestly?"

He examined the Mercator projection on the wall. Someone had already drawn the course of the flight on it.

"He'll be going overboard in another hour, Parr," said Oliver. "As soon as he gets out of the traffic in the Channel. That will be off the Irish coast. He'll have a motor launch. He will put his ship into a tail spin, and come down in his parachute. Then he'll have nothing to do for the rest of his life but to keep out of sight. Very sweet! Parr, he's making seventy miles an hour, with a load. He'll increase his speed a little. He ought to come down, with a nice three-point landing at Roosevelt Field at about eight o'clock Friday morning. There won't be standing room on Long Island at dawn! Remember the Bremen?" he asked. He resumed his chair. Parr said nothing, sat rubbing his blue chin, thinking of his barber.

"Parr," said Oliver, in his elaborately pragmatical manner, "one of the insufficiently—as yet—explored phenomena on psychology is the reaction of our perceptive faculties to the wish fixation; What we desire, we have. What we insist should happen, happens. I have seen it maintained that it is a dangerous thing to print discouraging bulletins when a great man lies ill. The whole world then gives him the death thought—and he dies! At least, so we are told by certain savants whose esoteric science we ignorantly call superstition. But, Parr, mark you this! The whole world at the present moment is giving this Martimo the success thought. By the way," he put in excitedly, "which one is the true Martimo—and which the paste?"

"The veritable Martimo," said Parr, "at the present moment is in the arms of my friend and collaborator, the sheriff. We checked his finger prints in the army records. I hate to demolish your theory, but I don't see how you can possibly hand him the success thought on his present predicament."

"He'll be reported in mid-Atlantic about eight in the morning," rattled on the bemused Armiston. "He should be off Cape Race about six in the evening. There's a moon. He will pass over the barking-dog corner about midnight. Maybe he'll drop a wreath or something. An hour or so later some of the keenest listeners among our down-east Yankees should pick up the thresh of his propeller. He'll be visible to the naked eye about four o'clock—flying high, of course—a mere glint reflecting in the rising sun. He can't get past Lewiston, Portsmouth, Waltham, Providence, without being seen. Great crowds will line the great-circle track at this end, pointing him out to each other. He will be seen. Parr, mark my word, and with plenty of substantiating detail. Remember the Bremen? We brought her as far south as New London, True. I admit she never, in the flesh, actually got farther south than Labrador, where she made a forced landing the previous morning. Nevertheless, the crowd at Roosevelt Field refused to disperse until long after dark. Parr," cried Oliver, challengingly, "what do you intend to do when he lands Friday morning?"

"Who?"

"Martimo?"

"Which one?"

"Either," said Oliver easily.

Parr chuckled. "I think I'll go fishing," he said. "Maybe the pond isn't working now."

He took down a telephone and, in that lordly way of his, ordered a cabin monoplane for tomorrow morning. He could transship to the mixed accommodation at Fredericton, and reach the railhead of the branch line by dark.

"Make two reservations," he said.

"I don't know but what I'd rather stay here and see the fun," said Oliver.

"No, the view will be better up there," insisted Parr.

At eight in the morning the deputy stepped from his car to a luxurious three-motor monoplane, and waited, with a smile of satisfaction, while his summer and winter overcoats were passed in. Inside he found Oliver in a deep chair by a table discussing the possibilities of breakfast with a white-coated steward.

"He is in mid-Atlantic," said Oliver cheerfully. He pointed to the morning papers. "Some day this success thought will get through!"

It was a fact that the captain of the Esthonia, a competent observer, especially at sea, reported at eight A.M., New York time, distinctly hearing the tearing thresh of an airplane propeller, evidently flying at a great altitude above a thin haze.

"This story will get out of the hands of the press before noon today," said Oliver hopefully. "It's too big for newspapers to handle. The press will have to move over to the curb and not cut out of line along with other obsolescent slow-moving traffic." His voice grew mysterious. "Do you realize Parr," he said, "that radio will distribute the news of Martimo's landing in less than one-seventh of a second after it actually occurs, to the farthest ranks of the unseen audience, no matter where they stand on the face of the earth." Radio will have a microphone in the cockpit before the plane stops rolling. And Martimo will be telling the world by word of mouth—by word of mouth, mark you!—the really vital things about the flight—whose oil he used, and whose spark plugs, and whose cigarettes. By the way, Parr, did you ever get so much as a single word of the preliminary messages between the two Martimos?"

"Not so much as a smell!" admitted the deputy. "We hadn't expected them to open up for another two weeks. They caught us flat-footed."

The same suant weather that wafted Martimo out over the Atlantic carried the three-motored monoplane to its destination without encountering a bump or a hole in the air. The passengers transferred to the mixed accommodation. When at dusk they stepped down at the shanty station at the railhead, wondering if they could pick up another reactivated flivver for thirty-five dollars, they were amazed to see the sheriff in their original purchase, at the milk platform. That he was awaiting them he at once made evident by reaching back and prying open the rusty door for them to step in and sit down. He concluded a conversation he was having with the station agent and started off.

"He's off Cape Race," said he.

Then he gave all his attention to driving. He was taking a short cut designed primarily for stone boats and the hardier kinds of buckboards, but he managed somehow to get through. And when, like a prudent mariner, he reached a spot where he could safely relax for a moment, he turned to reassure his passengers. He said to the rear seat, craning his neck:

"I've got a boy—my youngest boy, going on fourteen—something queer about him. Dogs don't bark at him." He shot a swift look at them. "I don't know why. Neither does the dog. That dog's sleeping with that boy of mine in the attic."

He tooled the car through a nest of boulders. Parr leaned forward, hanging precariously on the robe rail.

"When did you pick him up?" he shouted above the din.

"Daylight—yesterday."

A little later Parr yelled: "Gravel Meadow—what about them?"

"They high-tailed it out this morning!"

They came on barking-dog corner, tragically silent in the moonlight. Later they came on the sheriff's domicile, phosphorescent against the hemlocks, under a fresh coat of paint. From an attic window came a patient "ow, ow, ow," which quietly terminated at some word of admonition from inside, undoubtedly from the fourteen-year-old son, whose bed the faithful creature was sharing. The sheriff cut off the motor, and in ghostly silence it coasted down the gentle hill through the woods for a mile or more, and came to a halt at the former smokehouse.

Lights gleamed through the chinks. The flutelike notes of some long wave-arc or alternator wireless station were coming in—Carnarvon, Nauen or Arlington. The signals were drowned out in a rush of static, with its click, grind and crash. Then a birdlike chirping; the hoarse voice of a ship-to-shore spark; a sudden gust of machine sending at a terrific speed—and then, after a long pause, a fragment of a voice said:

"Halifax, at ten—very distinct—and moving southwest by south—"

Through a window they saw the two boys, Seth and Martimo, crouching over the bench, while Seth with the delicate fingers of a Jimmie Valentine, slowly turned the tuning dial, the two watching the slow movement of the calibrated arc with glazed fixity. There was a loud-speaker on a shelf above their heads, and under it hung the skull and crossbones warning of high voltage. Seth must have sensed their presence, for after a moment he quietly took himself out of his chair with that boneless grace that was a gift of this family. No sooner had he vacated the seat than Martimo slid over into it and took the dial. Seth tiptoed out, closing the door softly behind him. Without a word they moved over to the shadow of the trees.

"What's he got to say for himself?" asked Parr.

"Not a word," said Seth in a hushed voice.

"I expect he is doing a lot of thinking," said the sheriff.

Parr nodded. "He's got a lot to think about," he said grimly.

Seth turned to the deputy uncertainly. "You are not going—you're not going to take him up, sir?" he asked timidly.

Secretly the man hunter chuckled. He was thankful enough to be out of his own jurisdiction. But he temporized, studying Seth. "What's on your mind, son?" he asked flatly.

"You know they are double-crossing him," said the boy.

Parr nodded. "It's an old Spanish custom, widely practiced among crooks," said he dryly.

The boy began stoutly: "But this fellow isn't a crook at heart, sir! He's only a kid. He's got a fine record behind him. This is his first slip. They've caught him like a rat in a trap—"

"Are you sure," asked Parr casually, "that he didn't get a signal to hop?"

"His plane isn't out of his crate yet," interposed the sheriff.

Parr looked hard at Seth. "I'm inclined to let Nature take its course," he said shortly. "I wouldn't lift a hand, for my part. He's got to take what's coming to him."

"What's that?" asked the boy tensely.

"When they land, will there be any doubt in anybody's mind that they have made it?" demanded the deputy fiercely. "Can he walk out on the field and push the crowd aside and say, 'Wait a minute! I'm Martimo. You're cheering the wrong man'?" Parr chuckled. "Not! His cue is to fade out of the picture. What else can he do?"

Seth's eyes never left his face. "If they make it," said he tensely.

"They're making it!" cried Parr. "The whole world is giving them the success thought. Listen to your radio."

The boy said quietly. "And if they don't make it—what then?"

Oliver drew a quick breath. Adam turned his hawklike visage slowly on Parr, awaiting his answer.

"But they are crossing!" cried Oliver. "Everything is in their favor. That's why they took the chance."

Seth shook his head. "Nothing authentic has come through since eight this morning," he said. "The Esthonia picked him up at about thirty west longitude. There's nothing since—only the usual crop of rumors."

The flutelike notes of a big transatlantic wireless were sounding on the air again. They listened. Parr tried to pick it up, but it was too loosely abbreviated for him. It ceased as abruptly as it had begun.

"That's Halifax," said the boy. "The operators are rug chewing. They've got nothing. They are asking every ship within talking distance."

"It'll be another four hours before anything breaks," said Parr. "I'll snatch a cupful of sleep."

He went to the car and got out his topcoats, summer and winter, and helped himself to a local horse blanket.

"Seth!" he called softly. The boy went quickly to his side.

"Don't leave anything around loose that he can hurt himself with," muttered the deputy. Seth nodded. He had seen to that. Parr smiled to himself. He had that comfortable feeling that whatever happened, it would be adequately taken care of without his interference.

"How about your motor generator? He might accidentally start it up, and lean against it," he said quickly, at a sudden thought.

"I've taken out the brushes," said Seth gravely.

Parr put a hand on the boy's shoulder. "It's his problem," he said. "He'll have to work it out for himself. Just stand by, so he doesn't do anything foolish." He started off, then turned to say, "Don't let him know I'm here."

The night was fine. Parr rolled himself in coats and blankets, between the extruded roots of a great oak. Some time later. Oliver and the sheriff joined him.

Ages later, when he was turning over in his sleep, a familiar household voice roused him—so familiar, in fact, that for the moment he thought of himself as tossing on his cot in little headquarters uptown, where he occasionally rode out a murder mystery. The household voice was saying:

"The flight of Army planes, that took off from the Boston base to bring him in, as an escort of honor, are having trouble, because of the unexpected fog bank that has drifted in from the Sound. The Cuban ambassador has just arrived at the field—the city sent a special plane for him—and the mayor is greeting him. Wait a minute! For those who turned in late. I will repeat the last bulletin. Martimo has been reported on his course, at Lewiston, Portsmouth, Waltham. Providence—flying at an altitude of about ten thousand feet—"

The voice trailed off as the signal strength faded. Sometime later, it may have been seconds, or hours, another household voice said, talking to the very ends of the earth:

"There's nothing much happening just now—we're trying to till the gap while we are waiting. I might describe the crowd again. As far as we can see, in every direction—"

The next time Parr opened his cars, between gulps of sleep, a woman's voice, heavily modulated was speaking:

"Neighbors," she said. "I have a splendid recipe for buttermilk muffins for you this morning—"

Parr sat bolt upright. The sheriff was preparing breakfast over a two-by-six fire, built between stones. A small edition of Seth was breaking eggs in a pan, under the close supervision of an oversized bull terrier with a black nose. Parr prodded Oliver awake. The door of the radio shack stood open. It was empty. The sheriff followed Parr's look.

"Seth's got him," he said significantly.

Parr got up and went down to the shack. He twirled the dial. Burst of music, livestock reports, setting-up exercises, pure-food-and-drug talks smote his ears at familiar notches on the dial. He shut the thing off. Radio, after its brief illusion of grandeur, had fallen back into the morning ruck. Parr went back to the fire, watching with cringing stomach muscles the preparations for breakfast.

"What can we do for that fellow?" asked the sheriff suddenly.

Parr and Oliver exchanged a long look. The Martimo from the other side was, in all probability, at the bottom of the sea. The Martimo they had in charge was, in effect, a living dead man. At least the whole world, at this moment, undoubtedly believed him to be lost.

Parr asked, "Can Seth handle him for a few days, until—until he gets his bearings again?"

"Why, yes, we can hold him, as long as you want," said the sheriff, nodding agreement. "What then?"

Parr considered. "I think," he said lazily, "you might accidentally lift the surveillance when he gets so he can think calmly and realize—realize he's on the wrong shore!" He turned a full look on Oliver.

"And let him high-tail it?" ejaculated the sheriff.

"What can you hold him for—or on?" demanded the deputy. He shrugged his shoulders. What else was there to do?

It was the last week in July. Oliver's phone—the private one, into Parr's office—gang. It was Parr.

"They've found Martimo," said Parr. "We've just got the flash."

"No!"

"In person!" agreed Parr.

"Alive?" cried Oliver incredulously.

"So it seems," said the deputy.

It was true. The long-lost Martimo had come, so ran the story, out of the trackless wilds of Labrador.

He was naked, torn by thorns, his feet were bound by rags, he was all but starved. He had wandered blindly for weeks.

Aid was being rushed to him. Reporters, news-reel men, short-wave radio outfits, sound-reproducing mechanism, all were being rushed by plane for the astounding story.

Oliver considered a moment. He asked, in a low voice:

"Parr, which Martimo is it?"

There was a slight pause before the answer came.

Parr said, "I don't believe I'd raise the question."

The Pandora Complex

THERE is a concatenation of place, and especially of time—as some poet said somewhere. Events weave a counterpoint of their own, link themselves together in weird patterns utterly contrary to any plan, a sort of perverse miscegenation that defies not only the operation of orderly formula but even the law of probabilities. These curious, unpredictable matings of events are forever trailing through the news. See how the chain, even though some of its links seem for the moment missing, follows through: The cigar maker's mother was dead, and he asked the sandwich man to tend shop during the funeral. A customer tendered a five-dollar bill in payment for a ten-cent cigar, and the sandwich man handed it back, saying, "I'm a printer. I've been out of work for two years. Nevertheless, I am a printer."

They fell into talk about printing, and the upshot of it was that the customer offered the sandwich man a chance to go back to work as a printer again, printing five-dollar bills. The printer put in a new press, new inks, new paper; and when he achieved results to please his own discriminating taste as a printer, he secretly ran off a bundle of the counterfeits for himself and hid them in the bottom of his tool box at home. Of course, his wife found them; and being a conscientious soul, she extracted one from time to time, to pay off the more urgent small tradesmen. Those that passed current from hand to hand were unquestioned; probably are still moving innocently from till to till, gaining in good repute with age and decrepitude, as money will. But one went to a bank where a clerk who had been employed in the Federal Reserve noted something odd about the second letter of the serial number, and reported it. The bill was traced back through a Chinese laundryman to the printer's wife, to the printer, to the man who bought the ten-cent cigar; and thus a dangerous counterfeit was destroyed aborning, and a gang rounded up just as they were about to shove the queer. It would have been impossible to detect the weak link if the cigar maker's mother hadn't died, or if that printer hadn't been out of work, or if his wife hadn't suffered from the Pandora complex. Behind any of the ifs were cosmic causes which could be traced back to the Year One; and if any one of these causes had failed to come to pass, this particular band of counterfeiters would not have been caught when that particular Chinaman took his money to the bank.

Five days prior to the seventeenth of January, a so-called Alberta high—bar. 30.2—came drifting casually, as was its wont, across the international boundary line into the States; it edged through the Chinook Pass and down the slope onto the benches; moved over the bad lands, the plains of jumbo wheat, the iron ranges and the Great Lakes, in a generally easterly-by-southerly direction, actuated, in addition to its proper forward motion, by a feeble reverse English, related in some vague manner to the gyroscopic effect of the earth's rotation, which caused it to revolve slowly in a clockwise direction. The line of zero temperatures descended to the Ohio River valley and moved eastward along the flank of the isobars. A Gulf low that had wandered north by mistake had to lift itself to pass the advancing Alberta high, whereupon snow became general along the whole front, and due to the steepness of this front, it was accompanied by high winds which, with the zero temperature, recalled to old-timers the beginnings of the '88 blizzard.

Snow came sifting down on the city at one in the afternoon. By six the wind had risen to a half gale, and the snow swirled in wreaths like smoke around the chimneys and drove through the narrow streets across the island with the venom of a sand blast. If this had been '88, the police would have brought out sand boxes and blankets to help fallen horses. But there were no horses to slip on the icy pavement this day, and policemen, looking up at the luminous storm reflecting the city lights, said hopefully that if it got any worse all the "cans" would come out. The cans, in the parlance of Centre Street, constitute, as a genus, that ultimate bum's rush of broken-winded taxis that come limping out of the boneyard only when big storms sweep the streets bare of the usual cruisers. Ordinarily, there are too many taxis; at the theater hour there are almost enough; in a light drizzle there comes the pinch of want; and when a storm falls the hungry old 30-and-10 cans come creeping out of their burrows, seeking whom they may devour. Eight-o'clock platoons were sent out with the warning from their lieutenants to keep an eye peeled for cans. Most of the cans borrowed their number plates, tickets, insurance and even their rubber, and were worth watching.

At one in the morning, a sway-backed old Belleville, one of that ancient clan that sported a cylindrical hood in the days of peekaboo waists and willy strings, worked its way painfully eastward through wind-swept Twenty-third Street. It had been lying in wait at the ferry terminal, to pick up some gullible stranger and whisk him off to the wilds of Brooklyn or the Bronx by mistake. But the ferries had stopped running because of the smother, and the ancient Belleville prowled for victims in the more sophisticated areas of the island. But the same hand of fate that started this Alberta high on its slowly revolving way across the meridians, now intervened; as the taxi passed under the elevated, it began to buck and sputter.

Coincidentally, a sprightly young woman, tilted well forward on high-heeled pumps, in the sheerest of tan silk stockings, and a short caracul coat picked out in snow that muffled her to her ears, came beating against the storm out of the south under the elevated and dropped anchor, panting, at the all-night oyster bar tacked on to the rear of the corner building like a penthouse—in fact, it had been the penthouse vestibule, the family entrance of a thriving gin mill in the old days. During the oyster season, Joe the Oysterman could, at a pinch, accommodate two customers at one and the same time. During the months without an *r*, it was his shoe-shining parlor and pomade shop. Now its single gaslight showed like a sun dog through the frosted pane. The sprightly female out of the storm pushed open the door and thrust in her head, crying, as to a tried and true friend, confidently:

"Joe! Come quick! My water pipes have burst and I can't shut it off!"

She was a Miss Vinson, a budding sculptor with a studio on the top floor of an old brownstone around the corner—in fact, she was its only occupant at night. Not so long ago, she had come for Joe at three in the morning, to climb a tree to rescue a mewing kitten; on another occasion when Terry, the cop, had been sound asleep in the drug store, she brought Joe an alarum of burglars, and the chivalrous Joe had sallied forth and at them, loudly beating a dishpan.

So now, even in the teeth of a blizzard that blasted all outdoors, Joe gravely shed his long apron and ceremoniously handed it to her—for it was part of the bargain that she should tend bar in his absence—and taking her key, he stole forth to be a plumber. She dutifully put on his apron, polished a plate or two, and curled her slim legs around the rungs of his stool, to wait; it seemed that an oyster stew would be irresistible to a wayfarer on a night like this; but, there were no passers-by.

Through a hole in the frosting of the window the girl could see that the street was empty, save for a small coupé cowled in snow and seemingly abandoned to the elements. She waited and waited. Beyond the vague howl of the wind, all night sounds were muffled in the peculiar stillness of snow. The coupé wasn't abandoned; she divined that because there was no snow on the radiator. A point of light from a street lamp rested a moment on a polished headlight and shivered violently—the engine was idling to keep warm. A stray gust tore a crust of ice from one edge of the number plate, and revealed the first two characters of the number—1C. Snow instantly covered it again. ... Wasn't there a law, or something, against leaving a car with the engine running? ... Helen Bramsil had sold a pair of bronze doors to a historical society—doors replete with Indians, cupids and laurel intertwined; and immediately moved into the rented-limousine class, the chartered-car category! Anyone can own his own limousine, but it has certain disadvantages, among which is that your own limousine perceptibly ages with the passage of even small portions of time. A chartered equipage has eternal youth! It's like buying a new car every month, of the very latest model—in fact, every day if you wish. Merely complain, and a new car will be sent around in place of the one that was not so new. At afternoon receptions—even the most swagger—you can always spot the chartered limousines; they have the class, the air, flair; and prima donnas, cinema stars at gala first nights, divas and visiting premiers are sure to step grandly out of them. Well, some day she, too, would move into the chartered-car category—if she could only find a historical society in need of a pair of sixteen-foot bronze doors with Indians, cupids and laurel in bas-relief.

Pop, pop, pop—bang! Pop, pop. A decrepit old taxi—she could just make out the outline through the murk—was in difficulties, standing into danger. It strained, stuttered, bucked; by spasmodic little jack-rabbit leaps and bounds it finally got clear of the car tracks, inched its way to the curb, and, as if in its dying gasp, it disappeared around the building line in Twenty-third Street and became momentarily quiescent.

Nothing happened. After a time, her dreamy fingers subconsciously modeling imaginary cupids in a frieze she was making for the Beaux Arts competition, there came suddenly a crepitating rattle and roar from somewhere in her immediate neighborhood, which caused her to sit up in sudden alarm. Then she recollected the broken-backed old taxi that had come to a standstill just around the corner—the driver would be desperately prodding the throttle and adjusting his spark. As the engine raced with the sour din of overstrained machinery, the old Belleville back-fired with the staccato roar of a machine gun. That was it. It came again and again. There were moments of comparative calm. But just when things seemed to settle down for the night, that frantic taxi would let go again with a reverberating roar that split open the roof of the storm. Once the drug-store door, eater-corner, opened and the young cop on post looked out hopefully. But seeing only an old can in distress, he went back to the steam radiator.

Eventually Joe came back. He noted thriftily that the new snow was untrodden to his parlor door; but when he opened the till and counted the money, it held two dollars more than when he went away, and she gave him a dollar for his errand and went back home swearing eternal obligation to the oysterman. She stepped mincingly, like a kitten crossing a wet floor; the print of her French heels made it appear as if someone had stalked through the snow on stilts; the track led down the avenue, and west into Twenty-second Street, and into an old brownstone that stood back from the street with a little yard in front.

The old Belleville had anchored in front of an all-night novelty shop. This shop was brilliantly illuminated with dazzling white lights as if for a carnival. It sold everything, from sneeze powder and magicians' props of all kinds, to tambourines, chromium-plated souvenirs for the ferry trade, handball equipment, burned leather, glass pistols, mechanical bait, patent noise-making devices, fraternity emblems and phonographs, one of which was playing the same record over and over again, by virtue of some mechanical device, also sold here.

A clerk—the night clerk—who should shortly wake up and mop the paved floor with hot suds, was asleep behind the handbook counter where the neighborhood played the ponies with the aid of mathematical charts and systems for sale here. Another counter was devoted to a post office, with scores, hundreds of pigeonholes; the place did a land-office letter-box business for such persons, individual or corporate, as stood in need of a classy metropolitan address; and the mail that moved in here four times a day would have gladdened the heart of many a fourth-class postmaster.

At exactly 1:23 o'clock, the folding glass street door opened violently, and the clerk, wildly waving a steaming wet mop, rushed shrieking from the place. He called out "Murder!" and "Police!" He beheld the startled taxi driver and rushed violently at him. He seized him desperately, tugged at the startled fellow, tried to drag him into the store. But the taxi driver viciously shook him off, retreated warily before the wild onslaught. The policeman came running from the drug store. Exultantly, the gibbering clerk seized him and half dragged, half led him into the novelty shop. The taxi driver considered the situation for a moment. But only for a moment. Without a second look at his dying car, he dropped his tools and made off as fast as his legs could carry him. The irresolute old Belleville rolled over dead center once or twice, and then gave up the ghost. In the novelty store the frantic clerk was pointing at a trickling, dark stream that emerged from under the door of a telephone booth. In the booth lay wedged a dead man, like a horse cast in a too-narrow stall. In the adjoining booth was a submachine gun from which forty shots had viciously ripped through the intervening partition.

II

"Perfect timing!" said Parr, the police deputy, as his chilly gaze roved from Exhibit A to B to C. All the familiar landmarks in the topography of spot murder were present. This sort of thing was becoming standardized. "Everything clicked, as usual."

"Even the blizzard," put in Morel, his *alter ego*, who had just finished the preliminary interrogation of the clerk with the mop, and dropped the poor fellow, limp as a wrung rag, behind his counter.

"Oh, they carry their own weather service," said the deputy idly. His scientificos were swarming all over the place. Before anything was disturbed—even the dust—they would take it all down in photography, blue print and plaster. Cameramen were shooting Exhibit A, which still lay wedged, like a badly dressed clothing-store dummy, in the narrow telephone booth. They shot it from every conceivable angle.

"Ah, the trick car!" chuckled Parr, eying the dead Belleville at the curb, through the frosted panes of the street door. The ancient can was now decorated with hearselike plumes of snow.

" 'Trick'?" queried Oliver Armiston. Armiston, who was Parr's occasional collaborator in cases that did not yield to the usual hobnail methods of the police, had asked to be let in on the ground floor in the next spot murder, and this was it. He had been called out of bed and brought here in a police car, its siren whimpering like a panther with a sore paw as it coursed through the empty storm-swept streets. It was not yet dawn. The storm still lay flat, like a coursing greyhound, across Twenty-third Street, the coldest place on earth in a northeaster. A flock of shivering railbirds—for the rumor of murder would out, even at this chill hour—clustered, foot-stamping, in the snow across the street, watching with the titivating fascination that only fresh horror can contrive, every opening and shutting of the street door. Some of them tried to enter, but were brusquely put aside by two policemen on guard. Nevertheless, a wistful little tramp wrapped in four or five coats, and at least three pairs of pants and—lo and behold!—two pairs of shoes, shuffled up to the door and entered like a lord. Inside, he stepped out of his outer pair of shoes, which must have been designed originally for Primo Carnera, and shuffled over to the radiator. It was little Pelts, the elegant Morel's side partner. If Morel looked like a young dancing man just in off a late stag line, Pelts belonged to some shuffling bread line.

"Trick car, yes," said Parr, in answer to Oliver's question. "It's trained to backfire. It plays dead at the scene of the crime." He added vaguely, as he looked around: "This looks like a show of the No. 1 Road Company, working out of Chicago. They can put on their act any place in the country on twenty-four hours' notice."

He turned to the telephone booth, where the cameramen were rearranging Exhibit A, at last, for full face and profile. Parr studied the face, shook his head.

"Don't know the gentleman," he said grimly. Pelts and Morel gave no sign. "He seems to have passed out happy. They all do," he added. "These poor devils always know there is going to be a killing, but they never for a moment suspect they are elected. He came in, probably thinking he was tolling out the other fellow for the artillerymen."

Oliver said casually: "It doesn't seem to annoy you unduly."

Parr thought this over a moment. Then he asked gruffly: "Why should it?"

"It's murder," said Armiston with a gesture of completeness.

"Is it?" cried the deputy sharply; he glared at the telephone booth. "It's vermin—exterminating vermin," he added between his teeth.

"That seems to be the general notion," agreed Oliver. "A kind of rat virus by which Nature holds the beer barons and alky cookers in control."

"I'd like to have some of that rat virus," snapped Parr. "There are other species that need a shot!"

"Simple enough, the ingredients," said Oliver. "Submachine gun, trick taxi, telephone booth, stormy night. Touch off the gun when the car backfires. Then walk—don't run—to the nearest exit. No need to hurry. No one will follow. The police will arrive eventually, and survey the props with the air of connoisseurs. What rhythm! Perfect timing! Do you note that they carry their own weather now, Watson? Then you put on a Chinese chase. If by any chance you ever catch any one, you turn him loose for lack of evidence."

"If we don't," put in Parr amiably, "the judge or the jury does."

"It's safe enough—the formula," expatiated Armiston. "No danger of getting hurt—no one but the dead man—and as you remark, they arrange it so he passes out happy. Anybody could put it on. I could." He paused—a barely perceptible pause. "You could."

"In fact," said the police deputy, chuckling, "I do get a good deal of credit. Every time the vermin exterminators put on a good clean show— like this one—my admiring public write me letters thanking me for saving the county money. When they don't give me credit for the put-out, they always score me with an assist." His chilly eye ranged from Morel to Pelts, and he rubbed his blue chin thoughtfully. "In the banana bush in Central America," he said, "when a Jamockan black goes bad and annoys the white men, they take down their elephant guns some dark night and go alligator shooting." He eyed Oliver narrowly. "Is that what you are driving at?" he demanded. "That some of my hard-boiled babies in the Detective Bureau go alligator shooting occasionally?"

"I canvass the possibility," admitted Armiston.

Parr shook his head. "I'm afraid not," he said. "I've got some hard-boiled babies. I need them. But I fear they are not actuated by so lofty a sense of duty. Besides, we haven't got the props to put on the show with. It takes a company well rehearsed, with a good stage manager standing by, holding a watch on the cues. This sort of thing takes organization."

"I'm looking at it from another angle," said Oliver.

"What's that?"

"A one-man show," replied the extinct author. He was watching Morel in the mirror; the more sensitive face of the young dandy would reveal mental reactions which the less easily read countenance of the chief would withhold. Morel's eyes shifted imperceptibly, like those of a hunter listening with sudden intentness. Pelts yawned and turned his other side to the radiator.

Parr said: "He'd have to be—what's the word?—protean."

"Not at all!"

"How about your trick car?"

"Coincidence!"

"Your meteorological expert?"

"Another coincidence."

"The sleeping clerk?"

"Coincidence No. 3," said Oliver.

"And Joe the Oysterman being called off the job at exactly the right moment?" put in Parr.

"No. 4," said Oliver. "Think it over."

"And the young lady in the high-heel shoes who so carefully left indisputable evidence of her plausibility?"

Parr set up the, to him, essentials, one by one.

"Good Lord! You're not dragging her in for a part, are you?" laughed Oliver.

"Not that she is aware of," grunted the man hunter. "But she will be under observation, you can be sure. You are working coincidence pretty hard, aren't you?"

Oliver shrugged. "Everything that happens is a coincidence," he said. "Without coincidence there would be no history. But you lean over backward and declare that all things that happen simultaneously are premeditated by some master mind standing alongside and holding a watch on the cues. Everything clicks; I grant the rhythm," went on Armiston. "But don't you take too much for granted? Maybe someone is stealing their stuff. They can even count on you to play your part."

"Meaning the Chinese chase I am about to put on?" said Parr silkily.

Oliver nodded. He was watching the cameramen about the telephone booth.

"You take it for granted he is a beer baron or an alky cooker who accidentally, on purpose, stepped over into someone else's territory," he said.

"That's why he is here," remarked the deputy complacently.

At this moment the air was rent with a blood-curdling shriek. It was the clerk—the clerk who had calmly slept through the murder, but went frantic at the sight of a trickle of blood. Now he had regained his courage; he had dragged himself to a sitting posture and peered over the counter just as the cameramen posed Exhibit A for another full face and stepped back out of the way of the camera.

"It's the dominie!" he shrieked, beside himself with terror. "It's Mr. Ben-Benth—it's the Reverend Bentham!" Morel pounced on him, dragged him out, shook him till his teeth rattled. But all they could get out of the overwrought fellow was the name, Bentham, Bentham, Bentham, which he babbled over and over again.

It was gray dawn, with the tinkle of milk bottles on the air as its harbinger, before they isolated the Rev. Mr. Bentham. He seemed to have been a thoroughgoing knave who, up to this moment, had escaped attention of the police. His title was undoubtedly spurious. At least he had no church; he was even without a frock, for his wardrobe, though well stocked, contained not a single garment of clerical cut. He maintained an apartment in the new development by the river, but his business activities centered here around these rented mail boxes, of which he had a number on yearly lease, under various high and righteous-sounding appellations. He was a specialist in foreign missions. The morning mail brought many letters for him, many of them containing money. These people had been touched by his unselfish willingness to forward contributions for worthy foreign missions. He seemed to have operated the business with much thoroughness, going to the length of printing illustrated reports from Darkest Africa for the delectation of his clientele.

"Lone-wolf confidence man in the religious racket," said Parr. "One of the best. Look him up in the faro joints or the handbooks."

Gamblers always treat themselves to a busman's holiday with their ill-gotten gains. A faro dealer off duty usually moves around to the other side of the table. The Rev. Mr. Bentham merely moved across the aisle in the novelty shop to the local handbook, where he was an ardent student of form and system as applied to running horses. Most of the cash so gratefully tendered by his out-of-town clientele seemed to have passed back into circulation via this book.

III

The city is built on islands; to flee from it, one must cross water, either above or below. That is one reason why the morning line-up at Police Headquarters seldom lacks a cast for its revue. The tunnels and ferries and bridges are so many bottle necks through which fugitives must pass to escape to the mainland. And at the mouth of each of these bottle necks, Parr had picked men on duty twenty-four hours a day, like the guard at the gates of a walled city. They were highly educated in their calling.

Lynx-eyed Heinie, of Traffic Squad J, had picked up one hundred and thirty-eight stolen automobiles that tried to crawl through the bottle neck that was the Willis Avenue Bridge over the Harlem. Or was it one hundred and thirty-nine?

"It's a hundred and thirty-nine, Heinie," insisted the bridge tender, who was sweeping the tumultuous snow into piles about the gatehouse, to push it into the river; the hour was ten of the blizzard morning.

"It's a hundred and thirty-eight," said Heinie positively. Accuracy in figures was a religion to Heinie; his genius lay not only in visualizing combinations of figures but in isolating them into genus, species and variety.

"It's a hundred and thirty-nine!" insisted the bridge tender, jealous for Willis Avenue.

"Well, have it your own way," said the traffic policeman, pulling on his gloves and stepping out into the snow. "Here comes a hundred and thirty-nine now!"

He advanced to the middle of the plowed roadway and held up an imperious traffic hand. A magnificent equipage, almost too long to take a city corner without barking its fenders against the curbstone, came rolling to a puzzled stop. The chauffeur and the footman, with noses and ear tips pink from the biting cold, gazed haughtily at the interruption. It was of the town-car type, the crew being exposed to the weather on all sides, while the passengers rode snug in a bijou interior of satin and mahogany and silver with cut flowers, set well out on the rear axle. They were two charming young women—like kilties, much underdressed below the knees and overdressed above—they were engaged in such earnest converse that they did not notice the interruption.

There is a certain unbroken ritual in the lines and business of this sort of thing, like that of a scene in a well-matured play, or a spot murder. The traffic officer's opening line is: "Pull up to the curb, young feller!" accompanied by a wag of the right forefinger; but through ages of repetition, the words had become redundant, and the wag of the forefinger came to suffice.

The magnificent equipage drew up at the curb, climbing an upturned furrow of snow to do so. The hand of the traffic law now turned up, palm upward, and the forefinger wagged up and down with a come-hither gesture. The chauffeur had no difficulty in understanding this sign language. He unbuttoned several layers to get at his license and registration cards.

"I'll take your uniform off you for this!" he cried hotly, as he handed over his manifest. All chauffeurs say that. Now the policeman spoke. It was always his first spoken line, it never varied.

"The only thing you'll take off me is a ticket!" he remarked, with mild scorn. He examined the credentials. They were not in order. It happened that the cards were a year old. This chauffeur hadn't worn this ulster since the last storm, more than a year gone by. But Lynx-eyed Heinie passed this discrepancy for the time being. What held his eagle eye was that the number plate began with a big O. He got on the running board.

"We'll take a little ride, young feller," said he. "We'll visit the chicken coop first."

They got down at the police station without a look at the passengers. The two ladies, indeed, were deep in a discussion of the *cire-perdu* process, the lost-wax process of casting bronze, which had recently come into vogue again, after a hundred years of desuetude. They were oblivious of change. They had the abiding faith of a C. O. D. package in transit. One pompous carriage starter had tucked them in; another would apprise them of the end of their journey and break them out.

There was a lieutenant writing at the desk; Lynx-eyed Heinie took out his little book and wetted a stubby pencil and wrote at the top of a clean page the number, 139.

"This feller," he said, unfolding the chauffeur's papers and putting on his reading glasses, "is driving an O, without a clock!"

The lieutenant stopped writing in one blotter, and opened another.

"Wait a minute!" cried the enraged chauffeur. "I'm doing nothing of the kind! I'm driving a 1C. I'm driving a chartered car, not a taxi!"

"Tell it to the judge," said the lieutenant wearily. Humanity to him was just one idiot after another indignantly denying the most obvious facts. Any literate person could see with half an eye that this fellow was trying to take a private car out of town with a taxi-cab number plate. Only the lowest order of intelligence would attempt such stupidity.

"Sit down in the back room," ordered the lieutenant.

It was shortly before noon when Parr's private telephone in Armiston's study tinkled; and the man hunter, who had been drowsing before the fire after a long day put in before breakfast, brought himself wide awake in an instant and took down the instrument and gave heed. After a moment of utter silence on his part, he put the telephone back on its stand and resumed his sleepy regard of the coals burning on the hearth.

It had been his habit, since the insurance-widow case, in which his friend Armiston had supplied the dénouement, to make this quiet study in the secluded side street a port of call, the ambush from which to direct and observe the progress of his big cases. That was why he maintained his private phone here. It gave him not only a *point d'appui* from which he could move fast, but always, and equally important, it gave him a sort of human reflector for his mental lucubrations, in the person of Armiston. The mirror did not always slavishly give back the exact counterpart of his own mental images, but frequently embellished or even distorted them to good avail. Oliver lay back in his study chair, his head hammocked in his interlaced fingers, as he gazed at the ceiling and waited for Parr to arrive at the vocal point in his meditations. Finally the deputy sat up, rubbing his eyes.

"To resume," he said gruffly, yawning. "Coincidence No.—what number is it, by the way?"

"Seven," said Oliver. "What is it?"

"The high-heeled shoes in the snow."

"Ah, the young lady in search of a plumber reënters!" cried Oliver.

"And departs!" grunted the deputy. "By the Willis Avenue Bridge over the Harlem. Coincidence No. 8." He looked oddly at his companion.

"When I stop getting these breaks," he said, chuckling, "I'll resign and go to chicken farming. There are any number of other bridges she might have used for a get-away. But no, the imp of the perverse sends her to Willis Avenue—where the gorgon at the gate is none other than Lynx-eyed Heinie! He's been getting so much publicity for his eagle eye lately, that it is a matter of supreme egotism with him to let no wrong number plate escape. She was sporting a stolen taxi number plate on a brand-new sixteen-cylinder private limousine!"

"There is nothing so heinous about that, is there?" demanded Armiston.

"Oh, but there is!" cried the deputy. "You can't get away with rough stuff like that—not with Lynx-eyed Heinie on post, anyway! Heinie took the outfit to the station house. And when they finally look inside, behold, it is none other than the little dame who turned up at the murder scene at one o'clock this morning to take Joe the Oysterman off the job while the act was being put on. Neat, eh? Nothing Chinese about that chase, is there, Oliver?"

"How did they identify the girl?" asked Armiston. "She was not known to be a fugitive. There was no alarm out for her, was there?"

"That's another story," said the deputy, his eyes twinkling. "At the station house the discovery is made that there is a stowaway on board."

"Aboard the limousine?"

"The limousine! My man Pelts! Curled up in the spare tire on the rear deck!" He laughed outright. "He had assigned himself to shadow her. This limousine called for her, so he hopped a ride on behind."

"What has she got to say for herself?" asked Oliver.

"We're bringing her here for interrogation," said Parr. "You are to do the interrogating."

"Here?" ejaculated Armiston. "I?" he cried. It had happened before. On several occasions prisoners or involved persons whom Parr did not wish to subject to the white light of publicity entailed by a visit to Headquarters, had been quietly brought here.

"What am I to question her about?"

"Murder," said the deputy blandly. "You have a way with the ladies. I won't step in with my hobnail shoes, unless it is necessary."

He turned at a sound in the street. A long, low, profiteering-looking vehicle, as shiny as if it had just come out of a bandbox, hauled up in front of the door, accompanied front and rear by motorcycles, who, for once in their careers, were not working their sirens. It carried taxi number plates, which always begin with an O; Oliver could see that, now that he had been told. Otherwise he would not have noticed. Morel stepped out and handed to the street two elaborately befurred young ladies in high-heeled pumps and sheer stockings. In another moment they were ushered into the study, and Oliver stepped forward as the owner.

"I am Oliver Armiston," he said, fingering his single gray lock, a nervous gesture of his. "This is Mr. Commissioner Parr, of the police. This apartment," he added, rubbing his hands and glancing about as if inviting attention to the detail of the room, "is for the moment the chamber of the inquisition, where the question ordinary and extraordinary will be proposed to you." He smiled feebly.

"A very charming apartment," said the elder of the two, unfastening her fur tippet. "I didn't know the police maintained a private salle for the—what do they call it?—the third degree."

"Only in exceptional instances, madame," he said, bowing. "You are Helen Bramsil, the sculptress, I believe?"

"I see you have something of mine!" the elder one exclaimed. "That reassures me." She moved to the mantel and took down a small bronze Isis, turning it to every side. "It is really good, isn't it? I hadn't seen it for years."

"Splendid," agreed Oliver. "I have something of Miss Vinson's too. But it's only in plaster." From his secretary he produced a plaster cast painted to simulate the patina of bronze. It was a sleepy cat playing with a turtle. "I picked it up at an exhibition," he explained. "Sometime when you have it cast you must let me have a copy. Now, if you will take chairs, we might proceed with the more serious business." He paused awkwardly, seeking an opening. The elder woman, without a show of rancor, but nevertheless with a swift decisiveness, cried out:

"Is it a crime so heinous in the eyes of the police to be caught in the act of driving in a chartered car that happens, by some accident of which we are unaware, to be using the wrong number plate? Is that why we were detained for an hour at the police station? Is that why we are brought here under guard for questioning?"

"It isn't the fact itself," said Oliver, "although I will say it is a remarkable thing that you were able to proceed as far as you did before being stopped. There are sheep and goats among automobile number plates."

"I am aware of that," she said. "But why must I be dragged about the city like a felon?"

"The insignificant fact has its peculiar concomitant in this instance."

"Which is?" she demanded.

"Murder," said Oliver quietly. He studied their faces. But the word called up no qualms for them.

"We!" she cried incredulously. "Do you mean to say that we have been brought here to be put to the question in regard to someone's murder?"

"This young lady," said Oliver, turning to Miss Vinson, "is believed to have some information that will be of value to the police. ... Our information is that you were present, Miss Vinson, at the time a murder was committed."

"I?" murmured Miss Vinson. "Wh-when?" she asked blankly.

"This morning at one o'clock."

"But who—who was murdered?" she cried helplessly.

"The Rev. Mr. Bentham," said Oliver. He added, "Not very reverend, I believe."

Bentham. The name apparently meant nothing to her.

"You read the newspapers," said Oliver, as a matter of fact.

She said, quite simply: "No. I never—I do not read newspapers." She read books—all the latest ones—saw all the plays, kept *au courant* of all the arts, but she did not read newspapers. Oliver concealed his astonishment.

"For once, I ask you, please violate your rule," he said, "and glance over the headlines, at least." He handed her a morning paper. This spot murder did not occupy a very prominent place, nor a large amount of space. These machine-gun killings, horrible as they were, had become too frequent to be prime news.

The two sculptors knitted their brows over the headlines and looked up, more puzzled than before.

"You admit you were there," insisted Oliver.

"I?" she repeated vaguely.

"Let me refresh your memory," went on Oliver. "At one o'clock this morning you arrived home from a party at the Arts Club to find that your water pipes had frozen and burst, and the water was flooding everything. What did you do then, Miss Vinson?"

She stared at him, aghast.

"Maybe you can tell me," she said, at last finding her voice, "what I did then."

"I can do that," said Oliver. "You have a very accommodating friend who has served you in previous emergencies. Shall I name him? Joe the Oysterman. That is, he sells oysters in the *r* months; in summer he is Joe the Bootblack. It is a different identity, with the change of seasons. You gave him your key. He gave you his apron. You would tend bar for him, dish up oysters if any customers came along." He made the gesture of ladling soup, smiling. "He went to turn off the water. He was gone how long?" demanded Armiston.

She turned her troubled face from him to her companion, and back again.

"You are not asking me to inculpate Joe! You are not assuming that he left on my errand—to go and commit—commit—this—murder!" she stammered, breathless with foreboding.

"No," said Oliver. "No, not at all. Unfortunately, it is not so simple as that. Joe's time during his absence is fully accounted for. How long was he gone?"

"About twenty minutes, I should say," she replied. She stepped to Oliver's desk and picked up the newspaper, and looked at it a second time. "My geographical sense is not very good," she said. "Did this murder occur anywhere near that corner?" she asked.

"On the other side of the brick wall against which you were standing," said Oliver. He paused through several seconds. Then he added slowly: "There is reason to believe it occurred during the twenty minutes Joe was absent."

She took a deep breath, turned to her companion with a helpless gesture.

"And I am—I am actually under suspicion?" she stammered. "Under suspicion—of having committed this—murder?"

"You were present, and must be accounted for," said Armiston soothingly. "You were one of the coincidences. ... No. 5, I think, wasn't it, Mr. Commissioner?" he asked. Mr. Commissioner did not deign to reply. Oliver smiled reassuringly. "Coincidence is always under suspicion in real life," he said. "In my line of effort—literature—it is, I might say, our meal ticket. But with the police, a coincidence is a very questionable occurrence."

If he sought to ease the strain for her by persiflage, he did not succeed. She sank back in her chair. Helen Bramsil put an arm about her.

"Were you there, Beatrice?" asked the elder woman.

"I was there," said the young sculptress, nodding. "Yes, around one o'clock," she added.

"Did you see anyone in the street?" asked her inquisitor.

"No." She was positive about that.

"Did you hear anything?" asked Oliver. "Anything that sounded like a shot?"

She was thinking hard, growing more and more uneasy. She said, finally:

"There was a car of some kind around the corner—I couldn't see it. It was in trouble. They were working over it."

"They?" queried Oliver quickly.

"Someone," she said nervously. "It may have been one, or several. They were racing the engine. It back-fired terrifically!" Suddenly aghast again, she put her fingers to her ears, looked up, horror-stricken. "Could it have been the shots I heard?" she gasped. "There were shots, weren't there? It was a terrible din!"

"Possibly," said her inquisitor, almost carelessly. "There was a taxi in trouble around the corner at the time. There was nothing else you saw or heard?"

"Wait a minute," she murmured. "Let me think," she breathed. She put out a hand and took her companion's hand. She cast a nervous glance at Oliver. "I'm not implicating Joe; I wouldn't involve him if I could help it," she said timidly.

"You haven't, so far," Oliver assured her. "Was there something else?"

"Yes," she said, unexpectedly. "There was another car." Only the shrewdest observer could have noted the change in the atmosphere of the room. The two women did not. "It stood—it stood in front of Joe's place," she said, in the low tones of one telling herself something, for the hypnotic effect of her own words. "It was a little, closed coupé, rather shabby. There was no snow on the hood. I knew the engine was running, because I could see the bright work shiver when the light struck it." She looked up at her companion with a forced smile. "I was thinking of you, Helen, and your bronze doors; I was envying you. Do you know why? It's not very flattering—the mechanics of thought. It didn't come to me at the time, but now I see it all. The wind," she explained, "blew some of the snow off the number plate of that car, so I could read the first two characters of the number. They were 1C."

"1C," said Parr, speaking for the first time; he might have been an echo, for he relapsed instantly.

"I happened to know, before our unfortunate experience with your lynx-eyed person," she said, brightening a little, "that all 1C numbers are used for rented cars, chartered limousines. Miss Bramsil has been renting one lately," she explained to Oliver. "A 1C car. The thought fascinated me. It is so interesting to pick out the 1C cars in the street. They are so chic, élite; they have the air. This one, though, was very cheap and shabby." She laughed nervously at her own effervescence. She took her companion's arm. "That's why I was thinking of your bronze doors so enviously, Helen," she said. ... "She was on my mind all night," Miss Vinson explained to Oliver. "I called her up this morning. She came for me. We were on our way to New Haven when you stopped us about the number plate." She cried suddenly: "You stopped us for having a taxi number, instead of the usual 1C. How did it happen we had a taxi number? Why did that shabby coupé have a 1C plate?"

"Someone may have changed plates on the two cars during the night; for purposes of his own," offered Oliver. He added: "Coincidence No. 10—or is it 11? It does seem rather far-fetched, even for a coincidence, however. Was the coupé occupied, Miss Vinson, when you saw it?"

"The windows were clouded with frost; I couldn't see," she replied. There was a hint of uncertainty in the reply.

"But your impression was—"

"That it was not," she said.

"If I should tell you," pursued Armiston, "that there were no tracks in the snow in front of Joe's, except your own, coming from your home and going to it, and Joe's tracks, going to your home and coming back—that is, if I should tell you there were no footprints to the curb where you saw the car, what would you say to that?"

She thought a long time, eying him. "Then the car was occupied and someone was sitting in it, waiting," she said.

"And drove away without getting out?" queried Armiston's low voice.

"Yes," she breathed.

"Was it still there when Joe came back?"

"Yes."

There was a long silence. Parr shifted uneasily. He seemed almost on the point of breaking his silence. But things were going well as it was. Still, he turned and looked at Oliver uncertainly.

"You say you had no customer while Joe was gone?" asked Oliver.

"No one," she replied. She smiled. "You have just told me that there were no other footprints coming up to the bar. Are you trying to trap me?"

"No," said Armiston. He studied her for a long time. The ordeal she withstood easily now. She had completely recovered her poise. "You tended bar for Joe before when he helped you out in an emergency?" he asked.

"Yes. Twice—no, three times, I think, in the past two years. He is really very obliging."

"Did you ever serve a customer while you were tending bar for Joe?" asked Oliver.

"Yes," she said. "Once. I'm afraid I didn't acquit myself very well."

"Tell us about it," Oliver begged.

"There's nothing to tell," she laughed. "I know how to make an oyster stew, but I couldn't find his oysters, nor the milk. The customer got tired of waiting and went off while I was still looking."

"Did you find them afterward?"

"Finally, when it was too late," she said, laughing.

"I'm curious to know where," said he invitingly.

"You know, that place really isn't so small as it looks," she said. "There is a door behind those pots and pans; you have to take them down to see it! I did. Once I found that door, of course I had to open it and look behind it. The Pandora complex!" she laughed. A curious silence took possession of the room. No one moved. The girl, utterly unconscious of the change in tension, went on: "There is quite a hall behind it—an old dusty storeroom. There were his oysters, in a tub; and a big can of loose milk, like the big ones you see in the country. But it was too late," she sighed. "My customer—my only customer—was gone without having a chance to appreciate my special stew. But I put a quarter in the cash drawer for Joe," she concluded.

"What is your special stew recipe?" asked Armiston.

"Well, I bring the milk almost to a boil, and the juice to the same heat," she began methodically. "Then mix, and stir well. Then I add the oysters, two or three at a time, and bring it all to almost a boil again. About three minutes, no more. Then, lots of butter, salt, and paprika if you want it. And there you are!"

They laughed together.

"Your witness, Mr. Commissioner," said Oliver. "And a very frank one too."

Parr said: "Sorry we have annoyed you. We have to watch number plates very closely. Someone switched plates on your car. Probably some amateur; no old-timer would ever pick a 1C plate. They probably went to the extra precaution of not only stealing a car for some job of their own but an extra set of number plates too. They will turn up in the news some day soon," he said complacently. "Too bad you don't read the newspapers."

"How perfectly fascinating!" she cried.

"Morel," said Parr, "will you see that the young ladies are outfitted with regular plates and started on their way without further annoyance?"

Morel took them out, and the cavalcade, headed and flanked by motorcycles, moved off through the snow-filled street. Oliver and Parr started out in the official car. For the most part, the journey was made in silence. Once Oliver asked a question.

"What do you make of that phantom car with the 1C number plates?" queried he. "It certainly wasn't there when the police arrived."

"Coincidence," grunted Parr gruffly. He added, after a mental calculation: "No. 11."

They got down at the murder scene. There was a great crowd in the street now. They would be here for hours. Such is the fascination of horror to a neighborhood. The deputy spoke to several of his men and went at once to the oyster bar. Joe was asleep, or seemed to be; but when Parr, without a word, began taking down the pots and pans that hung against the rear wall, the oysterman very carefully opened his eyelids so he could see; otherwise he sat rigid. Parr uncovered the forgotten door of the ancient family entrance of the pre-Volstead gin mill. He peered in, sprayed his spotlight on the floor, then entered. Several seconds passed. The oysterman turned his eyes furtively this way and that; his breathing became labored. But when the sound of Parr's returning footsteps reached his ears he could stand it no longer. He slipped off the stool, crouching; he moved back the street door and peered out; then, with a half-suppressed cry of desperation, he sprang out—into the very arms of two policemen waiting for him. He fought frantically, hopelessly. He shrieked, "He stole my savings! He laughed in my face!" The crowd surging in front of the murder scene shifted from the street to the avenue like a great, sluggish swarm of bees. They could hear the poor fellow crying, "He robbed me! He robbed me, I tell you!" and among the crowd there were the usual thoughtless cries of "Lynch him! Lynch him!" Whistles sounded, sirens whined, police cars plowed furrows through the crowd—it was too slippery to use horses—and the reserves fought their way to the prisoner with whizzing clubs.

The story, in the end, which came swiftly, was pitifully simple. Joe was one of those legendary, gnomelike creatures to be found in every neighborhood, about whom, fantastically, had grown the usual tale of a miser's horde. Actually it was a slim little competence swept together by denials of wants unknown to ordinary mortals. And Bentham, the plausible rascal, had taken it from him with roseate promises. When Joe realized he had been the stupid dupe of the trickster, there was to his simple Corsican soul but one answer, death. The weapon was his only difficulty. But the night birds who patronized his bar helped him to that. Then he waited for his prey to come to the pay station, which he did almost nightly.

"Then he was wise enough to walk—not run—to the nearest exit," said Parr. "Perfect psychology, Oliver, even if it was subconscious. Naturally, the thick cops didn't suspect a get-away in that direction, because there were no footprints in the snow in the side street. That trick taxi didn't show up until after the murder. That helped. Then the girl came along and provided him with a perfect alibi in the Chinese chase the police put on. I'm glad she doesn't read newspapers," mused Parr. "She would feel bad about it."

"What was the break?" asked Oliver. In the chain of friendly coincidences that accompanied the oysterman on his vendetta there must have been one not so friendly.

"The guy who switched those number plates," laughed the deputy. "If it hadn't been for that taxi plate on the limousine, you never would have had a chance to ask her where Joe kept the oysters."

Unfinished Business

IN the village of Yorkville, the home of the *Hasenpfeffer* and broiled pig's feet, and *Kellners* in baggy Tyrolean shorts, much of the flavor of the older days among the people and their shops still persists under the thin film of metropolitan life that overflows it all. In the older sections there are still some of those shops where the proprietor lives with his business twenty-four hours of the day, coming and going, not by bus or subway, as is the usual urban custom in these latter times, but via a tiny circular staircase, rising out of the shop in the very middle, and leading to the upper regions, a squirrel-cage contraption not unlike the one we see in a firehouse winding itself around the brass pole. The new idea is to get as far away from business as possible, once the day is done. The old one was to sleep on the lot, with the added bondage of a night bell.

There had been one such establishment, a chemist's shop overlooking the rolly waters of Hell Gate, that Parr, the police deputy, had occasionally over a course of years glanced at with an inquiring eye. It was indubitably a chemist's shop. It had pills and pastils, unguents and emollients to sell. It had bright clean windows, limpid bottles of many colors; a gilded mortar and pestle hung over the door; inside, tiers of jars and bottles marked in gold leaf with occult alchemic symbols reached up to the very ceiling on all the walls. The business had been going on for years; indeed, into the second generation; for the legend, CHEMIST, and the date—Est. 1889—was picked out in colored brick against the façade between the second and third floors.

The proprietor—one Horatius Bounds—was a diminutive person, almost a dwarf, of comfortable middle years. He could be seen many hours each day, sitting at his desk or standing at his open door, always with a long pipe of tobacco, at which he puffed in absent-minded meditation. Many times each day he could be seen ascending the staircase, which was a tight fit for one of his prosperous girth. He had the august dignity of a professional midget and met all customers, or those who sought to become such, with a grave courtesy—and almost invariably with a regretful apology for being, as he said, a *drogerie*, and not a modern drug store.

It was so seldom he sold anything, that Parr had long since come to the conclusion that to retain his figure he must live on air. In other words, the establishment was regular in every way except that, contrary to all laws of gravity and economics, it had no visible means of support. This, of course, did not necessarily involve moral turpitude.

Just why the great man hunter's eye was arrested in the beginning by this establishment, it is doubtful if even Parr himself could have said. But it was a fact that throughout his city of seven million souls he had many similar points in his mind's eye to which he continually gave sly heed, much as the family cat keeps tab, in its apparently aimless meandering about its bailiwick, of promising mouse holes. Parr had this sixth sense for crime. It was so highly developed that he would find himself wondering how certain places and certain persons managed to resist the impulse they must possess, he felt, for crime and violence. It was the same subconscious protective sense that caused his confrere, the fire chief, to lie awake nights waiting for certain fire traps, card-catalogued in the back of his brain, to break out in spontaneous combustion.

A great editor, in slack times, makes news. Just so the police deputy, when his plant slowed down for want of raw material to grind, would hopefully nudge promising prospects. It was not that he played the *agent provocateur*. But there were always a certain number of rats of crime just about to come out of their holes; and the sooner they could be induced to emerge to be started on their inevitable journey to the big house up the river, the better. Every now and then he would tell off a bright young man, or a pair of them, to cast an inquiring eye over Herr Bounds and his plant, to ascertain, if possible, how he managed to violate the laws of gravity—what, as the prize fighters say, was holding him up.

"What have you got to say to me about it?" he demanded brusquely of shabby little Pelts, in three vests and two pairs of pants, and the general air of a dilapidated junk man. In slack times Pelts, when the jugs were empty and the big game lay deeper in the brush of their jungle, was apt to take cruises to nowhere—hunting, like the hound dog that he was, on his own. This morning he backed up to the rear entrance of Centre Street with a ding-dong junk cart and, ignoring the jeers of the nobby rookies clustered in the halls, made his privileged way into the presence of his master. He stood there ill at ease, hat in hand, his gaze wandering from one point of the room to another but never by any chance resting on his chief. Parr's senses quickened. These signs and omens were as so many signals to him.

"Well," he demanded, "what about it? He never sells anything. Does he ever buy anything?"

Pelts shifted uneasily in his ragged shoes.

"He buys old newspapers," he admitted. He gazed cockeyed at the coat of arms of the great city, that hung above the desk.

"That's frugal," said Parr. He eyed Pelts. There was something here; it must be taken out bit by bit, like a cork stuck in a bottle. "How old must they be?"

"He—he ain't particular," replied the one-man dog. "Anything that's secondhand."

"City newspapers?"

"And country newspapers."

"Where does he get them?"

"Buys 'em. Buys 'em—by the bale—from junkmen."

Parr said suspiciously, "You haven't been selling him any, have you?"

Pelts replied quickly, "No, sir. No, sir!" He added after a pause: "I bought some off him."

"Oh, he sells them too! By the bale?"

"Yes, sir."

The deputy drummed on his desk, examining his man with carefully concealed hope.

"Bring me a bale," he ordered curtly.

Pelts was gone like a shadow. In a moment two porters wheeled in a monumental, ragged bale such as one espies on pushcarts along the water front, and wonders what anyone could sell out of that one-half so precious as the stuff they buy. Pelts did not think it necessary to explain that for weeks in odd hours he had been lugubriously, and with enticing cries, trundling that cart to collect such precious trifles as poverty-stricken householders will hoard to sell; until, one fine morning. Herr Bounds had crooked a finger at him and frugally negotiated the sale of a bale of waste paper.

"Morel!" commanded the deputy sharply; and the handsome young Morel, dressed as if he were just in off a matinée stag line, instantly appeared. They broke open the bundle.

"They are clipped!" exclaimed Morel.

"Naturally," agreed Parr. "They are exchanges." He was wise in all callings. He held up a newspaper. It bore a machine-stamped postal address above the flagstaff on the front page—Exchange Editor, *The Post*. All newspapers exchange copies daily with hundreds of other newspapers throughout the country. This one had been clipped ragged. But what items had been snipped out by the professional scissors of the exchange editor, and what, if any, had been of such particular import as to merit the attention of Herr Bounds, it was impossible to divine. There were dozens, hundreds of exchanges, from all parts of the country, of dates running back a year and more. Parr shook his head dubiously. He cast them aside.

"Here we are!" he cried. "Here's one from the bunco-steerer's paradise!"

He held up a little country newspaper. It was two months old. He had never heard of its town, he had never heard its name. But to an archæologist such as he, forever delving in the detritus, the sedimentary deposits, the talus, that form and re-form in the everyday erosion of a great city, it was a find. It was folded, or had been folded, in that curious, fluted manner which the hawkers of out-of-town newspapers, in Bryant Park behind the Library, adopt as best calculated to catch the eye of a stranger in their midst.

These news merchants, playing on the yen of every traveler for news from his home town, display great panels of newspapers coming from all over the continent. At any hour of the day or night, you would find strangers standing there reading, rapt, their *Bugle, Clarion, Palladium, Mercury, Beacon* or *Blade*. The police kept a fatherly eye on these readers who so innocently advertised themselves and their habitat for the guidance of con men seeking to enter into friendly discourse with them with the object of selling them the Brooklyn Bridge or a share in the ferry tolls.

Fully a quarter of the bale consisted of these castoffs from the out-of-town stands. They were from cities and towns all over the East, of old dates. And they had all been clipped. It was fair to assume they had been clipped by our friend the druggist.

It was like a picture puzzle, Parr and Morel sorted them by town, date, geographical unit, fascinated by the speculation as to what gleaning from this broad harvest had attracted the little druggist without visible means of support. There were countless neat, little, empty squares, some only a few lines in length, others of a column, several columns. It was their daily routine to search for needles in haystacks, and it required merely the shadow of the shade of hope or that unweighable wish called a hunch, to stir the inertia of the impossible. In an hour there were a score of neat and carefully classified stacks of cast-off home-town *Clarions* and *Bugles* and *Dispatches*, and all had seen their brief day on the panels of Bryant Park and had been fortuitously arrested on their last journey to the junk heap, to be questioned here, under the ultra-microscope of crime detection. The only evidence they bore were neat rectangular holes carefully boxed in by column rules. These were negative images. It was but the turn of the hand for an overlord who had the police of the whole world at his beck and call, eager to exchange samples with him, to wire the score of cities and towns for complete copies of certain papers of specified dates. Then silent, ceaseless surveillance closed down about the *drogerie*, an invisible, impenetrable, imperceptible screen.

The Pines Crossing case, as it came later to be docketed, wore on. It was an afternoon in October, when the threat of early frost was in the air. The picture was undisturbed. Everything in the street was as usual. The august little old man stood in his neat doorway, smoking his long pipe, the while he watched with the wary eye of an owner uneasy for his plate glass—for a group of boys were noisily playing ball at the end of the little street. A junkman was haggling with an old woman at the corner. Morel, coming off the ferry on which he had become a regular commuter of late, was taking stock with a professional eye of the scene, of the foot passengers. An elderly gentleman in sober black, suggesting that modest degree of affluence which permitted him to patronize an old-fashioned basement tailor for his conservative attire, was approaching at the careful yet firm pace of the aged—a stout stick feeling the way ahead.

It was not the countenance, that was almost entirely concealed under a grizzled beard, nor the keen look in the eyes that peered out under the broad brim of a black hat, that caused Morel's pulses almost imperceptibly to quicken. At the moment he couldn't have told himself just what it was, but it was some iota of stored-away knowledge gleaned from the hours of constant riffling of pictures in the gallery down town, of readings and rereadings of the shoals of carefully classified data of persons and things which the police, in their guard over the peace and safety of their people, find it invaluable to set down in black and white. At some time his mind had drawn up and absorbed a particule, a drop, as if by capillary attraction; and in this moment that portion of his memory box came to life and said quietly, "This is it." Instinctively he passed the high sign to Pelts, who had taken up his cart again with painful cries for something old, anything old.

At that instant there came an alarm. At the sharp crack of a bat on a hard baseball, a wild yell went up from the boys playing their game at the end of the street. The hit was a line drive directly at the head of the feeble old man with the cane, who, in addition to being feeble, seemed further incapacitated by deafness, for apparently he did not hear the warning shout. But just as it seemed the ball was about to crush out his very brains, he put up a careless hand and caught it, caught it on the "meat" hand, as ball players say, without even taking the trouble to look at it. He carelessly tossed it back to the astonished boys without altering his pace. He turned in at the chemist's shop.

Old Bounds stood aside for him, bowing politely; and after a farewell puff of his pipe and a look up and down the street, he knocked out the ashes and followed his customer in. Morel did not check his stride or look behind. At the first telephone he put in a hurry order for two men.

An hour later he found the deputy sitting with Oliver Armiston, friend and occasional collaborator of the man hunter in the science of crime in its more abstruse aspects, in the latter's cozy study in the East Fifties.

"He had on his patriarch make-up," began Morel, broaching his story without informatory headlines. "See if you get this. Look! He walked like this."

The young dandy imitated the old man's curious, shuffling gait. The two stared at him.

"Maybe I don't do it right," said Morel. "Every bone in his two feet has been broken, at one time or another."

Parr had suddenly become all alive.

"The Barber?" he cried incredulously.

"At one time or another!" gasped Oliver, the untutored. "Good heavens! Had he been through the Spanish Inquisition, then, and been broken up bone by bone?"

Parr chuckled. "A ball player," he explained. "A big-league catcher—and a dandy in his day. He could peg down to second without taking either foot off the ground."

Morel nodded, smiling at his chief.

"But—broken feet?" blurted out Oliver. "Did he catch with his feet?"

"Foul tips, yes," said Parr. "In the old days, many a man who caught behind the bat got his feet smashed up. It finally put the Barber out of the game—made him a crook," he added grimly. "The Barber!" he exclaimed rapturously, with the gusto of a fisherman who feels the first tug of a big one. "Why, the last time I heard of the Barber, he was going straight—after he came out of Dannemora." He went on, amazed: "And he is conniving with the *drogerie?*"

Morel related the incident of the Barber carelessly picking the hot line drive out of the air not a foot from his head, without even deigning it a look. Man is the slave of his reflexes. The Barber's identity was certified in that subconscious act. The old ball player had become a notorious blackmailer, the king-pin in the nefarious badger game. His specialty was playing the part of the aged and outraged parent, arriving in the nick of time to save his darling daughter from a fate worse than death—in other words, for the pay-off. He got his nickname from his chatter behind the bat in baseball, and he carried it with him as a moniker through his career of crime.

"Morel," commanded the deputy, "we'll have a look-see upstairs in that shop tonight. Call out the fit-throwing squad. Better do the inside work yourself."

II

At nine sharp, with the moon coming up over Greenpoint, the ferry from the Island nosed up to the Correction Pier at the foot of the street and disembarked a discharged crew of workhouse addicts; and after a brief wait it took on a fresh cargo, men and women, from a fleet of Black Marias backed up to the stringpiece, and steamed off to deliver them to durance vile for their allotted stretch. There is always a crowd of the curious standing about when these petty prisoners come and go; and strangely, it is the discharged squad coming off the Island and turned loose ashore that presents the more abject spectacle.

For workhouse addicts rather like the Island, once they get in the habit, and feel as helpless as any professional pauper when they are turned loose. The wagons were backing and filling in the narrow street to make off across town for fresh loads of misery. Then there suddenly burst on the night air a shriek of mortal terror and agony from human lips. There was a squeal of brakes, a rush of feet; the shrieks rose higher. A swarm of policemen formed as if by magic at the tail of a wagon. Instantly a surging crowd was all about. Word passed from lip to lip—some poor derelict just off the Island was down under the great wheels; he had been crushed as it backed out.

"He's hurt terrible!"

"Back there! Give him air!"

"Call the bus!"

Police cut a lane through the crowd. They picked up the poor fellow and carried him tenderly.

"There's a drug store, blessed be!" said the sergeant. "We carry him in there, boys!"

Herr Bounds was taking the air at his front door, smoking his long pipe. When he saw the bearers heading for his establishment he cried out angrily:

"Take the bum away in your wagon! I don't want him here!"

But the man was dying, they said. They brushed Bounds roughly aside. Still the indignant proprietor continued to protest, until a lieutenant turned him over to two of his men and ordered them to take him outside and hold him.

"He won't even give the poor devil a place to die in," said the policemen contemptuously. They laid the moaning creature on the flag floor, bent over him anxiously. Outside, the crowds augmented, filled the street; the spreading rumor emptied the tenements for blocks around. It was fifteen minutes before the ambulance dashed up, clanging ominously for gangway. A stretcher figure was tenderly borne to the vehicle amid a hush, and drawn inside; the ambulance moved off, gathering speed. A block from the store, the stretcher case sat up, grinning.

"Maybe you'll tell me I ain't good, now!" he boasted, taking off his bandages.

"All clear?" asked the man in charge at the *drogerie*.

"All clear," said Morel, and he lost himself in the crowd.

"When the next poor devil does you the honor of passing out in your place, just be a little more hospitable," said the lieutenant to the still-irate Herr Bounds; he set the druggist free. In a few minutes the street was quiet again, except for here and there a late cluster making hushed inquiries.

Morel joined Parr in his closed car down the street. By exercising the simple though autocratic prerogative of running through every red light they came to, they shook off any possible shadows—for crooks shadowed Parr as he shadowed them—and drew up at Armiston's door, where Parr was wont, as he put it, to "make medicine" in special instances. He liked the mirror of a lay mind to counteract the prejudice of too close a view. In the passage across town, the following brief colloquy occurred:

"Did you make a clean get-away?"

"I think so."

"What did you find?"

"Just what you expected."

"Favorite sons?"—this from Parr, cryptically.

"And daughters."

They got down and went in. Oliver was poring over a blotter full of newspaper clippings arranged in neat piles like a game of Canfield. They were the returns from Parr's wire to police chiefs in twenty cities and towns. They were the "positives" of the yawning "negatives" that had been sorted so carefully out of the junkman's bale of old papers. Oliver looked up, brushing back his white lock.

"You know there's nothing you can't buy from a clipping bureau," he said. "I put in an omnibus order once for clippings on murder—anything, so long as it was murder, and had appeared in print."

Parr nodded. That order, suggested by nothing but curiosity on the part of the dilettant in crime as to what tools a murderer picks up instinctively when the moment arrives, had resulted in the uncovering of the murder of poor, overly rich Barry Dilk, and the apprehension of his kinsman, Comte de Sorges, as his killer. Parr nodded at the clips.

"Give us a guess," he repeated.

Oliver considered. He rearranged a pile of books on his desk. They were all those élite little publications in which the *comme il faut* are hall-marked— the lists as rigorously prescribed, even censored, by solemn-jowled trustees sitting in camera. If you are not in these lists, you are nobody socially.

"Someone is interested in the foibles of the rich," said Oliver. "No paragraph of their doings is too insignificant, so long as the person it refers to is rich and foolish. There has lately arisen a new type, that has been aptly referred to as the rotogravure section of high life—if you get what I mean." He smiled feebly. "These all belong," he added, nodding at the stacks of clippings. "This person may be assembling material for a piquant monograph on the Foibles of High Life; or The Error of Wealth; or The Anachronism of Primogeniture; or The Second Generation of the Great Fortunes. Most of these are young rakes burning up their inheritances."

"Favorite sons," put in Parr sardonically.

"Or," Oliver said, "it may be some ironic person viewing the American scene, or someone trying to get into society."

"That's a lead," said Parr, smiling. "How does it fit, Morel?"

"It's a clipping bureau for crooks," said Morel bluntly. "There are hundreds, thousands of envelopes, filed on steel racks, alphabetically. There is a card-catalogue system, with cross-indexing. The whole layout of a job is there—personalities, pictures, habitats, servants, even house plans. It's amazing what gets into print."

Parr grunted. Thirteen years, he was thinking. He remembered now, it was thirteen years since he began bending a professional eye on the *drogerie* of Herr Bounds, a vigil kept alive by nothing more tangible than a hypothetical sixth sense of crime.

"The Barber is coming out again," said Morel. "That's what he went there for this afternoon. He's getting his layout from Bounds. Another badger game, I think."

He looked from one to another.

"Any line on it?" put in Parr gently. Things were beginning to dovetail. Fragments, if you move them about long enough, begin to take on form and meaning.

"I think he is after Briscoe Jannison," said Morel, dropping the bomb lightly in his chief's lap. "The Jannison envelope was on old Bounds' desk upstairs; he had been sorting the clips."

It was the name of a gilded youth, a playboy of the Broadway side streets of the swell speak-easies and clip joints, who was industriously and notoriously throwing away a once-proud fortune. Parr took down his own telephone, which he had maintained here for years. He spoke quietly to some voice:

"Put two men on Briscoe Jannison. Quiet. Just nurse him along. The Barber is laying him out for a badger game. … Here's another. Trail everyone that comes and goes at the *drogerie*. Easy. Don't flush them."

There was a long pause.

"Any records of old jobs?" he asked.

"I think he destroys them," said the young man. "I think he burns everything. Here's a souvenir." He took out an envelope, from which he produced several partially burned clippings. "I raked these out of the fireplace," he explained.

Parr studied them, frowning, as a paleontologist studies a bone or tooth. He held a charred fragment up to the light. It was all but illegible.

"'Selah Pines,'" he read. The name meant nothing to him.

"He is dead," said Oliver flatly.

"You knew him?"

"I know his people. It's a rich Navy family. Every generation has had at least one rear admiral. Stiff-necked bunch. They live up in Connecticut, Pines' Crossing. Everybody in the town is a Pines, or is sorry for it. Always has been. This fellow was one of your 'favorite sons.' "

"He is dead? When?"

Armiston pondered.

"Good Lord!" Oliver ejaculated. "I wonder if this dovetails." They waited. "I'm a bit hazy about it. About six or eight months ago, he killed himself—in a suicide pact; there was some woman one never heard of. His mother didn't want him to marry." He paused.

"The woman—the woman," urged Parr.

Oliver shook his head.

"I don't remember."

"Did she die?"

"No. I think not—not then, at least. They got her out of the way. Very little in the papers about it. It was hushed up. You know," mused Oliver, philosophical even in the face of the picture puzzle that was unexpectedly taking form under his very eyes—"you know, there are some very proper people to whom certain things simply do not happen. Nothing touches them—not even statistics. They stand aloof from that part of the race that indulges in crime, violence, shame, disgrace, as if these misfortunes were reserved for a different race of beings." His companions were not following. They were regarding each other musingly, communing in that silent language of the learned. Oliver rambled on, nevertheless: "And when these things actually do happen to the stiff-necked bunch, why, they simply assume that they have not happened, and act accordingly. That's a picture of the Pines family for you."

Parr had down his telephone again, was looped through to the editorial rooms of *The Times*.

"Might I borrow an envelope from your biographical files, Mercer?" he asked. "Selah Pines. ... Yes, he is dead. I'll send a messenger for it. Thanks."

To his man in Centre Street, he said:

"Send me up the stuff on the Barber and Orphan Annie."

"Orphan Annie," said Morel, nodding at Oliver.

"Who is she? Where does she come in?" demanded Oliver.

"She worked with him in his last few times out of the stable," said the deputy. "It's got all the earmarks of a job of the Barber's. Rich young rake. Stiff-necked mother. Obscure, pretty female." He looked at Morel. "He's not a killer. Something must have gone wrong. Maybe that's why the Barber has been lying low so long. ... Where is Orphan Annie?"

"She hasn't been brought in, in months," said Morel. They paused over this trifle. Oliver watched intently. "She's got a step-brother—or a half-brother. A dip, isn't he? They call him Spender."

Thus the web wove its pattern under their skilled fingers.

"Bring in the Spender!" commanded Parr, rising.

III

The deputy was strolling, taking on his daily quantum of violet rays from the southering sun. Oliver Armiston, friend and occasional collaborator in those rare instances in which the human equation intervened, walked by his side. Parr looked at his watch. It was only nine in the morning. Although dirt farmers had turned out their cows hours ago, merchants on the Avenue were only now rattling open their shutters. They paused at the top of Murray Hill, piqued by the unwonted sight of the great thoroughfare in repose.

"I'm meeting a friend here," explained the deputy, coming to anchor against a lamp-post. At ten minutes after the hour, one of those extravagant boulevard cars that require one hundred square feet of traffic room to convey one paying passenger, drew up to the curb. A stoutish gentleman, very obviously just out of the care of his matutinal handler, to judge from his pinkish, overscrubbed look, nodded gloomily to Parr and looked askance at Oliver. Parr stared at the fish-faced young man at the wheel, right-hand drive. The exhaust rumbled a deep bourdon, suggesting at least three hundred horse power, which the pale youth tooled as if it were a feather. He was a gentleman chauffeur, for, in spite of the hour, he wore a béret and a dinner jacket. Parr's scrutiny caused him to stare at the deputy. The pale youth said, scarcely moving his bloodless lips, "So you think I'm a stool pigeon, eh? Well, let me put you right. I use cops. They don't use me. I take their buttons off when I don't like them. And I don't like you."

"Briscoe—now, Briscoe," pleaded the fussy old gentleman in the back seat. "This is the distinguished Mr. Parr, and he wants to save you from an embarrassing—I think I may say dangerous—situation."

"He thinks I'm a sucker, eh?" interrupted the young rake. "Well, I don't want his sympathy—or his help." He smiled at a pleasing thought. "I like being a sucker," he said genially. "Everybody tries to please me. You've no idea the favors they do me if I string them along. Oh, I loosen up," he said confidentially, "Sure, I've got to keep the con men contented. But let me whisper, brother; there's more gold put into the ground by prospectors than is ever taken out. ... Climb aboard," he invited, opening the door, "or we'll get a ticket for parking."

Parr declined the invitation.

"Take a little walk with me and let the young gentleman go home and rest his dinner jacket," he said to the august passenger. The passenger climbed out with many a sigh. Young Mr. Briscoe Jannison—for it was that celebrated playboy of the Broadway side streets—touched off his three hundred horse power with a jerk that almost tore the coat tails off his solicitor, the Hon. Addison Callamer.

"I've reasoned with him, Mr. Commissioner," the lawyer said as they moved along. "I told him what you told me—that the slickest of confidence men, aided by the most insidious of Jezebels, was plotting to badger him out of thousands, maybe millions—maybe his very life." He shook his head. "He pricked up his ears. He said to me, 'Badger? Badgers? Say, that's my meat. I can walk through a badger game backward, blindfolded, without barking my shins. The bigger they come, the better I like them.' And do you know," said the lawyer piteously. "I think he does like it. When I plead with him to work with the police, to help bring this band of rascals to justice, he is insulted—that a Jannison—a Briscoe Jannison—should be asked to be a stool! I don't know what to do about it," he concluded helplessly.

"Do nothing," said Parr placidly. "Let Nature take its own course."

He slipped a hand through the lawyer's arm and drew him along. They walked for a few blocks. The incident was closed. Finally the lawyer grew weary of this unwonted exertion and called a taxi. At a mystic sign from the deputy, another taxi that had been dogging their steps drew up for them, and they got in and drove down town.

The Spender was there, waiting for him. The pickpocket, the brother of Orphan Annie, the badger moll, was a miserable, timorous creature. Yet he had his rare moments of egotism—why work for a living, when you can steal it? He withered before the blank stare of Parr.

"You haven't got a thing on me, chief!" he wailed in the ready formula. "I'm going straight, chief! I swear I'm going straight!"

Yet behind it all he felt a certain pride, not only to be brought down town but upstairs. He was a small dip. But in the morning he would be stood up against a white, scored background under the glare of spotlights, and a droning voice in a loud-speaker would describe his face, his form, his bearing, his skill as a dip, and he would be turned loose to go back to his dens with an added éclat.

Parr said quietly. "There is something you want to tell me, Spender."

"I—who—me?" The Spender was all cringing humility. "I'm going straight, chief. I swear it, by my sainted mother."

"Swear by your sainted sister!" rasped Parr.

The man seemed to shrivel. His pasty face turned green. He looked around in an agony of fear, for some way of escape. His lips moved, but not to speak; they trembled with his chattering teeth. There was a long period of utter quiet.

"You've got something you want to tell me, Spender," urged Parr gently. The man remained mute. Parr said, "We are not after you, Spender. We want to help you." He went to his desk and immediately busied himself with the accumulation of unfinished business, new business, promising prospects; it was an unending stream, like water through a mill. He said over his shoulder, "Go inside and sit down, Spender. Think it out. Take your time." The Spender was led away and the door closed on him.

"I think she has kicked in—she's dead," Parr muttered.

"Who?"

"Orphan Annie, of course. Who else? Didn't you see how it hit him?" He asked, looking up from his work: "You know the admiral, don't you, Oliver?"

"Admiral?"

"Yes. Pines. Selah Pines' guardian. He's retired. He hangs out at the United Service."

"Oh, I know him, yes," admitted Oliver.

"Could you bring him in without ruffling his dignity?"

Oliver lifted his hands in protest.

"Parr, there are certain things that simply do not happen to a Pines," he began weakly.

"I could send a wagon for him," chuckled the deputy. "Tell him," he urged, "that we've got something down here we'd like to consult him about in the public interest. He'll come."

Oliver departed on the distasteful task. It was half an hour later, in Morrisania, that a police-box signal lamp winked twice. The man on post took down the phone and took the message. He strolled down the block where two of Parr's men were watching a house. The boss, he said, wanted them to bring him in. The two men waited, and waited, and waited. Toward eleven, the door they watched opened, and an elderly man in spats and a boutonnière came out, accompanied by a pretty young woman carrying a gay parasol. She looked up at the sky as if wondering what effect it would have on her complexion. The gentleman looked up and down the street, and noted the pair of young men opposite who were tossing an orange back and forth in a game of catch. As the couple stepped to the curb for a taxi, the game of catch became more violent. One throw got away, and the orange shot straight at the head of the young lady. She screamed. But her escort put out a careless hand and picked the orange out of the air not six inches from her head.

"Still good, eh, Barber?" laughed one of the detectives, running up and rattling a pair of handcuffs. "Can you still peg down to second without lifting either foot?"

The Barber looked from one to the other blankly.

"Do you want to wear these?" asked the detective. "Or will you be good and give us a ride down town in your taxi?"

"I'll give you a ride, boys," said the Barber. "What's on the ticket?"

They shook their heads. They didn't know. The three got in and drove away, and the young lady, with a shrug, walked off. It was a pleasant drive down town. There exists this curious camaraderie between the minions of the law and their quarry. But when the Barber was led into Parr's office and saw that glaring old sea dog, Beverly Pines, Rear Admiral, U. S. N., retired, sitting there, it was as if a cold hand closed over his heart.

"Do you know this man, admiral?" asked Parr politely. The noble scion of the tree of Pines, the patriarchal autocrat of this generation of that distinguished lineage, looked distastefully at the Barber. Then he stared, popeyed, for a moment, another moment; he paused—paused too long. He shook his head, glared at Parr.

"Walk, Barber," commanded Parr. "Walk back and forth in front of the desk." The Barber's knees trembled, his hands were sweating. At that moment, "Barber" though he was known to fame, he would not have trusted himself to speak. But he walked. There was no reason why a man should refuse to walk. He picked up and set down his broken feet with the odd, shuffling movement. He made no attempt to disguise his walk. Indeed, he was unconscious of his curious gait, had no suspicion that it betrayed him. The Barber came to a halt, trying to look self-possessed. Parr glanced at the old sea dog with a confidential smile. The admiral surrendered.

"Mr. Commissioner," he whispered in a husky voice, "there are certain things—You understand, our family—"

"Yes, yes, I know," said Parr soothingly. "There are certain things that simply do not happen to certain people." He said, after a moment of thought, "I don't think we'll have to drag you into it. The point is, you identify him."

"Yes, I will say that." The admiral glanced fearfully at the prisoner. "He is the father of the young woman who brought us so much trouble last spring."

"That's fine!" said Parr. "That will be all, admiral. I don't think we'll have to drag you into it. If by any chance we must, I am sure—you being the person of fine traditions and high sense of public duty that you are—you will oblige us. Thank you."

The perturbed patrician made hasty adieu.

Quiet settled again over the chamber of the inquisition. Parr worked at his desk. Oliver polished the head of his stick. After a time, the Barber began his chatter:

"Chief, I got something to tell you you'll be glad to hear. Things are going fine, swell. I got a house; I got a garden; I got a wife! It's good to sit home, at peace with the world, friends with the dicks, with an easy conscience. It warms the heart, it eases the mind. Sometimes, when I think of those poor benighted hustlers hovering in shadows, jumping at every squeak, waiting for a pinch around the next corner. I wonder how I stayed it out. But that stretch of mine up in the woods was good, chief—good. It gave me time to think, to take stock of my heart, to search my soul."

Parr raised an entreating hand.

"Sit down over there, Barber, and think," he suggested; and, crestfallen, the Barber sat down against the wall. Half an hour passed. Parr and Oliver started out to lunch.

"Throw us a line, won't you, chief?" pleaded the Barber.

"Someone wants to see you, Barber—wants to see you bad," said the deputy. He fixed a hard eye on the prisoner. "Think it over, Barber," he added, and departed.

"What have you got on him?" demanded the puzzled Oliver, outside.

"Nothing," admitted Parr. "We'll let it simmer on the back of the stove for a few hours."

He did not return after lunch. Hours passed. Meantime, in those two rooms in Centre Street, the two occupants sat alone with their thoughts, their hopes and fears. Men came and went, paying no heed to them. Nothing happened—that is, outwardly. But inwardly the mechanism of their brains moved ceaselessly, irresistibly, whether they would or no. They sorted their thoughts over and over again, classified them, codified them, filing and cross-indexing, rejecting, accepting, rejecting again; trying in vain to banish from the timorous counsel they sought to give themselves, the benumbing effects of hate, fear, despair, revenge, even remorse. At four, Parr came in with his *fidus Achales.*

"Bring him in," said the deputy to Morel. Morel brought in the Spender. The Spender and the Barber discovered each other.

The dénouement was almost electric. It was so simple; the mechanism of silence, waiting, of foreboding, had effected the subtle demolition so beautifully that to Oliver, standing there agape, the climax would have been almost ludicrous had it not been so rueful, so tragic, so final. The Barber, at the sudden confrontation, actuated by the reflex of an uncontrollable rage, sprang up with the howl of an animal; and seizing his chair, he swung it high above his head and rushed madly at the astonished Spender.

"You rat!" he cried, and in that one word he compressed the sum total of a thief's conception of dishonor. "You've ratted on me! You, and that damned, bungling sister of yours!"

Spender, with a shriek of terror, flung himself behind Morel, begging piteously.

"Save me! Hold him off! He'll kill me! He killed her! Yes, he killed her! He'll bash my brains in!"

Two men had the Barber firmly. He ceased to struggle. But his fury of speech was not to be controlled. He barbered incoherently:

"She lied! She bungled! It wasn't the first time she messed up one of my perfect lays! ... Chief, listen to me. You've known me for years! I'm not for the rough stuff! When I walked in on them—her and that fool boy—"

The Spender was mumbling in a frenzy of idiotic ecstasy: "I've got him! She asked me to get him! I've got him for her!"

"Listen," pleaded the Barber passionately. "When I walks in on them for the pay-off, this young fool Selah goes into a panic and pulls a gun. She grabs it and it goes off, and he goes down. It was his own gun—you know it was his own gun!"

"And then you pinked her—to make it look real!" cried Orphan Annie's half-brother. "You didn't think she'd live long enough to tell! Well, she told me!

I promised her to get you, Barber—and I've got you! I've got you!" He waved his arms exultantly.

Oliver oddly found himself looking at the second hand of the clock. Thirty-three seconds.

When the din had at last died away and the last of the sordid litter that adheres to the final booking of a prisoner for a solved crime was finished, Parr and Armiston sat alone.

"Thirty-three seconds, Parr," said Armiston. "In thirty-three seconds you established the heretofore unsuspected fact of murder, extorted a squeal from an unwilling witness, trapped the murderer into a confession. How do you do it?"

Oliver was thinking of Herr Bounds, the bale of old papers, the man with the limp, the fragment of charred clipping, and the curious, subconscious process of reading the significance of trifles as a chemist reads symbols.

"Thirty-three seconds!" snorted Parr. "What do you mean—thirty-three seconds? What's this building standing here for? What are nineteen thousand men doing, night and day? What about acres of pictures in the gallery, reams of dope, years of watching and waiting? Say the work of a lifetime!" He smoked awhile. "Good routine, yes," he admitted grudgingly. "And don't forget I've got a man named Pelts. After all," he said, making room on his desk for fresh endeavor, "it's just a small matter of unfinished business being brought up to date."

As for the august Herr Bounds, it is pleasant to record that he still continues undisturbed in the conduct of his *drogerie* in Yorkville. Parr wouldn't disturb that picture for the world. Nevertheless, a whisper is afoot in the dens of Herr Bounds' clientele—that too many layouts he sells to the trade go wrong. Too many of his customers start for the big house up the river sooner than, under the normal turnover of the profession, they have reason to anticipate.

At Early Candlelight

A high-vaulted automobile, tricked out in brass, of a vintage of the day before yesterday, stopped before an old weathered pine mansion in an elm-shaded street; and its Negro driver said, in a cautious whisper (though the street was empty) to the little old gentleman in high hat and shawl at his side:

"Here we is, suh. They ain't no one to home. They is all in cote. Only a foolish boy they left behind. I fetched candy for him. Is we going in?"

"Yes, Arthur," said the old gentleman. "A 'For Sale' sign is conspicuously displayed. The vendor implicitly forfeits the privilege of privacy and invites the closest scrutiny. Drive in at the gate and stop at the door."

The chauffeur helped him down and the master, drawing his shawl tighter, moved off on the grass as if he wished to see the outside before he saw the in. It was an old garrison house with overhanging stories; it had gambrelled roof, like a bee hive out of a fairy tale; and the windows were of tiny panes that shone opalescent in the morning light. When he came shuffling around to the front again, Arthur had coaxed the foolish boy out, and they sat on the porch step with a bag of candy between them.

"You can't go in there!" cried the boy shrilly, when the old gentleman put his hand on the knob. "Nobody can go in there. Everybody is in court. You can't go in there."

"He can," said Arthur, nodding confidentially. "You don't know him. He can go anywheres. I'll go 'long, see, so he don't tech nothing. You watch the car, close now, mind."

The interior was still in festal array. Some weeks before, it had been dressed for a wedding. But the cry of murder had echoed through the house and everyone had fled; and the bridegroom had been taken away in irons. The family had turned the key and now it was all for sale; as if, in one act of riddance, the proud folk would wipe the horrid blot from their escutcheon. It was to have been a Colonial wedding, with guests coming in old rattling chaises and creaking thorough brace coaches, as Continentals, Red Coats and Hessians; and Dolly Madisons and Molly Starks; and all the lights were candles. There were scores on scores of many-colored candles nested in chandeliers and wall sconces. The invitations had read "at early candlelight." Arthur opened the door to the left of the great hall, disclosing a long room made sombre by the vines that clouded the windows.

"This is where he kilt his uncle, old Zenas!" whispered Arthur, with rounded eyes.

It must have been a fine sight that day, with the great fireplace and its furniture at one end, and the fluttering light of a hundred candles playing on the stencilled walls and draped embrasures. It was bleak enough now. The candles had been forgotten in the horror of that moment; and they had burned on and down to their sockets, the grease guttering in streamers.

"He was a mean ole man," whispered Arthur huskily. "He was a peddler, with a pack on his back. Pore white trash! He w'ant wanted here."

"What did he come for?" said the old man, searching the shadows of the room.

"Just meanness," whispered Arthur. "He say he have a gift for the bride!"

"What was it?"

"Nobody never did find out!" breathed Arthur, eyes wide again. "It was something mean, anyway. Maybe young Mister Ozias throwed it in the fire, with the toddy iron."

"Toddy iron?"

"Yessuh, suh." Arthur's voice sank even lower. "Young Mister Ozias— he wuz a fine boy, suh—he kilt the old man with the toddy iron—whacked him on top of the haid with it. Hole clean as a gimlet! Kilt him daid quick." He plucked his master by a sleeve, and drew him to the desk in the center of the room. "Mister Ozias, he was standing here," he whispered, taking a stand before the fire. "The old man, Zenas, he sit by the desk. The old man, he was putting the hot iron in the toddy."

"Hot?"

"Yessuh, suh. Everything was ole timey that day. They put the hot iron in the toddy. It was just make-believe, suh. Then something happen quick! They hear the racket outside and break in the door. The ole man, Zenas, he lie daid there—right there! Young Mister Ozias, he stand here—nursing his hand—his hand was blistered something terrible from that hot iron."

"Where was the iron?"

"In the fire, red hot! Mister Ozias he say he take it fum the ole man and throw it there."

"You go out," said the master. "I'll come."

Arthur went back to the boy.

"You watched that car good, boy," he said. "I'll fetch you another kind of candy. The kind with barber pole stripes running from the bottom right up to the top."

His master came out and they got into the car and drove down the silent street. Nobody was about, all the houses were closed. But when they came to the court house square there was a great crowd, people pushing around the door. They had boxes and barrels against the windows to see in, and a sprawling oak by the jurybox window was clustered with laughing boys. It all had the air of a festival, the people fighting for points of vantage. No one noticed the old car and the old man with the shawl. It stopped at a door in the side street and the sheriff came running out.

"Why, it is Judge Alan Ebbs!" he cried effusively. "Judge, we're proud to have you here. You never sat here before, did you, Judge?"

"No, Sheriff," said the judge, getting down. "Emmons is sick and I took his circuit this term."

They escorted him to his chambers. Arthur took out his rusty black gown from a bag and shook it out.

"We got to get a new one, suh," admonished the Negro. "I got to comb your hair. You got to look nice. Suh, ain't we going to do something for Mister Ozias, suh?"

"The law," murmured the old man absently, "puts fresh arms into the hands of the injurer."

The clock struck ten, and Arthur opened the door into the court room. At this signal the lounging bailiffs suddenly screamed at the top of their voices:

"Silence in the court! Hats off! All rise! His honor the court!"

There was the rustle of rising, then a hush fell. Judge Ebbs arranged his chair and the tails of his gown. With rapt gaze, seeing nothing, he looked out over the upturned faces, and the rustle of seating died down to little whisperings. They watched him in mute awe, as if the symbol of his mere presence evoked the occasion.

"Proceed with the reading of the calendar, Mister Clerk, please," he said. The voice of the clerk became a drone of bees on a hot day; and the Judge took up a pencil. The pencil moved absently, picturing candles guttering in odd shapes. The vagrant pencil began drawing toddy irons, of odd shapes of ward, butt and bow. He looked up at the cluster of lights hanging from the dome, with eyes that still did not see.

"Empanel the jury," he said gently, nodding to the upturned faces within the rail.

It was the second day of the trial. You could hear the hounds closing in; you could feel the coming shiver of the view halloo on the still air.

"Old Zenas came to your wedding, uninvited?" said the Prosecutor, with curling lip.

"Yes," said the accused Ozias.

"Your uncle, among your fine friends, in his rags?"

"Yes," said the accused.

"He brought a gift to the bride?"

Ozias made no reply. A flush covered his face.

"Was it something shameful, that you destroyed it?"

"May it please the court, there is no evidence that there was such a gift," said Mr. Whitley, for the defense, "and I ask that this line of questioning be abandoned."

"I am producing it in evidence," said the Prosecutor, coldly. "Mr. Ozias Selden," he said, "you are rich. You come from a line of prosperous people. You were to marry a woman of fashion. When her ancestors first came to this town a hundred years ago, what was their condition?"

"I have no personal knowledge," said the witness.

"This will refresh your memory," said the Prosecutor. He offered in evidence a tattered writing, in a broken frame. The lawyers crowded forward to inspect it. As the Prosecutor held it up to the jury, Ozias, livid, struggled to his feet.

"I beg of you," he implored. "Do not read it. Isn't the evidence damning enough, but what you must besmirch others?"

"Silence!" commanded the Court. "Proceed."

"Your intended wife's family name was Furness?"

"Yes."

"Her great, great grandfather was Abner Furness?"

Ozias nodded, avoiding the eyes of the girl who sat trembling at the rail.

"This is a piece of writing," said the Prosecutor, to the jury. "The murdered man, old Zenas, framed it prettily, and brought it to the bride as a gift, knowing her love for old things. It is dated June 8, 1804, this town, and is a formal notice addressed to Ozias Selden, great grandfather of the accused. It reads:

" 'We hereby notify you in all friendliness that you brought into this town Abner Furness, his wife and six children, and left them, knowing them to be paupers and indigent persons. Under the laws of the Commonwealth, you are subject to a fine of Twenty (20) Pounds for each pauper aforesaid brought by you into said town, and we advise you to take thought unto yourself for your illegal act, and within ten days remove them beyond the boundaries of said town.' "

The court was in an uproar. The bride sank back with a low moan. Bailiffs rushed about, stilling the clamor.

"Motive? Motive?" snarled the Prosecutor, in a rising voice. "Do you ask for the motive that will drive a bridegroom to murder, at the hour of his wedding? Why, to protect the fair name of his bride, of course! To hide the fact that her proud family began life here as paupers, indigents, who were run out of town as common tramps!" He turned fiercely on the accused. "There is the missing gift! You tore it to bits, cast it out of the window into the shrubbery. And in your blind rage and shame, you tore the toddy iron from his hand, and beat him to death with it! Do you deny it? Good God, man, look at your burned hands! They damn you in the sight of man!"

Ozias was crying, unheard in the uproar, "No! No! I did not strike him! He struck at me. I tore it from his hands and threw it into the fire!"

"That's all," said the Prosecutor, sitting down, in the sudden surge of stillness. All eyes turned to the bench. Judge Ebbs seemed oblivious of the turmoil. He took up a book, found a place, read. Five seconds passed, ten.

He looked up over his spectacles and said in a small voice:

"The court will recess for one hour. You, Mr. Sheriff, you, Mr. Prosecutor, and you, Mr. Whitley, will you kindly attend me in chambers?"

He arose, and in an even deeper hush, the three surprised men followed him. "We make a little journey," said Judge Ebbs. "Get your things, gentlemen."

The stony-faced Arthur drove them in the old car to the old house, and when they got down and went in, the foolish boy stared after them, sucking at his candy.

"Mr. Sheriff, has this room been examined for any means of death other than murder?" asked the judge, pausing by the table. The sheriff nodded, everything had been done.

"I hope you have erred," said the judge wistfully. He sat down at the desk, patting the book he had read from on the bench. "The law," he said, "is a 'wilderness of single instances.' But there is a providence in all things. Gentlemen, did you ever know that a few years ago there was a great American general and statesman, who would not permit his name to go before the Presidential Convention?" They looked at him curiously. "I will tell you," he said nodding. "It is in this book. He suffered a brain injury, and his doctors advised him to retire from public life."

He looked up at the puzzled faces; no one spoke.

"I will tell you about the injury," went on the judge. "The general was seated at his desk—as old Zenas was—and above the desk hung a great chandelier—as this chandelier hung above old Zenas, gentlemen." He looked at them keenly, and their eyes sought the gaudy ironwork of the old candelabra.

"The General arose suddenly, unthinking, from his chair—like this—and the spike of that low-hanging chandelier—see it!—pierced his skull, narrowly missing, by a miracle, killing him—as this one could now pierce my skull! There is your murderer!" cried the judge, springing back and pointing. "See, that spike is round—like a gimlet—not square, like the bit of your toddy iron!"

"Lights! Lights!" cried the sheriff, in a terrible voice. He found the switch and flooded the old room with light. They gazed with horrible fascination at the spike of that murderous chandelier. It was all clear now. Old Zenas, rising in choleric wrath and brandishing his iron, when his nephew destroyed the shameful gift that exposed the bride as sprung from paupers, had impaled himself on that spike and fallen dead, even as the outraged Ozias having snatched the toddy iron from his hand, turned to cast it into the flames. That soiled spike still bore evidence of its terrible work, and under the red candle grease on the desk were drops of blood.

There could be no question, Ozias was exonerated, and returned to the arms of his weeping bride.

"He's a good man, Mister Ozias," said Arthur, as he drove the judge away from court. "I knowed we'd do something."

What Is the Goat's Name?

IT was a hick town, and a hick court.

"And a hick judge," said Soberski, marshal of the brilliant array of counsel for the plaintiff; he specialized in missing heirs. "Gentlemen, the hog-calling judge from Corn Hollow enters!" he intoned in a masked voice. "Arise and make your obeisances."

Judge Alan Ebbs came into the country dining room, taking off his silk hat, unwinding his shawl, blinking a little in the gloom. At his elbow followed Arthur, his Negro chauffeur, guiding him with motherly care. As the table rose as one man, and bowed courteously to him, Judge Ebbs smiled and nodded and said:

"Gentlemen! I hope you do yourselves well."

He was passing on, when the brilliant Soberski lifted a mug of foaming bock, the first of the season, and said in his beautifully modulated voice that could wring tears from a case-hardened jury:

"Your Honor, we make oblations to the goat!" And he quoted wistfully,

" 'Make me over, Mother April,
When the sap begins to stir.' "

Judge Ebbs paused, turning on his heel, and looking quizzically into the startled faces about the table.

"Goat, did you say, sir?" he asked mildly. Then his eye caught sight of a flamboyant poster featuring a goat on the wall, the bock beer sign; the landlord had just put it there to signalize the return of spring. The judge smiled, nodding, and passed on. But a few steps on he paused again, absently abstracted.

"He's forgotten his underwear," said the brilliant Soberski, *sotto voce*. Arthur was gently urging his master to his table apart. "Yessuh, suh, some nice lam' stew with dumplings," he urged in honey tones. "You'se goin' to eat yore plate clean today, suh. And I'se got you pill in my west pocket." He drew out a chair and seated the Judge and tucked the napkin under his chin. "And you'se goin' to take it!" he added admonishingly, producing the pill from a collection of tobacco tags, buttons and beech nuts. He went off to the kitchen. During the three days the Emberson will case had droned through its dry-as-dust testimony, Arthur had completely tamed that hotel kitchen. They stood around and begged for his nod of approbation now. Arthur sniffed the dishes with closed-eyed rapture and bore them in to the judge, watching the judge hawklike as he took his first taste.

"We's eatin' good now, Jedge," he said. "I got 'em skeered. Jedge, they's a lil' boy out back—"

"Go away, Arthur."

"Yessuh, suh."

The hotel dining room had filled now. It was the only place to eat in town. Never had the town seen such a distinguished assemblage of white shirts. It was a will case, of a secret son, involving ten million dollars, and all the talent was imported. Magnificent gentlemen of the bar, who came to the bushes only on affairs of enormous significance, were clustered thicker than flies on a dead horse. The residuary legatee, Miss Amelia Emberson, a drab little creature, who had made her handkerchiefs out of old bed sheets while her brother was alive, and probably would go on doing so if she got the ten million, lifted a veil to feed herself, at her table in a dark corner, with an uneasy lawyer to stand guard. In an opposite corner sat the secret son, in the custody of a fashionplate in a maroon shirt and an azure necktie, one of Soberski's trusty runners. The secret son, whom Soberski had uncovered in a traveling tent show and coached and furbished as befitted his character in the brief, was nervously palming the saltcellar and causing it mysteriously to disappear—for he was a prestidigitator by profession and his fingers were always busy. Soberski's trusty runner kicked him viciously under the table.

"Now, once more, you benighted acrobat," whispered the trusty runner. "Where were you born?"

"In a trunk cover, in a dressing room, in the sticks—"

"No, no, no, no," sighed the coach wearily. "Now, once more. You're on the witness stand, remember. Where were you born?"

"I get you now, shill," said the secret son. "I was born in Aurora, Illinois, in the year 1877—"

The distinguished array of counsel for the defendant occupied a long table in the center of the room. Jonathan Horton had come up hurriedly this morning to take command in the field. He ate nothing. He summoned one after another of his confreres to his side, and whispered with them anxiously.

Samuel Held, the chief of staff, was urging, in a mollifying tone, "Don't pull such a long face, John. They've got nothing but that birth record written in an old book. All the substantiating witnesses are dead."

"Look at the claimant," muttered the worried old lawyer. "Did you ever see a son who was a better image of a father? That rat Soberski ought to be in jail. What about the judge? What's he been doing for three days?"

"Just what he is doing now," said Held, with a covert smile. Judge Ebbs had finished his repast, and was drawing on the tablecloth. The tent-show claimant, the drab little residuary legatee, the high tension of the room that seemed almost at the breaking point, seemed to have no part in his thoughts. He was putting the finishing touches on a very passable copy of the festive goat in the bock beer sign. The diners were leaving, passing out through staring crowds of natives.

"Jedge, suh," said Arthur, removing the napkin and brushing off the crumbs, "there's a lil' boy out back—I want you to see him, suh."

"What's he got to see?"

"He got a goat, hitched to a waggin. Cutest lil' goat you ever see."

"Goat? I'll see it, by all means," cried the judge, rising. Arthur led the way through the kitchen, the help standing respectfully at attention.

"You, lil' boy, come here, come here," cried the proud Negro chauffeur, in a high seductive tenor. A small boy, driving a goat hitched to an express wagon, spoke to the goat in some private tongue and the goat lunged forward. The boy threw his whole weight on one line, and made a graceful admiralty turn of the barnyard, bringing up smartly at the kitchen hitching block. He touched his cap to Judge Ebbs.

"Want a ride, sir? It's ten cents."

"Ain't that pretty?" exclaimed the entranced Arthur. "Look at dat harness. Look at dem hames? Look at dose lil' hole-backs, Jedge, suh. Look at dese lines. What's de goat's name, lil' boy?"

"Bill!" said the boy, looking curiously at Arthur.

"Kin he back up?"

"Sure he can back up," said the boy. "You want a ride? It's ten cents."

Judge Ebbs picked up a small urchin sucking his thumb thoughtfully on the kitchen steps and lifted him into the cart. He produced a quarter for the driver.

"Give him two rides and a half," he said. "He doesn't have to take it all today unless he wants to."

He moved off down the alley to the street, one hand resting on his chauffeur's broad shoulder.

"Arthur," he said, "sometimes you startle me. Sometimes I think you possess mediumistic powers of a very high order."

"Yessuh, suh. Look out for dat step."

"It is trite to say," muttered the judge pensively, "that an idea can have no existence, without a mind to exist in. I sometimes doubt it. They are in the air, around about. Oddly enough, it was placed in my hands when I came in just now. But I looked at the giver, not the gift. Then you came to my rescue, Arthur. Thank you."

The distinguished gentlemen appearing for the defense broke out of a close huddle when the gavel fell, and Jonathan Horton arose to address the court. Mr. Horton said:

"Your Honor, I find myself in an embarrassing situation, and I am forced to throw myself on your mercy. I have just come into the case. I was summoned by wire this morning; and after consultation with my colleagues I find there are a number of loose ends that must be brought together. I have had no time to familiarize myself with the great volume of testimony, most of it of an expert nature, that has been taken. I respectfully request an adjournment. A week might suffice. A month would be more in keeping with the weightiness of the issues involved."

Instantly the brilliant Soberski was on his feet, but before he could speak, Judge Ebbs cut him off. He shook his head.

"I must deny your request. Silence, please, sir. Your client's interests have been brilliantly championed by the learned gentlemen, your colleagues. The case is drawing to a close. In another hour we should conclude the evidence. I will assume, sir, that you put your request for an adjournment in the form of a motion. I deny the motion and allow you an exception. We will proceed."

Soberski was grinning; behind his hand he whispered to his trusty runner, "There's life in the old boy yet."

"I thought he was cutting paper dolls," said the runner. "That was a goat he drew on that tablecloth. I went back to look."

"Recall the plaintiff," ordered the judge. A look of surprise passed across the faces of the defense. Across the faces of Soberski and his colleagues there passed a look of uneasiness, almost of consternation.

A hush fell in the court. Soberski prodded his client, whispered hurriedly to him, and the witness took the stand, nervously balling his handkerchief and palming it. Judge Ebbs picked up an old book, that had once been gaudy with gilt and tooling but now was a ruin.

"This book," he said, looking over his glasses at the upturned faces, "is the principal exhibit in the case before us. It is called, *Mother, Hearth and Heaven*, and contains suitable excerpts from the bible, the great poets, and some lesser ones. It is of a type commonly sold by book agents to country families. It contains several blank pages, framed with gilt, on which to inscribe the records of births, marriages and deaths. On one page is a writing which purports to be the record of the birth, on November 14, 1877, of one John Noah Emberson, as the son of John Noah Emberson and Sarah Tipton Emberson, both of Aurora, Illinois. The writing is signed with the names of the alleged father and mother, the minister who wrote the record, and two witnesses, all deceased. There are no county records in existence for this date. We have heard expert testimony as to the handwriting of John Noah Emberson, also been shown what purports to be samples of the handwriting of the others, deceased. This statement of mine is correct, gentlemen?"

There was a curious silence. The two hostile groups nodded acquiescence.

"It is evidently an English book," went on the judge. "The fly leaf is mutilated, but on the reverse side is the fragment of a line reading 'stationers' hall,' the usual copyright line of that period. Also the letter press contains English spellings, such as honour, kerb and cheque. That is conceded, gentlemen?"

They nodded again, Soberski whispered to his colleagues.

The bailiff carried the book to the witness.

"Are you the John Noah Emberson referred to in this document?" asked the court.

"Yes, your honor, I—"

"When did this book come into your possession?"

"When I was six years old, sir, in 1883. My mother gave it to me on her death bed. She told me it was—"

"Examine the book. How old is it? Is there a date of publication on the title page?"

"It's gone, sir. The rats gnawed it, sir."

"No publisher's name appears?"

"The rats gnawed it something terrible, sir."

Judge Ebbs looked sharply at the bailiff, who moved to within arm's reach of the precious volume.

"What is the name of the 'goat'?" asked the court, in a small crisp voice. An unfettered roar of amazement, then a loud guffaw, went up from the tense court audience. Counsel stared in bewilderment at each other, at the judge, who rapped for order.

"He's gone batty—paper dolls is right," rasped Soberski with a laugh. "Your honor—"

"Goat, yes. Goat," cried the judge. "What is the 'goat's' name?"

Silence fell, as swiftly as the uproar had come.

"Gentlemen," said the judge, "you evidently are not familiar with certain phases of the English law pertaining to this issue. In England, the printer is by law a party to a libel action; and he is required to put his name at the foot of the last page of every book or newspaper he prints. In vulgar parlance, he is commonly known in Temple Bar as the 'goat.' What is the goat's name, Witness?" he demanded. "You will find it, in the usual microscopic type, at the foot of the last column, last page—where no one has thought to look. There is the name and the date, 1887. That book did not come into existence until ten years after the alleged date of this forged birth record. The case is dismissed with costs. Arrest the plaintiff and arraign him before me for perjury, forgery—quick, Bailiff!"

What happened was swifter than the eye. The agitated prestidigitator dropped the book, caught it in falling, tore a leaf loose. As quick as a wink he had balled the leaf, palmed it. But the bailiff was on him from behind, seized his wrists, held them high in the air.

"—and for attempting to destroy legal evidence," went on the judge solemnly, above the uproar. "Prepare a transcript of the testimony for the District Attorney, Mr. Clerk. I shall recommend your conduct to the scrutiny of the Grievance Committee of the Bar Association, Mr. Soberski."

Murder in Triplicate

OVER a thoughtful pipe on the morning of September 17, Oliver Armiston expressed curiosity as to how an expert, a pundit in the historic art, would go about the job of murder in his own behalf. "Probably very badly," he offered, experimentally.

Up through the ages men (and women) had made a profession of the lethal art, some for zeal and even hope of heavenly grace, and some for pelf. Indeed, the very origin of the term assassin is religious. Murder, said Oliver, is a skilled service, to be hired, like valeting, dishwashing, or fumigating. Like other trades and professions, it becomes overcrowded at times, with consequent fee-cutting and splitting.

But these adepts always do their experting for others. Someone else supplies the motive, they merely do the killing. It isn't even murder, except by a fictitious extension of the criminal code, since killing without motive could not be premeditated. The demand comes from the outside; it is merely a delivery on consignment.

"Do these people ever take a day off and do a job for themselves?" asked the distinguished amateur, stimulatingly.

Parr, the police deputy, sat in his favorite elbow chair by Oliver's desk; his topcoat and jacket were open, his hard hat still rode his round dome, as is expected of a stage detective, and he idly twiddled a ragged stogy unlit, between his fingers. For some time he had been studying the utterly insignificant *objet d'art* on the fireplace shelf. After a time he turned his turret-like head on Oliver, and stared through him with the intent eyes of a microscopist.

"Say that again," said the man-hunter brusquely.

"It seems to be a law of nature that experts require external motivation," said Armiston. "There is something fatally prejudicial about motive. Maybe that's the reason, Parr, that clever murderers fail, whereas the stupid ones have a chance." He swung about and faced his rapt examiner. "You probably know more about murder than any other man alive," he said. "How would you go about a job, *in your own behalf?*"

"I know about murderers, yes," replied the policeman. "I have handled hundreds, thousands of them. But about *murder*, no. That is, if I get what you mean. You are talking about the man before the act?" He shook his head. "I have never had a specimen to examine. Unfortunately, they are not available." He smiled grimly over the thought. "By the time I am called in, he is a different person entirely. That's where they fail. It is impossible for them to foresee the psychic change the mere act entails. I use the word entail advisedly. With the murder he becomes another person, a man beyond the pale, a fugitive even if no man pursueth, to be overwhelmed, destroyed by a chance look, word, sound, act. One of the cleverest murderers I ever saw—clever because it seemed to be done so stupidly—was that of a woman housekeeper by a doctor in the Village. I went to tell him about it, and ask him about her. I heard him coming down the stairs to meet me. He paused halfway down, to get his nerves under control for the ordeal. In that cautious instant he revealed himself. By what possible system of foresight could an expert—and he was an expert—have foreseen that impulse?" Parr shook his head. "We had the case of a man who succeeded in utterly destroying his victim—she was carried out to sea, in a flood. I got a fur boa, the kind she had worn, and soaked it in a tub of water overnight. It was lying on my desk when the murderer came in to offer help. He saw it. He thought he had failed. He was lost before he could recover himself.

"So when you ask me how I, as an expert, would steel myself against self-betrayal, I say it can't be done, because there is no way of foreseeing chance. There are two hundred deaths a day in this city. One out of every four is investigated. Do you realize what a busy person the Medical Examiner is?" He reached up and took down his private phone, a direct wire he maintained from Oliver's study to Centre Street. He said, after a little pause, "Fetch them up here." He set the phone aside. "I'd undoubtedly be very clumsy at the job," he remarked dryly as he pushed it aside. "I know all the causes of failure. I'd have a fool for a client."

Shortly Morel, who with the crossmatched little Pelts constituted a sort of bifurcated administrative function for the manhunter's mental processes, entered. Oliver's housekeeper was all smiles, Morel being a dashing young man of the stag-line type. On the Deputy, on the other hand, she bestowed a disapproving glare—he looked the part in every line. Morel unwrapped a parcel when the door closed and displayed three bullets, one a .22 extra long, one a .32, and the last a punishing .45. They had been through the microscopist's hands, for bullets have fingerprints quite as readable as human thumbs. The two smaller ones were newcomers. But the .45 was a repeat; its picture was in the gallery. Its land-marks were identical with those of another bullet that had turned up in the course of a day's work three months previous. There is an odd theory about guns and those who use them. It runs that a gun which has killed one man is prone to do it again, as if, like human beings, one act of accomplishment invites another.

"Who was it?" asked Oliver, staring at the exhibit.

"We don't know," said Morel. "A man in the river."

"Which one killed him?"

"None of them. He was dead before they were fired."

"Drowned?"

"No."

"What, then?"

"We don't know."

The man certainly didn't kill himself. Why waste three shots on him, from three different guns, one with a record, after he was dead? Did three men fire the three shots, as if to share the jeopardy? Or did one man pick up three guns in succession?

Morel here produced a second packet, from which he extracted the wadding of a blank shell. Four shots had been fired, one blank.

"It looks like a formal execution," said Oliver. "Military," he added, glancing keenly at the others. "One shell is always blank in a firing squad—so no one can swear he fired the fatal shot."

"But he was dead before the shots were fired," interposed Parr pleasantly. "Now if you wish to examine into the mind of a murderer before the act, here is a mind worth looking into. Here is another fact worth considering. He took pains to have the body recovered. He dumped it in the Harlem River. The tide never gets out of the Harlem River. It swings back and forth between Spuyten Duyvil and Hell Gate twice a day. Let us assume he knew what he was doing." He looked keenly at Oliver. "Let us assume your expert was taking a day off, and doing a job for himself."

Morel said, "He tied a block of salt, rocksalt, to the body, to sink it. It's an old trick. The body comes to the surface days later, when the salt dissolves."

"Why go to that trouble?" cried Oliver, "Why not tie a rock or a grate bar for weight, and be done with it?"

"Maybe he didn't want to be done with it," said Parr. "There's experting for you!" He took up the bullets and examined them. "Everything here is obvious," he said. "They are obvious to us. They were probably meant to be. It rather suggests, doesn't it, that he wanted a little publicity? Murderers are like actors—they crave press notices."

"With the police!"

"Through the police," answered the Deputy. "He dressed it up, so it would get into the papers. Sort of gentle reminder to his followers. As if he said, 'You know what happened to A. This is what happened to be B. Now, C, D, and E, watch your step.' "

"What happened to A?" asked Oliver.

"The same thing, three months ago." Parr held up the .45 bullet. "This one was from the same gun. The others were different. Why change two, and not the third?" He paused for answer.

"Publicity," said Morel.

"It makes a very good story," agreed Parr. "I'll give it to the press. Usually," he added with a smile, "we like to go along with these people, to see where they are going."

"Does the cause of death correspond in each instance?" asked Oliver.

"In so far as utter absence of apparent cause is concerned, yes," said Parr. "That doesn't disturb us, however. There are methods, as you know, that elude even such an avid dissectionist as our medical examiner. The fashionable one, just now, in detective fiction, is to produce an embolism by injecting an air or gas bubble into an artery. Cyanide has rather gone out—it leaves its trace—and in real life it takes more of the stuff than in fiction. This happens to be real life."

"No marks of any kind?" pursued the amateur.

"Now we arrive," said Parr. "There are marks, yes. In both cases, the hands, arms, and face were spotted—like a rash. It was much more apparent in the first case than in the second. Dr. Wortly was very much excited at first. He thought he had stumbled on incipient typhus! That would have been a story for the front page! He made a number of blood tests, and such bacteriological examinations as he could." Parr shook his head. "I think he was disappointed. I think he had begun to hope that he had stumbled on a couple of cases of typhus to experiment with in his laboratory. He's got test tubes filled with the most virulent disease germs that he treasures above rubies. Not being learned in his degree," said Parr, "I suggested maybe the two cadavers had been journeymen house painters in their day, and had been putting on blue or purple paint in a high wind with an air brush. Perfectly workable surmise," chuckled the manhunter, "except it wasn't paint—it didn't come off."

He yawned and arose. He wrapped up his precious specimens and put them in a pocket.

"Well, Oliver, there's the fertilizing germ," he said lazily. "I think this might be the expert you're talking about, doing an occasional job for himself on his day off. If it is, I'll warrant he's got a fool for a client."

L ike adam of old, Parr the Deputy had indeed many children—flatties, dicks, guns, bulls, a moll or two, and, yes, stools, and highbrow scientificos, among other categories, to the number of nineteen or twenty thousand—but in particular, he had Morel and Pelts. They were as different lobes of one brain. Morel for the most part he had always with him, a sort of Ganymede to his immediate thoughts. Back in the shadows, beyond the immediate circle of his candle-burning, lurked Pelts, a shabby little fellow who had only one fault—he was hard to call off. When the Deputy walked abroad the little fellow, looking anything but a policeman, scouted the points and flanks. When a big case came to its inevitable stone wall, when all clues ran up blind alleys, there was always the comforting thought that Pelts was still out. Until he came slinking in, and curled up, wordless, in a dark corner, all was not lost.

About four that afternoon Pelts came in for a fresh sniff at Exhibits A, B, and C in the .45 case—as the affair of the two unknown men found swinging back and forth with the trapped tides of the Harlem River had been christened. He had on his make-up, if such it could be called. He was an ol' clo' man, no more sanitary than the law allows, attired in several layers of his stock, with a pleasing display of wares draped across one arm and a nest of hats from fair to hopeless on top of his head. Rookies grinned at him and winked at one another; uneasy prisoners who were left sitting for hours, almost for days, it seemed, to take counsel of their own forebodings, eyed him apprehensively as he passed through the halls of Centre Street; he passed on, and, with the privilege of a bootblack, pushed open the "big" door leading to the source of all power, and moved on into the inner sanctum, without even a by-your-leave from the white-collared gentleman on guard. Nor did he look at the scowling Deputy, or the pensive Morel who sat against the light of the tall windows. He took the sniff he had come for, of Exhibits A, B, and C, and quite as unceremoniously departed. One door shut with a soft thud, a second door shut with a soft thud.

"If that fellow could talk," said the Deputy—and left the utterance hanging elliptically in the air.

The fact was, Pelts couldn't talk. He was a roving tight-bellied hound with only a nose for an intellect who brought in bones, sometimes with meat on them. No one had said anything to him about the .45 case. It wasn't necessary; the mere fact that it was for the moment occupying the mind of the chief caused his own perceptions to be tuned likewise. Parr muttered impatiently:

"I wonder what's on his mind. This thing is blind."

"I might try following him," suggested young Morel with a guilty smile. But Parr shook his head. It couldn't be done. He would take cover. But later in the afternoon, through pure mischance, they got a lead. Busby, an operative attached to the District Attorney's office, came in with some papers, and in the course of passing the time of day he asked what Pelts was doing in the "alley."

The "alley" was a ramshackle block in Lafayette Street, hard by the courts and prison, the abode of gentlemen of the law, bailiffs, process servers, runners, and ambulance chasers. There were more telephones in that nest of rookeries than in any other block in town, and there were almost as many tears shed there between daylight and dark as there were across the street. It was the region of spurious hope for the hopeless.

"He's a runner," reported Morel incredibly the next day. The young man had smoked a social cigarette with some of his fellow social registerites on the D.A.'s staff, his feet in a dusty window, his eyes on the back street. It was a fact. Pelts had retired from the ol' clo' industry; he was now disguised in the hard-brushed neatness of the seedy; he was on the curb of the alley to pick up such crumbs as fall from the table of misfortune.

"A runner," said the Deputy, scowling. He ran over the names of the denizens of the alley in his mind. "For whom?" Morel didn't know. He thought Pelts was free-lancing. He and Morel smiled at each other—not at the aspect of Pelts in a new role, but at the aspect of themselves spying on the shabby little fellow.

"Let him alone!" commanded Parr, righteously. And he turned to other things.

But his thoughts kept coming back to the alley. A dozen times during the morning he looked up and stared at the opposite wall, and said "Lawyers," as if the words were written on his retina like a complementary image.

"Morel," he said, "who's in that block? Mordecai Cortez—"

"Bierstet, his suborner," joined in the ready Morel.

"Sally Levy—Abe Hoster—Winsmore—"

"Hanson—Borsel, the artichoke mouthpiece—"

There was riff-raff, the camp followers of every trial court. But there were among them some of those highly publicized counsellors nominated as brilliant. Parr nodded.

"Something is on his mind," he muttered. He was thinking of little Pelts. He was silent a long time. Then he said abruptly, "Give it another look," and hastily arose and took his departure.

It wasn't exactly cricket, of course. If it had been anyone else but Pelts, the obvious thing to do would be to call him in and ask him what was up. But one didn't do that with Pelts. Pelts probably couldn't have told. So the obedient Morel gave it another look. He had the technique of looking once, and again, and again—and again. It is a curious fact that the most simple, the most obvious, will gradually change, take on new meaning, if you look at it often enough—and at the hundreth view you begin to see something else that wasn't apparent at the first, tenth, or fiftieth examination. Morel found a room opposite, rubbed a hole for himself in the filmed window, and at odd times of the day and night he looked out on the alley. Occasionally he caught sight of Pelts, a drab figure among drabs that hived on the curb.

Every morning magnificent limousines, with cut flowers and liveried chauffeurs, drove up to the musty doorways, and dignified counsellors stepped out, amid awe, almost reverence. They climbed rickety stairways to shabby chambers, to scan the reports of their minions, to listen to stories that awaited the pen of a Dickens, to dispense with learning, ingenuity and cunning; and in the afternoon the brilliant men of the law would drive up-town to take a bath, as if the sordid grime of misfortune were susceptible to soap and water. Mostly these sacred confabulations were on a strictly cash and carry basis, in the hardest of hard money. It was not an unusual sight for an armored car to roll up to the rookeries with shot-gun messengers to carry off gold. One of them—Morel thought it was Bierstet who did the suborning for Mordecai Cortez—used police protection, telephoned for a policeman to ride beside him when he went to his bank. To the camera eye of Morel, there were mementoes for the morning line-up among the creatures who came and went in a never-ending parade. But as for Pelts—that aspect of the espionage was a blank. He gave it up.

The .45 case at this stage was purely of academic interest. A tempting police slip had been inconspicuously posted in the board room where ancient reporters and their veteran office boys checked up on the dragnet of police news every moment of the day and night. A floater out of the river was merely a floater—it seldom got as far as the dead hook on a night news desk. But two floaters, three months apart in point of time, but tapped by a slug from the same gun, caused a penny-ante game to cease and telephone lines jingled for a space. But at newsdesks there were mightier events for recording. In the making of publicity, there is a time to sow and a time to reap; and if the hypothetical experts experting in the case of the two .45's were keen for "press," they were lost in the glut of cosmic affairs.

Weeks passed, even months. Time is on the side of the pursuer. The fugitive drinks in fresh courage and comes out boldly again, no longer cowering at a look, a sound, a word. His defenses gradually lower. But all the time, behind the scenes, ceaseless forces are at work, with the patience of builders of coral rock.

"It's a dud," pronounced Oliver Armiston. "It hasn't any 'it.' It's merely two unknown men—unidentified and unidentifiable. The case has its points, yes—that .45! But you can't get any publicity. And nobody will work without publicity, these days—not even you, Parr. What are you doing about it?"

"Waiting," said Parr, placidly.

"For what?"

"Man coming across water," muttered the Deputy.

"Meaning what?"

"Chance," said Parr. His eyes gleamed for an instant and died down. "Someone—or something—always turns up. Maybe not today, or tomorrow, or next week, or next year. But eventually, in murder, the break comes."

Oliver looked at his watch and arose.

"I've got to meet a boat," he said. "I've got a man coming across the water this morning." he grinned. "Maybe he's your man, Parr."

"Fetch him around," invited the other, rising.

"I'm afraid he wouldn't fit—he's been on Deception Island for two years, far removed from the temptations of civilization. It's a whaling station," he explained. "He's a doctor. And, believe it or not, his name is Whales—Dr. Whales."

They drove downtown together. Parr found the Toxicologist, Wortly, hanging around waiting for him.

"Those spots weren't paint stains, sir," said the scientist plaintively.

"Good Lord! You're not going to revive the bubonic plague, are you!" laughed the chief. He himself had no difficulty in filing away unfinished dossiers for future reference, but these scientificos were harassed with the memory of elephants.

"I'm inclining to escharotics," said Wortly. "A caustic of some kind," He explained in response to a raised eyebrow. "The long immersion precludes detailed analysis. If," he said, timidly, "we could turn up another specimen—"

"Stick around," chuckled the manhunter. And at that moment the imp of the perverse caused the telephone to buzz. The Deputy gave heed. He grunted, hung up, pushing away the phone, called after the devout scientist, who was going back to his test tubes of bacteria and bacilli.

"Get into your rubbers and gas-mask, Doc!" he cried. "Here it is. The third floater! In the Harlem River!"

Number One was merely the Unknown Man, an extremely common person. Number Two was a Coincidence. Number Three—Parr laughed. He never know it to fail—eventually, the break came. This was the break. He had had the hunch in his bones. He left instructions for Armiston to be notified.

It was not until four in the afternoon that Oliver caught up with them, and it was at the Morgue. By that time Parr was in the throes of a relapse. Everything checked. It was a perfect replica of the other two. And there they came to a stop. It was the same blank wall—only blanker now, with the peculiar insistence of its own reiteration.

Oliver, of course, was delighted.

"You'll get some publicity now, Parr," he laughed, fingering the tell-tale bullet—that had not been the cause of death.

"Plenty," grunted Parr. He turned to meet Dr. Whales, whom Oliver had fetched along.

"He might help," suggested Oliver gaily. "He is not unversed in your lore—he is a savant with five Ph.D.'s. In his day he has seen police duty in Turkey. He was medico-legal expert for the Khedive of Egypt. For two years he has been sitting on the polar ice cap wiping his mind clear of civilized impressions. It should be a very sensitive surface."

Dr. Whales, a sturdy man of middle years, with a bald head, a torpedo beard, and piercing eyes behind thick glasses, acknowledged the flamboyant introduction with a smile.

"I'm rather out of practice, that's a fact," he said. "What do you want me to begin on?"

"The hands," said Oliver, "Look at the spots on the hands."

Doctor Whales turned to the specimen, and his eye ran over it in detail. It was a professional eye, Parr could see that. He waited, curiously, wondering if perchance there was something in Oliver's suggestion of a mind wiped clean and renewed by a prolonged absence.

"My experience," said Dr. Whales, rather shyly, "has been wholly of the East. Different races—different climate—different crimes." He turned to Specimen Number Three again. "Significances change with geography and the barometer. If I were in Cairo, Egypt," he added, turning away from the slab, "I'd say this fellow had been sweating gold as an occupation."

Blank silence met the mild gaze of the diagnostician. Pelts detached himself, and was gone.

"Sweating gold!" snarled Parr, suddenly ferocious with astonishment.

"Yes," said the ex-medico legal expert to the Khedive. "It's the spray of the acid they use—nitro-hydrochloric. The purple comes from the gold in solution." He looked at the startled faces curiously. "It's a common crime in the East—very easily spotted—no pun intended. I assure you! Over here I suppose you don't encounter it—no gold in circulation."

"But there is!" cried Oliver, exultantly. "There are tons of it—tons of it—being hoarded!" He turned triumphant, on Parr. "Parr," he cried. "This is the man coming across water!"

"Pelts! Pelts! Where is that blasted tramp?" cried the Deputy. Pelts was gone, like ice on a pond.

But he wasn't gone far. Before they got downtown he had finished his abrupt errand and stood waiting before Parr's desk, an abject figure. Parr grunted. Morel smiled. Oliver nudged his guest and winked. They all sat down. Pelts unbuttoned one coat, two coats, three coats; and from beneath a paper vest, he produced a bulky package which he laid on the desk.

"I just borrowed it," he said apologetically. "I got to take it back, if it ain't right."

"Right? What do you mean, right?" demanded Parr. He tore off the paper. It was a heavy .45 automatic.

"It's a cop's gun!" snarled the Deputy.

"Yes, sir," admitted Pelts.

"You're not meaning to tell me—" Parr glared.

"No, sir. I was just wondering. He happened to be on station reserve, and sleeping—I just borrowed it." Pelts wetted his lips. "I left my own in his holster, so he won't notice."

"What cop?"

"Name is Wickert—young cop—in the 17th precinct—" he paused.

"What about him? Out with it!"

"He had some spots—on his arms. I saw him playing handball one day—"

"And you've been tailing him, eh?"

"Yes, sir."

"In the alley?"

Pelts swallowed, nodded.

"What was he doing in the alley?"

"He's bodyguard for a lawyer."

"What lawyer?" demanded Parr, rising.

"Bierstet," said Pelts.

Parr took up the gun and beckoning Pelts, departed to the realm of Benson, the ballistics expert, to whom the internals of a rifled barrel were as engrossing as germs to the toxicologist. In five minutes they returned.

"The gun is *right!*" cried Parr, the gleam of exultation in his eyes. "Pelts! If you had my good looks, you'd have my job! Morel, this yellow dog, Wickert, will be outside in a minute. I've had him brought here. Fetch him in."

Wickert was a handsome young cop, just out of the police training school, lean, clear-eyed and graceful from hard conditioning. He came in jauntily. He had been summoned to the Front, which might mean anything an ambitious rookie could wish, preferably plain clothes. His jauntiness wilted a little at the sight of several civilians sitting there. At the sight of shabby little Pelts, he looked startled. But he came to a salute before the Deputy's desk very trimly. The gun lying there meant nothing to him. There was a thick silence. His eyes came back to the gun. It was one police gun in a thousand—twenty thousand. One arm moved imperceptibly until he could feel the bulge of the holster at his hip. He drew a careful breath, stood more rigid.

"Take off your blouse, Wickert," commanded Parr.

The man's jaw dropped.

"My—my coat, Mr. Commissioner?" he said.

"Take it off!"

The man took it off. The big gun bulged from the holster at his hip.

"Roll up your sleeves," rasped Parr. Dumbly the man stared about at the rigid audience. His eyes came back to Parr, as if from the hypnotism of that terrible gaze; and he slowly unfastened a cuff. He began slowly to turn up the cuff.

His gaze began to waver. He was staring at the window behind Parr now. The blood drained from his face. Then with a swift intake of breath a cry that rang through the room he sprang backwards, crouching, and drawing the weapon at his hip.

"Don't move!" he commanded, springing to a clear space. "Murder means nothing to me! Lift so much as a finger—" He motioned with the weapon; and quite obediently Oliver, his guest just in from Deception Island,

Morel, and Pelts put their hands in the air, and moved over to Parr's side of the room. Parr said nothing, did nothing. He and little Pelts exchanged one of their swift looks of understanding. The man held his position. He was regaining control of his overwrought nerves. He moved to the door, opened it softly, his beady eyes never wavering for an instant.

"I'm not alone," he said, in a whisper. "Murder means nothing to us. The first man to come out is a dead man."

None of them moved. He turned—and found himself confronted by two plainclothes men.

"Put up the gun—it isn't loaded," laughed one of them; and they both sprang at once. There was a struggle that instantly subsided, and the prisoner, gasping with realization of the utter and inescapable annihilation that had come on him in the space of an instant, sank limp and green into a chair. Parr arose and picked up the gun and handed it to its rightful owner.

"You think of everything, Pelts," he said gruffly. He turned to Dr. Whales, who in his old element again had gone over to the prisoner and rolled up a sleeve, professionally.

"This is a fresh batch," said the former medico-legal expert to the Khedive trying the purple spots on the man's arm with a fingernail. "They haven't begun to desquamate."

"Did you come all the way up from Deception Island just for this job, Doctor?" asked Parr.

"As a matter of fact," said the doctor, "I missed my English boat at Montevideo—and on the spur of the moment, I transhipped for here to see Oliver. We got in a day early."

"I'm glad you did," said Parr warmly. "Let's see what this fellow has got on him."

They found, among odds and ends in the man's pockets, a $20 gold piece which when examined under a microscope was found to be covered with the minute craters from the etching action of aqua regia. The coin had been sweated; five, possibly ten percent, of its weight had been removed by the smooth microscopic action of the only solute known to science for gold.

The first agony of Wickert's terror subsided, followed by a surly silence. Parr went in to talk with the prisoner later in the evening.

"We don't want you," said Parr. "We want your boss." He paused, but the man gave no sign. "You didn't kill those three poor devils. You merely mussed them up, after the job was done, so as to draw red herrings across the trail. And a very clever job you did of it too. Except for one detail. You used your own gun to sign the jobs with. Now do you want to go before a jury as the man who fired those three slugs—or do you want to come up for trial on the lesser charge as the man who carried out orders, and disposed of the remains after the job was done?" No answer. Parr smoked for a time. He leaned closer.

"What did he kill them for? Were they stealing the stuff they were sweating?"

Wickert said, as if he had been talking all along: "They couldn't keep their hands off it. There were shoe-boxes full of it, in that room upstairs. He had to rub them out—that was the only way he could cover himself."

"What did he use?"

"He's got some stuff in a bottle—he carried it in his vest pocket."

"Wickert, we want Bierstet," whispered Parr. "Where does he take that sweated stuff when you go along?"

"He's got a safety deposit box uptown. He makes the trip once a week, every Thursday."

"Have you got nerve enough to make one last trip with him—tomorrow? I want to find a box of it in his possession." When the man drew back, Parr urged: "We'll be right alongside."

At noon the next day Bierstet, known to the denizens of the alley, high, middle and low, as the counsellor who did the suborning for the big fellows, gaily called the police desk for what he was pleased to dub his shot-gun messenger—preferably that young fellow Wickert, if he could have him. He could, and did. Several tough frame boxes strapped with iron, each about the weight a man could handle, were put into the car, and Bierstet and Wickert, gun strapped on outside for publicity, got in and rode uptown.

Bierstet stepped out into the waiting arms of Parr, and a flock of bright young men, headed by Morel, relieved the lawyer of the box he was carrying.

"This way, counsellor," said Parr, invitingly, indicating his own car at the curb. "Or shall I call the wagon and throw you in?"

"For what?" inquired the lawyer, with a sneer.

"Murder—in triplicate," said Parr. "I believe you hold the record of 73 acquittals in first degree murder. You've never lost a case, have you, counsellor? Well, this time you lose. You've got a fool for a client."

The Man from the Death House

A few minutes before the hour of four, on the afternoon of the 18th (five hours after Isidore Carmen, the murderer, had his normal expectancy of life restored to him, on a writ of error), there came to a stop in front of an ancient though still elegant apartment house on the south side of the Park, opposite the job in the wall where the cab horses stand all day with drooping heads and one knee akimbo, first one equipage, then two, and immediately, a queue of limousines and taxis and towncars— separated out of the drifting eddics of traffic by that strange fractional distillation of common purpose. They were of the upper distillates, the more volatile fractions, as would have been foretold by a shrewd observer as much as half an hour before. Indeed, as early as three o'clock, in spite of a light snowfall and a chill crosstown wind, loiterers began to gather in little clusters before the house. By three thirty the concentration was sufficiently dense to attract passers-by.

"What's going on?" asked a citizen, noting the large number of loiterers.

The policeman appealed to shook his head. "Rubbernecks," he explained. He went to his call box and put in a call. And a moment later the nerves at Police Headquarters, functioning quietly, gathered ten policemen, playing checkers in a back room, and sent them to the spot, shivering in the damp chill.

But there was nothing to do. These rubbernecks are harmless souls. They attend all de luxe public functions, stand for hours in all weather—for the simple pleasure of staring, zoo fashion, as the great, the near great, and the merely fortunate, pass in and out. Via their grapevine telegraph, which never fails, they had been informed that Cloquet, the young Belgian genius of the pianoforte, was to privately unveil his rumored curve of the *cantabile* here this afternoon, for the ravishment of the very few—for Art, like Wall Street, has its way of discounting good as well as bad news. In another year or two the young man would garner the abundant meeds of fame; but today he was merely a hushed secret. There was no line in the newspapers. There were whole pages about Isidore Carmen, the man from the death house.

As the first arriving equipage came to a halt, a door-opener (one of those useless industries disallowed during the war but since restored) sprang forward with alacrity. But before he could turn the door handle and release the passenger, a swift almost military transformation occurred on the sidewalk. The loiterers snapped to attention and smartly boxed in a neat path leading from the door of the limousine to the doorway of the apartment house. If the passenger desired to enter, he must run the gauntlet. After a moment's timid inspection the passenger did so. Nothing happened. There was some slight craning of necks, but for the most part he was ignored. He was of the small fry, as early comers are apt to be. The second and third odd lots arrived and were lightered, with thumping doors. The rubbernecks had not long to wait. Almost at once the air was thick with celebrity. The greatest lions of the pianoforte, the fiddle, and the larynx passed in almost a solid stream. The human alleyway writhed, almost pinched itself shut in its delirious ecstasy at beholding so much celebrity on the hoof, as it were. In fact, so thick was the run of big ones this afternoon that after about fifteen minutes of it the more hardened among the rubbernecks began to feel assuaged with mere greatness and to pay homage in more exact change. Many a minor lion and fading star suffered the ignominy of being rated by utter silence.

Some were ignored altogether, as if they passed unseen. Such a one was a diminutive man scarcely five feet in height who seemed so fearful of being devoured as he ran the gauntlet that he held his fat fur collar together in front of his nose to hide his face. But he might have saved himself the trouble, for, as he took down his hand to turn the doorknob—the door-opener at the building line having decided to let him do it for himself—someone more alert caught a glimpse of the visage; and before the door slammed on the tiny figure, this triumphant one yelled raucously:

"That's one you birds muffed! That was Isidore Carmen!"

The name was like a gunshot. Isidore Carmen! Instantly the orderly alleyway formation of the assembled rubbernecks broke up. Actuated by one impulse they surged forward; they clotted in a huge boiling swarm about the entry, the name of Isidore Carmen on every lip. Even the stolid policemen took fire. They turned their faces, stupid with suddenly arrested attention at the sound of the name, and pushed their privileged way to the front of the mass, asking questions. Passers-by who usually walked around the rubberneck throngs with amused tolerance, now paused, catching the sound of the magic name. People came running from up and down the street; vehicular traffic stopped; the queue which had begun to grow ragged was now lost altogether, in the confusion. One policeman was ringing frantically at his phone for more help. The crowd about the doorway grew, like swarming bees. Isidore Carmen was inside! They settled down to wait for him to come out, with the fierce, tireless patience of wild dogs. Merely to see him—Isidore Carmen, the man from the death house—alive, in the flesh—became an inestimable privilege to be fought for. Such is the glamor when a man in the very straps of the electric chair comes back to life ...

It was into this scene that Cuyler Braxton, a society lawyer recently an assistant public prosecutor, and his fiancée, Estrelle—Estrelle, Inc.—

came driving, innocent as two love birds, in a taxi. Getting down, Estrelle noticed the dejected horses across the street.

"They are fewer and fewer. What becomes of them, Cuyler?" she asked.

Braxton, in his stiff-shirt way, was something of a wag, and couldn't resist the quip then current.

"I believe they are running some of them at Hialeah this winter," he said lightly. Looking about and seeing where he was, he called out: "Oh, I say! I hope you know where you are taking me?"

"Where?" begged the society dressmaker, smiling and taking his arm. She knew his weakness. Since his career in the Criminal Courts he had a most disreputable nodding acquaintance with criminals, and especially with the locale of crime. Set him down in any spot in the city and he would instantly orientate himself by recognizing the scene of some atrocity.

"This is the scene of the second act of the great de Mars murder of twelve years ago," said he. "I say the second act, because they usually find the corpse in the second act."

He pried a hole in the rim of the crowd with a powerful elbow, and went on to say, abstractedly, that there are those who hold that the scene of a great crime should be straightway struck and carted off-stage, once the police are done with it, lest it tempt someone else. At this juncture several policemen recognized Braxton and addressed him, proudly, as Mr. District Attorney—for one always holds that brevet with the members of the force, once he acquires it in any degree. They plowed a path for the handsome pair. One of the men whispered in Cuyler's ear.

"Carmen? Carmen! Inside?" Cuyler cried. He communicated the message to Estrelle.

"Here?" she cried. "How ghastly!"

"Why not?" said the lawyer lightly. "The music will lift him nearer heaven."

The privileged pair finally were thrust inside. They waited in a small entry hall of walnut and lincrusta-walton for the elevator. The door slid open. They stepped in. A little old man in a skull cap looked up dimly, and cried out, with effusive pride:

"Why, it is the Prosecutor, isn't it, sir?"

Braxton looked down at him. He put an arm about the bent shoulders and turned the ancient to Estrelle.

"This, my dear, is Zachariah Smith, not unknown to fame. He was the key witness for the defense in the de Mars murder trial," he said, by way of introduction. He shook his head dolefully. "I had to treat him a little rough, but I think he harbors no ill will."

"Oh, no, sir! It was in the line of duty," cried the old man, pleased.

"Your memory—I trust your memory has returned, Zachariah?" inquired the lawyer solicitously. "I thought so! I have known some marvelous cures to be effected by the successful termination of litigation. The house hasn't changed a bit, has it Zack? It still has the atmosphere!"

"We have the best people, sir!" said the ancient, in an awed whisper.

The elevator went up. They stepped out on a landing, and paused, breathless. The air itself seemed fairly to sway in time to the lacelike phrases of the E minor waltz. Rapt, they nodded to each other. The young man from Belgium had brought his curve with him.

There were three parlors *en suite*, filled with breathless celebrity. There was no applause, by request. In a lull they were seated. Cuyler disposed the skirts of his coat and turned so that he could talk in Estrelle's ear, over his hat and gloves, which he held in his hands clasping the head of his stick.

"I don't see him," muttered Cuyler, over the rim of his hat, as his eyes searched the audience. "Yet somehow I seem to feel him." The three drawing-rooms reflected each other like a hall of mirrors. A shadow passed over her face. "Oh, he's here, you can be sure," muttered Cuyler. "He's musical—I seem to remember he wrote a quartet for strings." He added, after a pause, "This is a queer place. Look around. What's wrong?"

Estrelle's eyes widened a little. She inventoried her surroundings. The proportions were massive, like a Parrish drawing. The rooms were heavily furnished and hung with tapestries, silks, and brocades. She recognized an Inness, a Carlsen, a Murphy, a Homer, a Sargent. But they all had tickets on. Every piece in the place was for sale.

"It's a racket," whispered Braxton, with a sly smile. He asked maliciously, "How do we happen to be here?"

"Hush," she cautioned. "Leocadie sent us her card."

She looked about. All the right people were here. The young man with the curve now struck a noble chord, and ripped off an arpeggio with steel tappets for fingers. With downcast eyes he played the A flat impromptu, nodding to that shadowy region beyond his left hand, cueing in the different voices as if it were a fugue. In the hush that hung on the echoes of the final cadence, Estrelle breathed:

"Listen to his thumbs!"

"Listen to your grandmother," murmured the barbarian lawyer. "I've remembered where I have seen her."

"Who?"

"The female whose hospitality we are accepting," said he. "The reconstructed dame, in black. She is looking us over. She is wondering about me. Think hard, old girl," he chuckled. "It was downtown. In the musty purlieus of the Criminal Courts. In a tall room with high windows that are never washed. Ah," he said, breaking off, "a newcomer!"

A lean tight-waisted young man, in the most correct of morning clothes, was politely crawling over the knees of an aisle of devotees to an empty chair, under the guardian eye of a footman. It was Morel, the competent young dandy from Headquarters, as much at home in a drawing-room as an English juvenile, and fondly preserved by his chief, Parr the deputy, for just such occasions as this. He parted his coat tails and sat down, staring insolently at his old friend Braxton without a flicker of recognition.

Just then the thunders of the A flat major polonaise burst on the air; and epochs passed. Braxton was wondering if the man had yet been born who would master it, when he felt the pressure of a fingertip on his shoulder. Turning, he found himself confronting the level gaze of the flunkey who had just seated Morel. The man indicated that the lawyer was to extricate himself and come with him to some unknown destination. Braxton scowled his displeasure. The lackey bent one eyebrow, in an all but imperceptible gesture of urgency; and the lawyer carefully broke himself out and arose, ignoring Estrelle's questioning look and the frowns of the others he disturbed.

He followed his guide down the deep-carpeted corridor. There were fourteen rooms here. She didn't have two slick dimes to rub together when they summoned her downtown for interrogation. He was thinking of this and trying to remember who she was and why they wanted her on that occasion, when the footman opened a door for him to pass through, into a luxurious boudoir. It was all period stuff, very correct, and all ticketed. It had the air, like the rest of the house, of being arranged not by a chatelaine but by a dealer, as if it could be bought by the piece or suite. That would account for the rent.

Then in a flash he remembered who she was—a Mrs. Corson, Mrs. deLacey Corson—whose specialty, since her husband disappeared from the deck of a transatlantic liner in midvoyage, was lending her name and undoubted connections to various fashionable "movements"—without asking too many questions. The police had "advised" her, once or twice. She was more or less openly available to occupy lavish suites in the newest hotels that were reaching for *ton*, where she entertained extensively—on a salary or honorarium. This outfit was undoubtedly put together to move some refractory antiques. She would occupy it nominally for a period, during which the salons would lend themselves naturally to *soirées* of an elité sort, like the affair of this afternoon. Then would come the discreet advertisements in the boudoir publications of the "private disposal of the distinguished personal effects of Mrs. deLacey Corson—admission by card only"—and the gullible would flock to buy. It was one way for an undoubted lady to face the world.

He passed on to a sort of state bedroom beyond the boudoir. The footman ushered him in, and drew the heavy door softly shut behind him. The principal piece was a vast Empire bed on a dais, in the center of the room. But it was not this he saw. He saw only Isidore Carmen, the lawyer, whose sinister talents had saved so many a client from the chair, and who had finally escaped himself by the skin of his teeth this very morning. Carmen sat at a slender, gilt writing desk, his head fallen over the blotter, his long arms sprawling. He was dead. There could be no mistaking the pose, or the misfit of his clothing—a dead man's clothes never fit him. Braxton heard a step behind him. The woman emerged from some shadowy recess and stood at his side, her fingers to her lips, her blank stare not on the dead man but on him.

The ex-assistant prosecutor was not unused to this scene. During his stay in Centre Street he had majored for a period in homicide. He had been on call day or night to view the latest corpus delicti *in situ*, so to speak. It is usually in the first lurid moments following discovery that the murderer reveals himself. Braxton could catch gusts of the battle piece penetrating this room, like the mutter of guns on a distant horizon; and thinking of that grandiose company out there he marveled, had there ever been so reprehensible a corpse! He never doubted for an instant that this was murder. Isidore Carmen was not the one to creep off here to die meekly like a sick animal, at the very moment he was gulping free air again.

He paced a slow circle about the writing desk, pausing to examine the scene from several angles. He looked at his watch. It lacked two minutes of five. They had arrived at four seven, and Carmen had just preceded them. It had all happened within the hour.

Braxton went back to the woman and stood for several seconds in silence, snapping the cover of his watch.

"When was he found?" he asked.

"Just now. One of the servants came in."

"You know who he is," he said.

She slowly shook her head, shrugging—as if it mattered! The lawyer lifted a morning newspaper out of a rack by the desk and opened it for her to see. A four-column story had for a top line, *Carmen Jury Locked Up For The Night.* Under it the pinched cruel face of Isidore Carmen looked out from beneath shaggy eyebrows. The woman stifled a scream. She gnawed at her knuckles, her stoicism gone.

There was a little commotion outside. The door opened. The footman was interposing himself before an intruder. But only for a brief moment. His face contorted suddenly with pain, he backed into the room, deftly propelled by Morel, who released him and closed the door softly and turned the key in the lock. Then he nicely dusted off his hands. He caught the picture in one swift look, and exchanged an understanding glance with Braxton. He paused by the desk, his practiced eye assembling the properties of murder. Then he went to a window opening on an old-fashioned areaway cut through to the street. He ran up the roller shade and drew aside the hangings. After a moment he made a pass across the pane. A keen observer below might have noticed one of the rusty cab drivers, clad in an ancient green coat of the hansom-cab period, and a battered old plug hat with a rosette, arouse himself from his day dreams and view his surroundings with the startled look of one just come up from sound sleep. It was little Pelts, Morel's sidepartner. Cuyler indulged in a secret smile. There wasn't a more capable team in existence than this cross-matched pair of sleuthhounds—one the elegant, the other always in rags and patches. The place had been under observation from the beginning. Although there wasn't a breath of change to the naked eye, the police had taken over. Every living soul within these walls was suspect. Braxton joined Morel at the window.

"How did he happen to come in here?" asked Morel.

"He didn't need a guide. He knew his way," said Cuyler. Morel looked up quickly.

"What do you mean by that?" he demanded.

"This is the room where they put on the second act of the de Mars murder, twelve years ago," said Braxton. "That was before your time, Morel."

"Yes. What about it?"

"Isidore Carmen was counsel for the defense," said the other, slowly. Morel whistled. "Morel," said Braxton, "in the de Mars case we had the corpus delicti, we had the motive, we had the man. But we never were able to prove what killed him. Carmen stood between us and the law."

"Too bad the Chief is away," said Morel. "This would please him." He studied the dead man stolidly. "Who found him?" he asked, turning to the room.

"I did, sir." It was the footman.

"Your name?"

"Herbert—that's my surname, sir."

"Did you see Carmen come in?"

"No, sir."

"How did you happen to come in here?"

"To take a call on the phone, sir."

"But you didn't take it?"

"No, sir, I didn't take it."

The footman looked at Carmen. The phone was within hand's reach of the dead man. At that moment the phone began to ring.

"Should I take it, sir?" offered the man.

"You seem rather calm for someone who has just walked in on a dead man," said Morel, not heeding. "Dead men don't seem to annoy you."

"No, sir; I've seen a good many in my time."

"Just how did you fill your time so full of dead men?"

"I was chauffeur and orderly for Sir William Prenton, a British surgeon, during the war, sir," said the man. "We worked pretty fast at times."

" 'We'?"

"We. Yes, sir. When there was a rush on, I did a little cutting and—plain sewing, myself, sir. Might I make a suggestion, sir?"

"Later," said Morel, silencing him; he turned to Cuyler. "Take that call, will you?"

Braxton took up the phone saying, "Hello," in his Supreme Court manner. There was a commotion on the other end. An incredulous voice cried:

"That isn't you, Cuyler?"

"It is."

The speaker was young Wainwright, one of the current society assistants in the District Attorney's office; his specialty was keeping the primadonna Justices of the Supreme Court in good humor.

"Is Isidore Carmen there?"

"Yes. At my elbow. Dead," replied Braxton in sepulchral tones. If he expected an explosion he was to be disappointed. Wainwright said crisply:

"Hold the wire, please."

The next voice was that of Colonel Wrentham, the District Attorney himself.

"How do you happen to be taking this call, Braxton?" he asked.

"They called me in from the recital just now, when they found him," the lawyer explained. "Morel saw me leave and followed me in here."

"Where, my boy?"

"Followed me to the room where de Mars was murdered twelve years ago. Recollect?" He paused. "Mrs. Corson is here—and the footman who found him. Did you telephone just now?"

"Yes. Is the concert still in progress?"

"He is playing the Butterfly Etude," said Braxton.

"How was it done?" asked the man who made a career of the study of method.

"Not a mark on him. It's anybody's guess."

"They were thoughtful enough to advise us—by phone," said the District Attorney. Braxton could not repress an exclamation. "Some assiduous accessory-after-the-fact," said the Colonel, "just phoned me anonymously from Brooklyn. The police are there?"

"Morel has taken charge."

"Howling swells?"

Braxton rolled off a few resounding names.

"Well, well! We can't exactly back up a wagon and haul them off to the House of Detention, can we?" mused the District Attorney. "I'll be along shortly. Will you carry on for me till I arrive?"

Morel here interposed himself, taking the wire, and asking to be put through to Headquarters, via the Centre Street switchboard. He gave instructions rapidly. Police lines were to be drawn at either end of the block. They were to avoid any alarm for the moment. No flying squads, no shrieking sirens. The reserves were to file in on the scene quietly, as if it were a church wedding overburdened with publicity. This thing is happening all the while, sidewalk jams standing siege for a glimpse of a famous or, still more delectable, a notorious person. The experts from the Homicide Bureau with test tubes, microscopes, and cameras, were to be smuggled in through 58th street. Meantime the soirée would be pinched off, without a whisper, and the lords and ladies of the pianoforte, the fiddle, and the larynx, would be permitted to disperse themselves without breaking the spell of the curve of the *cantabile* they had foregathered to appraise. Some few who had come on proxies would be startled to be politely requested to tarry. But this taking out of the goats from the sheep would be distinctly *sotto voce*.

So it happened that about five thirty, in the light of the street lamps on the snow which by that time was beginning to fall steadily, first one, then another, then a whole queue of equipages drew up at the curb in front of the ancient mansion, in a street now bare of people, save for dark, shivering groups behind police lines at either end of the block. And the great, and the near great, and the merely fortunate passed out as they had come, one and all in that exalted mood over the young man with the curve. The traffic was deflected into the Park, and there scattered to its many ways. The queue continuously fed itself as the front rank broke off with thudding doors, and drove away; and then, abruptly, it ceased.

Already the crowds behind the police lines, which had come to see Isidore Carmen, the man from the death house, walk out a free man under his own power, had begun to evidence the stirring of rumor. Whispers ran this way and that. It was impossible to say just how the rumor took form. But when a word of command finally released the police lines, the crowd surged forward with the word on every lip—Carmen was dead! His enemies had lured him here for death! Then from nowhere came newsboys, volleying through the throng, with the first news-flash: *Carmen Reported Slain Five Hours After He Escapes The Chair. Extra! Extra!*

The clock in the main salon was just striking the hour of six as the prosecutor entered. In the profession of law, among its more eminent practitioners, there seems to be two distinct races of men—a race of diminutive men, pigmies, like Isidore Carmen, who for good or evil are the most brilliant at the bar; and a race of giants, at once august and dominant. The Colonel was of this latter type. He got out of his coat, shaking off the snow, and surveyed the wreckage. The concert chairs still lay around in careless windrows; the litter of the audience still covered the floor; the grand piano, fetched across seas for the unveiling of the curve of the *cantabile*, stood open and undisturbed. Everything was in escrow for the time being—including the chatelaine of this ticketed establishment, the butler, and the three footmen who had been furnished on contract for the soirée together with the flowers and other trimmings; also ancient little Zack, engineer of the elevator; and several of the distinguished guests who had come on cards not their own. They were being interrogated in the dining-room by the police. This would go on for hours—sometimes it lasted for days—fresh relays of interrogators being constantly brought up from the reserves to ask the same questions with maddening repetition.

Morel and Braxton came out.

"Where are the hounds of the press?" asked the Colonel in his deep rumbling bass. He seated himself with slow dignity on a small concert chair. He took out his reading glasses, and in the purblind manner of the bifocal, felt for the bridge of his nose and put them in place.

"The reporters are sniffing at the door crack," said Morel, with a dry smile. "We have rather violated the rights of the privileged gentlemen—but we need elbow room."

"Has none of them been inside?" demanded the prosecutor.

"Not one," Morel said.

"Have you talked to any of them by phone?" Colonel Wrentham's tone had a steely quality.

"No, Colonel. I'll see them shortly."

The prosecutor, he knew, had gubernatorial aspirations, and an eye on the press. Wrentham drew an extra from his pocket, a replate of the Wall Street edition of the *Times-Herald*. He spread it out, and cried:

"Don't trouble yourself. Here is the complete story of the murder! It is already in print and on the street. I bought it at the door, coming in."

Morel and Braxton started forward, with gasps of astonishment.

"It is impossible!" said Morel. "Nothing has been given out. And no one has been admitted."

Nevertheless it was all there. The entire upper half of the first page was occupied by headlines of almost monstrous effrontery, in the calm assurance and specious dignity which the headline carpenter knows so well how to assume. Across the page shrieked the legend:

ISIDORE CARMEN EXECUTED AT 4:07 P.M.

Private vengeance acts swiftly when machinery of the law fails to function in the case of twice-convicted murderer

The lower half of the page was taken up by two boxes. One gave the complete list of the celebrities present for the unveiling of a new genius—celebrities who did not suspect that under cover of their ecstatic absorption the "execution" was being carried out in an adjoining room. The other box contained an exact plan of the apartment, including the lethal chamber. *X* marked the spot! The architect's drawing of the rooms had been amplified and elaborated, in the manner of newspaper artists, with dummy figures occupying the vital points. A dotted line showed Carmen's manner of approach to his doom; he had not taken the elevator—he had walked up the stairs, and proceeded directly to the murder chamber. The detail of the telephone on the writing desk was shown. A number of radiating lines issuing from it suggested that the telephone was violently ringing at the dead man's unheeding ear. Another dotted line, of implied electrical activity, led to the office of the District Attorney, and that dignitary was shown at his desk in a futile effort to save the life of the man, a life which he had asked three separate juries to hold forfeit to the law. And leading from the prosecutor's office was another dotted line of electrical communication, carrying to a telephone in Brooklyn whence the first casual alarm had emanated.

Colonel Wrentham turned the page. The second page consisted entirely of a detailed account of the crime. The details could not have been more specific if the murder itself had been personally conducted by the reporter who wrote it. The colonel looked at his watch and took up the telephone on the table. He called for the *Times-Herald's* editorial rooms, and was immediately connected.

"At exactly what hour did you issue your extra on the Isidore Carmen murder?" he demanded.

"We haven't issued an extra!" said the voice. "We have nothing but the rumor."

"Thank you!" grunted the prosecutor, and hung up.

He tested the weight of the paper of the first page between thumb and finger, and compared it with an inner page.

"A dummy first page superimposed on the regular Wall Street edition!" he muttered, with a shrug of grudging admiration.

Morel examined it in detail. He smiled.

"We will be able to trace it," said he. "It doesn't err from the regulation format by a hair. Only a newspaper compositor could have set that type. And only a newspaper press could have printed it."

"I wish you luck," said Wrentham sarcastically. "There are only six thousand newspaper compositors out of work at the present moment. Any of them would be glad of a job."

"But it would be impossible to fake it in the time that has elapsed," protested Braxton. "No printing plant on earth could put that dummy out in one hour—even if they had the facts of the story. And they've got the facts!" he cried, excitedly banging the paper. "Do you doubt for a moment that this is a true account of the murder of Isidore Carmen? No. It's the absolute truth!"

"How long do you think that story has been in type?" challenged Wrentham.

"Hours!" said Morel glibly.

"Days!" cried Braxton.

"Weeks!" boomed the Colonel, pounding the table. "They have simply bided their time, waited for us to fumble. How long has this list of invited guests for the recital been extant?"

"A month or more," said Braxton. "It was postponed once or twice."

"Is it reasonably correct?"

"With a few last-minute changes, I should say yes."

"Then there is nothing, barring the actual date itself, that couldn't have been set up and printed weeks or even months ago." Wrentham examined the date line of the bogus extra. He laughed dryly. The date was mashed, the type illegible. "Gentlemen," he said, ponderously, "I have been misfeasant, malfeasant, incompetent, incapable, ineffectual, and a moon-eyed dodo in office—so it is said. But if you will fetch me this murderer, I promise that even my latest assistant deputy assistant will have no difficulty in establishing premeditation." He tapped the bogus extra dramatically.

"Braxton, what killed de Mars?" he asked. "My mind is rusty on that old murder."

"We were never able to find out," said the former assistant. "The cause of death was never determined."

"Then it is no longer a mystery," cried the prosecutor; and adjusting his glasses again he read from the account on the bogus newspaper page:

" 'The most astounding feature of the execution lies in the fact that both the apartment used and the manner of dealing out death to the victim is identical with that of the celebrated de Mars mystery of twelve years ago. This fact is especially significant when it is remembered that the de Mars case was the first of a long series of abortive murder trials in which the accused invariably escaped punishment, due to the brilliant chicanery of their counsel, Isidore Carmen, the criminal lawyer who is the victim here. The lethal method in the de Mars case, and in the Isidore Carmen case today, was by spinal analgesia.' "

"What is spinal analgesia?" asked the prosecutor.

"A moment," interposed Morel. He went to the dining-room and stood for a moment looking in. It was a sorry spectacle. The police flowed over everything; all was confusion. The unfortunate *grande dame*, Mrs. Corson, who in her efforts to make a living and still retain the full measure of gentility she thought her due, had been made use of by sharpers and clever opportunists, and now finally by what looked like a murder syndicate, was at that moment under interrogation.

"Terry," called Morel sharply, and a brisk young detective approached.

"We're barking up the wrong tree," said Morel. "Don't overlook anything—but don't put on the screws too hard."

Morel caught the mildly inquiring eye of the competent footman, and summoned him with a gesture.

Closing the door behind him, Morel led the way into the drawing-room. He nodded to Wrentham and Braxton.

"This is the footman who found him," he said. "Now, Herbert, disregard the fact that we have gone over this before. These gentlemen know nothing of it."

As part of the play, Morel disposed himself comfortably on a concert chair, and carelessly lighted a cigarette. The footman's stance was easy, there was no embarrassment in his manner. He waited.

"How did you happen to go in there?" began Morel.

"The telephone was ringing, sir."

"This one?"

"No, sir. The calls were switched in there, so as not to disturb the concert."

"But you could hear it, in here?"

"Just a dull thudding sound, sir."

"You are sure it was the phone?"

"Oh, yes, sir. It was still ringing when I got there."

"And Carmen was dead?"

"Yes, sir."

"What killed him, Herbert?"

All three men looked at him.

"It looked to me like a case of spinal analgesia," said the footman. He paused, looking from face to face, all of them skilled in concealing their thoughts. After a moment he went on: "There is something unmistakable about it—death from spinal analgesia. During the war I saw a great many accidental deaths from it—due mostly to haste, or incompetence, or impure chemicals. You realize we had to operate in emergency stations behind the lines and under the severest conditions."

"We?" queried the prosecutor, looking up from under his shaggy brows. "Do you class yourself as an experienced anesthetist?"

"Yes, sir."

"And you've had them die in your hands?"

"Yes, sir. There is a certain percentage of fatal cases, even under perfect conditions. There is something about a death from this cause—I'm not a medical man, I can't describe it. But I think I can recognize it at a glance. And this case has all the symptoms."

"Analgesia," interposed the prosecutor. "You mean anesthesia, don't you?"

"It is a method of local anesthesia, sir, by injection in the spinal column."

"Cocaine?"

"I believe they use some special derivative, sir."

"What happens?" demanded the prosecutor.

"A momentary paralysis of the areas affected, sir," replied the man. "If the puncture is too high in the spinal column," he added, absently lifting one hand and touching the back of his neck, "the action of the heart and lungs ceases—and death ensues."

Morel said: "Herbert called my attention to what looked like a pin prick in the back of the neck."

"What does your medical examiner say about all this?" Wrentham asked.

"Plausible," said Morel.

The prosecutor rose and kicked the rumples out of his trouser legs. He paced up and down among the broken aisles of concert chairs, finally stopping in front of the footman.

"Go on," he invited casually.

"That's all, sir. I took the liberty of suggesting it because I thought it might otherwise pass unnoticed in the autopsy."

Wrentham said dryly:

"There seems to be a general inclination in this case to prevent the police from overlooking any of the finesse. They have gone to nonsensical lengths to be impressive—these murderers! If they must execute him, why go to the trouble of fetching him here? Why fill the house with celebrities? Why furnish printed directions with the corpus delicti?" He glared at the bogus extra. He turned to the footman. "Did you see him come in?"

"No, sir. No one seems to have seen him. I think he must have come late and walked up, after the concert started. I stood at the top of the staircase until the program began." Herbert paused and smiled oddly. "Then I was guilty of a bit of imprudence. He—that is, Cloquet—was playing the posthumous waltz—"

"Posthumous?"

"The E minor, sir, yes. I wanted to see his fingering—"

"Oh, you are a virtuoso, too?"

If the flippancy found Herbert, he gave no sign.

"I left my post—there was no one coming—and went to a spot behind the hangings where I could see his hands."

"And during that convenient absence of yours, Carmen entered unseen and went direct to his doom?" Wrentham's tone was casual. But he suddenly barked: "Why did he come in here?"

The footman said innocently: "You mean you want my surmise, sir?"

"Let's have it."

"I should say he was directed by one of the servants," replied the footman. "He follows, quite unsuspicious, thinking he is being taken to the cloak room."

"Ah! And then, without disturbing three hundred sensitive souls who are on a hair-trigger on the other side of the wall, we execute him, eh, by jabbing him in the neck with a needle!"

"Yes, sir," agreed the footman, solemnly. "Have you ever noticed the utter abstraction of an audience under the spell of a great master?"

"Yes," said Wrentham flatly, "they can hear a pin drop!" He fixed his keen eyes on the servant. "Now we are about to anesthetize our victim," he said. "How would you go about it, Herbert?"

"A skillful operator could do it while he was helping him out of his coat, sir," said the footman. "Let me illustrate how simple it would be." He took up Wrentham's greatcoat and poised it for him. But the colonel shook his head. Directions were a little too specific in this case; he was no lay figure.

"And then what?" he pursued.

"The bogus servant merely puts aside—"

"Oh, he is bogus, is he?"

"Why, yes, sir! He puts aside his slight disguise and joins the guests. He might mingle with the late comers who were waiting at the head of the stairs by that time. He would have been unnoticed. He would be dispersed without interrogation with other celebrities."

"Oh, he is a celebrity, eh?"

"He may be."

"Or a footman?"

"Oh, yes, sir. Except that his privileges for escape would be curtailed, if he were a menial."

"Quite so. But in any event he is someone skilled in the use of the needle?"

"Yes, sir, necessarily. Everything was timed beautifully," replied the footman.

The District Attorney rubbed his chin thoughtfully. He turned on Morel and Braxton, eyeing them wordlessly. Several seconds passed. He studied the servant through another spell of pregnant silence.

"I hope your past is an open book, Herbert," he said finally. "Is it?"

The man hesitated. For the first time since he came into the room he seemed embarrassed. He said, rather awkwardly:

"I've been out of a job for the last ten months, sir."

"That's where you got the lock-step," remarked the prosecutor dryly. "I wondered." He nodded to himself at some thought, then turning to Morel he said, "Your witness," as if he were in court. Morel sent the footman back to the dining-room.

"That's your man!" muttered Colonel Wrentham, looking after the servant. "But you are a long ways from hanging him."

It was two months later that Parr, the deputy, came back from abroad, and in the course of time he called for the dossier of the Isidore Carmen case. All the holes had been carefully caulked up by Morel and his cloud of operatives. It was a matter of deep chagrin to the handsome Morel to have failed so dismally in his first solo flight.

Parr turned the sheets in the high stack of documents. He paused here and there, and Morel watched him.

"I sometimes think," said Parr, apropos of nothing, "that human nature never learns, except by experience. We can be told, we can see others stub their toe; but inevitably we have to actually stub our own toe, in exactly the same way, before we take the lesson to heart. Take the case of Isidore Carmen. He spent his life, with his utterly unscrupulous cunning, in rescuing clients from just punishment for crimes of cupidity, passion, and violence. Wouldn't you think he would be wise enough to avoid those same fatal pitfalls in his own conduct? Not at all! He makes the same mistake himself. He writes fool letters to a woman. And as if that wasn't enough, he murders her when he fails to get the letters back."

That was ancient history. It was Carmen the murdered man in whom Morel was interested, not Carmen the murderer. Parr, turning many pages, looked up again.

"Have you checked up everything?"

"Yes, sir. I've gone over it time and again."

"Name your possible suspects," commanded the chief. Morel named them, one by one. The list began with Herbert; it might be said it began and ended with Herbert, because the others were insignificant. And there was never enough evidence against the footman to accuse him, formally, of complicity. Parr went over the names, scowling.

"No one else?"

Morel shook his head.

Then Parr asked, slowly: "*Is there no person so obviously innocent that you would immediately dismiss his name, if by chance it occurred to you?*"

Morel gaped.

Parr continued, just as deliberately. "Doesn't it strike you there is too much of the obvious in this case? That fake extra, for instance. It depicts every step in the murder. And correctly. If it is 99 per cent correct, you are apt to accept the remaining one per cent without being too curious. Think. What have you overlooked? What have you taken for granted?"

Morel knitted his brows. He passed the people of the drama mentally. There was no one.

"Suggest something, sir," he said.

Parr drummed on his desk.

"Did you check up on that anonymous telephone call from Brooklyn to the District Attorney's office?"

"Good heavens!" ejaculated the startled Morel. "And why should I?"

"There you are!" said Parr. "Why should you, you ask? You are so positive in advance that it will lead nowhere. Yet he tells you he is informed by an anonymous telephone call from Brooklyn. And you simply take his word for it."

"But—the District Attorney!" protested Morel, staring at Parr.

"For the last twelve years," said Parr, harshly, "Isidore Carmen has made the District Attorney's office the laughing-stock of the state. Wrentham wanted to be governor—they have turned him down; his record of convictions isn't good enough!" He added, in a lower tone, as if he spoke to himself alone: "Thwarted ambition can be a motive."

It was two weeks later that Parr, taking his cane for a walk up Fifth Avenue for his daily quantum of sunshine, managed skillfully to cross the path of the District Attorney, walking solo from his club to his home.

"That's a clever man, that Herbert of yours," said Parr, as they fell into step. He spoke idly, in the tone he used when he was about to tell a murderer he was under suspicion and would shortly be brought to book.

"Mine?" said the colonel. "Why mine? I have no interest in him."

"Except to get employment for him later, as chauffeur for the Maitlands," said Parr.

"It's true I spoke for him," said the prosecutor. "The poor fellow had been out of work so long."

"That isn't where he picked up the lock-step, though, Colonel," said the deputy, still mild. Wrentham shot a look at him. He said nothing.

"You recognized him, of course?" asked Parr. "When you encountered him in the Carmen murder?"

"Why should I?" asked the other.

"Before you came to New York, Colonel, you were a rising young lawyer in Illinois—before the war, in a tank town below Ottawa. Did you ever hear of a forger named Heberton? A young college man with a fine record. He enlisted in the ambulance corps in 1914. You defended him, didn't you, and got him a curtailed sentence? The fingerprints are the same."

"I may have defended a person of that name," said the colonel. He turned to Parr, and stopped. "I'm leaving you here," he said shortly.

"Not quite yet," said Parr, putting up a friendly yet insistent hand. "Let me tell you something. Despite my best efforts I was never able to trace that telephone call—the anonymous telephone call to you—from Brooklyn. Do you want to know why I think we couldn't trace that call? Because there never was any anonymous call from Brooklyn to the District Attorney's office that day! Do you follow me?"

"I'm afraid not," said Colonel Wrentham. "I bid you good day."

"A moment," said the deputy. "We never learn, Colonel, except by harsh experience, do we? Your entire career has been consecrated to upholding the law—dealing out punishment to those poor weak human beings who break the law or take vengeance into their own hands. There is no wrong without a remedy at law—so you lawyers say. And yet, when the great crisis in your own life hits you, when you realize that your dearest ambition has been thwarted, that this rascally shyster, Isidore Carmen, by his clever chicanery, keeps you from being governor, then you forget there is such a thing as law, a legal remedy; and you become a poor weak human being yourself, and take vengeance in your own hands. Oh, we haven't got you yet," added the deputy, "but we are closing in on you, and your clever confederate."

Parr turned and looked after the colonel some little distance off. He noted, with something like awe, that the distinguished military carriage of the colonel was gone. The massive shoulders had bowed; he felt for his footing with his cane; he looked up and down, with the purblind helplessness of the bifocal, as he stumbled across the street.

Sources

"The Purple Flame." *Adventure*, November 1912.

"The Phantom Alibi." *McClure's Magazine*, November 1920.

"Wild Honey." *Saturday Evening Post*, November 26, 1921.

"The Footstep." *Saturday Evening Post*, November 28, 1925.

"The House of Many Mansions." *Saturday Evening Post*, March 17, 1928.

"Hangman's Truce." *Saturday Evening Post, Saturday Evening Post*, September 1, 1928.

"Vivace-Ma Non Troppo." *Saturday Evening Post*, March 16, 1929.

"Thumbs Down." *Saturday Evening Post*, June 28, 1930.

"The Two Martimos." *Saturday Evening Post*, November 15, 1930.

"The Pandora Complex." *Saturday Evening Post*, May 7, 1932.

"Unfinished Business." *Saturday Evening Post*, February 4, 1933.

"At Early Candlelight." *American Cavalcade*, May 1937.

"What is the Goat's Name?" *American Cavalcade*, June 1937.

"Murder in Triplicate." *Ellery Queen's Mystery Magazine*, December 1946.

"The Man from the Death House." *Ellery Queen's Mystery Magazine*, January 1951.

The Phantom Flame and Other Detective Stories

The Phantom Flame and Other Detective Stories by Frederick Irving Anderson is edited and introduced by Benjamin F. Fisher. It is set in Garamond and printed on 60 pound Natural acid-free paper. It was published both in full cloth and in trade softcover. The cover design is by Gail Cross. *The Phantom Flame and Other Detective Stories* was printed and bound by Thomson-Shore, and published in September 2016 by Crippen & Landru Publishers, Norfolk, Virginia.

CRIPPEN & LANDRU, PUBLISHERS

P. O. Box 9315

Norfolk, VA 23505

Web: www.crippenlandru.com

E-mail: info@crippenlandru.com

Since 1994, Crippen & Landru has published more than 100 first editions of short-story collections by important detective and mystery writers.

This is the best edited, most attractively packaged line of mystery books introduced in this decade. The books are equally valuable to collectors and readers. [*Mystery Scene Magazine*]

The specialty publisher with the most star-studded list is Crippen & Landru, which has produced short story collections by some of the biggest names in contemporary crime fiction. [*Ellery Queen's Mystery Magazine*]

God Bless Crippen & Landru. [*The Strand Magazine*]

A monument in the making is appearing year by year from Crippen & Landru, a small press devoted exclusively to publishing the criminous short story. [*Alfred Hitchcock's Mystery Magazine*]

RECENT PUBLICATIONS

The Columbo Collection by William Link.
New stories written by the creator of television's greatest sleuth. Trade softcover, $18.00.

Ten Thousand Blunt Instruments by Phillip Wylie, edited by Bill Pronzini. Lost Classics Series.
Wylie's stories were, in the words of editor Bill Pronzini, "controversial, provocative, iconoclastic." His detective fiction was among the most ingenious and innovative of his generation. Full cloth with dust jacket, $29.00. Trade softcover, $19.00

The Exploits of the Patent Leather Kid by Erle Stanley Gardner edited by Bill Pronzini. Lost Classics Series.
The Patent Leather Kid is an elegant crook, hiding his identity with mask, gloves, and shoes made out of black patent leather. In truth, he is a wealthy, seemingly indolent socialite, who becomes a terror to the underworld. Full cloth in dust jacket, $29.00. Trade softcover, $19.00

Valentino: Film Detective by Loren D. Estleman.
Valentino has a perfect job for a film buff – he is a film detective who locates lost movies so that they can be preserved for future generations. And often he has to become an amateur sleuth as well. Full cloth in dust jacket, signed and numbered by the author, $43.00. Trade softcover, $17.00.

The Duel of Shadows: The Extraordinary Cases of Barnabas Hildreth by Vincent Cornier, edited by Mike Ashley. Lost Classics series.
"One of the great series of modern detective stories." So wrote Ellery Queen when he introduced American readers to the writings of Vincent Cornier. Full cloth in dust jacket, $28.00.

Shooting Hollywood: The Diana Poole Stories by Melodie Johnson Howe.
Melodie Johnson Howe was "one of the last of the starlets," making movies with Clint Eastwood, Alan Alda, James Caan, James Farentino and others. Hollywood is brutal, and it is a place, as Marilyn Monroe said, "where they'll pay you

a thousand dollars for a kiss, and fifty cents for your soul ..."
Diana Poole finds crime in that world of glitz, glamour, and
greed. Full cloth in dust jacket, signed and numbered by the
author, $43.00. Trade softcover, $17.00.

The Casebook of Jonas P. Jonas and Others by E. X. Ferrars, edited
by John Cooper. Lost Classics Series.
  Stories by a mistress of the traditional mystery. "She remains,"
wrote one reviewer, "one of the most adept and intelligent adher-
ents of the whodunit form." Full cloth in dust jacket, $29.00. Trade
softcover, $19.00.

Nothing Is Impossible: Further Problems of Dr. Sam Hawthorne
by Edward D. Hoch.
  Dr. Sam Hawthorne, a New England country doctor in the
first half of the twentieth century, was constantly faced by murders in locked rooms and impossible disappearances. *Nothing Is
Impossible* contains fifteen of Dr. Sam's most extraordinary cases.
Full cloth in dust jacket, signed and numbered by the publisher,
$45.00. Trade softcover, $19.00.

Night Call and Other Stories of Suspense by Charlotte Armstrong,
edited by Rick Cypert and Kirby McCauley. Lost Classics
series.
  Charlotte Armstrong introduced suspense into the commonplace, the everyday, by writing short stories and novels in which
one simple action sets a series of events spiraling into motion,
pulling readers along, breathless with anxiety. Full cloth in dust
jacket, $30.00. Trade softcover, $20.00.

Chain of Witnesses; The Cases of Miss Phipps by Phyllis Bentley,
edited by Marvin Lachman. Lost Classics series.
  A critic writes, "Stylistically, [Bentley's] stories ... share a
quiet humor and misleading simplicity of statement with the
works of Christie .... Her work [is] informed and consistent
with the classic traditions of the mystery." Full cloth in dust
jacket, $29.00. Trade softcover, $19.00.

Swords, Sandals and Sirens by Marilyn Todd.
  Murder, conmen, elephants. Who knew ancient times could
be such fun? Many of the stories feature Claudia Seferius, the

super-bitch heroine of Marilyn Todd's critically acclaimed mystery series set in Ancient Rome. Others feature Cleopatra, the Olympian Gods, and High Priestess Ilion blackmailed to work with Sparta's feared secret police. Full cloth in dust jacket, signed and numbered by the author, $45.00. Trade softcover, $19.00.

The Puzzles of Peter Duluth by Patrick Quentin. Lost Classics series.
    Anthony Boucher wrote: "Quentin is particularly noted for the enviable polish and grace which make him one of the leading American fabricants of the murderous comedy of manners; but this surface smoothness conceals intricate and meticulous plot construction as faultless as that of Agatha Christie." Full cloth in dust jacket, $29.00. Trade softcover, $19.00.

The Purple Flame and Other Detective Stories by Frederick Irving Anderson, edited by Benjamin F. Fisher.
    Previously uncollected stories by one of the premier mystery writers of the 1920's and the 1930's. Full cloth in dust jacket, $29.00. Trade softcover, $19.00.

Lost Classics